SCRAPING THE TOAST

By Anne Main

Scraping the toast

Set in Cardiff this is a story of love, loss and family secrets as seen through the eyes of young Sarah Matthews, a child in the sixties and seventies.

Visiting her grandparents in their shabby Victorian home in Cardiff, Sarah revels in the freedoms she finds there. But all is far from idyllic in Alma road, dark currents run beneath the surface.

The house is crumbling and as the years pass even Sarah notices the increasing decline into squalor. Clifford, her dominating, disabled grandfather is confined to the ground floor and rules his small domain with a degree of control that borders on bullying.

Sarah and Gran, co-conspirators often seek escape from Grampy's critical gaze. "What the eye doesn't see the heart doesn't grieve over." Is Gran's motto.

In Sarah's eyes Gran is perfect. But is she?

Why doesn't Gran ever want to leave Alma road despite its hardships even after Clifford dies? Why is she so devoted to her bad-tempered husband when her own life is such drudgery? What is Gran's dark secret?

As an adult Sarah uncovers a shocking secret about her darling Gran hidden in her late mother's private documents. Its a secret that throws into question everything Sarah thought to be true.

But that's the thing about secrets... once you know them do you keep them?

Scraping the Toast

The small brown suitcase lay wedged behind the water tank...... A faded luggage label- Mr and Mrs Harris c/o The Grand Atlantic Hotel Weston Super Mare.

Sarah

In the drab, colourless weeks after mum died, I found my Gran. She whispered to me from quiet, papery shadows that dismal summer. I unearthed her secrets and her lies from an unassuming grey box file tucked away in mum's bedroom.

I'd spent days sorting through my mother's things; clothes that she would no longer wear, ugly ornaments that she no longer needed and nobody wanted, piles of bills and bank statements begged for my attention.

Death is a time-consuming process.

In the end it always comes down to sorting through piles of, what can only loosely be called stuff.

That morning, I'd decided to tackle that most tricky and daunting task for the sorters and rubbish pickers of the deceased; the document pile... Mum's private papers.

Gran, was to be found lurking amongst a rag-tag jumble of papers, photos, announcements and knick-knacks. Tucked away on the top shelf of a wardrobe in a large box file, just waiting to for me to find her.

We all have secrets and Eleanor's box of secrets was hidden deep amongst the rest of my mother's memories; away from prying eyes and awkward questions.

As the eldest daughter, the job of sorting out our mother's affairs fell to me. Well that's what Bea, said when I looked to her for support.

"Oh, come on Sarah, I'm hopeless at paperwork!...
You know what I'm like; give me a bank statement and I've
lost it, trust me with a certificate and I use it to write the
shopping list on. Important things just seem to disappear the
minute I get my fingers on them.... No, it would be best if you
did it, really it would ..." Beatrice wheedled and won.

"Besides Sis, you've got a bit more time on your hands
than I've got..." Bea left the rest unsaid. It didn't need saying
really.... She was right... I did have plenty of time on my
hands.

Bea took full advantage of my time-rich status as the
older, widowed, sister, when she looked for favours. Recently
redundant at the awkward age of nearly fifty-five, my free
time had proved very opportune.

Unlike me, Bea had all the pressing demands of a
glamorous, hectic family life and finding time to look after an
ailing mother had always been so very inconvenient for her;
Bea was just so busy, busy, busy.

Bea always relied on me to have time to deal with things,
especially over the last two years as we watched our Mother
descend into the grey, wobbly world of Alzheimer's disease.

Beatrice just didn't do unpleasantness; it was as simple as
that.

Bea didn't mean to be selfish; she just couldn't help
herself. She would be fifty in November; the party and face
lift were booked, along with the cruise up the Nile. So much
to do and so little youth to do it in.

So, I sat with a coffee, that sharp September morning,
leafing through faded photographs, cuttings and papers that
Mum had kept safe for years. On top of one pile stuffed into
that battered grey box file was a snippet of yellowing

newspaper; Eleanor Fowler, born July 14th 1906 Inkerman Street, Cardiff.

Gran. My darling Gran.

As a child I had loved my jolly, plump Gran with a fierce loyalty that saw no fault. To me she perfect.

My grandparents muddled along in an uncomfortable time warp of a house in Alma road. Their dingy terraced home a mere three streets away from where Gran had been born in another shabby road, of identical terraces teetering on the edge of Cardiff.

That morning, as I sat surrounded by our Mum's documents and bank statements, I found out that I didn't really know Gran at all. She'd lived a life and a lie.

To this day, I can conjure up that small, Victorian, house in my mind's eye. If I close my eyes it comes to me, with its cold, dingy rooms and lino floors graced with red Turkey rugs that didn't show the mess or the spark burns from the sulky fire.

It was a house of distinct and unusual smells. Lifebuoy soap and Brasso competed with the steamy, dish-cloth aroma of boiled jam roly-poly and chips cooked on the hob in lard.

Tom cats always pee'd on Gran's front step, spraying their foul calling card up the majolica tiles of birds and flowers. The lingering, pungent aroma offended my Grandmother, who had a nose for such things. She railed against their disgusting antics. "I'll swing for those bloody cats!"

And my Grandfather pee'd in the sink when my Gran emptied his night bottles down the Belfast in the morning. This brownish-yellow liquid mingled with drained Savoy cabbage water on a regular basis. The sour tang coming from the plughole did not seem to offend her like the cats did; well, if it did then she never passed comment.

To this day the dusty, sweet smell of loose tea reminds me of my Grandparents' home. It wasn't ever their house, but it was their home. It was the place my mother Jean grew up in and, eventually, couldn't wait to escape from.

It had been my haven.

Twelve Alma road was a shabby, terraced property. For fifty years they paid their rent to a miserable stick of a landlord, the never-to-be-mentioned, Mr Pugh. Over the years, until Gran died in 1979, the house slid slowly into rack and ruin. Time and progress left it behind. The plaster crumbled and creeping damp grew webs of dark fungus on the walls.

But, for all its failings Alma road was her home and the only home that Eleanor ever knew after she married my Grandfather; the handsome Clifford, Aubrey Harris in March 1928 just seven months after her 21st birthday.

My childhood was shaped with memories of Alma road; the only house in the street allowed to keep its wrought iron railings during the war.

CHAPTER 1

1965 Alma Road

"Nelly...Nelly!... Can I smell burning out there?" Clifford barked his enquiries from his armchair. The brown moquette chair was placed in its usual position beside the dusty fireplace. He glared at the smouldering, nutty slack that refused to warm him. "Dear God what is that woman up to!"

He muttered under his breath. The small fire had been banked up overnight and still clung on to life.... *just*. It needed attention. "Nelly!"

Clifford noted with a flash of irritation that the grate hadn't been black-leaded for weeks and the clinker underneath the grate was choking the life out of the fire. It just wasn't good enough the room was starting to chill...

Clifford's stomach gave a small rumble. He gathered himself for another bellow. Where was Nelly with that toast? He could feel his impatience rising to a crescendo. *"Nelleee....Can I smell something burning out there?"*

That morning Clifford was wearing his second-best cardigan; it already had several small, worsted darns worked on to the elbows. Clifford always wore out the elbows way before the rest of the cardigan even showed signs of wear. Nelly would mutter about the insubstantial nature of *elbows* in merino wool cardigans as she worked her repairs over a darning mushroom.

Even accepting Clifford's culpability in the matter of worn-out elbows, it irked her that many a good garment looked *so* shoddy *so* quickly. I, on the other hand, who could not sew, marvelled at the craft as a newly created patch of warp and weft reinforced the bald surface and gave it a new lease of life. As Gran's watchful apprentice seated at her feet, I always had the job of threading her needles-*" young eyes" being* best for the purpose. My mother would have thrown the cardigan away.

Clifford waited for the response to his question and paused to listen to the familiar lie that Nelly trilled in from the outside yard. He knew that she lied to him. She lied to spare him, she lied to deceive him; sometimes she lied just because it was easier. Today it was easier.

"No, Clifford." The rhythmic, metallic *"scrinch, scrinch... scrinch, scrinch,"* sounds drifted into the parlour from outside. The tell-tale noise of a knife working its magic on singed bread.

"Nelly!... Can you hear me?... What on earth are you up to? That fire needs seeing to." He craned his neck to see what was visible of their small scullery.

If Clifford leant hard enough to the left in his armchair, he could almost glimpse the white Belfast sink that hovered tantalisingly out of his range. He could not, however, see his small wife hidden around the corner next to the outhouse and the drooping rambling rose; one of the few sickly plants to grace their scrubby yard.

"Nelly!"

Nelly chose her spot well to remedy the consequences of her inattention to the bread under the gas grill. *Scrinch, scrinch.*

"Nothing's up Clifford.... just a minute...I'm coming... It'll be right there." She called through the doorway.

Gran entered the scullery; dropped her dwindling fag end into the washing up bowl with a small hiss; disguised the toast with a liberal slick of butter and dark marmalade and handed it to me.

"There you go Sarah, take it to your Grampy for me... theres a love.... I've got to sort that fire out for him." She gave a smile and a conspiratorial wink as the toast, best side up, was sent in on a pretty china plate to my grumpy, grandfather.

I used to be in awe of the fact that Gran could work out in that tiny scullery with a cigarette dangling from her lips that invariably supported a huge, drooping, grey caterpillar of fag ash clinging on to the filter for grim death. This delicate balancing act was, it seemed to me, a skill to be proud of.... but I knew it was another one of her secret talents that was not to be commented on. Sometimes the loosening caterpillar appeared to defy gravity; occasionally it made its way into the food to be flicked away or stirred in; *"what the eye doesn't see the heart doesn't grieve about Sarah.... here you go, take that in for your grandfather."*

As a small child I knew that my Gran was the best fun with such a wicked laugh. She drank "mother's ruin" in the scullery, topped off with a large slug of Robertson's orange squash. She breezed over rules that didn't suit her and hid her Craven A cigarette butts in a large, ornamental jar in the hallway when returning from shopping.

But of course, she didn't smoke -Grampy disapproved of smoking.

To my young eyes she was impossibly glamorous; she wore a slash of Rimmel red lipstick whenever she left the house -always wearing her carefully adjusted hat.

I also knew that Gran fibbed, great big whoppers... and she fibbed a lot!

From the age of about eight, I loved visiting my grandparent's home on a Sunday morning. Unaccompanied by the watchful gaze of my censorious, rather strait-laced mother I basked in the freedoms of Alma road.

My mother was forever *busy* with my sister Beatrice; a whiny, sickly three-year-old child, whose nose wore a permanent green candle as she clung limpet-like to my mother, demanding attention and sucking her patience. All Mum's energies were channelled into Beatrice, so I turned to Gran -*my* Gran.

My mother did not wear makeup; very occasionally she would powder her nose and smear on a touch of pink lipstick if it was a dressy occasion, but she *never* slicked on the bold, crimson red of my Gran.... I would have been shocked if she had.

Mum had a firm set of rules that brooked no argument.

"Just do as your mother says," Dad advised. "There's no point in debating the matter. If your mother has put her foot down, then that's your answer. No point asking me."

A biddable child, at eight years old I was considered old enough and sensible enough to make the short journey unaccompanied to Alma road. I was trusted to buy the little pink ticket from the conductor and then walk the few hundred yards from the bus stop in Albany road to Gran's house.

"No talking to strangers. No going to the top of the bus where the smokers sit and no sitting on the side bench seats... you might slide off. Always sit next to a lady, keep your purse zipped up and your knees together.... wait until the bus stops before you get off. Oh...and if you've got a problem always ask the conductor." Mother's instructions never varied.

After being seen onto the double decker by my mother, a visit to Alma Road was always worth the effort. Naughty and enjoyable, *"out of sight out of mind"* as Gran used to say, whatever the crime.

Co-conspirators we ate damp strawberries dipped thickly in sugar, left the crusts on our sandwiches, buttered our Rich tea biscuits and kept secrets. With hidden treasures in the middle room and untold exploits in the upstairs back room I looked forward to my weekly visits and, most of all, the freedom.

At home order reigned; things had to be tidy, put away *"a place for everything, and everything in its place, don't go upstairs empty-handed Sarah."* Tea towels were ironed; dust was moved around and lies were punished with a slap on the legs; inside the four walls of 12 Alma Road the rules were very different and I loved it.
I loved her....

By my mother's standards my Gran's approach to doing housework was positively sluttish. I loved writing in the powdery, grey dust that covered the furniture. If I made a comment about the dereliction of dusting, I was handed a duster, but if I didn't.... then I could write my name in the dust as much as I liked. I never made a comment. as an intelligent child I was quick to learn the house rules.

The upstairs dust was the best of all; always at its thickest and most rewarding, particularly in the back-box room which was my domain and play room. Dust lay everywhere in that haven. The only exception was in the jumble of the middle room where a chipped, plaster statue of the Virgin Mary stood in a dust-free polished circle on the tall boy. It seemed only right that I dusted around Jesus's mother; otherwise, the rest of the tall boy remained untroubled by the duster.

But then only Gran and I knew about the dust upstairs.... so, it didn't matter.

Alma Road had two sets of rules. Grampy's rules and Gran's devil may care rules.

"Here you are Grampy," I angled the toast to its best advantage. He rearranged his chair area to receive the offering. Newspaper folded in three and tucked to the left, bone china teacup and saucer placed on the side table to his right.

"Ah my breakfast...Thank you Sarah," he gave a delicate sniff.

He took the toast with a suspicious look and placed it daintily on his lap tray.

His tray was complimented with a small, starched linen napkin. My Grandfather had standards. He liked things just so.

"Do you want me to bring you in anything else Grampy?" I was bobbing and twirling slightly for him to admire my Sunday best dress. I was a vain child and rather proud of the puffed-out skirt that floated out to best advantage with a twirl.

"Not at the moment." He shook his head and ate his breakfast offering. Patting his mouth with the napkin held in his soft, white hands.

I waited to see if he commented on the singed toast, which was a regular failing, but to my amazement he never did. It didn't matter how scraped and piebald its appearance he *never* mentioned it. My Grandfather could not abide burnt toast and so it went without saying that my Grandmother would *never* serve it to him. It was quite simple really.... when you understood the rules.

"Will you make me some boats today please Grampy?" I pleaded as he munched silently on the rescued toast.

The boats of Alma Road were a rare treat that never happened at home; small armadas of carefully folded newspaper allowed to sail and then scuttled in the white Belfast sink.

It was bliss to use the yellow, rubber, nozzle jammed on the end of the solitary cold tap and then direct the fierce jet onto the flaming craft as they drifted around the edges of the porcelain sink. Grampy used to think they just floated and sank.... Gran knew they blazed gloriously.

Gran never commented on the black sodden mess that had to be retrieved from the sink or complained about the smoky pall that settled over scullery with its tiny window and low sloping roof. Funnily enough the acrid smell never wafted into the back parlour where my Grampy sat reading his paper, it remained firmly in the scullery before drifting its way obediently out of the back door. If it hadn't, I felt sure he would have mentioned it.

"I'll think about it, Sarah, when your Gran has sorted that fire out ... it needs riddling and mending.... before it goes next door."

"How can a fire go next door Grampy?" I asked genuinely puzzled by the concept. At home we had flick -o-the switch fires that didn't need coaxing and talking to, our fires were reliable, clean, soul-less. The art of making, rescuing and managing fires in Alma road was a source of intense fascination to me.

I learnt the craft of scattering sugar onto a sulky fire; coaxing it back into life. Oh, the joy of being allowed to hold a broad sheet newspaper over the grate opening to cause a roaring updraught; the increasing sucking of the paper hinting at the new life that was drawing through the coals then timing it just right before the yellowing paper almost burst into flames. Many a time the paper started to singe as the fire leap into life and Gran would rescue it from disaster, "Oops careful...We don't want a chimney fire Sarah Jane, do we?"

My Grandfather was an intelligent man who enjoyed nothing more than solving puzzles, posing riddles, teaching things and I was his willing pupil. He taught me chess, mental arithmetic, Origami, a way to say the alphabet backwards and how to whistle. He believed a child should be instructed; a young mind must be moulded through education. I was his protegee.

This concept of retreating fire hinted at a distinct lack in my knowledge base.

He laughed.... A sharp mirthless bark, which was all the more surprising because I don't ever recall him laughing about anything.... ever.

"It's a turn of phrase child. The old back-to-back houses had shared flues, if not looked after a fire could find itself looking to go next door... for attention so to speak...."

My Grandmother appeared with a heavy zinc bucket of best coal and a grubby wet rag. "That fire's nearly out Nell. You shouldn't let it get so low, it's almost out" He said accusingly as she knelt before the hearth on creaky knees.

I watched as my Gran riddled and coaxed the small fire back into life using choicer nuggets of anthracite. The black, slate hearth looked momentarily glossy as she ran the damp cloth over the surfaces. A tarry smell of hot soot filled the air as the cloth sizzled across the two side stands that waited for the kettle. Little bobbles of water fizzed and crackled as they bounced across the hot surfaces.

"That grate needs black leading too. I've been thinking for days now how dull it's looking." He chipped away as she flicked and wiped.

"Yes Clifford...." On her knees she gathered a shovel full of cinder and ashes from under the fire basket, ".... I'll need to pop out to the shops and get some Zeebrite first; we ran out last week."

She gave the tiled frieze a desultory swish over with the grimy rag-*a lick and promise*. Job done, she tottered off into the garden with the brimming bucket to dispose of the hot cinders on the clinker heap and to have another secret cigarette.

I hovered patiently by Grampy's chair, holding a pile of old newspapers. I would not ask a second time; Grampy was a busy man. He would answer in his own good time and I knew that if he said No, then the answer was No and there would be no boats. Grampy was resolute in his decision making.

"When your Gran has finished cleaning out the fire bucket in the garden, she can get the card table from the middle room."

My heart gave a little skip, the table *was* good news. Knowing Gran, it would be at least another ten minutes before the folding green baize table was erected, but at least there *would be* boats!

"We'll need to make some fire-lighters first though," he added as he eyed the large pile of newspapers in my arms "We can't have you using all the newspapers for boats, not at this time of year when we need the lighters for the fire."

When I first saw Grampy's nimble, manicured, fingers rolling, folding and plaiting the paper lighters, I was eager to learn the craft. At first my clumsy fingers would not co-operate. I had many failures before I mastered the task of delivering the perfectly straight, tightly woven paper lighter, to my Grandfather's exacting standards.

After intense tuition in the art of fire lighter construction I finally knew the drill; a broad sheet of newspaper, placed lozenge side on, would be rolled from one corner to the other creating a stiff wand. After a fold in the middle the two ends were repeatedly placed over each other at right angles until a firm, sculpted stick appeared with two little ends tucked in neatly at the top to complete the job.

"I'll fetch the lighter box for you then Grampy," I said as I jigged from one foot to the other resisting the pressing urge to go for a pee.

"I think that you'd better spend a penny first, my girl," Gran said as she drifted into the room and recognized the signs.

I would hold on to my wee as long as possible in Gran's house. Sometimes in the cold weather I would wet my knickers, just a little, but the dreaded outside lavatory was to be resisted until the very last second.

At home we had an inside toilet in the upstairs bathroom, it was warm and safe in our bathroom with soft pink toilet tissue on a roll and an electric strip light. I never wet my knickers at home.

In Alma Road toilets were very different ... but not in a good way. The toilet grew spiders, big twiggy -legged ones that nestled in the ivy that crept around the door frame, they lurked malevolently with their sticky webs in the dark, undisturbed recesses behind the high flush cistern. Sometimes they emerged from the ivy and walked towards me, daring me to cross their path.

In winter a small night light balanced on the cistern to stop it freezing over. The wooden seat took on a greasy, damp, slipperiness as my small bottom hung over its cold edge. In my mind a large, watchful spider hid under the rim, waiting for me. I prayed for the day that my legs would long enough to allow me to hover over the hole without touching down on the seat.

But most of all I dreaded the horrid lavatory paper. It sat in a china holder on the back of the toilet door.... A small cardboard box of shiny, slippery, medicated San Izal sheets that reeked of Jeyes fluid and defied all my efforts to clean myself up. The sheets reminded me of tracing paper that scratched and prickled... Wiping my bottom became an ordeal that I had discussed with Gran.

"Gran.... why do you and Grampy have that *really* hard toilet paper?" A petulant whine entered my voice.

"Your Grampy likes it Sarah." She said as if that were the end of the matter.

"But *why* does he like it Gran? Mum and Dad like the soft paper that we have at home... and so, do I." I bleated.

"I've got a *really* sore bottom now.... look Gran!" Anxious to prove my point, with childlike innocence I dropped my pants, bent over and displayed my red, inner cheeks.

"I've tried *scrumpling* it like you said, but it *still* hurts." I wailed.

The week before when I had raised the vexed issue of "scratchy" bottom wiping, my Gran had suggested scrunching and *scrumpling* the paper sheet before use to take the bite out of it. I was obviously no good at scrumpling and my pink, raw bottom bore testimony to my ineptitude.

Gran took pity on me and after giving me a small hug we went upstairs to *sort things out. S*he applied some Vaseline and a light dusting of talc to soothe the chafe and the following week a roll of soft, pink tissue mercifully appeared. The coveted roll was placed on a shelf in the scullery cabinet for me to help myself.

Nothing more was said on the matter and of course, it went without saying that I didn't mention the matter of soft toilet tissue to my grandfather.

The Izal box remained in the lavatory, resistant to rot, damp and falling apart. Its sheets billowed and floated with brown streaks like some hideous jelly fish; defying the flush

20

and lingering to tell a tale from a previous occupant. But I, at least, did not fear it now- only the spiders.

"Come on Sarah Jayne Matthews *you* need to spend a penny before anything else.... Off you go whilst I put up the card table for Grampy....Be smart about its Miss or there won't be time for boats."

My Gran only ever used my full name when she meant business. No shouting, no smacking, no threats to tell Mum, just my full name and a beady stare over the top of her glasses. I trudged out reluctantly to do battle with the spiders.

The folding, baize covered card table was pressed into use for games and past times on a regular basis; Scrabble, Old Maid, putting stamps in albums, jig saw puzzles and Grampy's paperwork.

But whilst Grampy and I engaged in after lunch past times, I never ceased to be amazed how often Mrs James, tapped the wall during my visits. For some reason the triple rap on the party wall about two o'clock on a Sunday afternoon was particularly irksome to my grandfather.

"Mrs James is knocking again Nelly." Grampy called through to the scullery as Gran tackled the washing up. Leaving the pots to drain on the wooden draining board, Gran scurried in removing her pinny. She rapped the wall three times. Grampy glowered.

"Ooh hoo Mrs James," she called melodiously, "just coming!"

"I'll just pop around to see what the old soul wants Clifford.... Won't be long." and with that she would disappear. Gran would usually be gone for about an hour before dashing back just in time to make a small afternoon tea prior to my trip back to the bus stop.

"Here we are then," Gran she would say, as if we had all been somewhere. "I'll make us all a nice cup of tea. I've bought some of your favourite biscuits this week Sarah.... Milk and Honey creams."

Sometimes it would be Battenburg cake, or *on* the rare occasions when Mrs James didn't need Gran, we would make Butterfly cakes with sherry butter-cream fillings and if I was *very* good, I got to lick the bowl. Mum would never let me lick the bowl.

Gran didn't have electricity in her tiny scullery except for the overhead light bulb. She was untroubled by the sockets and everyday electrical appliances that my mother's kitchen seemed unable to function without.

Gran didn't have them, so I supposed *she* simply didn't need them for the job.

A turquoise, gas-powered washer-mangle stood in the corner; I never saw her use it but a thick crust of Omo lurked on the rim, so I supposed she must have done sometimes. Butter was kept fresh and cool in the water chilled "Osokool." Milk bottles stood on the marble topped washstand that served as her work area and everything was within reach.

Even as a small child I was allowed to chop vegetables with razor sharp knives, grate nutmeg and fingernails into the rice pudding, light the gas with matches and test out "*concoctions*" of ingredients.

"I love your kitchen Gran; Mum won't let me play in hers." I said devotedly as I sieved flour in mounds and knocked the lumps through the sieve with the back of a tablespoon.

I did not feel disloyal dismissing the blue and cream Formica glossiness that was my mother's pride and joy in favour of Alma Road's scullery.

It was simply a fact... I did love it.

Gran's enamel gas cooker wore an ancient, blackened, knobby coat of grease that softened and obscured its angles like candle wax. The greasy mess worried me

"Oh, don't worry about that... protects it from rusting Sarah." She explained.

Every few months I helped Gran by lifting the chip basket out of its black pan and scraped the glutinous blackened residue from the bottom of the solidified lump of lard that poked through the basket mesh.

"That's a good girl Sarah. Just to freshen it up a bit luvvie before I get your Grampy's tea."

Gran's chips *always* had tiny black speckles all over them and they were the best chips ever-double fried in deep yellow fat that saw service for years. Many a piece of long eaten haddock relived its glory days when that fat was heated up for egg and chips.

The green enamelled, kitchenette unit located in the scullery contained everything Gran needed; she would set to creating marvels whilst Grampy sat reading his papers by the fire.

Gran's cakes were a revelation; feather light creations whipped and creamed by fork and wooden spoon. Her plump arms would jiggle and flap as she beat the sugar and butter into creamy, white peaks, folding eggs and flour until just the right consistency emerged.

With my best dress protected by a tea-towel wrapped around my waist, I would wait to dollop the fluffy mix into fluted paper cases, licking my "dolloping" finger between each spoonful.

"Look Gran they're all done, and I've tried to get them all the same," sticky cake mix coated my top lip.

It was a skill to get the mixture evenly divided between the twelve bun tins so that nothing was left over, and all the little cakes turned out the same size.

If I got the buns *just* right my Gran always observed "Perfection.... you'll never get married my girl."

"Why won't I get married Gran," I had asked as the last pale ooze of mixture completed the twelfth case at just the right level.

"Oh, it's just a saying Sarah." Gran spoke through the dwindling cigarette butt dangling on her bottom lip; her mouth pulling down on one corner to let the smoke and words drift out.

I felt that being able to smoke, balance a butt on your lip and talk at the same time was a prodigious talent equivalent to ventriloquism. I had tried practising the complex art at home for ages in front of my bedroom mirror with a stubby pencil hanging from my mouth secured with a liberal dab of spit, that was until my mother caught me. My mother gave a loud disapproving tut, slapped my legs hard and said that "she would be having words."

Today the cake distribution passed scrutiny and I, it seemed, was destined to remain unmarried again.

"When your judgement is *that* good my girl, it means you will always see a man's short comings." She said with a wink. Gran was a good winker.

Making cakes was hot work and Gran would have her orange squash mix after *testing* the sherry to make sure it hadn't gone off since the last time, we made butterfly cakes. Luckily for us the sherry never did go off, but Gran did remark that it had a tendency to evaporate in certain weather conditions, which was unfortunate.

CHAPTER 2

Winter 1967

Beatrice was in hospital having her tonsils out. It was the school holidays, and I was to spend a few days at Alma Road.

Beatrice had red jelly with ice cream, and I had Gran... all to myself.

My father delivered me to the house early on Monday morning in his ageing Ford Prefect. He was on his way to work: the detour was making him tetchy.

I arrived with a few essentials for my four-night stay, all neatly packed in my small case. I was under strict instructions from my mother to *mind my Ps and Qs* and to help my grandmother by not getting under her feet.

Gran said that "*I was always an angel and never any trouble*" so I had no worries on that score.

I was starting to grow my hair long. Mother fretted about me going to bed with damp hair in what she described as "that mausoleum of a place".

I asked Gran what a mausoleum was, and she said it was where cheeky cats lived, or at least I think that's what she said.

All through primary school I sported an unflattering, pudding basin bob.

I was mortified by the blunt ugliness of my appearance. Motherly lectures on nits fell on stony ground. I moaned about the unfairness of it, especially since Bea's hair was longer than mine. Apparently, Bea's *was too curly for a nice, neat bob and it needed some weight to keep it under control.*

All the princesses in my fairy tale books had long, wavy locks spread artfully across their pillows as they slept, my ugly mop could not even manage a small set of bunches, no matter how hard I scraped and pulled.

"Mum it's so not fair. Ever body is growing their hair long...Please Mum. Can I...can I? Please..." was my regular refrain.

It was only when I reached double figures that Mother relented and allowed my hair to creep past my ear lobes. This particular visit I was under instructions to remind Gran to wash my hair on Wednesday evening, the regular hair wash night in the Matthews' household.

"We are going shopping later this morning poppet, whilst your Grampy does his ablutions," Gran said as she hung my warm winter coat on the hall stand.

Ablutions were a mystery that never happened at home.... but they did happen in Alma road. After the laying out of towels, soap and hot water, Grampy would requisition the scullery for at least an hour as he performed them. Gran would clear up after Grampy, but for the duration of ablutions the scullery, and the route through it to the garden, was strictly out of bounds.

I would always be instructed to spend a penny beforehand just to be on the safe side.

Gran led the way up the stairs into the front bedroom where she and I would share a bed later that night. The big front bedroom had a frigid air that allowed us to play puffing billies with our breath; pale gasps of steam accompanying my every word, *haa...haaa*.

I helped her straighten the bedclothes; crisp, cotton sheets and scratchy woollen blankets were tucked in firmly, all topped off with a sateen quilted eiderdown and a heavy chenille bedspread. The little fireplace was boarded up to prevent draughts, and the windows bore lingering evidence of the early morning frost on the inside of the grimy windowpane.

"Jack Frost paid us a visit last night Sarah," Gran said as she unpacked my case.

I regularly huffed and blew on the sash windowpanes creating holes in the opaque glitter. Gran didn't object to smeary windows like my mother.... sometimes she would even use her own thumbnail to scratch patterns on the ice to create fairy writing that would fade as the frost melted.

"Let's pop down and make your Grampy his tea and toast before we go out to Albany road," she said as she set off down the landing with a brimming porcelain gazunder retrieved from under the wooden bedstead. She draped a napkin over it and carried it down the steep stairs.

Grampy was sat in his usual place beside the fire waiting for his breakfast; that morning he was cutting his nails.

Grampy's nails formed beautiful, rounded squares at the end of his elegant white hands.

My own father's hands were rough and scratchy with nibbled nails and a persistent orange, greyish-black tinge around the fingers acquired from gardening, nicotine and engine oil. The stains defied the scrubbing of the nail brush and his callouses made tickling prickly.

Once as I watched Dad turn over heavy clods with his spade in the garden, I asked why he couldn't have nice, soft hands like Grampy did.

"I prefer my workers hands any day of the week my girl... yep any day" he said "but don't *you* go saying that I said so Miss."

"Gran shall we make some fairy cakes today?" Monday was not cake day. but I lived in hope.

"No not today Sarah, we've got to do a few errands. And..." she added with emphasis ".... your Aunty Molly is coming this afternoon. She always visits Grampy on Monday and Wednesday afternoons." Gran said.

A visit from Aunty Molly was *not* good news. My face fell a little.

The words *come and give your Aunty a kiss* posed a dreadful dilemma in my mind. Did I aim to the right of her face and risk touching the witchy pale, brown mole that graced her chin and sprouted a solitary curly hair? Or did I lean slightly to the left and risk brushing the grey bristle on her top lip.

I *hated* kissing Aunty Molly and I had told my mother so one day.

Mother had shaken me by the arms and said that Aunty Molly was a lovely, sweet natured lady who had had a hard life and that I should count my blessings. She had added darkly that Aunty Molly had been a very pretty girl once and that I ought to *"watch my step."*

I certainly didn't want to step in whatever Aunty molly had stepped in.

Aunty Molly was tall, thin, and worryingly bristly. She wore her mouse-grey hair in a tight bun at the nape of her neck and adopted a dress code that even to *my* young eyes seemed somewhat bizarre. Long pleated skirts and shapeless jumpers hung off her spare, angular frame and even in winter she wore beige ankle socks with her flat brown brogues.

Aunty Molly's drab, lean, colourlessness was in such stark contrast to my bosomy, vibrant Gran with her neatly coiffed hair that defied the grey, smart heels and red lip stick. Gran laughed and chuckled, Aunty Molly simply smirked occasionally when she scored particularly well at Scrabble.

Aunty Molly came to visit my Grandfather and *he* enjoyed her company. Gran however usually "got on with things" on Mondays or went to a whist drive in the church hall on Wednesdays.

I found it impossible to believe that Aunty Molly was my Gran's sister. I felt it was even odder that for sisters they always had so very little to say to each other.

Bea and I chatted incessantly and quarrelled as much. Gran and Aunty Molly merely exchanged a few pleasantries each time their paths crossed.

My Gran was all twinkle and gaiety, Aunty Molly was dour, prim and plain.

Molly's only concession to ornament was a huge, sparkling sapphire and diamond ring that she wore on her right hand. I admired it fiercely.

Mum said once that *"Aunty Molly had paid a heavy price for that ring"* so I knew it must be *very* valuable indeed.

The short journey to the shops usually took us nearly an hour each way as we progressed in a stop, start fashion a few gossipy yards at a time.

Gran knew such a lot of people, mostly ladies, who enquired after my grandfather and passed on information about neighbours and their current affairs.

Sometimes I struggled with the conversations littered with references to sharp little ears, chatterboxes and *pas devant les enfants.* It seemed to me that "affairs" were very tricky to understand if you were young.

That particular morning we spent absolutely ages in the green grocers picking over the carrots and sprouts; rejecting any that fell short of my grandmother's high standards.

"Here, you hold this paper bag up for me Sarah whilst I get to the bottom of these sprouts." Gran started placing a line of withered, yellowing sprouts along the display edge.

"It appears that all the old tired ones have been stirred through the fresh batch." She said loudly, catching the sheepish eye of young Evan serving behind the counter.

"Well, I'm not buying stale old sprouts and that's fact!" The bakery was to be our last stop. Gran chatted companionably with the gossipy Mrs Evans behind the bakery counter, as she nimbly boxed up some pink and lemon French, fondant fancies, Aunty molly's favourites.

I was secretly amazed that for such a thin lady Aunty Molly had such a *very* sweet tooth; she even sprinkled sugar on her tomatoes. Fresh red tomatoes disappeared under a liberal crunchy dusting of sugar that she devoured with gusto.

I thought Aunty Molly had very ugly teeth; snaggle toothed, grey and gappy.

When I asked Gran why Aunty Molly's teeth were so grey and wonky, she said it was because *Aunty Molly liked indulging in a bit of humbug,* which rather explained the black and white stripey nature of them.

I much preferred Gran's even, white teeth especially when the top set floated so prettily in little bubbles in the glass beside the bed.

If I was looking bored or glum when Grampy insisted on *some quiet for the football scores,* or a *bit of hush for the shipping forecast, she* would "drop" her top teeth for me from the two fangs that anchored them into place. It was a rare treat that inevitably brought me out in a fit of the giggles...my grandfather *never* found it amusing.

"Come on then tuppence we need to get a wriggle on or your Grampy will be cross," Gran extinguished her cigarette in the hall stand urn and breezed down the narrow passageway. The heels of her small shoes clicked purposefully on the hall tiles.

"Off you go Sarah and show him your school report while I get the lunch.... Oh, my goodness just look at the time its nearly quarter past twelve," she said as if I had been dawdling all morning, causing her to be late. "Your

Grandfather likes his lunch at one o'clock on the dot... I'll need to get my skates on."

My heart sank at the thought of my report. The "C+ for Conduct and the damning conclusion *"It appears that Sarah is easily distracted in class and she must try harder to stop chatting."*

My school reports were always presented to my Grandfather, who went through them line by line. The phrase *"could* or *must try harder"* was one of his pet hates implying idleness and a lack of care.

Ultimately it was the small copperplate comments that drew his eye as he passed judgement and there were rather too many references to *"chatting too much and not giving my full attention to the task in hand."* I knew that I was heading for a lecture.

Mercifully the potatoes caught on the bottom of the pan when they boiled dry in the two minutes Gran said she that popped out for a tinkle.... the nutty, smoky aroma this imparted to the mashed potatoes, even with a bit of trimming, distracted Grampy from any more lecturing about the dreaded C+ and *"trying harder."* We ate our lunch in gloomy silence.

Aunty Molly arrived at just before three o'clock, wearing a beige beret and a long, grey, gaberdine mackintosh. By the time my Aunt had walked the one mile from Inkerman street, where she lived with Miss Ruth, her lodger, the mac had warmed up just enough to give her a distinctly rubbery odour.

Aunty Molly was tall and thin with huge, ugly feet. Her sensible, flat shoes looked *massive* to me, compared with Gran's tiny size three and a half.

Gran wore neat, dainty court shoes that I used to covet and play with as a small child; perfect high heels for make believe.

Aunty Molly had enormous feet. *Fowler feet my* mother called them.

My own mother followed Gran and had the dainty feet and the short stature of the Benson side of the family.   But Aunty Molly was a Fowler through and through.

One Saturday as we shopped for some new school shoes, I was mortified to be accused by the assistant of going up a whole size since my last pair; my feet it seemed were growing at an expensive rate.

My mother observed that I would probably have *feet like Aunty Molly.* That day I went home and cried bitter tears over my hideous feet.

Princesses *always* had small, dainty feet that slipped beautifully into glass slippers. It was the un-loveable ugly ducklings with big feet who had to cut off their big toes to fit the prince's beautiful shoe.

I concluded that *that* was probably the reason Aunty Molly wasn't married.... Big feet!

"Clifford.... how good to see you, I'm sorry to say that it's pretty foul outside this afternoon. That low has moved in far quicker than forecast." Aunty Molly always discussed the weather in some technical depth with my grandfather who took a great interest in such things; sometimes a discussion about isobars could last for an hour or more.

"Miss Ruth thought you might enjoy this jig saw puzzle of south Devon cottages, so I brought it along for us to do. I've counted the pieces-*twice,* so we won't have any mishaps like before." She said, alluding to the infamous *missing last piece fiasco* that caused my grandfather to fly into a rage and seethe for days.

She placed the box on the side table as she bent to give Grampy a peck on the cheek.

"Ah Sarah.... how lovely to see you! Come and give your Aunty a kiss."

I aimed for the mole.

*

The jig saw puzzle was a great success and the three of us worked for nearly an hour and a half on a large tray on the card table. Meanwhile Gran "got on with things" in the scullery; a faint whiff of tobacco drifted into the room as she made the sandwiches.

My "job", so Aunty Molly said, was to find all the edge pieces and to find all the pieces with blue sky on them. The pieces were filed into two piles ready for assembly.

Grampy's "job" was to tackle all the difficult areas such as the thatch or sky; apparently it needed a certain sort of intellect and patience to do large areas of similar colour. I thought the sky was the most boring part of the puzzle.

Aunty Molly and I could only tackle the easy bits of the puzzle, our role was to help and assist. Grampy always had the honour of putting in the last puzzle piece; after all he'd done all the hard work.

My father would never have sat doing jig-saw puzzles.

Aunty Molly left just before six o'clock with a promise to return on Wednesday afternoon for a game of Scrabble with Grampy.

On Wednesdays, donning her best hat and lipstick, Gran went out to her weekly Whist drive held in the local church hall. Whatever the weather Gran never missed her game of Whist and the juicy gossip she gleaned over cards.

After Aunty Molly left, the rest of the evening was spent quietly in front of the fire playing "Patience" as Grampy had paperwork to do. Gran aired my winceyette nightie in front of the fire over the wooden clothes horse and as a final insurance for a good night's sleep she made me a mug of Horlicks.

That night as I lay tucked up in the big cold bed, my feet searching out the pink hot water bottle, I wondered why Aunty Molly and her whiskers kept coming to see Grampy every week without fail?

Later that night Gran crept into bed and her warm comforting bulk slumbered next to me with soft snores until morning.

When I was woken up by the familiar clink of milk bottles settling on the doorstep Gran was already up and gone. She would be hard at work tackling the morning chores ahead of my Grandfather's breakfast and his appearance in the back-sitting room.

"Come on Imp stop trying your Grampy's patience," Gran said as she brought Grampy's morning cup of tea into the front sitting room where he slept. I sat in my nightie on the small sofa asking questions about this, that and the other.

The single bed occupied much of the small front room, which was by far the nicest room in the house; it even had a little gas fire in the modern tiled grate and a view of the street if you squinted through the net curtains.

If my Grampy was in a particularly good mood he would let me play the feet game. That morning I was pestering for permission to play.

The game involved me standing on the small, tiled heart and chilling my toes and feet as I cold as I could bear them. Then I would quickly jump into the bed and plonk them onto Grampy's nice warm legs to see if I could make him squeal.

My father *always* squealed that I was a little monkey who had feet like ice-blocks.

But Grampy never so much as batted an eye lid no matter how cold I made them. It wasn't fair...... He always won.

I had just asked him if we could play the game when Gran brought in his tea. One day I felt sure that I would be the winner but this morning it was not to be.

"No more pestering your Grampy Sarah, your porridge is ready. Run along now and eat it up while it's nice and hot.... I've put the cream off the top of the milk on it for you."

Having the thick cream off the top of the Jersey gold top milk was a big treat that usually fell to Grampy's portion. But this morning Grampy said that he would prefer a boiled egg. The buttery yellow liquid was to be all mine. I scooted off into the back room.

Later that morning Grampy was doing his paperwork. I sat next to him fetching and carrying little articles to and from the small bureau. It was always easy to find anything that Grampy requested because the bureau was arranged with military precision in the small drawers and slots that formed the bureau's interior. Nothing, absolutely nothing was allowed to be moved from its designated place.

Once I had picked up a small, colourful post card that I found in the stamp drawer to ask him about it.... he promptly summoned my Grandmother to ask her *why* she had put the offending card in the wrong place and sharp words had ensued.

How could he possibly hope to know where things were if people moved them or didn't put them back in their proper places. He raged.

The stamp from Malta, destined for his collection, had not been soaked off yet and until then, and not before, the post card had *absolutely* no business being in the stamp drawer.

Compared with the chaotic jumble in some of our drawers at home it seemed such a very small transgression, but Gran said meekly that she was very sorry and that it wouldn't happen again.

As I carefully sought out the ball of rubber bands for Grampy to add to, I pondered a family conundrum that had started to thread through my mind. I had recently attended a wedding with my parents of a distant cousin, and it had occurred to me that I did not know what Gran's name was when she was a little girl. The concept of changing names had caught my imagination.

"Grampy what was Gran's name when she was a little girl." I asked passing the neatly entwined ball of rubber bands.

"She was called Eleanor... Eleanor Fowler when she was growing up and then when we married in 1928, she became Mrs Eleanor Harris." He replied without looking up from his documents.

I allowed this nugget of new information to seep in before progressing my enquiries .... "Oh, so Aunty Molly is really called Molly Fowler, then," I said with certainty.

Grampy looked up with his nut-brown eyes. "No," he said slowly, "no.... your Aunty Molly is called Margaret Smith.... Molly is a diminutive... or a pet name if you like." he added by way of explanation, already anticipating my next question as the unfamiliar word "diminutive" trickled past me.

This revelation about Aunty Molly's name a stopped me in my tracks. *Not only was Aunty Molly not a "Molly" but it seemed that she wasn't a Fowler either.... Perhaps she wasn't even Gran's sister.*

"So, Aunty Molly isn't really Gran's sister then.... I mean if she's not a Fowler?"

My Grandfather shook his head at my childish logic.

"That's incorrect Sarah.... Aunty Molly *is your* Grandmother's older sister, and she is called Margaret Smith because she married a Mr Archibald Smith in 1927."

He looked towards the scullery where my Gran stood in the doorway with two cups of tea, listening.

"I was just explaining to Sarah why Aunty Molly was called Smith." He said levelly.

"So, I gather," she said. "Well now Sarah, if you have finished helping your Grampy, then perhaps you would like to help me bake some fairy cakes for tea."

The thought of helping Gran with the baking, especially with it being a Tuesday, drove all thoughts and chatter about Aunty Molly straight out of my head.

Later on, that night as I lay in bed, cuddling my hot water bottle, I thought about Aunty Molly and the newly discovered, mysterious, Uncle Archibald. I resolved to ask

Aunty Molly all about it the following afternoon when she came to play Scrabble.

On the Wednesday morning of Aunty Molly's visit, it rained .... relentless, driving stair rods that plunged the small house into gloomy darkness and me into pestering boredom.

By eleven o'clock, I had explored the button box, and made some fire lighters, but no boats.

By raiding the scullery and the larder I had peeled off and found ten Golly labels from the jam and marmalade jars, just enough for the saxophonist-Hooray! And discovered that I could produce loud Kazoo noises on a piece of Izal toilet tissue wrapped around Gran's tortoise-shell hair comb.

I had twiddled, twirled, skipped and hummed until my Gran suggested that I should give Grampy a bit of peace and play upstairs in the little back bedroom where the dressing up box lurked.

In the tiny, dusty haven, that was the back room, a large jumble of old clothes and unfashionable hats lurked in a battered tin trunk that was covered in peeling labels. A tatty, fox fur stole with staring glass eyes and scratchy dangling claws used to frighten me a little with its musky smell; cracked leather pads and rather goofy expression.

A satin embroidered Kimono, pink and black with trailing leaves and exotic butterflies wandering across its back was a firm favourite. But my absolute delight was my mother's 1950's wedding dress. A tiny ballerina length lace dress with a Peter Pan collar and pointed sleeves that buttoned up the arms almost to the elbow. In that fairy tale dress, which on me nearly reached to the floor, I became

Sleeping beauty, or Cinderella or even my very favourite - Rapunzel; I just needed to work on the hair.

"Now don't thump about though Sarah, otherwise it will sound as if you are coming through the ceiling," Gran cautioned. "Run along and don't make a mess, there's a good girl.... I'll call you when it's time to come down and wash your hands for lunch."

With that I scampered up the stairs into a world of make believe and fairy stories.

After posing in a series of old hats in front of the small, foxed mirror, and practising some graceful marching and bowing with my arms akimbo in the Kimono to capture the beauty of the back embroidery, I reached deep into the trunk for *the dress*.   As I slipped it over my head the familiar smell of faded rose water delighted my senses.

I twirled and preened in the wedding finery complete with peep toe shoes and a short-battered veil neatly attached to a small Juliet cap; I felt like a princess.

I thought about Aunty Molly. I still found it incredible to believe that she had once been a young bride; I resolved to ask her all about it.

Curiosity killed the cat, Gran used to say darkly whenever I pestered her with Why? Why? Why Gran?

But satisfaction brought it back, we used to chant back cheekily at school. I never knew what that answer meant either.... I never dared say it to Gran.

After our lunch at one o'clock of fried egg and chips, Gran cleared away the dishes, removed the tea cloth from the card table, made up the fire, and sliced and prepared the ham sandwiches which she wrapped in grease proof paper.

At just after two o'clock Gran put on her best hat and gloves to go out. The Whist afternoon started at two thirty. I watched admiringly as Gran fastened up her best, blue winter coat with its rabbit fur collar that looked like mink.

She applied her red lipstick from its gold sheath and dabbed powder on her nose from her Coty compact. She looked beautiful.

"I'll be back just before five o'clock to serve the afternoon tea. Be a good girl for your Grampy and listen out for the door knocker. Aunty Molly should be here in about half an hour. Now don't open the door to anyone else Sarah, there's a good girl."

It went without saying that only "expected" visitors were welcome on the Harris doorstep and even then, the rules of visiting etiquette must be observed.

It was always *very* important to enter or exit 12 Alma road at such times, and in such a manner, that did not disturb my grandfather's viewing and listening schedules.

Grampy had fixed opinions about visiting times. Regardless of age or relationship he would *shush* and glare at any offender with such ferocity that ensured silence endured. Even poor old Father John, on a courtesy visit from St Bartholomew's, felt the need to observe a few minutes contemplative silence during the tail end of the weather forecast.

"I've put a kettle on the hob next to the fire so it should be all ready in a jiffy when I get in, "she said. With that Gran gave me quick kiss, collected a large umbrella and left for the mysteries of the afternoon whist club.

Aunty Molly was due arrive at just before three and today; I had the job of answering the door. Usually, Gran would leave the door on the latch for Molly but today the rain and wind made it preferable to keep it firmly shut against the weather. I sat and listened for the tell-tale sharp, triple rap.

If ever I was in the house alone with Grampy and the door was knocked when visitors were *not* expected I was not allowed to answer the door. Grampy was very particular about callers, and only the chosen visitors to Alma road knew the special triple knock. Unexpected visitors threw him into a grumpy tizz.

Aunty Molly arrived punctual and bristly as usual; we settled down to play.

After a while the game of Scrabble slowed somewhat; Grampy was spending rather a long time trying to work out how to get his "J" and "Z" onto a double word or triple letter. It was boring.

I sat impatiently waiting for my turn, which was next, but I knew better than to try and hurry Grampy.

Aunty Molly sat impassively waiting for her turn, every so often she would create a gentle *click* as letters were moved around on the grey plastic ledges.

I decided to tackle the Uncle Archibald conundrum.

"I was playing at dressing up this morning Aunty Molly," I said by way of an opening salvo.

"Oh, that's fun Sarah and what were you pretending to be?" She scrutinized her letters and plotted her moves. *Click*

"Well first I pretended I had a hat shop selling hats to pretty ladies, then I was a Chinese lady who sold tea." I said.

"Ah I see that you must have found Uncle Albert's kimono that he sent to our mother when he went to the far East.... so actually, Sarah you were a *Japanese* tea lady" she said. *Click*

My Grandfather shuffled and re-arranged his letters several times but still made no attempt to place them on the board.

I absorbed this latest nugget of information. My father said that Uncle Albert was Gran and Aunty Molly's younger brother. Dad had said that Uncle Albert had served bravely in the second world war and had died in Malaya fighting the Japanese. It was curious that he had sent home a Japanese Kimono. But I unwilling to be distracted from my quest for Uncle Archie, I let it go.

"And after that, Aunty Molly, I pretended that I was Cinderella going to the ball in Mummy's lovely wedding dress...." I paused slightly before taking a deep breath....

" What was *your* wedding dress like Aunty Molly? Did you feel like a princess when you got married to Uncle Archie?"

A small silence descended. Scrabble tiles knocked together. *Click, click.*

Aunty Molly barely blinked her lizard eyelids as she said evenly. "Oh goodness... *that* was such a very long time ago Sarah... I've quite forgotten all about it.... but I'm sure that you would think it very old fashioned.... things..." she said obliquely, "things were very different in those days.... Very different indeed."

Grampy, after consulting a small, battered dictionary, clattered down all his letters onto the board. "Well Molly I think that is the best I can do under the circumstances -

Jezebel for forty-two." He said as he totted up his impressive score.

I was puzzled by the word, "I thought we weren't allowed names Grampy?" I dared to suggest as he slotted the strange word neatly into place. *Click, click.*

"A Jezebel *can be* a name, Sarah but it also means a loose or fallen woman.... a temptress. It's in the Scrabble dictionary," he said with authority.

If it was in Grampy's Scrabble dictionary, then that was the end of the matter. I contented myself with refocussing my attention on Uncle Archibald.

It was my turn to play, within two minutes I had used Grampy's "Z" to make Zoo with my two letter "o's.

"Well Sarah that was quick! Is that really the best you can do? I don't think you thought about that for very long.... I mean it does seem a bit of a waste that you just miss reaching a double word score by doing that." He said accusingly.

I rummaged in the bag to find two new letters. Grampy hated "wasted" opportunities; particularly at Scrabble; it smacked of a lack of concentration.

"I'm fine Grampy I had a lot of "o's on my tray to use up. It's Aunty Molly's turn to go now." I said, keen to drop the conversation about wasted Scrabble letters.

I wanted to resume my line of questioning before the moment was lost. Aunty Molly sat quietly contemplating her letters and the state of play. After a few moments I interrupted her thoughts.

"Aunty Molly.... What happened to Uncle Archibald? Is he dead too?" I added; still thinking about Uncle Albert and the Japanese.

My Grampy sucked in a large hiss of irritation through his front teeth. "Sarah you are being rather impertinent today Miss..... pressing your Aunty Molly with personal questions, especially when she is trying to concentrate!" His tone was stern, his words clipped.

I glanced sheepishly at Aunty Molly to see the effect of my crime.

"That's all right Clifford, the child has a right to ask," she said as she shuffled letters. *Click.*

"Your Uncle Archie.... for that was what everyone called him.... went to work in Malaysia in 1934. The 1930's were a hard time for many families.... in more ways than one," Molly said slowly choosing her words with care.

I listened quietly as a *new* Aunty Molly took shape before my eyes.

"And then the War came a few years later Sarah. .... All in all, it was a terrible time," she added thoughtfully as if recalling some distant horrors.

"Your Uncle Archie was still working abroad when war broke out.... and.... and like many other women with men overseas at that time, I... I didn't hear from him again.... So, in answer to your question Sarah," she said without looking up.

"Yes, I believe your great Uncle Archie to be dead now, after all this time.... He is dead to me." She sounded sad and flat.

I felt sorry for her.

Aunty Molly placed her remaining letters on the board and sat lost in thought as we finished the game. I knew better than to ask any more questions.

Grampy won as usual.

The following week at home I told my father that I knew about Uncle Archie and that Aunty Molly had told me "that he was missing presumed dead." My father listened carefully and said that he had always known that Uncle Archie "had jumped ship" and so I supposed that it probably amounted to the same thing.

CHAPTER 3

Spring 1970

It was four o'clock and I sat quietly with a pile of blank questionnaires and my project note pad waiting for Grampy to finish his tea and Welsh cake.... *my Welsh cakes*. The little crumbly circle studded with raisins and dusted with sugar was being savoured and evaluated. a product of my afternoon's baking with Gran. I hoped fervently that *my* amateur effort was up to my Grampy's high standard; too dry, too thick, too plain or.... worst of all scorched would sour his mood for the rest of the afternoon.

I had chosen *his* cake with particular care from the pile as they were flipped and turned on the black bake stone; early ones in the batch were often a little pale or doughy; later ones had a tendency to be dark and crisp as the stone grew more intense, but the ones in the middle batch were often perfection.

A soft, golden brown, middle specimen was being eaten.

The mantle clock ticked as he chewed thoughtfully on the offering. If I wanted a good interview with my Grandfather, I knew there was no point in trying to rush the matter. He would be ready in his own good time and not a moment before.

Gran had popped next door to see Mrs James for a few minutes so I was to start with Grampy, she would join in with her thoughts later on.

"Not *too* much later Nelly," grampy had added as Gran had tidied her hair to leave. Now she would not stay long.

The day had been gloomy and cold. The sky had that greasy, grey light that had promised rain which never arrived. Inside the back parlour of Alma road, the remaining daylight was fading fast.

I knew better than to switch on the little lamps before my grandfather felt in need of them, *money doesn't grow on trees Sarah. Bills need paying.* So, we both sat in the dwindling daylight, that struggled to crawl through the one side window servicing the small room.

The narrow sash window was located directly opposite my Grampy's chair giving him a view of the side wall of next door's parlour and occasionally a glimpse of the cat that slept on top of the coal store roof. Even on the best of days he couldn't really see the sky from his armchair.

I had started my new secondary school in the Autumn and now, with all the toadying enthusiasm that came with having a crush on my History teacher, I was anxious to get a good grade for my Easter project work; "Modern 20th century social history."

"*Now Class you have a very exciting opportunity this Easter holiday to take part in a social History project,*" Miss Jervis announced with a smart clap of her hands.

" *All of you must try to find a senior member of our community, such as a neighbour, or grandparent, who is willing to share their memories of living in a different time with you. A portal into the past!*" She beamed enthusiastically at the lively class.

For Miss Jervis it was her first appointment to a teaching post, she was of the view that History should be brought alive for the pupils. Dates and dusty statistics were *so* yesterday. She was determined to make her mark in the department.

"*So, boys and girls, you may consider, for example how this person's house might have changed over the years as the world and technology has changed? Or you may try to ask them why they lived where they did? Was it because of their job, were they born there? Think really hard, any aspect of social life is acceptable.... and.... the best project will win a small prize.*"

Miss Jervis made this final part of her announcement with such a dramatic flourish that it sent shivers of excitement down my spine. A prize... I *so* wanted to win that prize.

There had been much fidgeting and giggling as boys and girls suggested *victims* who might be sacrificed on the altar of their school project. I immediately thought of Gran and Grampy.

I was dubious about how much my grandparents' house in Alma road had actually changed over the years. To me the house *always* looked the same; same scullery, same carpets, same wallpaper, same furniture, same outside toilet, same spiders.... Same Gran. A part of me loved the comforting sameness of it. A visit to see my grandparents' home never varied significantly from the tracks that were their settled lives.

Sometimes Aunty Molly hoved into view with her bristles and halitosis for a game of Scrabble and cards. Uncle Archie had been put back in the too sad and difficult box, not to be mentioned again, and occasionally my sister Beatrice came with me, when she wasn't pirouetting through ballet or drama classes or any one of the other numerous clubs and hobbies that she seemed to attend most days of the week.

"Remember boys and girls to be polite and respectful at all times to your interviewees, but most importantly, you may only repeat or tell anything about your subject's life with their permission. I'm sure you will all find it a very rewarding experience and I hope we will be able to share each other's valuable memories. Remember this our chance to have a window on the past... Happy hunting!" Miss Jervis trilled as we gathered up our questionnaire sheets in tatty handfuls.

Grampy put his cup and saucer on top of the now empty plate. "Yes... that was very nice... a good effort.... thank you, Sarah. Now, be a good girl and take these plates out into the scullery for your Gran.... you may switch on the lamps and *then* you can tell me about this project of yours."

I leap up to remove the plates, my heart did a little flip as I recognised my golden opportunity to catch my grandfather's good humour. I'd made *a good effort*, that was the highest accolade I could hope to achieve in my Grampy's eyes. I had tried my best.

As I sat with my pen poised over the questionnaire, I was dithering about how to get started on the meat of the project. I'd filled in his full name, date of birth and occupation: Clifford Aubrey Harris born in Cardiff 1903 retired. Former occupation; senior shipping clerk for Cardiff Docklands corporation.

I knew that Grampy hadn't served in either war; too young for the Great war, not fit for the Second World war, I decided to try to get him to talk to me about living at Alma road.

"So, when did you and Gran come to live in Alma road and why did you choose this house?"

I felt this question was an easy, opening gambit that could lead to more promising material. I waited several moments whilst he crafted his reply.

"Your Gran and I rented this house from Mrs Pugh in August 1930, just over two years after we had got married in March 1928; your mother, Jean was nearly nine months old at the time and we wanted a home of our own."

He rattled off the timeline with the same precise exactitude that he brought to everything he did.

"It was quite hard for a young couple to find and afford accommodation in those days especially since your Gran and I wanted to stay near to the family, who all were all living in this area at the time," he said.

My ears pricked up, Grampy never usually explained his actions; they just *were*. I wrote *"close family support network"* in my best script.

"The house belonged to a widowed lady called Mrs Olwyn Pugh; of course, she is dead now, but the house still belongs to her family and we rent it from them." He added for clarification.

This nugget of domestic detail was also news to me as I had assumed that the house was theirs. *A rented house!*

"We were told, at the time by a neighbour, that Mrs Pugh was looking for a respectable young couple who would rent the property *and* take care of her things whilst she was living away for a while. Apparently, we fitted the bill." He said, a faint smile flickered on his lips as he recalled the memory.

"But why did Mrs Pugh move away.... and why didn't *she* sell the house?" I asked keen to mine this particular seam a little deeper.

Clifford chose his words with care; recalling a long distant memory, a snapshot of his youth, when hope was so bright.

"The 1930's was a difficult time for many people.... and it was a particularly difficult time for the Pugh family, Sarah.... Mr Pugh had been killed in an industrial accident when he was working at a munitions packing factory in 1917. Then, a few months after the tragedy, their only son James returned home injured from service on the Western front, in 1918," he spoke slowly as I scribbled copious notes trying to capture a world that was alien to my own. *This sounded exactly the sort of living history Miss Jervis wanted.*

"But *why* did they have to leave Alma road?" I asked, unsure where this part of the story might take me.

"Because, poor James Pugh, like many hundreds of other miserable devils at that time, had suffered a mustard gas attack in the trenches on the Western front.... mercifully, for his mother, he came back.... but he never fully recovered; he was a broken man with poor health.". He paused a moment to collect his thoughts.

"Gas was a terrible weapon Sarah that kept killing for decades to come; twisting its knife into many a man's lungs 'til he gasped his last; robbing him of his health and choking the joy out of his life." He spat his words out with a bitterness that I had never heard in my grandfather's voice before.

"By 1930 Mrs Pugh had decided that with James' health declining, she should take him to live beside the sea for the sake of his lungs; a nice little bungalow with no stairs and a veranda for James to sit on. Fresh air was considered the best medicine in those days," he added by way of explanation. "This house was to be let out to fund their move and when, *or if*, James improved Mrs Pugh said that they would move back to be near the family in Cardiff....they never moved back."

The forty-watt bulb in the lamp struggled to lift the shadows that were settling over the small room; the sinking fire gave a grudging glow.

I pushed my hair behind my ear as I scrawled notes on the greying page. "That's very sad.... especially for Mrs Pugh. I mean all those bad things happening to one family meant that you and Gran got to live in *their* house instead of them.... it still seems very unfair when you think about it." I said chewing the end of my Biro.

"No-one ever said that life was fair Sarah. One person's misfortune can open up an opportunity for another to seize their chance. No body actually *wants* the bad things to happen but, since they *do* ... then it's a chance for the opportunists to take their own stab at happiness; grab it with both hands and live.... A cancelling out of the misery, if you will." He said as he lifted his gaze from the flickers that flared and fluttered in the grate. I had the uneasy feeling that somehow, he had forgotten about poor Mrs Pugh.

He pressed on, ".... sometimes other people get their feelings hurt along the way; casualties of unhappy events if you like.... No body *means* it to happen, but it does just the same.... One person's loss is another person's gain in life.... And that's about the long and the short of it.... Isn't it...? Eleanor?"

Clifford looked across the room to the small figure standing poised and listening on the threshold.

Absorbed as I was in my work, I had not heard the click of the front door, or the clack of the shoes in the hall, or my grandmother enter the little back room. She stood in the shadow of the hallway door.

As I turned to follow my grandfather's gaze, I saw an expression cross Gran's face that I struggled to interpret; gone was her bounce and glow fuelled by a tid-bit of news, buoyed up as she usually was by a natter with Mrs James. I saw a glimpse of pain, sadness and a tiredness around the eyes that made her look bone weary.

Gran looked old as the shadows lengthened.

CHAPTER 4

1974

"Sarah pop up stairs with that bag of linen for me, there's a love. Your father has left the laundry bag by the hallstand.   He seemed to be in in a bit of a rush today, no time to pop in.... you go on up and I'll be up to put it away properly in a minute."

Gran called out her instructions from the kitchen as I sat in the back-room parlour waiting for my grandfather to finish his ablutions.

These days Grampy seemed take far longer than he used to "going about his business."

I had spent the last fifteen minutes waiting for him to appear from his activities in the scullery. With nothing to do, I was bored. The weekly trips to Alma road were beginning to turn into a bit of a chore for a restless teenager. Sometimes I tried to dodge the scheduled visit.

"Oh, come now Sarah....you know that Gran and Grampy always look forward to your visits. Its only a couple of hours of your time whilst your father takes Beatrice for her piano lesson. Surely that's not too much to ask is it?" Mother wheedled accusingly when I raised the prospect of meeting up with friends in the local park instead of my duty visit to Alma road.

"Besides your father must return the bed linen; it's all washed and ready for her. You can hardly expect your father to go on his own and then just drop it off without popping in to see your Grandparents can you now Sarah?" Mother piled on the guilt, brick upon brick, crushing resistance.

"Besides, Gran will be expecting you, won't she?" Mum let the question hang in the air.

My mother always managed to get her own way. As a teenager I put it down to the only child syndrome. For my mother there never was any squabbling with a demanding sister who squawked at the top of her voice if I borrowed her Jackie magazine without asking. No competing for Dad's time as he shuttled between Bea's ballet classes and her thousand and one hobbies. No, my mother was used to wheedling *and* getting her own way. Spoilt only child syndrome.

Yes of course Gran would be expecting me, what other answer was there. They had their rhythms and routines, and I was one of them. "Ok, ok.... I'll go then," I muttered reluctantly. My mother smiled triumphantly; job done. Of course, I wouldn't let Gran down.

Even the promise of collecting my weekly pocket money from Grampy was starting to lose its appeal now that I had a Saturday paper round. It went without saying that I did still love seeing Gran, but Grampy's incessant quizzing about exam results, the latest maths tests, essay marks and "O" level predictions felt rather like being under the microscope; a struggling insect placed on a slide and examined in minute detail.

Under pressure I would sometimes try to fob him off with airy, vague comments of making good progress and teachers being pleased with me, but Grampy always lighted on the detail. The exact turn of phrase was invariably winkled out of me; he missed nothing.

Grampy always found out what he wanted to know in the end. That was the one unfailing truism about my grandfather; *nothing* escaped his notice and he *always* got to the bottom of things in the end. If he ever appeared *not* to know something it was because he simply chose not to.

As I trudged up the steep, creaky staircase with the fresh white linen I noticed a froth of cobwebs making skeins across the ceiling. The dusty webs housed clusters of ethereal, small, bodied spiders with hideously long gossamer legs. The creatures crouched in the greying corners of the ceilings making the place look grubby and unkempt.

I tried to recall the last time I had been upstairs. Everywhere I looked seemed shabby and forlorn; the paint work on the banister rails chipped and peeling. Beneath the dado rail the ugly, knobbly creamy paper covered in stylised flowers and leaves was thick with grime, the collected dust throwing the unfashionable pattern into high relief. The red patterned stair runner was bald in places and an unfamiliar sweet, woody odour invaded my senses as I climbed.

I headed for the chilly box room. I had not been into the cramped back bedroom for quite some time; my childish forays into the glamorous world of make believe and dressing up boxes was long past. The room looked smaller than I remembered it.

A jumble of boxes containing the discarded old shoes and dressing up clothes was now piled haphazardly against one side the in the alcove next to the boarded-up fireplace. On the other side of the fireplace a net curtain wire draped with a blanket was stretched and sagging in front of a large copper water tank.

The tank was wearing a tatty, grey, padded jacket tied on with string in a vain attempt to conserve the precious hot water generated by the parlour's feeble back boiler. Two wooden slatted shelves rested above the tank and served as Gran's airing cupboard. Apart from a few grey bath towels shoved to one side, the shelves were otherwise devoid of laundry.

In the right-hand corner of the top slatted shelf sat a large zinc bucket brimming with water. A sizeable, creeping brown stain ran accusingly across the left-hand corner of the room, a piece of ceiling paper had helpfully come away in a triangle, the paper now acting as a conduit down into the bucket. I stood staring at the make-do arrangement.

From the colour of the staining and repeated wavy brown patterns fanning out like bark on a tree, it was obvious that the leaks had been progressing for quite some time. I dithered about where to place the crisp, clean sheets.

"Ooh...do be careful what you're doing with those clean sheets Sarah love. "Gran said as she came up behind me in the back room. "I think I might need to empty that blessed bucket again before you put the linen away for me; just give me a moment."

I stood speechless as Gran took down the heavy pail and lugged it off to the washbasin in the next-door bathroom.

"Righty oh Sarah, now we can get on with putting those things away." She carefully positioned the bucket back under the sagging paper. "Make sure those pillowcases go well over to the left for me please, there's a love."

I stood clutching my mother's freshly laundered linen, reluctant to place it on the musty wooden shelf.

"Gran, don't you think you ought to get that leak mended?" I eyed the mouldy wallpaper with a thinly veiled look of disgust. A small silver fish louse scuttled behind the wallpaper seam.

"Oh, I don't like to bother Mr Pugh with worries about the house. It's fine as long as you empty that bucket regularly.... if we have a fine patch of weather it doesn't need emptying for ages." Gran busied herself stacking the linen well away from the drip.

"Anyway Sarah, I keep most of the spare linen in that chest in the middle bedroom. Once I've changed the bed with this clean laundry it will be empty in here again, so a little drip or two is no bother at all really." She said, as if it was the most natural thing in the world to catch water in a bucket in the corner of her back-bed room.

I was aghast at the squalid wrongness of it all- nobody should live like this, especially not *my* Gran. The woody aroma of damp and mould seemed even stronger now that the drip bucket had been moved.

"But Gran that bucket was almost full! It's hardly an occasional drip."

Gran re-folded two pillowcases.

"You might have some tiles off the roof... or something. It's probably soaking stuff in the attic as well." I added lamely.

My grandmother kept her back to me, humming a tuneless refrain that often accompanied her tidying and sorting.

"Does Grampy know about that leak?" I persisted undeterred by her lack of response.
At that she turned, her face wore a stony expression.

"I never worry your grandfather about things he doesn't *need* to know about my girl." She started to leave the small airless room...." So, I'll thank you for minding your own business Sarah Jayne."

She resumed her gentle humming as she made her way down the creaky stairs to make my grandfather a fresh pot of tea.

Later that afternoon as I journeyed home in the car, I raised the subject of the box room and the leaks with my father. Whatever Gran said I was determined that something ought to be done about it.

"Dad... Gran has got a real problem with leaks in her back-bed room. I mean it's awful; the paper's hanging off the ceiling, and it smells horrible; all fusty and damp. Even the laundry shelves are turning mouldy.... It really needs fixing. "

I waited for a few seconds before adding, "and... and for some reason she doesn't want to tell Grampy *or* Mr Pugh about it."

My father kept his eyes on the road.

"Couldn't you do something for her Dad?" I pressed, keen to get an ally.

My father shook his head.

"I've been on at her about those blessed leaks for at least a year now. It's a load of rubbish about her *not wanting to bother Mr Pugh....* I've offered to go up in the attic myself to see where the rain is getting in Sarah. Your grandmother has told me *very* firmly to keep my nose out of *her* business.... you can't help some people Sarah, especially if they don't want to be helped." He added.

"At this rate the whole place will gradually fall down around her ears-still on her own head be it; it's her choice.... Your grandmother can be a very stubborn old woman when she wants to be." He paused for a few moments.

"She isn't going to change her ways now Sarah... more's the pity." He added under his breath.

Sarah digested this nugget of information- so Dad *had* known about the leaks for ages. She felt certain that she'd never heard him mention the matter before - it went without saying that her mother would know about the problem as well.

A wave of irritation washed over her. Gran's obstinacy over seeking help *was* ridiculous. Why on earth wouldn't she want someone get up in the attic and get a bloody leak fixed?

CHAPTER 5

September 1977

With all the hectic, selfishness of youth I had neglected my grandparents of late. Shopping trips with my best friend Judith, a steady boyfriend, study rotas and exams. So many things had a greater call on my time; days flew by, weekends disappeared. Visits once so eagerly anticipated became a chore; I repeatedly found pressing reasons to skip going to Alma road... after all Bea hardly ever visited. But this Sunday was different; I was off to Bristol university the following week. I needed to say good-bye, especially to Gran.

"Let's not keep Grampy waiting; be a love and take this tray in to the table for me Sarah, I just need to pop to the lavatory.... I'll be back in just two tics." Gran swatted a bluebottle away from the cheese and cucumber sandwiches that were already curling at the edges; she handed me the tea tray.

"It's quite heavy... so be careful how you go there's a good girl." Gran took a cigarette from a packet kept in the cutlery drawer and lit it from the gas cooker. She headed for the sweet spot next to the toilet her swollen legs moving in a slow and creaky fashion.

It was Sunday afternoon, and I was bubbling over with nervous excitement at the prospect of leaving Cardiff to go off to University; freedom beckoned! Outside the day was bright and still warm for the time of year, inside the house felt cold and gloomy.

Grampy was of the view that, regardless of the weather, early September was far too early for a fire. Alma road ran according to my grandfather's agenda, not the capricious vagaries of the seasons.

Today there was no tarry odour from a coal fire to compete with the familiar scent of damp walls and stale urine that was Alma road. The less I visited the more I noticed the smell; an old smell that was never mentioned or questioned-*have you burnt the toast again Nell? Is that bacon singed? Nelly.... I'm sure I can smell those potatoes boiling dry!* But never "Why does that sink reek?" I was complicit in the lie.

A small bunch of blowsy dahlias perched on the bureau caught my eye. The brash red, orange and yellow blooms, so redolent of impending Autumn, added an unexpected splash of colour to the tatty sitting room.

Unless it was a birthday, flowers didn't often make an appearance in Alma road, especially dahlias.

Gran hated dahlias, *only earwigs and Aunty Molly love dahlia's* she had explained when I had once pursued her dislike of the flower. Grampy sat with a crocheted rug over his knees to ward off the chill. I settled the tray on the tea table before pouring the tea.

"Uh... where shall I put this for you Grampy?" I said, spying a new jumble of small white boxes that covered the side table next to his chair. He swept them aside with his carefully manicured hands and cleared a small space for the bone china cup and saucer.

"Thank you, Sarah.... I *told* your grandmother to remove those this morning," he said with emphasis, gesturing towards the offending boxes.

"Nelly.... Nelly!" he bellowed towards the kitchenette knowing full well that she was in the garden. "Nellieee!...."

"Coming Clifford.... I'm coming..." she trilled. Gran bustled into the room accompanied by whiffs of smoke and a few flakes of grey ash clinging accusingly to her cardigan.

"My goodness can't I even spend a penny in peace now?" She stood four square in front of my grandfather, "now what on earth is all this fuss and noise about Clifford?" She said with a surprising amount of good humour in her voice. I sat nervously in the armchair waiting for the storm to pass. My grandfather's irascible outbursts were legendary. I felt sorry for Gran living with such a bossy and demanding old man.

"Boxes!" he said grumpily. "How on earth can I sort things out with all these blessed boxes cluttering the place up.... there's no room on the side table to put anything down. I told you only this morning to move those boxes

Nelly." He glared at her with his nut-brown eyes, a dainty china teacup perched elegantly in his soft white hands.

"Sorry Clifford, I completely forgot about them," Gran said meekly as she stooped to pick them up. Her bones seemed to creak as she eased herself to her knees grasping the side of the mantle-piece for support. I rose to help her but Grampy flapped his hand for me to sit down again.

"It's all right your grandmother can manage.... Now then Sarah..." he said as Gran scrambled on her hands and knees to reach one small box that had bounced under his armchair, "tell me *all* about this course you are embarking upon at Bristol."

At that moment I was sure that I hated my imperious grandfather with his demands, rituals and nagging criticisms. How my poor Gran put up with it all I just couldn't fathom. The injustice of it made me burn with resentment and I yearned for the visit to end.

His praise for me and encouragement to write to him fell on death ears. I vowed inwardly *never* to write to the miserable old stick. Never.

The tedious afternoon dragged on. Over tea and stale sandwiches all the details of my course had been explored, picked apart and analysed. Finally, reassured that studying Art history was not leading me down a pointless educational cul-de-sac populated by long haired hippies and degenerates, Grampy wished me well.

I hugged my little Gran long and hard in the kitchen. "You take good care of yourself my luvvie." She said as she clung to me. "Don't be too hard on him Sarah... He's a good man your grandfather.... and he loves you, always remember that" she added firmly.

It was the first time my Gran had ever referred to Grampy's irascible behaviour and yet it was obvious from her tone that she would brook no discussion on the matter. I let it pass.

"I'll be back to see *you* soon Gran," I said with emphasis as I untangled myself from her bosomy embrace.

I gave Grampy with a dutiful peck on his cheek and muttered vague noises about hoping to see him soon.

Gran watched my leave taking from the kitchen doorway as if rooted to the cracked linoleum; she looked small and lost; a prisoner waving goodbye at the end of visiting hours.

"Sarah... just before you go... I want you get me something from the bureau?" he said. I tried not to sigh with impatience as I halted in my tracks and turned to face him.

"Of course, Grampy."

"Mind those Dahlia's don't topple over when you open the bureau front, that catch is getting a bit stiff" he warned, " in fact I think you had better give the vase to your Grandmother for a splash of fresh water, it's been nearly a week since Aunty Molly brought them from her garden, I think they could do with a bit of a top up."

I dutifully handed the vase to Gran, the meagre inch of opaque green water gave off a foul, tangy odour as it swirled around the rotting, fleshy stems.

"Now pass me that yellow envelope Sarah please... it's on third shelf down on the left... careful you don't disturb the bill pile," he said with his customary precision.

Each item was still filed in its exact place waiting to be summoned for his use. I resisted the spiteful urge to pull a few sheets out of order.

I handed him the small stiff envelope. On the front, written in his beautiful precise copperplate handwriting, was *Miss Sarah-Jayne Matthews.*

"Good luck in your new endeavour Sarah... this is from your Grandmother and me with all our best wishes." he said as he formally handed me back the yellow envelope.

"Thank you Grampy," I said dutifully, tearing open the seal. As expected, a small fussy Good Luck card covered with black cats and shamrocks appeared; it had been personalised with stick on foil letters neatly placed along the top-*Sarah Jayne*.

Unexpectedly inside the card, nestled five crisp, twenty-pound notes; a small fortune, money they certainly could not afford. I was overwhelmed with the generosity of the gift.

"Oh, my goodness... thank you.... thank you so much," I kissed them both and cursed my mean-minded thoughts. Grampy gave my hand a small squeeze, imparting in that small gesture more affection and warmth than I would have expected from him.

"You're very welcome Sarah... very welcome. Take care and we'll see you soon." he said.

"Of course, you will Grampy" I said, "after all its only ten weeks and then I'll be home again...It will be nearly Christmas and I'll have such a lot to tell you both.... Bye... I must dash now, or I'll miss the bus."

CHAPTER 6

December 1977

It was almost five o'clock, the evening was chilly, and already dark.

"He's going out with the tide Sarah. I'm sure he is. I know your Gran's very worried about him." Her mother twisted the knife.

In a urine scented red phone box on the corner of Whiteladies road, my thumbnail worrying at the flaking window paint. I listened to my mother's garbled family updates.

What tide? Why did she have to be so bloody cryptic? Any way Gran always fussed over him.

My afternoon had whizzed by in a frenzy of shopping; a collection of carrier bags crowded the small booth. I willed the phone call to end.

My two new best friends, Cheryl and Judith, waited outside the cubicle in a fog of moist, breathy, giggles. They were stamping their feet against the cold. Cheryl gurned at me through the dirty glass.   I signed... *only two more minutes.*

"Sarah...?"

"Err I can't be too long Mum... someone else is waiting for the 'phone. What do you mean Grampy's going out with the tide?"

Newly off the parental leash I had been having the most uproarious time in Bristol. The three of us had spent our afternoon splurging our meagre student funds on Christmas gifts we certainly could not afford.

On occasions Cheryl had proved shockingly resourceful. Browsing in the gilded beauty hall of House of Frazer, Cheryl confidently slipped a glamorous black and gold compact into the pocket of her parka coat.

"Me Mam loves anything Channel," she excused in her broad brummy accent.

"I abhor naked consumerism and absolutely believe in the redistribution of wealth," she had opined later in a lofty tone over a cup of tea in the marketplace. To prove her point she surreptitiously shovelled copious packets of sugar and paper napkins into her pocket.

"Sign shouldn't say help yourself if they don't mean it." She reasoned.

Cheryl, a confident sassy redhead, and Judith a buxom brunette who believed bras were the devices of masculine oppression, were both studying Politics and Social history. The two young women occupied the same student hall of residence as me, and we had met in the small, shared kitchen that serviced the eight rooms. I was dazzled by their stroppy confidence.

Cheryl had been topping up a milk bottle with water from the tap to replace the pilfered inch that now swirled in two mugs of steaming coffee.

"You can only do this once to each bottle otherwise people notice; works best on silver top especially if you give it a shake," she advised, as if it was a vital skill every new student should know. Guilt free she carefully replaced a jar of ersatz coffee back on a shelf marked Angela Rawlings.

"Hi...I'm Cheryl Jenkins, room six. I'm sharing with Judith Cooke... Uh...I don't suppose I could borrow some of those biscuits of yours, could I? I'm starving." She eyed the packet of chocolate digestives in my small pile of provisions I was unloading onto my allocated shelf.

"And I shouldn't leave those in here though, people steal things all the time.... especially the good stuff," she said with a wink as she grabbed four biscuits from the pack.

My Nescafe and biscuits became Cheryl's Nescafe and biscuits and within days we had become firm friends.

Our shopping afternoon had been such fun until now. Standing in a grubby phone booth the Christmas sparkle was starting to wear off and I was beginning to feel as flat as a deflated party balloon.

"But like I said Mum, I'll be coming home for the Christmas holidays in ten days' time anyway. It's not long 'til then is it?" I cursed the whine creeping into my voice. Mum was laying the guilt trip on me and I really didn't want to go back home and miss the end of term fun.

My thoughts ran selfishly to the student ball scheduled for the following Saturday. It was the highlight of the student calendar, an event I had been planning for weeks. I simply couldn't miss it or, more importantly, miss the chance of flirting with the gorgeous Daniel Pearce. My heart was set on the long-haired Geography student from Devon and the Christmas ball was my big chance.

Daniel had caught my eye in fresher's week, and he was everything that my father would have hated; a cool, laid back hippy with cheeky grin. With dark hair tumbling onto his shoulders, a silver earring, blue denim flares and a penchant for smoking weed, he made my heart do flip flops every time I bumped into him around the campus. *Gorgeous, gorgeous... drop dead gorgeous!*

Playing cool had not achieved the desired result; the black, daring plunge front evening dress, bought that afternoon, was in the words of Cheryl *bound to get his dick to take notice.*

"But what do you *really* mean by going out with tide Mum?" I hated it when she was obtuse.

The line crackled and fizzed with static.

"It's the end of the year... it's a turn of speech, you know... the ebb and flow of life and all that... surprisingly it often proves to be a truism," Mum twittered annoyingly.

"Grampy's been rather grumpy and off colour for weeks now Sarah.... your Gran's really *very* worried about him.... Couldn't you come back just a few days earlier than planned? I'm sure the college will understand under the circumstances...." She paused for dramatic effect. "Please Sarah...it would mean a lot to Gran."

"But Mum I've got such a lot on at the moment, we've still got lectures until Friday *and* you know that I have to pack up my room at the end of each term.... so, I really do have loads to do." I lied smoothly.

My grandfather being grumpy, so no change there then; and apparently a bit off colour... well it didn't exactly sound urgent to me.

"Tell you what Mum, I'll come home next Sunday afternoon.... that's a few days earlier than I had planned, and I can still finish up things here."

And it's after the ball... and... hopefully, after a night of rampant sex with the gorgeous Daniel, black dress permitting. I lusted in hope.

"I will pop around to see them as soon as I get back... I promise... Look Mum I've really got to go now... a queue is forming and I'm nearly out of money.... So, I'll see you Sunday then?"

"I suppose so... I mean if you really can't come back any earlier than that Sarah, then I guess it will have to do" she said slowly. Her tone dripped with the maternal disappointment, that I had come to recognise over the years. It was a tone that showed she had lost the argument.

The following Thursday morning a telegram arrived at my hall of residence:

"Sarah- Grampy died of heart attack last night.
No need to rush back. Funeral a week on Friday.
Mum xx"

I packed my bags and got the next coach home.

CHAPTER 7

Going Home

December 1977-Cardiff

Sarah ran the folded pink bus ticket under her thumb nail and chased out the pellet of blue-grey grime that lurked beneath. Her hands were grubby from newsprint and her hair hung greasily on her shoulders. Sarah needed a good long shower.

She turned away from the unflattering reflection in the condensation-streaked window.

In her rush to catch the coach there had been no time, or hot water, for a shower. The hall of residence showers was notoriously cranky and busy in the mornings with girls getting ready for the day and this particular morning proved no exception. She felt unkempt and guilty.

She had to make do with a lick and a promise as Gran used to call it and she knew it would be noticed.

Her jeans sported a fresh coffee stain that she knew for certain her mother would spot and fuss over the minute she clapped eyes on her.

She could almost hear her mother's voice ...*Oh Sarah dear ....it looks like you've split something... we'd best get those jeans in the wash as soon as possible before the stain sets in.* Her mother's eagle-eyed scrutiny was suffocating.

The journey back to Cardiff seemed to take for ever. The coach battled the Bristol traffic, chugged over the Severn Bridge and then lurked for an hour in the Newport bus station before finally trailing into the busy Cardiff terminus at 4 o'clock.

It was getting dark. Through the steamed-up windows, she could see groups of Friday shoppers, bags bulging with presents and the inevitable rolls of wrapping paper. Gaggles of women huddled inside bus shelters to avoid the sleety drizzle that was starting to fall softly over the City.

Ropes of gaudy, festive lights snaked down the city streets and around the shops. In a couple of hours streams of workers would cram the bus station on their way home from the shops and offices. She needed to get a move on.

As Sarah stepped out from the fug of the coach the cold, damp, Cardiff air hit her. With any luck, at this time of day, she would not have to wait long for the next bus home. The depot was busy with red and cream buses regularly sweeping into the bays disgorging passengers and picking up new ones. She yearned be inside in the warm.

A part of her was dreading arriving to the gloom and implied criticism. She knew there was nothing she could have done, but a guilty nag told her she should have gone home earlier. *Grampy dead.* Last night her head had throbbed with the possibilities.

All Sarah had ever known was an Alma road with Gran *and* Grampy; Gran never venturing more than a mile or so away from the doorstep, Grampy, eagle eyed, watching the clock until she returned. Ruling the roost from his chair.

Gran's whole world and timetable had revolved around Grampy's incessant needs and wants, "*.... Oh, my goodness loos at the time, we really must get back!... Don't dawdle Sarah... your Grandfather will be expecting his tea in ten minutes.... take those scissors into your grandfather Sarah he wants to cut something out of the newspaper.... pop around to the post box for me, there's a good girl, Grampy wants this letter to catch the mid-morning collection....*"

Precision, rules, doing things *his* way to his schedule, keeping things from him. Now all that was gone. There would be no more hiding away in the scullery smoking Craven A's and drinking Gin. No more scraping the toast.

The funeral of Clifford Aubrey Harris was well attended. Gran's status in the close-knit community was well observed. Neighbours remarking with admiration on the turnout and eagle-eyes noticing the few that didn't make it.

Such a marvellous woman that Mrs Harris... all those years with him, and him being like he was... Oh Yes...a saint she was.... I never heard her complain, no never ever complained did she, and him... no wish to speak ill of the dead but he was ... well you know how he was.... To be charitable it couldn't have been easy for him either, but by

God he would have tried the patience of a saint. Oh yes, a marvellous woman.... simply marvellous.

Numerous elderly neighbours from Alma Road struggled into the gloomy chapel of rest to pay their respects to a man few had met or seen outside the house for many a year. Curtains all along the street were kept closed for two days after his death and on the morning of his funeral. Gran, in her grief, appreciated such things.

Mr Savage, the butcher expressed his heartfelt condolences as he picked out the choicest ham for the funeral sandwiches; he generously added an extra slice on top for bunce. Gran was a loyal customer.

The milkman doffed his cap with murmured words of regret for her loss when he called to collect the weekly bill and insisted that she accept a carton of double cream.

On the morning of the funeral, Gran's whist club members fluttered along to the service in a flap of black hats and sombre coats smelling strongly of mothballs.

The elderly ladies, solemn faced, perched in an orderly row on the back pews of the church out of respect for the family members and in order to secure the best view of the whole proceedings. The ten fluffed up women, heads nodding, eyes darting, reminded Sarah of group of brooding crows.

No, no.... It's a murder Sarah-.... The collective noun is a murder of crows not a group.... it's a murder! She could almost hear his voice, precision sharp, correcting her as she kept her eyes focussed on the blonde wood coffin in front of the altar aisle.

He's a good man Sarah... and he loves you...always remember that.

A brittle shard of guilt needled away at her. *I'll be back soon Grampy.*

After the service a fresh-faced Father Lawrence, who had only been in post six months since the death of old Father Thomas, patted Gran on the shoulder and reassured her that God would indeed hold Mr Harris to his bosom and make him whole again. Mr Harris, he opined professionally, was free of pain and suffering now and his friends and family should rejoice that he was now walking with angels.

Gran, stony faced, clasped her rosary and sniffed into a damp, lace hanky. She blessed herself.

It was a day of ritual, muttered sympathies and observances. Crushed with remorse, Sarah longed for the day to end... she didn't think for a moment it would end the way it did.

Above the clattering of dishes in the kitchen Sarah could hear raised voices. Sharp squawks punctured her thoughts. Earlier she had sought refuge in being useful, retrieving fallen napkins, proffering extra sandwiches, making tea and now washing up her grandmother's best tea plates.

Gran's raised voice grabbed her attention. She never recalled Gran raising her voice, ever. Sarah moved to the doorway to see the cause of the commotion.

"You have no right... absolutely no right at all to say that... how dare you!" Nelly rounded on her victim. "What makes you think you have right to come in here.... into.... Into our home and criticise him?" She hissed.

The unanswered challenge hung in the air as Sarah's mother stepped in and put her arm around Gran's shoulder.

"It's all right Mum... shh shh now, don't get yourself upset Mum, not today of all days." Jean soothed. "Mrs Evans didn't mean anything by it Mum... did you now Mrs Evans?"

Sarah glanced at the small mousey looking neighbour from number eleven who was sitting in the corner of the room. The offender, still resplendent in her hat, muttered *sorry* several times, eyes pleading for others to come to her aid.

"Mrs Evans was only saying what many people must have thought over the years.... Come on Mum, we all know that Dad could have his...." She let the word hang in the air. "...Have his moments.... Not that he could help it of course, what with his condition and everything" Jean added hastily.

"But please don't upset yourself Mum, you must know Mrs Evans didn't mean anything by it. She's always been such a good neighbour to you and Dad over the years... She wouldn't want to hurt your feelings, not today of all days... you know that don't you?" Jean reasoned.

The poor unfortunate Mrs Evans sat, cowed into silence, nodding her head in agreement.

"Oh, really Jean!" Gran drew herself up to her full five foot two inches and turned on the room.

"So that's it is it? Apparently, *many* of you.... and others "she said darkly looking towards her daughter, "seem to be under a miserable misapprehension that I've spent my life as a martyr.... a martyr shackled to a tyrant, and... and it's *apparently*" she dragged the word out laden with anger "apparently a weight off me...ME.... that my husband Clifford is dead!"

Her eyes scanned the room daring them to protest.

"So, *if* that's what you're all thinking, then I want to put the record straight...."

All conversation stopped; cups returned loudly into saucers; the room sat in rapt attention. This was better entertainment than many could have hoped for under the circumstances.

"Clifford was the best husband any wife could wish for. The best!" Faces swivelled towards the small stout figure commanding the room.

"None of you have the right to judge him.... None of you knew him like I did." Her eyes darted accusingly around the room, daring people to contradict her.

"Clifford was such a good, patient and kind man.... and I wasn't worthy of him." Nelly gulped deeply.

"If Clifford had lived to be a hundred, even then there wouldn't have been enough time for me to make up to him for all he had to suffer!" Her voice fizzed with rage.

"I loved him.... he was my rock, not my burden." With that she burst into loud guttural sobs.

"I loved him … loved him...." she said over and over again as tears ran down her bewildered face.

"There, there Mum... you're getting yourself overwrought. Come and sit down... It's been a very long, stressful day for all of us." Jean guided her mother to sit in the battered fireside chair.

Eyes drifted down into laps as an embarrassed hush draped over the room.

"I think it's time for you to get some rest now Mum. Sarah can show your visitors out whilst I'll make you a nice fresh pot of tea."

Taking their cue from Jean, the room emptied. One by one the neighbours left the house murmuring their condolences. They departed, each pressing Sarah's guilty hand and urging her to take good care of her grandmother.

"Don't worry now...No offence taken.... It was just the shock Sarah... that's what it was... definitely the shock, what with yourgGrandfather dying so sudden like." The guests filed out through the narrow hall and stood in the street to gossip.

"Crazed with grief she was.... See I told you she was a martyr to him, a fair martyr...

A fine woman that Mrs Harris, and a good Catholic too... Course she knows in her heart of hearts he was a bit of a tartar, but marvellous that she wouldn't have a word said against him...simply marvellous.... But then haven't I've always said that woman's a saint?"

CHAPTER 8

September 1979

"A bit of good news Sarah…. Your Gran's eventually agreed to go into the Forest Fach nursing home…. it's really very nice Sarah…. very nice indeed."   Her mother's tone was bright and up-beat.

Sarah's mind reeled, was this supposed to be good news?

"Oh, it will be such a weight off my mind I can tell you…. Gran's even getting a nice view of the garden from her room," her mother added hastily.

Sarah's weekly phone call home to her parents had taken an unexpected turn.

"Everyone speaks very highly of the place…. and the staff are lovely too, all chatty and so good with the old people…. really lovely." Her mother said swiftly.

Sarah listened dumbfounded… Gran leaving Alma road! She couldn't believe her ears. Of course, she knew something was up. The letter from her mother suggesting that they "must *have a little chat about Gran,*" the timed rendezvous for a phone call home. Yes, she knew something was definitely up...but she hadn't expected this!

"You know, well we *all* know that she couldn't carry on living in that old mausoleum any longer Sarah, certainly not now the weather is getting colder.... I mean to say, it's falling down around her ears.... it's freezing cold and leaks like a sieve. It's a positive health hazard!" Her mother paused for dramatic effect.

Sarah watched the rain trickle down the glass panes of the telephone box and waited for her mother to add weight to her argument.

Gran actually going into a care home.

The question of getting Gran to move out of Alma road into a flat, or some such pensioner accommodation, had dripped away for two years now since her grandfather had died. Constant niggles and digs from her mother about "the state of the place" always fell on deaf ears or were met with a brusque "It suits me fine, thank you very much!"

Now it seemed, that her mother had got her way over the matter; but then she always did.

"I mean to say Sarah, it's ridiculous and... and positively embarrassing her living the way she does. It's not something anyone would want for their mother is it? Not in this day and age."

"The place is positively Dickensian, and it smells! You've got to admit the place positively reeks of .... Well, you know what I mean Sarah... it reeks of all sorts."

"Oh, come on Mum...!" Sarah squawked loyally. It was true- the place did smell.... but then it always had.

Her mother steam rollered on, barely pausing for breath.

"I've often wondered what on earth the neighbours must think about it, what with the state of the place and all.... I said to your father that this should have happened months ago... years ago even.... but then your Gran is always so stubborn, and she never listens to me anyway."

Sarah didn't know what to say to the startling revelation that Gran was leaving Alma road. Her Gran was as much a part of the fabric of Alma road as the walls and windows. She just simply couldn't imagine Gran being anywhere else.

The revelation hit her like a body blow and set her mind racing-*Why for God's sake? Gran had always been adamant she never wanted to live anywhere else...so why now?*

Her mother chattered on. "Of course, the health visitor, Miss Phillips, has been an absolute angel... simply marvellous about it all."

Sarah was speechless.

"Miss Phillips said that she wouldn't hear of Gran going back to Alma road... told her straight she did, that she simply would not allow it. She made some enquiries and found Gran this nice bed in the Forest Fach ...and so that was that.... It's a weight off my mind I can tell you!" Her mother said with a flourish.

"What health visitor Mum? Why has Gran got a health visitor?" Sarah was struggling to make sense of it all. Her mother's twittering was adding to the confusion. Her head was spinning.

"Oh, I'm sorry love, of course I forgot, I haven't told you all the latest.... but then I didn't want to worry you, what with your final exams and everything and at first Gran said she didn't want people making a fuss.... those were her very words; *stop fussing Jean, I'll be fine.*"

A chill gripped Sarah's heart.

"Your Gran has had a few days in hospital.... just to carry out a few tests about that dreadful, hacking cough of hers. Honestly, it was like pulling teeth to get her to even agree to that! You know how she never listens to any one unless it suits her." Her mother's voice sharpened with exasperation.

"Eventually the doctors at the hospital did manage to persuade her that a bit of bed rest and a course of antibiotics would help her pick up a bit. So, after a bit of argey-bargey she agreed to go into the Heath hospital for a few days. They got the health visitor involved in her case .... A lovely young lady; a Miss Phillips." Her mother barely paused for breath.

"And it was *her* professional decision that Gran shouldn't be discharged back to that old house in Alma road. Miss Phillips was very firm about it *"not under any circumstances Mrs Harris."* That's what she told her.... those were her very words Sarah."

"What... do you mean Mum.... will she *ever* go home?" Sarah held her breath.

Her mother hmmmed and haahed a bit before answering.

"Well, we've told her that your father and I will keep paying the rent on Alma road.... just for a few months... you know just to keep her options open, so we aren't saying to *her* never ever.... But in all honestly Sarah she won't be going back there, not with her condition." She said

"What do you mean *her condition* Mum? What's her condition?" Sarah felt her world crumbling.

"She has cancer Sarah; breast cancer and it's spread to her lungs.... ridiculous isn't it all those years of smoking like a trooper and she gets breast cancer." Her mother gave adtry toneless laugh as if Gran had planned to be as awkward and contrary as possible to the very last.

"But surely Gran can get treatment? Can't they at least do *something*?" Sarah's voice took on a pleading tone, her heart hammered in her chest.

"No, no they can't Sarah... not at this stage. The doctors have said that it's too far advanced. Your father and I have agreed that there is no there's no point in upsetting her with nasty operations and the like. It's just a matter of time now and keeping her comfortable."

Sarah listened as her mother read out the death sentence.

"You know what she's like Sarah.... She should have sought treatment years ago then maybe something could have been done, but not now. It's just too late now. Typical of your Gran, she was always too busy always looking after your Grampy to bother about looking after herself...... Never even so much as mentioned to me that she had a lump.... goodness only knows how long she's had it.... probably years." Her mother mused.

Sarah stifled a sob. *Too late!*

"Don't go upsetting yourself love. She wouldn't want you to get upset. There's really *nothing* anyone can do now except make sure that she lives out her life as comfortably as possible... and that *certainly* doesn't include going back to that draughty old house in Alma road.... no, under the circumstances, this is for the best."

"Poor Gran....does she know?"

"I think she has always known something wasn't right Sarah.... but if you mean has any one explicitly told her the prognosis, then no... no they haven't... and we are not going to." Her mother said firmly.

"The doctor said there was no point upsetting her. Your father and I have told her that she has had another one of her bad chest infections and that she needs to rest and get over it in a nice nursing home where they will look after her. After we explained that the house was still going to be there for her, she seemed to accept things. Gran will go into the Forest Fach on Monday."

Sarah started to sob, deep painful gulps.

"Try not to fret.... You know Gran wouldn't want you to get upset, especially not when you've got studying to do for your exams. I wanted to tell you because I thought you might want to pop home and give her a little visit.... you know when she's settled in like. She's been asking about you such a lot lately. I think a little visit would do her the world of good... But don't leave it too, long will you?" Her mother's voice took on an anxious tone

"Any way let's just say she'd love to see you. In fact, we all would it's been a few months now since your last visit.... maybe see if you could manage it next week-end?"

As she hung up the phone Sarah felt numb. Alma road without Gran....

Mindful of previous sins she spent the evening packing and caught the early morning bus home.

Chapter 9

Gran

The following morning Sarah was due to see Gran at the Forest Fach. As she sat up in her old bedroom, she was beginning to wish she hadn't come home at all, the tension in the household was palpable. If it wasn't for her promise to visit Gran, she'd get on the next bus back to Bristol she thought miserably. *Bloody parents.*

Sarah couldn't help but overhear her parents arguing, their shrill voices drifted up through the ceiling. Even over the jingles and dulcet tones of the television it was clear they were rowing about Gran.

The argument had been brewing all evening. Her parents had barely contained themselves over dinner, so as soon as she had finished her meal, she disappeared upstairs to let them get on with it.

She crept to the top of the stairs to eavesdrop.

"She's got to face the facts Jean. We all know the writing is on the wall... It's absolutely pointless paying the rent on a property that we all *know* she'll never go back to.... we aren't made of money you know," her father sounded exasperated.

"It's an expensive charade, that's what it is, nothing but a bloody charade.... we can't this up for long you know!"

"But George, I can't tell her that. She only agreed to go to Forest Fach on the promise of keeping up the rental. We can't back out.... It would kill her.... I'm sure it would."

"The cancer is killing Jean and paying her rent *and* paying for this fancy nursing home is killing me.... Well, it's your choice and if you insist on keeping up this stupid nonsense then we won't be having a holiday this year.... and that's a fact!"

Sarah could hear her mother weeping.

"Well, I'm certainly *not* visiting her tomorrow; I've got lots of things to do .... I'll drop Sarah off but that's it!"

A few moments later she heard the front door slam.

The following morning Sarah got ready for her visit to the nursing home with a heavy heart; the atmosphere between her parents was still strained, sentences clipped and polite with her father spending most of the morning outside washing and polishing his car.

Sweet, spicy smells had drifted upstairs even before she had gone down to breakfast; her mother had taken cover in the kitchen and baked a batch of welsh cakes as a little gift for Gran. Sarah was grateful for the prop, at least she would have something to talk about on her visit. Freshly baked welsh cakes were Gran's favourites.

In the afternoon her father dropped her outside the Forest Fach, clutching the small tin of cakes. Her nerve was starting to fail.... what would Gran be like, it had been several months since she had last seen her... what on earth would they find to talk about for the next hour and a half?

She made her way through the swing doors into a large, bright communal area served by notice boards and signs. Wheel chairs were stacked in rows like so many supermarket trollies. Large lifts disgorged shapeless old women wrapped up in blankets being pushed along by staff. An elaborate, everlasting flower display attempted to cheer up the waiting area.

"Err, I'm here to see my Gran.... umm she's Mrs Harris, Mrs Eleanor Harris" .... Sarah addressed a plump young lady sitting at the reception desk. "Err....Which way do I go please?"

Without looking up the girl in the blue uniform scanned the register and handed Sarah a pen. "All visitors must sign in." The girl glanced at her watch. "Mrs Harris will have been taken through to the day room for the afternoon.... down the corridor and first left.... Visiting ends at four thirty. Tea is not provided for visitors and smoking is not allowed anywhere on the premises," she added as if reading from a script.

Sarah made her way down the antiseptic corridor. From rooms off she could glimpse the skeletal outlines of old ladies lying in their beds surrounded by railings. Some poor souls lay calling faintly for "nurse, nurse," others lay dozing with their mouths open and spittle drooling down their chins. Away in the distance a tea trolley clattered and clanked on the lino floors.

Sarah spotted her instantly. Gran was seated slightly apart from the other residents, with her chair angled towards the window. Despite it only being just past three o'clock she was wearing an unfamiliar dressing gown with tartan slippers sporting small fluffy pom-poms. Gran's hair looked uncharacteristically flat and utilitarian, devoid of her favourite waves. She looked so very old.

"Hello Gran," Sarah bent to give her a kiss. "I've brought you some of Mum's Welsh cakes." She sat down on a small stool by her grandmother's swollen feet.

"Oh Sarah, what a lovely surprise. I thought I saw you in the car park a few moments ago through the window; at least I *hoped* it was you." She smiled a gappy, toothless smile. The staff hadn't bothered to put her teeth in.

I'm so pleased to see you, I really am my luvvie," Gran beckoned to Sarah for a cuddle.
Sarah's heart contracted; Gran had been waiting for her.

"Let me have a good look at you.... My, my you have turned into such a beautiful young lady.... but then you always were such a pretty child." Without her dentures Gran's voice had a soft lisping quality.

"Tell me all about your university.... you know your Grampy and I always loved to know what you've been up to." Every so often she punctuated her sentences with a small sharp cough.

"I'm fine Gran, it's all going well, it really is. My tutors are pleased with me and I'm hopeful of a 2:1." She looked into her grandmother's rheumy eyes waiting for the next question. They chatted and skittered around the topic of her university life until Sarah could bear it no longer.

"Never mind talking about me all the time Gran, more to the point *what* have you been up to?" Up close Sarah could see that the dressing gown didn't fit; the sleeves had been rolled up several times and it obviously belonged to someone else.

Her grandmother fixed her with a knowing stare.

"Sarah you have always been such a bright girl. Bright and perceptive. You and I both know that I'm not long for this world.... no, no let me finish what I have to say." Gran flapped away Sarah's brief attempt at protest. Another bout of coughing ensued.

"Your mother, on the other hand, must think I'm simple or something not to realise what's what.... A chest infection indeed!" She dismissed the ridiculous pretence with a wave of her hand.

"I'm not gaga whatever your mother might think. I know I've got cancer Sarah and what's more I know there's nothing anyone can do about it. So that's it really." she said firmly.

"I'm getting very tired of this world. We all have to go and my time has come. I don't intend to linger any longer than I have to." Her voice was calm, without a tinge of self-pity.

"Gran....please don't talk like this," Sarah pleaded.

"Tsk tsk Sarah, just ask yourself would *you* want to live out your final days in an institution, wearing clothes that don't belong to you, eating tasteless slop because they've lost your teeth and missing your own bed? I don't think so.... and neither do I." she said with emphasis. "I've had my innings and it's time to go, I'm only glad we've had time to say goodbye."

Sarah sat stunned; she hadn't expected this. "But Mum doesn't know.... I mean she doesn't think that *you* know." She gasped.

"All her life your mother has only ever seen what she wants to see. She likes life to be in neat, organized boxes and the one thing I've learnt is that it rarely is."

In the hallway a bell rang, visiting time was coming to an end.

"Kiss me Sarah before we say goodbye and …. and try not to judge me too harshly will you my love?" Gran squeezed Sarah's hand.

"What do you mean…. judge you Gran….Why would anyone judge you? Don't be silly, you've been the best Gran ever. You *are* the best Gran" she corrected herself. "I love you Gran," Sarah felt the tears welling up.

"And I want you to always remember Sarah Jayne, that your grandfather was a good man; the very best…. never forget that." She kissed her granddaughter on both cheeks, wiping away Sarah's tears with her knobbly fingers.

"And we both loved you too, more than you will ever know. Goodbye my precious. Make sure you give me a wave…. I'll be watching." Gran said as she turned towards the windows.

Sarah left the day room sobbing as if her heart would break. From the car park she could just glimpse the faint outline of a little old lady waving good bye at her through the windows. She waved Gran good bye for the last time.

Two weeks later her parents received a phone call from the nursing home to say that Gran had passed away in her sleep. Everyone, except Sarah, agreed it was a blessing.

Sarah

Cardiff September 2012

Later that morning as I tried to bring some order to my mother's documents, I discovered the narrow, rusty, brown plait, coiled in a small wooden cigar box. It nestled like a dull bronze snake alongside a tatty photograph of my Grandmother and her famous waist long hair.

Slim and laughing in a knitted bathing suit that clung to her unfashionable curves, Eleanor tipped her head back so that her thick wavy hair nearly reached behind her knees, a cascade of lustrous beauty. All that remained of its fabulous length was a small brown pigtail tied with red cotton.

On the reverse of the tiny, battered photograph was the date- August1927.

CHAPTER 10

Nelly

August 1927

"Come on Molly do let's go in.... It's empty.... we won't be seen. Be brave for once!"

I attempted to drag my sister by the hand into the small doorway on the corner of Queen's street.

Molly stood transfixed by the awful prospect of being seen entering the shop. Her face was tense; her eyes darted to and fro as she scanned the street nervously; fully expecting the awful prospect that someone they knew would hove into view at any moment and witness the crime.

Clutching her purchases in a delicate package tied up with string Molly looked racked with indecision. She hovered on the threshold of the barber's shop. Faint wafts of spicy fragrance drifted through the doorway; bergamot pomade and tobacco mixed with tangy lime and soap.

Molly, my sweet, gentle sister, wore her fair hair in a soft bun, at the nape of her neck. Her hair was fine and golden like her nature. I had the fiery temper and fiery brown hair of my mother's family, the Benson's, thick wavy hair that my mother called "Titian."

My sister Margaret had the air of an angel, she wouldn't look out of place in some romantic Victorian painting; a wistful Madonna or devoted heroine.... soft, gentle and winsome; a daring warrior she was not. Molly looked terrified by the prospect of what might lie ahead inside the gloomy barber's shop. My skittish behaviour that hot and sticky afternoon was the final straw.

"You can't Eleanor …. what would Mother say?" She pleaded. "We *really* should go home Nell... I've finished my errands for the afternoon...... Please don't spoil things Nell...for *my* sake please let's go." Molly screwed up her pretty face and looked as if she was about to burst into tears. She wore the mantle of grownup sister heavily and I was a trouble to her with my flighty ideas and willfull nature.

Molly would hesitate in life, I would jump straight in, both feet, no regrets, grabbing the moment-it often got me into trouble as Molly too frequently reminded me.

It was a hot August day with the sort of languid stickiness that caused flies to bite and tempers to fray. My hair hung unfashionably long and heavy, like a bell pull down my back. I longed to be free of it.

My sister had been shopping for ivory lisle stockings for her wedding to her newly acquired fiancée; Mr Archibald Smith. She was due to be married in three weeks' time and as the day approached, she had had a few errands to complete.

Molly was fiercely proud of her new status as a fiancée and even more proud of the beautiful sapphire and diamond ring that Archie had given her to wear. Not given to show Molly had cried when she saw its vivid beauty on her narrow fingers.

Today she had wanted to put the finishing touches to her trousseau and I was to help her with the choosing. The fine stockings were to compliment her cream, drop waisted dress and cost an extravagant 3/9d a pair.

Our young brother Albert had insisted on giving Molly five shillings from his meagre savings as a wedding present. Blushing at her own daring, Molly decided to spend the unexpected windfall on her "delicates" for her wedding day.

The hosiery department had been a delight of beautiful gossamer fabrics that slid seductively through the fingers. I had been in heaven and lingered over the fine silk stockings in exotic colours; some jewels costing over one guinea a pair.

Molly, ever sensible, kept her eyes on the rayon and lisle. In the end she settled for a pair of fine knitted lisle stockings and a practical set of crepe-de-chine flesh-coloured cami-knickers. Archie would be pleased she said with a faint blush that spread prettily across her throat.

"Can't we go home Nell?" She pleaded.

"Oh, for goodness sake Sis it's only hair! Well... I'm going in, even if you're not you... you cowardy custard," the taunt would test my timid sister to the limit. "I've made my mind up Molly and I'm going to do it. I'm twenty-one now.... no-one can stop me." I let her hand slip through my fingers and strode into the cool dark shop.

With that Molly burst into tears. She trailed miserably in my wake.

"But what will Clifford say? You're getting married soon.... it'll never grow back in time. Just think what this means Nell! It's your crowning glory." Molly persisted in throwing remarks at my back as I marched defiantly into the small empty premises. The row of empty red leather chairs beckoned.

Molly's pleading and appeals for reason fell on deaf ears and in just under an hour and a half I emerged "shorn" with a daring, shingled bob and finger waves slicked into place with a dab of Brilliantine.

Liberated, I revelled in the draft that cooled my pale exposed neck. I kept a small plait of my hair as a trophy to give to Clifford and the rest of my crowning glory lay in coppery piles on the floor. Molly was speechless.

Later that evening, I paraded my "new look." My darling Clifford said that I looked exactly like the divine Miss Tallulah Bankhead, who was a roaring success on the London West End stage. I was thrilled. It was *exactly* the effect I wanted. I decided to take up smoking the following week to complete the look.

Our mother cried bitter tears over my racy transformation and the loss of my hair. My father eyed me darkly and said tersely that it was a blessing that I was already engaged to be married to Clifford as he feared for my moral compass.

CHAPTER 11

Molly

September 1927

It was the morning of Molly's wedding day, a warm, Indian summer lingered with the promise of fine, settled weather for the next few days.

I was buzzing with excitement at the prospect of my sister's wedding to Archie; so excited in fact, that I was starting to aggravate my sister's already frayed nerves.

Molly sat motionless in her lace, drop waisted bridal gown waiting for me to dress her hair. Her slender frame looked fashionably elegant and I, who despaired of my bouncing bosoms that defied binding and ruined the line of my pale pink outfit, had to admit, that I had never seen her look lovelier. Clifford had said that he thought that my bosoms were fun when I complained that they jiggled and ached as I danced.... the cheek of it!

"Oh, Nelly do stop twirling and chattering on so.... my poor head is starting to pound." Molly pulled a little moue as I jigged about the bedroom. The morning was racing away and the *jitters* had sucked the life out of her.

Molly was blessed with a quiet and gentle nature, whereas I drew my father's ire with my love of fripperies and dancing. He had muttered to my mother on more than one occasion that *will-fullness was sure to lead that girl astray-you mark my words.*

Consequently, my engagement to Clifford had been met with family sighs of relief all round. Even though I had just turned twenty-one my father felt that I was in imminent danger of turning into a liability, and if I was, then it was one that he would much rather hand over to Mr Clifford Harris to deal with-hair or no hair.

Mother and father liked Clifford, they thought he was a polite, sensible fellow who was showing promise in his clerical job. The family hoped that he would have a calming influence on my hot temper and *flibbertigibbet* nature.

Clifford, with uncharacteristic vulgarity, said to me one evening that he would have more luck trying to piss into the wind than trying to tame me. I collapsed with giggles at the very thought of it.

By one o'clock that afternoon Molly would be Mrs Archibald Smith. At five thirty-three she would leave on a steam train from Cardiff Central station for a four-day honeymoon in an hotel on the Torquay Riviera; The Imperial.

To me it all sounded heavenly, but *Molly's* nerves were fraying just at the very thought of the night to come.

Archie had been courting my sister for nearly two years. Their engagement had been announced in the local papers at

Easter, just after Margaret's twenty fourth birthday. Father had agreed to the engagement and given his blessing. By Fowler standards Mr Archibald Smith was a man of some substance; and Margaret, in father's opinion, was certainly of an age when she *ought* to be married and starting a family of her own. Father was reassured by Archie's good manners and attentive nature; his little Molly was making a good match.

Archibald, Archie to all who knew him, was tall, dark and handsome with a sprinkling of grey at the temples and twinkling, liquid-brown eyes that caused Molly's heart to beat a little faster. His upright stance hinted at his time served in France with the South Wales Border's in 1917, his only injury was a missing top section of his middle finger on his right hand and a tendency to cry out in his sleep when the "sweats" were upon him.

Archie knew he had been lucky, he had lost so many friends to wounds, disease and battle fatigue; unlike them he had a chance for a new and positive future and he intended to grab it with both hands. He needed to settle down with a wife and hopefully, in God's good time, have a son to carry on the family business and the family name. At nearly thirty-five he was almost eleven years older than Molly, and as his old father had observed, it was high time he was married.

Yes, sweet Molly was the perfect choice.

Archie's father owned the small tobacconist's; Smith and Son, that straddled the corner of Queen's Street, a busy thoroughfare that did a good trade.

A neighbour, Mrs Simmons, had once made some snippy, obtuse comment to Mother about *it was no secret that old man Smith employed Bookies' runners* but Mother said that

Molly was a lucky girl to be asked by Mr Archibald Smith, and that other people always envied good fortune.

Mother held her head high and sailed past Mrs Simmons the next time she saw her whilst shopping in Queen's street.

It *was* a good match and a step up in the world for Molly. Archie was set to take over the family business when old Mr Smith retired; he assured our father that Molly would be well provided for, and so the deal was done. Archie was welcomed into the Fowler fold as the new son-in-law in waiting and no-one could dispute that they made a very handsome couple.

An impressive sapphire and diamond engagement ring, that had once belonged to Archie's late mother, now twinkled on my sister's delicate hand. Its extravagant beauty hinted at a prosperous future for sweet Molly and I was truly glad for her.

But for all my good wishes I couldn't hide the fact that I *was* hugely envious of the fact that after their wedding Molly and Archie were to live in the small flat above the tobacconist shop in Queen's street. A home of their own from the moment they were married.

After our wedding Clifford and I would have to make do for a while with the middle bed room of Inkerman street. We would be rubbing along with Mother, Father and my brother Albert until we could afford to move out.

I knew that mother would think that I was ungrateful to scorn the middle room but I was so desperate to escape the claustrophobia of my father's ever watchful eye and I longed for a place to call our own.

Clifford promised me that the arrangement would not be for long as his job as a shipping clerk at the burgeoning

Cardiff dockyard was progressing well. "Soon Nelly we will have a place of our own; very soon... I promise......Just have some patience; it *will* be very soon."

I bit my lip and tried to be patient.... patience was not in my nature.

Molly's wedding and honeymoon plans all sounded terribly glamorous and I couldn't wait for my time to come.

Clifford and I had decided on a small, early spring wedding the following year without any show or fuss. Father had fretted about the cost of another wedding and anxious to secure his blessing Clifford and I had agreed on a simple affair in late March when the worst of the weather should be over.

I wore my small diamond solitaire with pride... Mrs Clifford Aubrey Harris certainly had a smart ring to it. We would make our own luck!

That morning of Molly's wedding the house was a bustle of preparation for the big day.

Molly sat for the last time in our small bedroom that we shared as sisters. She perched on a stool in front of the small dressing table and mirror looking more like she was waiting to be led to the gallows than a church.

Molly nervously twiddled her lace handkerchief, embroidered with blue forget me nots, her eye lids lowered trying to avoid eye contact with me as I helped her get ready for her special day.

"Well then just promise me you'll tell me all about *it* then when you get back from Torquay Molly!... I'd tell you if it was the other way around, honest I would...." I was trying not to sound cross at Molly's refusal to let me in on the big secret of *it*.

I didn't want to quarrel with her on her wedding day but for heaven's sake, she was being infuriatingly *close.*

Molly sat blushing as I pressed her again and again about the mysterious art of being a married woman. I brushed her long, fair hair with sweeping strokes until it shone and shimmered like spun silk.

"Pleeeese Molly....."

I knew that Mother had had a few words with Molly the evening before to prepare her for the wedding night and that she had sworn her to absolute secrecy.

"I *really* can't say anything Nell...Oh please stop pressing me...you know that I promised mother faithfully that I wouldn't say anything!" Molly said stiffly for the umpteenth time. So, despite all my pleadings she absolutely refused to give way on the matter.

If the truth be told, for Molly the awful improbability of the "Act" just didn't bear repeating. Molly felt sure that she must have misheard, or at least misunderstood her mother when the excruciating *marriage* talk littered with euphemisms had taken place the night before.

Molly had listened mutely as her mother struggled to do her duty by her daughter and so Molly's ignorant fate about the mysteries of the marriage bed was sealed.

In only a few hours Molly knew that she would certainly find out if Archie knew what to do about *"it"* .... the embarrassing prospect loomed large and didn't bear thinking about.... Her cheeks burned at the awful prospect of what lay ahead. Molly wished that Nelly would just shut up; her head throbbed.

"Look Moll, I'm getting married to Clifford in six months' time," I pleaded. I was the only one who ever called her "Moll" and I knew it would tug at her loyalty. "Please Moll..., I'm your sister after all... *and* I'm going to know about *it* soon enough enough....and I'd much rather hear it from you than from mother......" I wheedled.

"*Go on* Moll, I won't say anything, I promise I won't. Cross my heart and hope to die."

Molly shook her head miserably, twisting her handkerchief over and over in her hands.

"Oh Molly, I'd tell *you* if it was the other way around... It's just not fair.... You're being beastly and... and a prig!" I said petulantly, hoping my sister would relent.

In a tense silence I coaxed Molly's honey-coloured hair into a soft bun, the creation was held into place with a beautiful old mother of pearl comb that belonged to our grandmother. The coil sat at the nape of her neck under the borrowed lace cap and veil that I secured with hair pins onto her lovely head. A faint pink glow tinged her cheeks and her cornflower blue eyes glittered as she stared mutely into the mirror at her reflection.

"There, you look *absolutely* beautiful Molly, really you do.... Archie is a very lucky man." I said as she smiled shyly back at me in the mirror. Molly suppressed a small tear that she dabbed away with her handkerchief.

"We mustn't quarrel on your wedding day but...you must at least tell me what *it's* like then when you've done the awful deed Molly...." I said as I held her gaze in the mirror. "Promise?"

"Promise." She said softly.

CHAPTER 12

Nelly

24th March 1928-

We stood waiting to board our vessel, surrounded by our few guests on the passenger quay of the bustling Cardiff docks. Eager to be off and leave my old life behind, I was so impatient to be gone. In between the casual social chit chat that marked the event, I kept looking at Clifford as we waited to embark on The Waverley, an elegant paddle ship that gleamed in the sunshine.

Soon it would be just the two of us. No more furtive kisses and Albert, our reluctant chaperone. The keen anticipation about our night to come made me tingle with pleasure. Just us!

Everyone agreed as they waited to wave us off that, for the time of year, the weather had been remarkably kind to us. The brisk breeze fluttered the colourful bunting decking out the paddle steamer. It was a handsome vessel with its huge twin funnels and massive paddles getting up to steam in the middle of the deck.

The pleasure steamer was quite busy with day trippers and was taking Clifford and myself over to Weston Super Mare for our honeymoon. Four blissful days in the Grand Atlantic Hotel.

We planned to stroll in the newly opened Winter Gardens, indulge in side shows on the old pier and the crowning glory of our visit was to be a trip to the theatre and dancing on the fabulous New Pier. For days I had driven everyone mad with my noisy enthusiasm. Clifford said I was like a *Whizz Bang* the way I clattered about the place causing mayhem.

It was a chilly afternoon, but I was too fizzing with excitement to feel any nip in the sharp March breeze. I stood proudly next to my new husband; him tall and handsome in his best suit and me in my new lemon and caramel going-away outfit topped off with a delicious felt cloche hat.

Mrs Clifford Aubrey Harris, I turned the words over and over in my head. I was married at last!

Earlier that morning a keen wind had blown away the clouds giving rise to a sparkling day. After a simple wedding ceremony, followed by a wedding breakfast for twelve in the Cardiff Central hotel we had all caught the tram to the docks.

I was giddy with happiness. I kissed every one for love and luck as they waited to see us off on our honeymoon

I hugged Molly ferociously as she stepped forward looking teary-eyed, "Come on Sis.... I'll be back soon. Be happy for me."

Molly held me for a few seconds and whispered *good luck fervently* in my ear as if I were embarking on some intrepid expedition. *Good luck Nelly...you'll be alright.*

"And if not there's always our little secret...lots of Gin," I whispered back jokingly.

Only a few months earlier when Molly and Archie had returned from their own honeymoon, I never seemed to be able to talk to my dear sister for more than a few minutes on my own. She was so elusive it was almost as if she was avoiding me and our promised pre wedding chat. The deep secret of *It* still eluded me.

So, one day in December I had seized my chance to get to the bottom of the matter. With our own wedding day only a few months away, I was desperate to learn the secret of married life. I managed to collar Molly when I went around to their flat to deliver some spare linen from Mother.

Thankfully Archie was out and about getting new stock for the shop. I found Molly sitting on her own marking sheets with a household laundry marker. It was the chance I needed. I had been determined to hold her to her promise to tell me all about "it" before my own big day. Today was my opportunity.

"Come on Molly then.... spill the beans.... you promised," I said chirpily as I helped her fold the crisp laundry into neat oblongs.

Molly kept her eyes low, intent on making a clear mark on the inside hem of each sheet.

"I'm sorry Nell, I don't know what you mean," she said quietly working away.

"What do you mean, *you don't know what I'm talking about*... Molly you know perfectly well what I mean," my tone was filled with exasperation as I gazed at my sister's bowed head.

I had sat through numerous family afternoon teas, in company. We had met several times at church amongst the congregation and we had had a light luncheon with Clifford and Archie at a Lyons Corner house in Albany road, she couldn't have been more surrounded by people if she had arranged it on purpose. I felt she was avoiding me.

That afternoon was the very first time I had had her all to myself in weeks. How could she have forgotten her promise?

"It" Molly .... you promised to tell me all about "it", *that's* what I'm talking about as you well know." I sat waiting for an answer. She obstinately kept her eyes on the bed sheets.

"Come on Molly," I said with a slight nervousness creeping in to my voice, "Surely "it" isn't that awful is it?" I left the question hang in the air as I sensed her misery; her head still bowed, avoiding my gaze. "You know you can always tell me anything Molly... I'm your sister after all." I wheedled.

"I don't know," she snapped, "We...I mean.... I haven't done *it* yet either! We've been married nearly nine weeks Nelly and I'm still a virgin.... and it's all my fault... so there.... now you know!" My sweet, sensitive sister promptly burst into tears.

Over a cup of tea Molly unburdened herself of her shameful secret... she and Archie were yet to consummate their marriage and what was worse she said was that Archie was beginning to lose his patience with her.

"Oh, Molly, sweetheart.... what shall you do now? Have you spoken to Mother about it?" I suggested, although I had to admit the idea of discussing things of a personal nature with mother was always a somewhat vague and unsatisfactory experience.

"Oh, for heaven's sake Nelly.... *you* know what she's like!" Molly cried. "Mother just said that these things in married life *take a bit of getting used to*, and that nature would take its course, or, I don't know.... something like that...after all the other shocking stuff she was trying to tell me I think, at the time, I was just wanting her pre wedding advice to end...oh God it was just so embarrassing!" Molly shivered with revulsion and searched her sleeve for a handkerchief.

"But....but I just take one look at Archie and I just can't.... you know.... I just can't do it." she sniffed miserably.

I secretly wondered if Archie had some hideous war wound that repulsed her but I felt it would be too indelicate to ask. I simply said," Oh dear," and squeezed her hand.

"Look sis.... I know Mother said it was all part of God and nature's design and that there was nothing shameful in it, but honestly Nelly, I just can't believe that I can be expected to let him put that...that huge.... *thing*, inside me.... I just can't." She burst into broken dry sobs, as if her heart was breaking.

I sat wide eye-eyed and speechless as she related tales of a startlingly enormous male appendage that grew beneath the sheets whenever Archie kissed her.

"I like kissing him Molly, really I do.... And I don't mind if he wants to feel my breasts a little and...." she added, "and I said that I wouldn't mind so much if his manhood stayed soft and little and we tried to do *it* then. But when I said that Archie laughed at me and said that I was being a prize dunce... And that if I *ever* wanted a sweet little baby of my own then I had better get used to the idea of having a man do *it,* as real babies weren't really found under gooseberry bushes." She said hopelessly.

My heart bled for Archie and Molly locked in this private misery.... I could only imagine what led him to make that hateful, desperate comment. Everyone knew that my sister Molly loved babies. Whenever we spied a small bundle in a park being aired in its perambulator Molly could never resist cooing and fussing over tiny little fingers and cute little noses. Molly longed for a baby of her own.

"He's beginning to get so very cross with me Nelly, and I know it's all my fault. Archie said the other evening that a wife had a duty to submit to her husband's needs.... and that I should remember my wedding vows. He had been drinking then and....." I waited with baited breath as Molly gathered herself together.

"And what Molly?" I asked.

"And I thought he was going to force me Nell." She said wide eyed at the memory.

"Oh, Molly he didn't?" I said horrified that my poor sweet, sensitive sister would be claimed in that way.

"No... But Archie was so cross with me that when he left, he slammed the door so hard I felt sure it would come off its hinges.... so, you see I've got to do something about *it* or else......" Nelly trailed off leaving the rest unsaid. She sat looking a picture of misery.

"I know" I said brightly; desperate to help "we'll try Gin and courage .... Molly you *will* be a wonderful Mother.... I just know you will. We just need to break your duck that's all and then it will be fine.... After all, even our mother worked out how to do it with Father. Stands to reason that *it* can't be so very terrible doesn't it?" I chucked her under the chin and tried to coax a smile.

"Come on Molly, Archie loves you to bits, you know that don't you?" Molly nodded, bleakly.

"So, you must tell yourself that you *will* screw your courage to the sticking post, and that you *will* lie back and think of England, helped along by a few large tots of Mother's ruin.... You can do this Molly!"

So, it was decided that, come hell or high water, Molly would allow Archie his conjugal rights the following Friday evening. Meanwhile, I would help her sneak some Gin into the flat for medicinal purposes which she would add to some cordial just before bed. I had convinced her that if she was a bit squiffy then she wouldn't mind the whole business quite so much.

 Gin certainly took the edge off most things in my opinion, so Gin it would have to be.

Molly had brightened a little at the prospect of a solution to doing *it* at long last and vowed earnestly to see the plan through.

"Thank you, Nelly, you're a life saver.... I was beginning to feel such a failure. I will do this, really, I will.... and you must promise, on your honour, not to breathe a word.... not to anyone! ... Promise me!"

"Of course, ... I promise. Our secret"

And so, the deed was done. The following Wednesday over tea Molly had whispered to me that she had at long last broken her duck, but added that "*it* was still taking a bit of getting used to, and that a large slug of Gin had certainly helped in the proceedings."

At least Archie looked a little less grumpy the next time I saw him. It all appeared to be working out for the best. I kept my fingers crossed that Archie and Molly would be blessed with a baby soon. A little blessing that would put the sparkle back into her sweet nature.

And so, they had all waved us off as we stood on the deck of the spankingly smart Waverley.

As we plied our way with a loud a chuff of steam out into the channel, leaving the crowded quay behind, Clifford kissed me.

"I love you Mrs Harris...."

"I love you too"

Sarah

September 2012

As I spread the assorted contents of the grey, box file on the dining table I began to see a timeline emerging from amongst the stack of faded ephemera. I knew Bea would love to see this archive of family history, so I tried to put things into appropriate piles, taking extra care with the ragged, fragile, handwritten Births Death and Marriage certificates.

My Grandparent's wedding certificate nestled in an envelope complete with unsent post cards of the gloriously elaborate Grand Atlantic hotel and the winter gardens. A cluster of dance tickets and a cinema ticket for "The Jazz Singer" tumbled out of a theatre Bill for "No No Nanette" from a musical production on the elegant Weston Grand pier.

A small rent book for 12 Alma road dated August 1930 also lurked amongst the plethora of bits and pieces with a receipt for: Two light oak armchairs 2gns, one oak bedstead with worsted overlay mattress and washstand £3-10s-6d.

So, there it was, the first items of furniture that my grandparents set up home with, and then lived with all their married life. It even including my Grampy's fireside chair.

A fragile, yellowed clipping taken from a local newspaper caught my eye amongst the scraps, announcing the birth of a son; Leonard William Smith 5lb 4oz. Born to Mr and Mrs Archibald Smith on July 1st 1929.

So, Aunty Molly had had a baby after all; baby Leonard.... But no-one in the family had ever talked of Aunty Molly and the mysterious Uncle Archie having a child... So, what had happened to baby Leonard?

A faded black and white picture showed Leonard; a tiny, rather grumpy looking baby swaddled in shawls. Leonard was being held in his grandmother's arms against a background of full-blown summer roses. The somewhat sickly-looking child, probably only a few weeks old, was glaring at the camera as the two proud parents stood by.

It looked so like another world; a world spanning the old and the new, a world where Edwardian looking grandparents looked old beyond their years and the young looked to the future, unaware of the hardships and horrors that the next decades would bring down upon them.

An implausibly young Molly and Archie stood flanked by Clifford and Eleanor. Gran looked beaming and plump with a swelling abdomen that heralded the arrival of my own mother Jean and Aunty Molly looked shyly beautiful as she stood by her young husband in her sprigged summer dress.

CHAPTER 13

February 1930

An ordered calm draped itself over Inkerman street. The house was quiet. Our Jean, who Clifford said was the sweetest, most adorable cherub ever put on God's earth, was having her long afternoon nap. At only six weeks she had slept through the night like an angel and had captured her father's heart. Now as the months passed, she was turning into the most placid natured baby any mother could wish for.

Mother sat knitting little Leonard a matinee jacket whilst keeping a watchful eye and ear out for Jean and I had been granted the luxury of two whole hours freedom to pop around and visit Molly.

Mother had noticed Molly's increasingly slender, exhausted appearance and had decided that a little sisterly company and some home baking was in order. I was sent around with a batch of welsh cakes fresh off the griddle.

"That girl to needs to get her strength back up." mother had observed as she packed the welsh cakes in a small basket.

In the gloomy light of their flat Molly did look tired and pale as she bustled about making some tea to go with the cakes. A mountain of ironing sat in a corner awaiting attention.

Before laying out the china she hastily draped some little terry napkins to air on a wooden clothes horse to finish off drying in front of the fire. "I won't be a moment Nell, these nappies will never get dry at this rate, and then where would I be?"

"Oh, my goodness!" A look of alarm crossed Molly's face.

"That's the tripe...it'll be ruined." The persistent rattling of a pot lid called urgently from the kitchen.

Molly left the question of damp nappies hanging in the air and dashed off to attend to Archie's supper of tripe in milk and onions simmering pungently on the stove.

It was obvious, especially to me, that Molly was swimming hard to keep her head above the turbulent waters of domestic life.

"Here we are at last...." She set the tea tray down, "I think we've got a few minutes peace and quiet for a nice cup of tea before Billy starts fussing for his milk." Molly's beautiful blue eyes looked like saucers in her fine, delicate face; grey shadows smudged underneath her lashes casting her cheekbones into high relief.

"Please come and sit down for a few minutes Molly and take the weight off your feet.... mother says you really should try and rest a little more...." I urged as she fussed and bobbed like a small bright-eyed bird. "At the rate you're going you'll wear yourself out and then where would Archie and Billy be? ... Do sit down."

Molly perched reluctantly on the edge of a dining chair ready to spring into action if baby Billy needed her. Motherhood sat so heavily on Molly's shoulders; the worry and the demands of it caught her every breath. Feed times, colic and gripe water obsessed her, stiff nappies were rubbed between her fingers to raise and soften the nap until her skin was raw; and her pretty hands were almost spoiled. The hearth rug had almost lost its pile where she paced up and down and patted little Leonard's heaving back for hours at a time.

"Come on Sis, relax a little.... sit down and pour us both a nice cup of tea...Baby Billy is doing so well now.... I mean just look at him trying to sit up on his own.... And he's got such a lovely little smile." I reached over and straightened up little Leonard who lolled against some large soft cushions in the armchair next to the tea table; his fierce little face broke into a rare sunny smile.

This small, fleeting reward lit up Molly's face and her heart melted at the sight of it,

"Billy darling.... what a good boy for your mummy you are." She cooed as she sprang up and rushed over to plant a large kiss on his cosseted brow.

Little Leonard William, or *Billy* as Molly chose to call him, was the sun, the moon and the stars to them both and it was a heavy responsibility for Molly to bear.

Billy had been a sickly, colicky, demanding child from the moment he flopped blue-lipped and unresponsive into the world. The midwife had grumbled that the lazy little mite needed at least three sharp smacks on his bottom to get

118

him to launch his first pitiful wail into the world. Now, it seemed, that having mastered the knack of it, Billy hadn't stopped wailing for more than a few moments in any one day or night since he was born. It had frayed my sister's poor nerves terribly but at long last it looked as if things were slowly turning a corner.

Despite Molly's maternal cares she did have something I longed for...a home of her own. I was deeply envious of the neat little two bedroomed flat above the tobacconist shop. Of course, it wasn't exactly *all* theirs as Molly pointed out, they still had the business of the shop paraphernalia to contend with. Archie regularly had the book keeping and paperwork scattered all over their little sitting room, their one big cupboard that dominated the small sitting room was entirely taken up with logs and receipts.

Old Mr Smith said that they still had to store some of the spare stock boxes upstairs in Billy's bedroom, but since Archie put up the curtain divider, even that seemed no real imposition at all. Molly was mistress of her *own home* and I wasn't.

I *so* longed for a home to call our own. The strain of having Jean and all our possessions cramped into middle bedroom at Inkerman street, and then by day all of us clustered together in one small sitting room throughout the dreary winter with Mother, Father and Albert, was beginning to take its toll.

We tried to make the best of things as we all muddled along together. Luckily Jean was a placid baby but even so galvanized pails of steeping muslin and nappies encroached into the scullery, little baby things festooned the clothes horse in the back room, elbowing out father's shirts.

Albert often grumbled about being tired as he trailed off to work when Jean had had a wakeful night teething. At the end of the day of work my poor, darling Clifford had to make do with a hard chair in the tiny parlour which struggled to accommodate three grown men, two women and a baby. We so longed for a place of our own one day, or at the very least just a little *more* space.

"You are *so* lucky to have this little flat Molly.... I mean I know; we mustn't grumble and Clifford and I are so *very* grateful to mother and father, but when all's said and done their house does feel so …. so very lived in!" I nibbled the Welsh cake; a plain one sliced with a little stewed apple in the middle.

Mother had said that dried fruit was becoming ruinously expensive and scarce in the shops now; father blamed Mr Mac Donald and his useless National Government. Albert said that there was everything for the having under the counter if mother kept in with people a little more, which she didn't, Whatever the reason the Welsh cake was plain.

"I know Jean is an angel but even she can't help crying and getting a little cross sometimes...." I let that thought hang in the air as Billy reverted to form and started grizzling; his face screwed up into a red scowl that demanded his mother's attention. Molly gave a tired sigh and hoisted Billy onto her thin hip.

"Still we must count our blessings," I said brightly, "at least Clifford still has a good job in the shipping office and we have enough to get by on; we are even managing to save a little after we've given mother our weekly dues." I said proudly.

"Clifford told me that he saw more than twenty men queueing for work outside the docks yesterday, and Mother said that Mr Alwyn Jones's eldest son, Rhys has left to seek work in Bristol because he has been laid off at the factory. Times are hard for a lot of families." I said.

My frazzled sister shushed and patted. Molly dipped a moistened finger in the sugar crumbs and let Billy suck and soothe himself on it. "I know Nelly," she murmured sympathetically before adding darkly "and Archie says that things are going to get an awful lot worse before they get better," Molly swayed her hips in a soothing rhythm as she talked. "Archie says that there are just too many men chasing too few jobs, especially those poor devils too damaged and unfit to tackle hard work since fighting for their country; it's only a bit of tobacco that gives some of them the will to live."

Molly shook her head at the thought of the grey scarecrows that were an everyday sight hovering on street corners and leaning against the dock walls, hands cupped around cigarettes for warmth; patiently waiting for non-existent jobs.

"You won't believe it Nell" she added, getting into her stride as the baby's eyes fluttered into sleep, lulled by the swaying, "but Archie even caught young Jack Edwards trying to steal some cigarette papers the other day! Apparently, Archie said that Jack goes around the streets with his five-year-old brother collecting discarded dog ends and then he makes them up into "new" cigarettes to sell to the men waiting in line at the docks." Molly shook her head at the tragedy of lost youth; little Jack couldn't have been more than eight or nine years old.

"What did Archie do with him? Did he call the police?" I couldn't help but feel shocked at this turn of events. The Edwards' family were well known locally; they were a good, hard working family, times were tight, but *stealing!*

"No, he wouldn't do that," Molly said sadly, "Archie knows that Mr Edwards lost his job in the meat packing company some three months ago. With four small children to feed and another baby on the way soon, the family are really feeling the pinch.

"Archie took Jack home with a flea in his ear and told Mrs Edwards not to worry about sending her weekly shilling for the slate until things picked up a bit. Mrs Edwards said that she would see Jack was spoken to by his *Da* when he got back from looking for work." Molly gave a rueful smile, "the really sad thing is Nell.... Archie knows that it was almost certainly Jack's father who set him on the enterprise in the first place."

Later that evening I snuggled up in bed with Clifford in our little room. Jean, with her arms in a position of quiet surrender above her head, lay warm and milky in her crib. I cursed myself for being the impatient, ungrateful wretch that I was, always wanting more.... I was happy in our own small world as I lay in the crook of Clifford's arm tuning into the quiet sounds of the house at rest.... I must stop trying to force life or surely, I would be punished for it.... Whoever said "nothing good or bad lasts forever" knew such perfect golden times as this would pass. In the black of the room with its shallow breaths and snuffles, I felt a sense of panic....

Please God don't steal things away from me.... I am grateful for what I have... I am, I am.

Father was snoring through the walls and Albert's bedstead springs were creaking as he tossed and turned in the little box room on his narrow bed and I really did try to count my blessings.

I thought of poor Mrs Edwards burdened with debt, worries and a needy family and thanked God for what we had; our beautiful baby, our good health and each other. I said my contract with God over and over like a rosary trying to ward off ill fortune and still the small terrors that started to grow in my mind.... *Thank you, God, for all I have... thank you, God, for all we have.... thank you, God....thank you.*

There would be time for our own home soon enough.

Sarah

Cardiff September 2012

During my foray into my mother's papers I began to uncover such interesting treasures amongst the jumble of bits and pieces.

The tiny china fairy doll with its grey gauze skirt was missing one arm, it lay wrapped in silvery pink tissue from an almond macaroon, to protect it from harm. The faded Christmas beauty was nestled in a small Turkish Delight box for a bed; lined with a single tiny knitted, woollen booty threaded with a scrap of lace, a few grey-green pine needles were lodged in the threads.

Happy memories of Christmases long past? I smiled as I smoothed out the papery wrapper. Gran loved Turkish Delight, little pink and lemon cubes packed in sugar powder that clung sweetly to teeth and perfumed the breath.

I put the little doll back in its box to show Bea and started a separate pile for odds and ends at the other end of the dining table. The box was soon joined by some pressed rose petals dried carefully between thick, folded cartridge paper.

The petals had bled and oozed to leave frail, beige, slivers that clung to the page headed in my Gran's beautiful copper plate hand "September 1930-Our first Summer!"

I unfolded another piece of paper, foxed and grubby. It looked like a small poster or flyer for an event; a puzzling advertisement for a "Valley's Red Run" dated October 14th 1932. The quartered bill was tucked up in a manilla envelope; a cascade of assorted newspaper clippings fell out from between its folds, brow. Dead whisperings floated noiselessly in small, grey drifts onto my mother's cream carpet. Headlines and articles that told of fierce spring floods and even fiercer destitution. Starving miners marching to London and angry shouts of protest; sodden weather, winter freezes and deadly influenza.... Human misery.

The ghostly echoes landed into my world with a deafening crash.

CHAPTER 14

Alma road

August 1930,

Clifford tapped gently on the door of the house in Alma road. Eleanor took in the wonder that was to be their new home. The little, red-brick, terraced building stood solid and unremarkable in its row. The bay-fronted design almost the mirror image of her mother and father's house in Inkerman street. It presented a smart, uniform face to the world. Eleanor loved it.

Ranks of similar little houses had sprung up over Cardiff in the last sixty years. They formed regiments and flanks in the narrow city streets that proudly commemorated battles and dignitaries; Balaclava, Sebastopol, Raglan, Nightingale, Ladysmith, Cardigan.... The humbler soldiers' names were simply etched in hearts if not brick.

Nelly had been in such a rush and a fluster that very first morning to get little Jean settled and left with her mother.

Now as she stood on the threshold, she wanted time to un-spool in slow motion; to savour the joy and anticipation of seeing around this house, *their* house; their first real home together.

"It looks wonderful Clifford," she said, "But can we really afford it?"

The brass knocker gleamed softly, testament to Brasso, lint and elbow grease. The step was freshly scrubbed and the colourful majolica tiles that flanked the door were glossy and clean. She turned to admire the clump of ice blue forget-me-nots, tumbling over the border behind the low privet hedge; a small gesture of welcome on our first day. *Our home!* She thought as her heart skipped wildly in her chest.

Olwyn Pugh came to the door wearing her out door coat. "Do come in, Mr and Mrs Harris."

They were ushered through the front door into the narrow hallway. The black, white and ochre hall tiles formed intricate geometric patterns against the high skirtings and creamy lincrusta wall paper under the dado rail. Three panelled doors and a set of steep wooden stairs covered in a smart red runner came off the long corridor.

Mrs Pugh juggled a set of keys as she showed them the bare front sitting room that was to be all theirs. Nelly imagined sitting in the small bay window and watching the world go by as Jean slept upstairs in her cot.

Mrs Pugh proceeded to the open second hallway door with a large key. "As we agreed Mr Harris, this middle room will remain locked at all times during your stay, but I thought you should at least see inside." She smiled kindly.

They respectfully poked their heads around the door frame as the door swung back to reveal a small room stacked high with a spare bedstead, boxes, trunks and a few other sticks of furniture.

"None of this will give you any bother Mrs Harris.... it's just a few things that James and I don't need for the moment. Our little bungalow in Porthcawl doesn't have much space; so, as agreed, we'll leave these things here with you for another day." Mrs Pugh quickly glanced around at the piles that represented a former life and backed out the room. She locked it behind her with a sharp *click*.

"Everything is all packed up with camphor to guard against the moths and the like," she said, "so it shouldn't bother you at all...no, not at all."

Olwyn Pugh seemed a little distracted as she showed them around the rest of the small house; her tiny back parlour with its lovingly black-leaded grate that gleamed a soft graphite sheen, a small, scrubbed scullery with red quarry tiles, white Belfast sink and bleached deal drainer.

It all seemed perfect; Nelly squeezed Clifford's hand with joy. Immaculate nooks and cupboards were opened for us and displayed to the best effect; Nelly was so happy she wanted to laugh out loud.

In the yard, the coal house was flanked by a brick privy and a beautiful, blush, rambling rose cascaded along the garden wall and over the low slate roof, heady with late summer perfume.

Nelly's heart sang with happiness. *I will dry the fragile petals and scatter them in the linen drawer,* she thought to herself. *Little Jean's bed will smell of sweet roses, Clifford's pillow will remind him of this summer; the summer we had* _our_ first home. Her heart raced with joy at the prospect of their future life together in Mrs Pugh's house.

The little house did not have a speck of dirt or grime anywhere. Even so, every so often, out of habit, Mrs Pugh would run her finger across a surface and note its cleanliness with a small nod of satisfaction.

Upstairs the front bedroom seemed cavernous compared with the cramped middle room in Inkerman street. Nelly hugged herself at the thought of their new bed sitting proudly beside the small fireplace. Oh, what fun they would have in their very own bedroom, no father snoring through the walls, no Albert tossing and turning, no Jean in with them.

Clifford gave her a conspiratorial wink.

The little box room with its trailing rosebud wallpaper overlooked the yard; this was to be Jean's room. The sun was glancing through the sash window and a shaft of light illuminated a cascade of motes that danced like sprinkled fairy dust in the empty space.

A small, functional room with a glazed door, was tucked in the crook of the landing; it housed a vast, white porcelain bath with just enough space to squeeze in the small, china washstand that Clifford had been obliged to purchase. Clifford had made it _quite_ clear that he did not expect to wash and shave in the scullery of a morning like some docker; no, he would use their very own bathroom for his morning's ablutions.

Mrs Pugh took a deep breath, and then tackled the ordeal that was "the middle bedroom." She rifled through the household bunch of keys and unlocked the door.

"This room.... this _is_ James's room," she said firmly.

The cosy middle room looked as if someone might walk back in to claim it at any moment. A line of books, ranged in height order sat on a small shelf in the alcove next to the tiny grate, a pair of outdoor walking boots, rich with dubbin, nestled under the single bed that was neatly made up with blankets and coverlets. An oak tall boy stood in the corner topped with a selection of small picture frames and a small swing mirror. A well-thumbed Bible sat on the bedside table.... In the corner a clock ticked.

"It's very.... er... very nice.... and very *tidy* Mrs Pugh." Nelly managed to say, as she glimpsed inside at the quiet order that draped over the room like soft lint.

"Yes, well, that's the way my James likes *his* things.... Since serving his King and country Mrs Harris." she said proudly. "He's *very* particular about order, he can't abide, dirt, bad smells and disorder. No, no everything must be just so.... And that's my view on the matter too," Olwyn Pugh said loyally.

She closed the door with a gentle click. "It will stay *just* the way he likes it until we come back.... I've promised him that."

"Of course, it will Mrs Pugh," Clifford said as he took her hand. "Eleanor and I will take *very* good care of everything for you and, as you say, it will all be here for you when...... When you feel the time is right."

Olwyn Pugh fought back a small tear as she stored away the last few memories of happier times in her heart. She adjusted her hat and shook hands on the matter.

"Ah well, we will all have to see what the good Lord has in store for us now Mr Harris. I know you will look after things for me Mrs Harris.... and I wish you both *all* the luck and happiness in the world.... it does my heart good to think that there will be a lovely little baby in the old house again." She said generously.

And so, we found our first home. We signed for our set of house keys from Mrs Pugh and paid the first three months rental in advance. Clifford tucked the buff rental book inside his breast pocket for safe keeping as we waved Mrs Pugh goodbye.

We watched her small, brave figure retreat up the road, bag in hand, towards the Cardiff bus station and a new, uncertain future with her son James in the bracing coastal air of Porthcawl.

Once she was fully out of sight Clifford turned to me and smiled, "There is just one more thing to do Mrs Harris, before old Mr Jackson's horse and cart brings our furniture around," and with that he scooped her up effortlessly and carried her over the threshold. "Welcome to our new little home Nelly.... I know we are going to be *so* happy here."

CHAPTER 15

Nothing lasts

The year mellowed and turned towards a ripe Autumn and for some poor souls it crept darkly into a bitter, hard winter... In the midst of an uncertain and changing world *our* little family prospered. Happy, laughing visits from Molly, Archie and baby Billy cemented my bond with my sister; we were mothers now with our own homes, each mistress of our own domain; sharing new skills, confidences and chatter that entwined us and drew us ever closer....

Rhythms of domestic life settled over us. Little family teas proudly served to doting grandparents. Father helping Clifford prune Mrs Pugh's roses and erect shelves, whilst mother re-lined cutlery drawers with ironed brown paper.

Small gifts of spare linen and china generously appeared and eked out our own. And so, plate by plate, shelf by shelf, almost imperceptibly we grew into Alma road... and each night we made love.

Our first magical Christmas in Alma road was marked with our very own little tree and a china fairy; she leant so firmly to the left in her white gauze skirt that she caused Clifford to observe that "he was worried that she was of a socialist persuasion." Jean tugged at her father's heart as she tottered her first chubby steps; little tumbles and scrapes, mixed with laughter and tears.

We felt complete in our own sweet kingdom. As the months went by my terror of Mrs Pugh turning up on the doorstep with piles of baggage and a sepulchral James by her side receded.... I dared to hope that we would never have to leave.

Clifford and I joked that we were like old Darby and Joan as we drank our cocoa of an evening by a warm winter fire. We felt lucky and blessed.... It felt almost *too* grown up to be real, *too* perfect to be true... and a niggling thought of Mrs Pugh whispered *too* good to last.

That winter that dragged us into 1931 was particularly wet and bleak; a spiteful rain slicked down the factory walls as men sheltered there waiting for work, hands cupped around their pencil thin roll ups.

A cold wind blew hunger and hopelessness down from the Valley coal pits to the idle dockyards, and other families felt its chill; clothes became too big as spare, pinched frames shrivelled and accused the worn-out shirts and trousers that hung off them.

Everyone "made do and mended "turning and patching until there was nothing left to turn and patch and then cutting and shortening until trousers became breeches and shirts became little smocks.

And in our little home we counted our blessing and watched our daughter grow and thrive. We paid our rent to old Mrs Pugh and still poor James's lungs rotted and coughed up his awful legacy.

The year rolled on.

Summer 1932

Billy and Jean splashed and played through that last, long, hot summer. The dappled shade of Roath park gardens offered a cool respite from the dusty August heat for Molly and me. We ate our picnics, drank sharp lemonade and fed crusts to the idle ducks.

Lulled by the buzz and hum of metallic, blue and green dragon flies hovering effortlessly over the ornamental lily gardens, we strolled hand in hand with our little ones; meandering through the shimmering, afternoon haze into the cooler wild-flower meadows that flickered with daisies.

To Billy's delight, jaunty little boats navigated the Scott memorial in the Roath park pleasure lake; yellow, red and blue flags fluttering gaily in the lazy breeze.

Jean wore garlands of daisy chains around her plump little neck and collected fistfuls of brassy, golden buttercups as we passed through the blowzy formal borders.

The massive, tropical glass houses located at the far end of the park, steamed with exotic orchids and liana swagged palm trees. The glittering palaces disgorged pink visitors; clutching their sun hats and parasols as the heat claimed them and they sought refuge in the common man's flower beds that were a riot of patriotic red, white and blue nodding blooms. A loud buzz and hum of bees flitted through the military ranks of red and yellow-faced snap dragons that edged the paths. The day felt hot and lazy. Time seemed to move slowly.

As Molly and I sat resting on a small rug on the grass, I noticed how many young men in worn out clothes there were out and about in the luxuriant gardens that day. Some men were sleeping curled up under bushes on the dry leaf litter, others were taking their rest on wooden park benches, heedless of stares; all of them surplus and tired.

I watched as one skinny, weasel faced youth, no more than ten years old with huge shifty eyes the colour of bruises, slipped up to the shaded area where the fat swans gathered and shooed away the pampered birds. He darted in on a raiding foray and scooped up handfuls of dried crusts into his pockets before he charged off into the undergrowth.

"Did you see that poor lad Molly?" I said anxiously. I craned my neck to follow his shameful zig zag across the grass. Soon he was lost in the dense shade of the bushes flanking the far side of the lawn.

Molly turned languidly to follow my gaze across the cosseted grass, "What? What was I supposed to see Nelly? Oh, do you mean *that* boy?" She pointed to a small figure struggling to evade the grasp of a fat, uniformed park keeper.

The boy had been caught foraging in a park rubbish bin; he was being pinioned by his shirt collar. The ragged collar ripped away and the lad ran full pelt for freedom, clutching a half-eaten apple as his prize.

On the other side of the green, the park keeper was now blowing his whistle furiously at the receding back of the scraggy lad; the boy scampered for dear life across the immaculate, striped lawns.

"Oh Dear, that is *such* a shame Molly.... that poor lad must be starving to steal bread from the park swans.... I wish we had given him something to eat... I'm sure we could have spared a little of *our* meal," I said guiltily as I looked at the sleeping golden heads of our own dear babies.

Billy and Jean were napping plump and content on the picnic blanket, with the fragments of our bloater paste and cucumber sandwiches wrapped in wax paper, spoiling in the sun.

"It's more than a shame Nell.... it's an absolute disgrace. Archie says the poor men are becoming quite mutinous about the lack of work, especially when they can't put any food on the table.... First it was the pits, then the steel works, then the farmers and now half the docks are standing idle because there's no goods to shift. What with the closures and the protectionism in America, Archie says there's no work to be had in Cardiff now for love nor money, no matter how hard the poor devils look, ... it's bound to lead to trouble for everyone in the end, mark my words." Molly said sadly.

And so, Molly damned us all that hot August day in our summer dresses and hats with our sandwiches and our security.

CHAPTER 16

Billy

That September it rained; thunder cracked storms, that broke the heat with long glancing needles. Water bounced off the dusty paths running in rivulets down the dusty gullies.

It rained in pounding, heavy drops that battered and mashed the fields into ooze and slop, washing out the root crops and flattening the standing grain. It rained in torrents that swelled the Taff and cascaded into the little houses with filth and sewage. It rained day after miserable day.

Preachers from the local chapels stood on street corners in the City centre, offering hope and repentance and yet still it rained in biblical proportions. Newspaper headlines spoke of hope lost; of epic floods, crop failure, famine, deaths and strikes. That September God seemed to forget about the poor scarecrows of Wales.

The world was grey. Day after day the rain sucked the life out of families who had little left to give. Rumours spread of a whole family of nine walking into the water and drowning themselves one night in the foaming Taff; folk said that the poor mother held her baby under the murky waters to lessen its suffering. Three weeks later a small fish-nibbled corpse bobbed and peeped from out of the twisted willow roots at Taff weir. The others were never found.

October 1932

Molly sat in our little parlour that cold Wednesday morning dandling little Billy on her knee, "Look Aunty Nelly.... little Billy is going to *Ride a Cock horse to Banbury Cross, to see a fine Lady upon a fine horse...*aren't you my strong soldier?" She sang and crooned in a sing song voice to the golden-haired child she bounced on her lap.

"You ought to be careful about lifting Molly, little Billy is getting such a big, heavy boy now.... Aren't you my angel...? come sit on Aunty Nelly's lap for a *cwtch* and give your mummy a little rest?" I held out my arms to Billy who was scrabbling awkwardly over Molly's meagre lap.

I had been a bit concerned of late about Molly's pale skin and slender bird-like frame; she had developed a distinctly peaky look about her that I hadn't seen for a long while. Whereas I seemed to get plumper with more energy by the day, Molly just seemed to be drained. I threw myself into my chores and motherhood with gusto.... I felt so alive.

Clifford joked that I ought to be a farmer's wife carrying a stout ewe under my arm and a sack of grain on my back the way I effortlessly swung Jean high above my head, whipped and bashed my potatoes into fluffy mounds of submission and walloped clouds of dust out of our rugs with such vigour.... *Good strong arms Nelly.... we could have you carrying sacks of potatoes or pushing wheelbarrows full of turnips if you'd rather use those muscles,* he teased.

But soon all was clear; that morning over a cup of weak tea a wan looking Molly had confided to me about the baby. She was absolutely sure now that another little brother or sister for Billy would be arriving in Spring time. I was delighted for them both.

Secretly Clifford and I were hoping and praying for an addition to our own small family sometime soon and I hoped that my sister's good fortune would rub off on us. I too longed for another baby.

Molly sipped her tea and nibbled a dry biscuit in an effort to stem the swelling tide of nausea that afflicted her each morning.

"Archie is *so* pleased about it Nelly.... and I do so want another baby." she glowed with happiness as she spoke, a pink blush brightening her sickly pallor.

"Even so... I just can't help the fact that a part of me feels guilty somehow because we are so happy," a small look of terror crossed her face "you know Nell, when I think about all those other families that are suffering so badly, I just feel.... well guilty.... It can't be wrong for Archie and me to be so happy can it Nelly?" She opened her beautiful, luminous eyes wide at the thought of somehow being cursed for being too happy. I shook my head, poor sweet Molly.

139

"I know I'm being silly Nell, it's just sometimes that I want to cry because I'm so happy... and then I want to cry because others aren't." She gently ruffled the long golden curls that were starting to form into ringlets at the back of Billy's head; he sucked his thumb and started to drift into a doze on my lap.

"But Archie says we must grab our happiness where we can and be thankful for it.... After all none of us knows what the future has in store do, we?" She pleaded as if somehow doing a deal with the fates.

Archie was right.... none of us knew.

Just before that grey dawn on Friday October 14th the posters went up around our streets. Shunning the cold; eager, wet hands stuck them on lamp posts, notice boards and church hall doors. Nobody dared remove them.

Before the world started to go about its business that day, the hunger marchers had left the valleys. Like a gathering snowball, pale, hopeless men were swept up to join them along their route. And so, they pushed on; swelling their ranks to hundreds; shabby clothes and gaunt faces, desperate lads and defiant angry men.

The clatter of their boots and clogs drummed a tattoo that heralded their coming as they marched relentlessly on. People lined to streets to cheer them on and wish them luck.

Boys, heralding the protesting army, ran ahead of the men and handed out the red and white bills of defiance. A "Red Run" from the valleys was passing through Cardiff that day and then weaving its hungry way onwards through the streets all the way to the city London.

The National Hunger march was scheduled to pass up Queen street on its deadly route before making its way through to the gathering point at City hall. As Billy slept upstairs that afternoon, Molly stood on the doorstep of the tobacconists watching the ragged army march by. She clutched her coat tightly as the wind guttered around the corner slicing through her.

Row after row they came, some tipped their hats as a mark of respect to the young priest who stood in prayer at the corner of the street; most stared blankly ahead. God was not with them that awful day.

Then towards the end of the rag-taggle line came the women; wives of miners and farmers who were too sick or exhausted to march. These back markers struggled to keep up the relentless pace of the men. Molly saw one poor woman with a tiny pinch-faced baby strapped to her breast in a plaid shawl. The woman strode out defiantly in workers overalls as she cradled her sickly child that was clinging monkey-like to her scraggy frame. Molly's heart went out to her.

And so, the deed was done.... Molly rushed back into the flat to grab a hunk of crusty bread and cheese for the woman. After all, it seemed the least she could do as one mother to another.... Molly felt sure it would help sustain the mewling child if its mother had some food in her belly and some milk in her breast.

Molly pressed the small offering into the woman's hand "take it... Oh please take it," she said as the poor child started wailing and coughing; deep guttural coughs that caused it to writhe and moan piteously.

"Thank you, missus, my 'usband's too ill to march, but I'm not. I want those bastards in London to see what they are doing to us up in Cyfarthfa with their means testing... wicked it is.... I hope they all rot in hell. "She spat out her curse.

"God bless you..." She clasped Molly's hand in gratitude for the small act of kindness before moving on; the march wouldn't wait.

On the Sunday morning Molly felt too sickly to go to St Bartholomew's with Archie and little Billy. Waves of nausea still swept over her every morning as she retched and heaved over a china basin. This morning though was the worst ever. Her head ached and throbbed; hot waves passed over her leaving her sweating and shivering. Her legs felt like lead and her bones ached.

Billy had been fractious and cried and grizzled all through the night demanding her attention; she felt exhausted with it all. "Go without me Archie," she pleaded miserably, her eyes barely managing to open as she spoke. "I'm sure Father Edwards will understand.... and I don't think mother will be surprised now that she knows our good news... I just feel *so* rotten this morning, I can barely get my head off this pillow it aches so." Molly groaned as another wave of nausea crashed over her. Beads of sweat covered her brow; she struggled to resist the overwhelming urge to vomit.

Archie knew that he could not exactly be described as a natural or even particularly devout Catholic, having assumed a "flag of convenience" in order to marry Molly. But he tried to do his duty and attended mass on a fairly regular basis. He

142

knew that Mr and Mrs Fowler noticed when members of the family were missing. *Words* were said.

This morning Archie could easily get out of going to mass. He had to admit though that Molly did look very peaky; her cheeks had a bright high spot of colour against her pale skin that he hadn't noticed before, and her eyes looked quite dull and listless. He was worried about her. Perhaps she was doing too much.

"I think I'll stay home with you Moll.... you stay in bed now and I'll read little Billy a story when he wakes up and then I'll get his breakfast. He's still asleep at the moment; I'm sure God and your mother could excuse us all for just this once." Archie said dutifully.

Molly closed her eyes and ran her tongue around the edges of her parched lips. Feeling helpless in the face of illness, Archie topped up her glass of water.

"Don't fret now.... I can always ask Dr Thomas to pop by later on to take a look at you if you want me to." He watched her roll back into the middle of the bed clutching her stomach and groaning piteously. "Try to get some rest Moll and then I'll bring you a nice cup of tea a bit later on after I've seen to Billy. Maybe you could manage a bite of toast, when you've come to a bit?"

Two hours later as Molly lay dazed and groaning on the rumpled bed, Archie fetched Dr Thomas. The diagnosis was stark, Influenza. The deadly virus, that was gripping parts of Cardiff and causing havoc in the valleys, was now upon the Smith household; Molly was its first victim.

Over the next four days unable to get out of bed; Molly shivered and heaved; sweated and tossed until at last Dr Thomas pronounced that she was out of immediate danger. Little Billy however sank rapidly and buckled under the curse of the virus; the second household victim. Newspapers were full of reports of the influenza that was sweeping the old and the weak away in its vicious path. Archie was wretched with worry.

The note to our parents had been brief; it sent the whole family into a state of agitation and despair.

"Dear Ernest and Kathleen

Molly's been so very ill with the influenza but, God willing, she is out of the woods now. Billy is still very sick and Dr Thomas is concerned that he may not pull through unless he turns a corner soon. I think you need to come soon Kathleen, if you feel that you can. Archie."

Our mother rushed straight to Molly's side with broths and tasty little morsels to raise her spirits and strength. Father agreed that it would be best if mother stayed with Archie to help nurse Billy until the crisis was over. Dr Thomas had forbidden visitors to come to the house; so, all the rest of us could do was wait, hope and pray.

Our little household carried on as normal. There was nothing anyone could do now except put our trust in God. I attended mass more often than usual imploring Him to save Molly and Billy; to keep them safe; to look after the new baby to...... to fix all of it.

"Holy *Mary Mother of God, pray for us sinners now and at the hour of our death Amen."* Eyes screwed up in blind, tearless pleading that tried to do a deal with The Almighty. Hours spent on my knees in front of our little statue of Mary in the back room, doing penance for any wrongs; real or imagined.... Promises that we would all try harder to be good Catholics; surely Our Lady would hear my prayers?" *Hail Mary... Just listen to me... Holy Mary... please God!"*

I clasped Jean close, fearful of a vengeful God and gave silent thanks that my own family was safe from harm. Local newspapers continued to recount tales of whole families succumbing to the influenza.

But soon, over the days other headlines of unemployment and hunger overtook them, the disease was no longer fresh news and the stories of influenza slipped off the front page.

Clifford was caught up in his work for the shipping company; working long hours and often coming in late for his supper. With slack docks and fewer employees now in the shipping office than in previous years, he felt that it was important to shine; make himself indispensable, be a key part of the dwindling team.

That Autumn Clifford had taken to going swimming every Thursday evening. His early enthusiasm had blossomed into an intense desire to be part of the team of regulars.

Thursday was "work's night" at the Cardiff Corporation baths and he joined in with the rest of the men from the shipping company. Some of the more able men were in training for a local swimming Gala and Clifford quietly hoped that he too might be picked to represent the company.

Clifford had settled into a rhythm of doing numerous lengths that built up his strength and stamina; honing his lean body and calming his mind. The rhythmic ploughing back and forth in the lanes was starting to pay dividends; improving his muscles and developing his lung capacity to such an extent that he could now easily tackle a length under water. Clifford felt part of the team and Nelly was proud of him.

The Guildford Crescent baths offered the men the chance to exercise and socialize in the pool and steam rooms; everyone equal with their clothes and grime stripped away. He enjoyed the manly environment; the sheer physicality of it. He never missed a training session.

"Oh Nelly, I've done it, after three months of practising.... they've only gone and made me a full team member." He gave Nelly a big hug; triumphant. He beamed with pleasure. "Aren't you happy for me Nell? Is something up?" he looked at her anxious face. He could see that she had been crying as she sat by the light of the fire.

"I saw Archie today in Albany road today Clifford.... He looked terrible, poor man. He said that Molly is getting a little stronger now, thank God," she crossed herself superstitiously, "but the bad news is that little Billy is still so very poorly with the influenza.... Dr Thomas has warned him that Billy might not survive the week unless he turns a corner soon." she shook her head in disbelief at the dreadful enormity of it all. The prospect of losing Billy was too awful to contemplate.

"Archie is so worried about them both. He says that my poor sister spends every waking hour pacing the boards with Billy trying to get him to sleep for a little while; the poor mite's not feeding and his poor little chest is so weak with coughing."

Clifford noticed the catch in her voice as she struggled to hold back the tears.

"Apparently Molly won't let go of Billy, not even for a moment. Neither our mother nor Archie can take over and give her some rest.... the poor darlings. My poor sister must be beside herself." She said as she sat by the fire twirling a small, damp handkerchief between restless fingers.

"I do *so* want to go and see them Clifford; just to give Molly a hug." She caught his anxious look and quickly cut him off before he could say anything. "But I know I must think of Jean.... I told him that I was praying for them all, but I can't risk it.... I mean I couldn't forgive myself if I put our own little Jean in danger.... I just feel so helpless.... They must feel so miserable and.... and abandoned." With that she burst into hot tears of rage and frustration; inwardly railing against a heartless God for ignoring her prayers.

Clifford held her close, wrapping his arms around her protectively. Nelly was so small in his arms, such a little woman, so much fun and spirit and yet with such a tender heart. He hated seeing her crushed by all the worry about Molly and Billy. He was just grateful that his own family was safe. As he stroked her head and hushed her sobs, he silently anticipated that the worst may be yet to come. If old Dr Thomas had said that he expected worst, then surely it would come.

The local newspapers still carried articles about deaths from the influenza that stalked the families of Wales; but it was the growing announcement columns that showed it was the weak, the old and babies who were being swept away in its deadly wake. Now all any of them could do was hope against hope that Billy wouldn't be yet another small addition to the mounting toll of victims.

CHAPTER 17

Molly

That Monday morning, the 2nd of November, was chill and grey. Clifford made his way to work on his bicycle; the thin tyres jolting and rattling over the lumps and bumps in the scabby roads. As he cycled past the tobacconists on the corner of Albany road, he glanced up at the front left-hand window that served the sitting room of the little flat.

Clifford saw Archie staring bleakly out through the pane of glass, smoking. He gave Archie a small wave. Suddenly the sash flew up and Archie called out to him, "Oi... Hey Clifford... wait!... Please wait.... I need to speak to you."

The sash clattered down and within moments Archie appeared and began, unlocking the shop. Clifford stood a little way back from the door as an exhausted looking Archie appeared on the threshold.

His clothes looked rumpled and grubby; hair raked back from his forehead in greasy strands; the man that stood before him was unrecognisable from the normally dapper Archie Smith.

"How are things Archie old chap," Clifford said softly as the gaunt figure of his brother-in-law propped himself on the door jamb.

"He's gone Clifford.... our little Billy he's...." Archie's voice trailed off; dry guttural sobs seemed to be wrenched out of the very heart of him; his face screwed up against the pain that tore through his body. He wrapped his arm around his middle; fingers bunched and clutching at his thin pullover. Archie sobbed uncontrollably and slumped down onto the floor with his head in his hands.

Clifford propped his bicycle against the shop front and helped Archie up. "Come on Archie.... you've got to be strong. Molly needs you now." He saw the flare of anger in Archie's eyes.

"And I *need* her, "he spat "and I needed Billy... my darling Billy. She shut me out Cliff, she bloody well shut me out... Me his own father!" Guttural sobs wracked his body.

"No-one could get near him; I never got to hold him alive when he was so poorly... not once and now.... even though he's dead, she won't let me near him. He's been dead since dawn and she... she...." His eyes were wild with grief.

"And she won't lay him down, not for a moment... she still keeps pacing around with him in her arms, singing and rocking, bloody worrying at him... As if that will bring him back. Can you believe it? Our poor child" Archie shook his head in despair.

"What shall I do now Clifford? Tell me. What do I do?"

Clifford felt for Archie as he paced about outside the corner shop as if afraid to go back inside and confront the horror of his dead son.

"I'll fetch Dr Thomas... he'll know what to do.... Hold up Archie; you've got to bear up for Molly... she is obviously still unwell... it's the shock. I'll tell her parents and Nelly... We'll all help." Clifford added.

"Go back to Molly, Archie.... she shouldn't be on her own... not now. I'll be back as soon as I can old man." Clifford called over his shoulder as he grabbed his bike.

Clifford cycled at full pelt to the small surgery in Queen Street to summon Dr Thomas, then he flew back towards Inkerman street and Alma road.... *Nelly and her parents would need to know as soon as possible.* He churned words over in his head as he cycled trying to find a kindly phrase to soften the blow... But what could he say? *Billy was dead.* He dreaded being the bringer of such sad news especially to Nelly.

The grey morning draped itself over him; a soft drizzle swept in greasing the streets and clinging to his clothes as Clifford went about his miserable task of spreading the word.

When the news broke of Billy's passing, a dreadful hopelessness settled over the whole family. Three households united in grief. Archie shut the shop for three days and Molly took to her bed under Dr Thomas's strict instructions that "she must rest and think of the new baby."

It had smashed hammer blows into her heart when Dr Thomas had lectured her that Billy was beyond help now and that she must take care of herself and think of the new life growing within her... What did he know?

For Molly these well-meant phrases were mere platitudes and she blocked them out. Without her darling Billy she felt dead inside, and nothing would ever fill that void in her heart. Nothing.

Later that same day, when Billy's corpse had been taken out of the flat, Archie had held Molly tight to stop her from blocking the funeral directors from taking his little body to the chapel of rest.

Pinned by his arms she stood furious in the hallway. Billy's small corpse seemed to weigh no more than a feather as she watched the undertaker carry it down the narrow stairs wrapped in a grey blanket; his perfect porcelain face peeking out from the folds with purple lips and blue shadows on his once rosy cheeks.

She hated him then; letting their child go to that cold place; to be laid out and washed by other hands when it should be her hands, to be dressed and buttoned by other fingers when they should be her fingers. Oh yes; she hated them all, especially Archie.

She had howled and moaned like a stricken animal until the horse drawn van with Billy's body in it had disappeared out of sight down Queen street. Dr Thomas gave Molly a sedative to calm her nerves and help her sleep. That morning they put her to bed in a fog of drugged forgetfulness.

Archie drifted from task to task and day to day; subsumed in the miserable drama of it all, he went unnoticed. All eyes were on Molly. *"You've got to be strong for her Archie... she needs you the poor girl.... It's your job to look after Molly now."*

He buried his own grief deep within him; cast into a role he never wanted to play, a role that he didn't know the words for.... Inwardly he screamed and howled for his son; his hopes his dreams... *His son.*

Neighbours and friends of the family came around to Inkerman street with murmured words of condolence for the Fowler family, curtains were closed, blinds drawn down in the houses along the terrace as a mark of respect.

Kathleen and Ernest worried about their eldest daughter as comforting platitudes were offered up by kindly neighbours and swapped on the street corners by well-meaning friends; *"such a shame about poor little Billy, but then she's still young....there'll be plenty of time for others...Influenza they say....terrible news, the poor soul... such a pretty little boy too... a real shame."*

With Molly so distraught and on bed rest, Nelly and her mother tried their best to help Archie with the funeral arrangements.   The awful bureaucracy that surrounds a death had to be dealt with and would not wait. Announcements were to be made; forms were to be filled. Life dragged on.

Billy's small life became reduced to three short lines in the Western Mail; Leonard William Smith deceased 1/07/1929 - 2/11/1932. Much loved son of Mr and Mrs Archibald Smith. Funeral service to be held at St Bartholomew's Church, Queen Street, 11am Monday 16th November.

CHAPTER 18

Archie

As the dead days slid by before Billy was to be laid to rest, another small life slipped silently away. On the Sunday morning before the funeral, Molly knelt in prayer and anguish beside Billy's little wooden cot; his teddy and toys just as he had left them... She hardly noticed a slick ooze trickle wetly between her legs, staining her nightgown. As she convulsed in tormented grief for her lost golden child, bloody gobbets made their way down her inner thighs spattering the small rug and floor.

When Archie entered the bedroom with a cup of tea, he saw Molly sitting on her haunches, pale faced and mute. Drained and shattered she said nothing to him; *after all what could she say that made any difference now? She felt cursed.*

In her hands he saw there was a tiny, pink creature that could have been a bald nestling chick, resting on a scrap of torn liver.... She offered it to him.

Whilst Dr Thomas saw to a broken Molly in the dark and lifeless bedroom, Archie waited nervously in the small parlour. The horror of the morning imprinted on his mind.... Molly with her hands bloodied, her face wretched with pain. He tried to shut out the image that kept looping through his brain.

In his haste he barely recalled the blur as he raced around to the surgery to summon Dr Thomas. He desperately tried to gather his thoughts as he made the slower sad cycle to Inkerman street, to tell Molly's parents and Nelly about the latest turn of events.

As he rode past rows of calm houses, it had all taken on the feel of a bad dream. He felt shattered inside, more tears, more heartache, more pain. It felt as if his world was being hollowed out by a spiteful God. All he had left now was Molly; Molly who was locked away from him; unresponsive and distant.

Nelly was quickly despatched by the family to sit with Archie and help out. She felt ill-equipped for the task and a small, selfish voice within nagged that maybe the Smith bad luck was catching. But father and Clifford insisted that she go and so go she did, saying several Hail Marys for her own wicked thoughts.

Archie sat in the pokey kitchenette with his head in his hands, a smouldering cigarette dangling between his fingers. Nelly regarded the messy ashtray that overflowed onto the table. The urge to smoke herself overcame her and she reached into her handbag for a small packet of Craven A's.

"What will you do Archie... you know about tomorrow?" She drew on the cigarette for support as she tackled the thorny subject of Billy's funeral planned for the next day.

She watched as his fingers raked nervously through his fair hair; he did not look up.

"Mother thinks Molly shouldn't go... but if she doesn't what will she do?" Nelly paused to look at him hoping for some response. "I mean it doesn't bear thinking about not going, but *how* can she under the circumstances?" She stared at his bowed head.

"Oh, Archie this is all so awful.... for both of you... Tell me.... what we must do?" Nelly willed Archie to look up. He needed to be strong now; Molly needed his strength more than ever. She waited for his answer.

Archie roused himself into response. "She'll go Nelly, unless Dr Thomas forbids it.... We'll leave it to him, let him decide. If I tried to stop her, she would never forgive me... She'll go all right." He spoke without looking at her, his voice low and measured. "I'm worried about her Nell, she hasn't said anything for hours.... she just keeps looking at me. She isn't even crying... Nothing, not a word, just bloody silence." He took another Woodbine out of its packet and used the still smouldering butt to light the next one.

For a few moments Nelly said nothing; she joined him smoking in a taught, awkward silence.

"It must be the shock Archie, what with poor Billy and now *this*," She waved her hand in a vague gesture towards the bedroom door; unsure how to tackle the subject of Molly's failed pregnancy. "She'll come around when it's had time to sink in.... She just needs a little time... you both do." she added hastily. She felt out of her depth; words felt trite, clumsy, pointless even. Platitudes tripped off her tongue and she hated herself for using them. She stared at Archie.

Archie looked like a hollow man, he dragged deeply on his cigarette; his tired eyes squinting, as if seeing some other figure in the room.

Nelly could think of nothing useful to say. She closed her hand over his with a gentle, comforting squeeze. What could anyone say?

They sat and waited with just the tick tock of the mantle clock punctuating the silence. The curtains shut out the vague, wintry brightness of the November afternoon as the world outside went about its business. In the gloomy, smoke filled room, there was nothing to say and nothing to do now, except wait.

Dr Thomas gave a small knock and entered the sitting room. A kindly, yet practical, old man he knew the Smith family needed answers; life was about the living. He had seen countless similar sad events in his long career but in the end the small tragedies all boiled down to the same eternal dilemma.... What happens next?

Nelly hastily stubbed out her cigarette as the doctor entered.

"She's going to be all right Mr Smith; I've given her a sedative to calm her nerves and help her get some sleep. Mrs Smith just needs plenty of sleep now and then nature will do the rest it its own good time. She's young... there will be time for other babies." Dr Thomas cleared his throat. "I'm sorry about the loss of little Leonard, Mr Smith.... please accept my condolences." He spoke in a practised manner the words slipping effortlessly out of his tight mouth.

"Thank you, doctor," Archie mumbled. "What shall we do now?... You know about the funeral." Archie's hands twisted and turned over and over as he grappled with the pressing matter of Billy's funeral service. "It's being held at St Bartholomew's, eleven o'clock tomorrow morning... I mean *is* she well enough to go?" His words were awkward and forced, he knew that he was shifting the decision onto Dr Thomas' slender shoulders. Damned if he did and damned if he didn't.

They both looked at Dr Thomas waiting for the verdict.

Dr Thomas shook his head slightly." Of course, she isn't well enough to go but...., having spoken to Mrs Smith, I fear that she must go." Dr Thomas looked directly at Archie. The decision was made.

"I've advised your wife that I will pop in on my rounds to see her first thing in the morning, just to check on her condition. If she is no worse then, she may go to the funeral." Archie gave a small nod of acknowledgement. "But" Dr Thomas said with emphasis, "but afterwards I absolutely insist that Molly must come straight home to bed. She must rest completely for at least a week; no lifting, no housework and no stress.... Is that understood?" Archie and Molly nodded meekly. "I will come and see her every day to make sure she is recovering *and* obeying my orders... to the letter!" He gathered up his bag. "I'll be back at 9.30am tomorrow.... Don't worry I can see myself out." He shut the door behind him with a small click and left the family to its misery.

That terrible Monday of Billy's funeral it rained; a persistent heavy, drumming rain that slicked down the windows and swirled rubbish down the streets to block the drains. Cold, miserable, relentless rain.

Early that morning as Nelly waited to leave for St Bartholomew's she stared out of the rain-streaked window in Alma road. Her head pressed against the pane; she stared at the blind terraces. The houses opposite had closed their curtains as a mark of respect; tatty old velvets with faded edges not quite meeting in the middle. Mrs Jones at number 9 peeked around the edge of the drapes before they twitched together.

The unwelcome spectre of poor, broken James Pugh invaded her thoughts as she contemplated the empty street. She felt flat and hopeless. Motherhood was a beautiful and a terrible thing.

Nelly was dreading the day, the ghastly rhythms of funeral music, black hats, tears and incense. *Bloody awful all of it* she thought as she followed the path of rain overflowing the iron shuttering and sluicing down into the gutter. They would need umbrellas.

Molly, Archie and the entire family were caught up in the overwhelming awfulness of it all. They were all being carried along like the mess of rubbish that was flowing down through the streets. She watched a small collection of twigs and leaves gather around the drains causing the water to bubble up over the pavement edge.   Nelly raged in her heart against events; Molly and Archie didn't deserve such sadness. She pulled the curtains together and sealed in the misery.

The second, tiny life went without remark or mourning that day, except in Molly's heart.

The family gathered at the church surrounded by a few neighbours as they went through the solemn rituals of death and burial.

Nelly felt strangely detached throughout the service. She stood next to Clifford watching her sister and Archie stiff and tragic at the front of the church; her own mother looked slumped and old as she leant on father's arm for support.   It was if she was a bystander caught up in a bad dream watching familiar characters playing out unfamiliar roles.

Nelly studied her sister, catching a small glimpse of her pretty face as she mumbled her way through hymns and prayers. Molly, pale and fragile looking, appeared to bearing up remarkably well as she stood next to Archie grasping his arm for support. But Nelly knew that deep inside Molly must feel if she was dying; her still bleeding body a reminder of her loss. Nelly willed her to be strong.

The rest of the awful day passed in a blur of tears and hushed platitudes *"so sorry for your loss... if there's anything we can do... He's gone to a better place...Everybody is thinking of you my dear.... Poor, poor Billy."*

Before the day could grind to a close, they must all endure the proprieties of a small tea and sandwich reception at Inkerman road.

Tea and sympathy. What does that ever solve? Thought Nelly bitterly as she dutifully handed around a plate of sandwiches to neighbours who sat polite and stiff backed on the hard chairs of the back parlour. She smiled and nodded as she passed through the small gathering, accepting murmurings of condolence soothed with tea and biscuits. She willed them to leave.

Molly sat wrapped in grief as Archie thanked friends and neighbours for their kind words. By three o'clock it was nearly dark and with hushed tones and well-meant words the neighbours departed; the room was set to rights and the ordeal finally over.

CHAPTER 19

Decisions

With Billy buried we all settled into a dismal rhythm that sad November.

The year was rolling to a close and it felt impossible to contemplate our family Christmas under the circumstances. Molly sank within herself and the family sank with her.

Molly had drifted further away from us all and I feared for her. I tried to cheer her up with chatter and distractions, but the very sight of our own darling Jean toddling around on her plump little legs caused her to break down in pitiful sobs.

She was inconsolable in a world without Billy. For Molly, Billy was everywhere; he haunted her. Occasionally she would start at the yells of small child in the street, pausing to listen with cat like watchfulness at the squawks and wails of a thwarted toddler. Peering around curtains to spy on the world below that seemed to be filled with babies and children.

Archie was left to fend for himself as the chores went undone and night after night no meals appeared on the table. Molly, always slender, became wraith like as she drifted around the flat clutching at memories of Billy; the little scuffs on the skirting boards where his push-along-horse had collided with the wood; the bedroom full of toys that she would not allow to be touched.

Even when I visited on my own, Molly refused to come out of the flat; everything reminded her of Billy, and it tore at her. Leaving the flat meant leaving Billy.

Nothing seemed to get past the void in her heart that was swallowing her up. Molly spent her days gazing forlornly out of the window as the world went about its business, a world without Billy.

Then it happened; one awful Monday morning things just came to a head and our whole world came crashing down.

"I know you don't *want* to do it Archie, but if Doctor Thomas says it is for the best then you *must* listen to him.... It's been over four weeks now since little Billy died, we all *know* in our heart of hearts that she's been getting worse.... Things can't go on like this... especially now...." Kathleen paused to let her words sink in.

Father sat stern and unblinking next to mother as the thorny topic of *what to do about Molly* was tackled. An awkward silence settled over the room; everyone reluctant to add their two penneth worth.

With Molly on bed rest at home under the watchful gaze of old man Smith, the rest of family sat around the Fowler dining table conspiring; decisions had to be taken about Molly's future and quickly.

Only hours earlier Dr Thomas had strongly advised Archie to allow Molly to be admitted to Whitchurch hospital for psychiatric treatment. *"It's for her own good Mr Smith... otherwise I won't be responsible for the outcome."*

So, we all gathered in Inkerman street to decide Molly's fate... family business. It was a decision that Archie couldn't make alone.

"I just can't put her in *that* place, Mother. I hate the very thought of my Molly in a.... an asylum." Archie looked around the assembled family for support and caught my eye.

"Nelly, she didn't.... you *know* that she didn't *mean* to do it... Molly wouldn't hurt anyone; especially not a baby... It's not her fault!" He pleaded helplessly.

Lost for words Archie burst into tears of impotent rage.

"We *know* it's not her fault Archie.... nobody's blaming anyone...but..." Kathleen paused for a moment to allow Archie to compose himself. "But as her husband, it's up to you to do what's best for her."

Weeks of Molly's increasingly bizarre and irrational behaviour had come to a head; something had to be done.

That very morning Molly had slipped out of the flat and scooped up a dozing baby from a perambulator parked outside in the wintry chill. Oblivious to the drama, the baby's mother was busy doing her errands in the green grocer's shop that flanked the tobacconists' front shop-window display.

Whilst the young mother chattered and shopped, Molly took her baby.

When Archie had gone into the back-bed room to get some more stock for the shop, he found the little mite cocooned in a blanket and fast asleep in Billy's cot. Molly was sat next to the crib singing a soft lullaby; the infant slumbered oblivious to the drama unfolding on the street below. Molly rested in the nursing chair with her small, useless, dried up breasts exposed.

"Billy was cold Archie... I couldn't let him get cold..."

The frantic young mother of the missing baby boy had screamed blue murder when she discovered her loss. The police were summoned. Only the swift discovery of the baby safe and sound and the intervention of Dr Thomas promising to *"get poor Mrs Smith the treatment she needed"* had calmed the situation.

The policeman, a kindly man, had insisted that Molly must be dealt with, one way or the other; taking other people's babies was a very serious matter that could not be overlooked.

Within hours of the incident Dr Thomas had found Molly a place in the City asylum at Whitchurch; with Archie's permission Molly could be admitted as an in-patient later that afternoon. Dr Thomas now awaited their instructions.

Clifford looked at me before finally taking the plunge, "Ahem," he cleared his throat. "I say Archie old man... It *is* for the best... I mean if you *admit* her then she can leave the er... the hospital when she's ready. But if on the other hand if you wait for her to be committed by the authorities then who knows.... she could be in there for a very long time." Clifford waited a few moments. I squeezed his hand under the table.

"If Doctor Thomas says that he thinks that Molly *will* get better with specialist treatment then surely you can't deny her that treatment .... can you?"   Clifford ploughed on.

"As Doctor Thomas said it was Molly's cry for help; we all know that she meant no harm by it... Science has moved on so much these days Archie; there's such a lot they can do now. There's no shame in getting help." Clifford scanned the room. Silent faces looked back at him.

"We will all take it in turns to visit her every day until she's ready to come home, Won't we Nelly?" I nodded vigorously.

"You won't be on your own in this Archie... families must pull together at times like these." Clifford added. "You know it's for the best." Faint murmurings of assent went around the table, even father said a brief *aye* after mother gave him a small nudge.

Archie nodded miserably. And so, the deed was done; just three weeks before Christmas Molly entered the City asylum and mental hospital as a voluntary in-patient. We all agreed it was for the best, whatever *the best* meant.

I felt that I lost my sister that day. It would be several miserable months before Molly would be allowed to come home to us; a part of her never did.

CHAPTER 20

Archie

February 1933

"Yoo-hoo.... Is anybody home? Archie are you in?" I called up the stairs of the flat as I let myself through the front door. I was greeted by silence.

Even Clifford had noticed Archie's increasingly dishevelled appearance of late, his cheek bones were now razor sharp with mauve hollows under his eyes.

It was decided that we should take him under our wing a bit more. What with visiting Molly and a business to run, Archie was definitely letting things slide.

Without Molly the flat was taking on an unkempt, unloved appearance. When, on a recent visit, Mother discovered mould growing inside Molly's best china tea pot; it was the final straw. It was obvious that we all needed to do more to help Archie now.

Despite Archie's protests a family rota was agreed: Mother said that she would tackle the groceries and three times a week she would plate up a nice supper for Archie. I was to tackle the cleaning and the laundry whilst Mother minded Jean; between us we would all keep a much closer eye on him.

I had purchased carbolic and disinfectant to give the place a thorough going over; Molly couldn't come home to such a poor show. The very act of keeping the place fit for Molly's return felt a step towards her recovery: not *if* but *when* Molly came home.

I had so hoped that our Molly would be quickly returned to us, but her progress was painfully slow. She seemed vacant and apathetic; nothing seemed to cheer her or get inside her shell. It was as if a light had gone out inside her. But Dr Thomas said, there *was* progress and so we all clung to it like a drowning man clings to a life raft.

This afternoon, armed with cloths and a basket of cleaning essentials, I planned to clean out some kitchen drawers and tackle the grimy windows; I had plenty of time before I needed to get back to Alma road. After work that evening Clifford would be attending his weekly swimming practice at the Corporation baths. The works Gala was now only weeks away and Clifford was keen to keep his place on the team. I set to work on my hands and knees.

The front door slammed and a heavy slow tread up the stairs marked Archie's return from visiting my sister.

"Yoo, hoo Archie... it's only me... I'm in the kitchen." I wrung out a cloth and wiped over some painted surfaces sticky with grease. "Shall I put the kettle on and make us a nice cup of tea?" I did not hear a reply. "Archie? "

He sat in the armchair by the window; he looked worn out and my heart bled for him.

"Archie, is something the matter?" As soon as the words were out of my mouth, I regretted them.

"Everything is the matter Nelly... just everything... I mean just look at it.... look at all of it." His eyes blazed and he swept his hands around in a large expansive gesture. I failed to see his point, the room was ordered, I'd dusted yesterday and a small fire was laid in the grate.

"She should be here with me Nelly... Here in our home... our bed; not sitting in a hospital ward, gazing out of the window all day." He sprang out of the chair, "How long is this supposed to go on for? Dr Thomas says she's making progress.... Progress!" he spat bitterly. "So, she gets out of bed and gets dressed by herself now... is that what *you* call progress? I want *my* Molly back... I just don't recognize her any more Nelly; she's changed *so* much."

I raised an eyebrow at this last remark; it struck home. Only the week before when I visited the hospital, I too had seen a *new Molly*.

Molly's beautiful hair had been shorn; not stylishly cut, but chopped close to her head in a limp approximation of an Eton crop. The remaining few inches of hair clung unflatteringly to her scalp culminating in a short wispy fringe that grazed her eyebrows.

Molly's delicate features had been thrown into sharp relief by the loss of her crowning glory; the savage crop gave her a pinched, hard-faced expression. Without the subtle golden highlights of her long tresses, her hair now looked mousey, nondescript. My poor sister looked old beyond her years.

When I had tackled the ward sister about this brutal, utilitarian hair style, so unlike Molly's favoured chignon, I was left reeling.

"Mrs Smith cut off her own hair Mrs Harris....it was her own decision." Sister said crisply.

Further questioning revealed that Molly had felt that it was a foolish vanity to be fussing with her hair when her son was lying cold in his grave and so, she had decided to rid herself of it. One morning she had simply hacked off chunks off her beautiful hair with a pair of toe-nail scissors borrowed from another patient's locker. The resulting close-cropped style was the final work of a kindly barber, who regularly visited the men's ward; he'd been asked to "finish *the job and tidy things up a bit for poor Mrs Smith."* Molly had left him very little to work with.

"Archie she can't help it; she feels she is to blame for ...." I caught his eye and left the words unsaid. Dr Thomas was certain that Molly's overwhelming sense of loss and guilt was at the root of all of her problems.

"When she's better things will look different, really they will. We've all got to be patient Archie.... they say that time is a great healer." I added lamely. "I'll make us some tea before getting on with my few chores, shall I?"

"Nelly, nothing is going to bring our Billy back... nothing... I loved him too! Surely if I can live with it, then she can?" He broke down and sobbed bitter angry tears, balling his fists with rage.

I gave him a small hug; his once powerful arms felt thin and wiry under his grubby shirt sleeves. Poor Archie.

As I lay in Clifford's arms that night I couldn't sleep. The alarm clock on the mantle-piece irritated me with its incessant loud metallic tic. I willed myself to relax before the night slipped away.

Archie's bitter expression niggled away at me. He was still a young, handsome man, it must be so cruel to watch Molly drifting away from him. I lay in the dark listening to the relentless tic of the clock; and Clifford, exhausted by his swimming practice and our love making, snored contentedly in a deep slumber.

I offered up a prayer for Molly and Archie.
The next few weeks drifted by. Day by day Molly grew calmer, more settled; the hospital routine seemed to soothe her. Her fits of weeping gave way to a subdued, meek composure.

Molly drifted about the wards like a colourless wraith, quiet, listless, biddable. Eventually she was trusted with small tasks such as serving the afternoon tea to other residents; there was talk of acceptance and even maybe just *maybe* being able to go home if she continued to keep it up.

I crossed my fingers and prayed that Molly would come home to us all soon. As spring crept towards us, we had a tiny glimmer of hope.

Clifford was now practising three nights a week, honing his technique in readiness for the swimming Gala, now only a week away.

"We've got to get that shield Nell; it's company honour after all." Clifford spread out his swimming costume to dry on the clothes horse. "Do say you'll come and watch us on Saturday. There will be fifteen teams from all over Cardiff... It's only for a few hours.... Please Nelly. I do so want *you* to be part of it." he said eagerly.

Eleanor felt torn. Mother had hinted that, God willing, Molly would be coming out of Whitchurch hospital on Maundy Thursday. Someone would be needed to help Archie *keep an eye on things as* she had so euphemistically put it; looking after Jean on Saturday would be out of the question. But then, it *was* only the one afternoon and it did mean such a lot to Clifford; she resolved to beg a favour from Mrs James. "Of course, I want to come, you just try and stop me! "she grinned.

"I'll be cheering louder than anybody *when* you win that shield."

"Don't hex us Nell-*if* we win you mean.... If"

"When!"

CHAPTER 21

Homecoming

The stairs appeared mountainous and dark; Molly hauled herself up to the sitting room, grasping the handrail with grim determination; willing her heavy feet to follow one step after another.

Molly's legs threatened to buckle under her and her heart pounded so vigorously in her chest she felt sure that others must hear it. A small blue vein pulsed in her temple as she fought the urge to dash back down to the open front door and out into the bustle; to hide amongst the crowd, to run; to do anything except face Billy's room.

For weeks Molly had dreamed of this moment; dreaded this moment. The smell of him, the softness of his little clothes; the cardigans she had knitted with pride, the toys hugged and loved by his tiny plump hands. Only the presence of Dr Thomas silhouetted against the street outside stopped her flight. She knew she was being watched.

"Come on in Molly and put your feet up.... I've put the kettle on to make us all a nice cup of tea; it will be ready in two tics.... I'm sure we could all use one." Nelly chirped brightly.

I caught Archie's nervous glance as he stood on the half landing watching my sister plod silently up the stairs. Keeping her eyes firmly ahead of her, Molly walked past the door of Billy's bedroom and headed for the parlour.

"Mother's sent around some fresh Welsh cakes for you with plenty of currants in. Old Mr Collins magicked a quarter pound packet up from under the counter... and she's put a nice sprinkling of sugar on them for good measure; they're just the way you like them." I said forcing a chirpy brightness that I did not feel. "I'm sure you won't have had any half as nice as these in the...in uh... I mean... in a while."

I knew I was babbling, filling the gap. Molly had barely said two words to anyone since her discharge from Whitchurch; this dull, stony-faced silence was pure torture. I was desperate to coax her into life. Archie looked worried. Dr Thomas followed Molly up into the cosy sitting room.

"Do take a seat Dr Thomas," Archie gestured towards two brown moquette armchairs that hugged the small bay window.
Dr Thomas gently led Molly by the arm and escorted her to the other armchair facing him. Archie and I sat at the table. What next?
Molly's quiet compliance was unnerving; a small muttered *thank you Dr Thomas,* was the only indication that she was aware of her surroundings. Molly gave a slight nod of her

head and sat down; thin hands folded over a shapeless, brown woollen skirt that hung off her spare frame. She reminded me of a dowdy old primary teacher who once taught us both; Miss Lyons-careworn and colourless.

The angry whistle from the kettle sent me scurrying to the kitchen to mash the tea and fetch the milk jug. As the small ceremony of tea making took place the awkward silence reigned.

Fluttered, white hands from Dr Thomas declined sugar, a small nod from Archie accepted just the right amount of milk, Molly gave a slight motion of her mouth that wavered between a grimace and a smile when I placed her cup beside her. Nobody spoke, I wanted to scream.

So, we sat, just the four of us. I passed Molly a Welsh cake on best flowered china. As she reached out to take the proffered plate, I kept hold of it. A small look of surprise flickered across her brow as she felt the tug of resistance.

"Oh...." Her eyes met mine, feelings of anger welled up in me *for God's sake Molly say something-anything. Fight!* I held her gaze; refusing to surrender the plate until she at least acknowledged my presence. I smiled at her.

"Umm... thank you... thank you Nelly, I can manage it." Molly said coldly; her dull, fish-like eyes barely flickered as she took the plate from my grasp. I felt as if she had slapped me, her tone was clipped and formal as if addressing some sort of house maid. Archie shot me a helpless *do you see what I mean now* look.

As the afternoon ticked by, we talked around Molly, through Molly and to Molly. Answers were monosyllabic, closed and polite. Awkward pauses seemed to last interminably. The tension was giving me a headache.

Eventually it was almost time for me to go home; Jean needed collecting. Clifford would be home in a few hours expecting his dinner. Anxious to escape the suffocating tension I sought refuge in the kitchen; I washed up the tea things and cleared away. Soon I could leave.

I had tried to draw hope from Dr Thomas' quiet assurances of Molly's continuing progress; I listened to his platitudes about *early days, not expecting too much and time being a great healer.* But in my heart of hearts, I felt sure we were all in for a very long wait. Poor Archie.

The door clicked behind Dr Thomas and Nelly as they left. Archie heard their footsteps retreating down the stairs and he felt adrift, hopelessly out of his depth.

So now it was just Molly, or rather a shadow of Molly, and himself with a vast gaping void that was Billy in between them. The light was starting to fade and the fire burn low in the grate. An early evening gloom settled over the room and the awkward silence was suffocating him.

He so wanted to hold Molly, hug her to him, but she sat statue-like; rigid backed looking out towards the street below. What was she searching for?

Don't rush things Mr Smith Dr Thomas had said to him *give her time, things will all work out in the end. Things.... what the hell did Dr Thomas mean by things!*

Suddenly, without so much as a word, Molly sprang out of the armchair with an energy and purposefulness Archie hadn't seen for many months.

"Are you all right Moll?"

She headed towards the landing.

"Molly... what's up... are you going to lie down for a little while?"

She marched, grim faced, past their bedroom and towards the little spare room. His heart sank.

"Don't Molly... not today...Please. For the love of God let it be." Archie willed her not to turn the knob.

Molly took a deep breath and entered the small room. Billy's room.

A jumble of cardboard boxes was now stacked high against one wall; shelving and brackets sprawled across the bare floorboards. The rag-rug was gone, the nursery toys were no longer there and the space where the cot-bed used to be was filled with old newspaper bundles. She had walked into a storeroom.

All of Billy's little things were gone; this was not *his* room. It was as if he had never been, he was erased.

"What have you done?" She hissed; a horrified expression crossed her face as she turned to confront him. "Oh my God Archie....What the bloody hell have you done?" With that she burst into tears, hot sobs and gulps welled up from within her; the wound raw, as fresh as the day it was made.

In vain Archie tried to console her. "Dr Thomas said making a clean break from the past was for the best Molly; new beginnings and all that." She shrugged off his embrace.

"Molly do at least try to see reason. Dr Thomas said it would be for the best...for you...for both of us."

She shot him a withering look.

"I thought I was doing the right thing," Archie added lamely. "Some things are only packed away at your mother's ... We can start again... you know when you're ready.... when the time is right."

Molly felt in her heart of hearts that the time would *never* be right. Billy was dead and it was all her fault

CHAPTER 22

Kathleen

June 1933

"Are you making Mummy some nice perfume?" Kathleen sat and watched her tousled-headed grand-daughter selecting fallen rose petals. The child was carefully placing the petals into her little tin bucket, layer upon layer; absorbed in her task Jean simply nodded as she bent to pick up another choice petal to add to her collection.

A showy cascade of candy pink and cream blooms tumbled over the roof of the lavatory and along the small garden wall; in their abundance the earlier flowers were now showering their petals in thick drifts on the path.

Jean concentrated on the task in hand as she toddled on chubby legs around the small garden collecting up the papery dry whisps.

"Daddy will be home soon are you going to make him some of your beautiful perfume too?" Kathleen teased,

"Shall we make him smell of roses like a princess in your story book?"

Jean shook her head and giggled at the thought of it.

Small hover flies skittered along the flower bed; velvety bees hummed diligently in and amongst the Antirrhinums and spicy Sweet Williams that flopped over the small border. A musky, rich scent filled the afternoon air.

It was a glorious Saturday afternoon and Kathleen had popped around to see her granddaughter. Earlier that morning she had visited Molly and there was much that Kathleen wished to discuss with Nelly; so much that worried her.

"Here we are Mother," Nelly placed a small tea tray onto a folding stool that served as a table, "it would be a crying shame for us to be inside on a glorious day like this," she handed her mother a delicate cup and saucer, sprinkled with sprigs of for-get-me-nots, before taking her seat on a dining chair placed in a sunny nook by the back door. The two women sipped their tea companionably in the warm sunshine.

Clifford was at swimming practice; it was the third training session that week and the coach was pushing them to the limit; coaxing every last ounce of effort from straining muscles. Earlier that morning Clifford had grumbled about his legs being tired and stiff as he set off on his cycle ride to the corporation baths. The men were training so hard for the up-coming City Gala. Nelly knew he would not be home for at least an hour or two yet; they had plenty of time to themselves.

"So how did *you* find Molly when you saw her today Mother..." Nelly ventured. "Did she seem more..." Nelly was unsure of the words she wanted, "more you know... more like her old self?"

When Nelly had seen her sister earlier in the week; they had quarrelled. She had not mentioned the fact to her mother, but she had fled home in tears from the vicious tongue lashing meted out by Molly. Bitter accusations of *smug complacency* and her *perfect life* had hit hard.

Clifford had consoled her with kisses and reassurances that Molly couldn't help but envy their happiness, but the barbed comments had wounded Nelly deeply. She still smarted at the injustice of it.

"Molly has changed, and the way things are going, I don't think she will ever be her old self," Kathleen said evenly, "but I'm beginning to think she is choosing to wear this hair shirt. It's as if she *wants* to wallow in in her misfortune-*their* misfortune ... Archie is at his wits end with her and I don't blame him." She added firmly.

"What do you mean.... *choosing?*" Nelly gasped "Surely you can't believe Nelly is *choosing* to be like this?"

"Well, she's *not choosing* to alter the way she is and that's just about the same thing in my book," Kathleen added tartly. "We all know that what Molly needs is another little baby to call her own, but the way *things* are I can't see it happening...."

Jean toddled over with the gift of a crushed, pink Sweet William flower held between her sticky fragrant fingers.

"Oh, thank you my angel, that's beautiful. But don't pick any more of Mummy's pretty flowers now... just collect the rose petals from the path, there's a good girl," Jean gave a sunny smile and toddled back to her bucket.

"There's many a family that lost sons and husbands in the Great War *and* many a mother that's had to bury a baby. It's time she pulled herself together Nelly, it really is. I said as much to Archie only the other week." Kathleen was getting into her stride. Nelly cringed inwardly; she knew that her mother could be very forthright when dishing out advice.

"I said to Archie that what Molly needed was another baby to help heal her heart.... I mean these things take time and she's not getting any younger," Kathleen lowered her voice fearful of being overheard by Nelly's neighbours. Nelly leaned forward, listening intently.

"But apparently Molly has moved out of their bed and insists on sleeping in Billy's old room... and what's more Archie says that she intends to stay there... The poor man doesn't know what to do about.... well, as a married woman Nelly you know what I'm talking about," she shot her daughter a knowing look, Kathleen waved her hand vaguely, reluctant to tackle the delicate subject of marital relations.

"So, I tried talking to Molly about it this morning and got my head bitten of for my pains.... she actually raised her voice to me Nelly... me her own mother!" Kathleen shook her head sadly.

After her own tongue-lashing Nelly found it easy to imagine that her sister had snapped. The old sweet, gentle Molly never used to be so... *so angry*.

"Other mothers have lost their children and had to start again, so why can't our Molly?" Kathleen added. Nelly sipped at her tea waiting for her mother to continue.

"Molly will *never* have another little baby unless she changes her ways. She looks like a walking scarecrow.... she refuses to let her hair grow and she throws on her clothes with no thought of what she looks like. It's almost as if she wants to look as unattractive as she possibly can." Kathleen scrutinised the tea leaves at the bottom of her cup as if hoping to find some answers amongst the brown dregs before tossing them on the flower bed.

"The sad truth is that your sister is clinging to the past and shutting out the future and no good will come of it Nelly, you mark my words.... choosing a life of misery that's exactly what she's doing *choosing*. We *all* miss little Billy, especially Archie, but now he's missing Molly. The past is the past and none of us can alter that... but we can *choose* how we approach the future.... whatever it has in store for us."

Nelly decided not to mention the argument with Molly.

"Nelly...Nellee...."

"We're here. In the garden Clifford." Nelly called over her shoulder. She sprang up to give her husband a hug as he popped his handsome head around the back door. "My goodness you're back early. Mother and I have only just finished drinking our tea; we weren't expecting you for another hour or so at least... Jean look Daddy's home!" Jean rushed over to her father, holding out her bucket for him to admire.

"My, my what a lot of rose petals," he ruffled her golden hair, "petals for a princess. Come and give your Daddy a kiss," he scooped Jean up and swung her high about his shoulders, whizzing her up and down with his powerful arms as the toddler giggled hysterically.

"Clifford!" Nelly said with mock sternness, "you'll make Jean sick whirling her round like a dervish... and just before her time as well...Goodness me, what *is* your Daddy thinking about?"

"Sorry Mummy," Clifford gave Nelly a wink as he deposited a giddy Jean on the path where she promptly sat down with a bump.

"Well don't let me interrupt you ladies, I'd better get on with my chores," he delved into a small Duffel bag before hauling out a sodden costume that needed attention. As he wrung it out water dripped and splodged on the tiled path creating ugly wet patches.

"Anyway, don't blame me for interrupting your cosy afternoon chat, I'm afraid you have the Cardiff corporation to blame for that. Apparently, some stuffy official insisted that they shut the baths early this afternoon and that was the end of things... *everybody out of the pool and no arguing!*" the chap said. "Closed until further notice on the orders of the Council"

"And what's worse," Clifford grumbled, "they've even cancelled the City Gala! All that work and training for nothing. They were even posting up a notice about it on the doors as we were all leaving."

Clifford draped his soggy costume over the line that looped across the passage. "Oh well it looks like I shan't be needing this for a while. Cancelling the City Gala, it's a rum do and that's a fact! Nobody knows quite what to make of it." Nelly felt a small shiver of worry trickle down her spine.

CHAPTER 23

Clifford

The next morning Nelly got up early to tackle her chores before going to church; she bustled about purposefully in her small scullery waiting for the kettle to sing. The pink-blue skies were streaked with silver that promised another glorious summer day, the morning was already warm, a few early bees were flitting through the sunny flower beds foraging for the best blooms. A glimpse of the pink rose bush hanging its heavy dew laden blooms over the wall made her smile; there would be plenty more petals for Jean's potions today.

Little Jean was still fast asleep and the house felt blissfully quiet; Nelly loved these special times; snatched moments of calm before the bustle of family life began in earnest. The kettle called and she made herself some tea, putting just enough leaves and water in the pot for one cup.

Clifford had had a restless night complaining of going down with a summer cold; he had tossed and turned and moaned and groaned before eventually drifting off to sleep in the early hours. She crept out of bed leaving him to doze for a while longer, with the curtains pulled shut against the early morning light he could rest for a few hours. Poor Clifford.

The evening before he had even rejected her attempts at love making saying his muscles felt achy and weary; he teased her and called her wanton before turning his back on her, desperate to grab some sleep.

"Not tonight Nelly.... the spirit is willing but the flesh is weak," he had joked feebly as she attempted to coax him into life. Nelly so wanted another baby; she had been hopeful a few times recently when her monthlies had been late, but each time it had been a false alarm and a disappointment.

The mantle clock chimed the half hour. Still only 6.30am she would let him lie in for an hour or two longer before taking him his tea in bed. He could always miss church if he didn't feel up to it; Mother would understand, after all father had had a nasty cold only a few weeks ago and even *he* had cried off going to mass. There was a lot of it about.

Perhaps Clifford would feel better in a day or two, especially if he rested. She would buy some honey to make him a soothing honey and mint drink. They had plenty of time to try for another baby.

Mother and father were coming for Sunday lunch after church. Molly bustled about in her dressing gown, mentally ticking off a to do list in her head; there was such a lot to do. Suet pastry was top of her list; suet was a tricky devil but a steamed steak and kidney pudding with lashing of meaty gravy was one of Clifford's favourites. She so wanted to get it right especially since her father was ever quick to point out the merits of her mother's own feather light pastry. *You'll have to go a many long mile to find a better cook than your mother Nelly!* He father was fond of saying. Nelly was determined to get his approval.

Nelly carefully skimmed the congealed fat off the pan of cold stewed meat and onions with a slotted spoon. *Hmm....* she would certainly need to prepare plenty of vegetables to help eke out the meal with two hearty men to feed. Even with a generous lump of kidney the chunks of beef for her pudding were in short supply. Good meat was so ruinously expensive and so hard to come by these days; still it would just have to stretch, she thought to herself as she broke up some of the larger chunks with a fork. *The flavour was there and that was what mattered,* she mused as she stirred gravy browning and seasoning through the mixture. She started to measure out the suet and flour into large china mixing bowl.

The massive crash and thud reverberated throughout the house. A clench of anxiety gripped her chest as she strained her ears for the source of the commotion before dashing to investigate. In her haste Nelly dropped powdery suet granules all over the floor; they lay like so many maggots on the red quarry tiles.

"Oh God!" she gasped "Oh my God what on earth has happened?" her heart pounded; visions of falling furniture flashed through her mind. "Jean, Jean.... mummy's coming, don't worry Jean... mummy's coming." She yelled as she flew along the passageway and sprinted up the stairs as fast as her legs would carry her.

Fearing the worst Nelly clattered into the small back bedroom.

Jean lay fast asleep in her bed; early morning sunlight shimmered through the curtains casting slanting shafts of gold across the child's face. Nelly's breathing slowed as the band of fear that clutched at her heart loosened. "Oh, thank God," she murmured.

Then she heard a small groan from across the landing. "Oh no..... Clifford!"

Nelly pushed against the back of their bedroom door with all her might. Panting and heaving she shoved the door open a few precious inches as the obstacle barring her entry gave way a little. Peering around the edge she discovered that the bedside cabinet was now partially blocking the threshold; through the small gap she could see tips of Clifford's fingers.

"Ahhhhh...Ohhhh...." His voice sounded feeble and weak. A throaty, chewed up garble "...lly...ulp..."

"I'm trying to help Clifford, really I am," She called around the door to him. "It's just that I can't get to you, the door is stuck," she pushed and shoved at the door to no avail, it wouldn't budge so much as another inch.

"Can't you try to move away from the door Clifford? You're blocking it..." His groans were tearing at her.

"Answer me.... Clifford.... For the love of God!" Nelly could feel the tears brimming up as she pushed hopelessly against the immovable door.

It was useless she could not hope to gain access through the door; there was nothing for it, someone would have to get in through the upstairs window. "Just give me a minute to fetch Mr James from next door. I'll get him to bring his ladders. Don't worry Clifford, I'll be back as quick as I can."

Nelly clattered down the stairs and out into the street in her slippers. Next door the curtains of the James' household

were all still closed against the morning. It was only 7am.
Still, it couldn't be helped, Sunday or no Sunday, she had to
rouse her neighbours.

Nelly hammered vigorously on the brass door knocker
and rattled the letter box impatiently with her fingers; *"the
noise was enough to wake the whole street"* Mr James would
later recall; *"I thought the whole world must be coming to an
end or something."*

The broken windowpane was a small price pay. As
Nelly steadied the ladder for Alf James, he gingerly removed
the shattered shards of glass. Alf slipped his hand inside the
frame and lifted the sash. A short, tubby man, he grunted
and puffed as he clambered through the window into the
bedroom.

As soon as Mr James had gained access, Nelly rushed
back into the house. Her thoughts were whirling; she was
trying not to panic.

Mr James removed the toppled bedside cabinet blocking
the door and let Nelly in. Clifford was lying on the floor in a
tangle of bedclothes; a bright flush covered his throat and
face; his breathing was rapid and laboured; greasy beads of
sweat gathered on his brow, his dark eyes flickered.

A small dark trickle of blood ran down Clifford's cheek from
a cut just above his eyebrow. "I think you'd better summon
Dr Thomas, Mrs Harris.... looks like Mr Harris has had a nasty
fall, and that cut might need seeing to, it looks quite deep to
me," Mr James dabbed at the wound with his handkerchief.

"I reckon that he must 'ave hit that blessed cabinet before
he hit the ground... nasty business. Look I'll stay with him if
you want to get yourself dressed like," his voice was kindly.

"Ask Mrs James to come in and stay with Jean whilst you get Dr Thomas... We'll have this all sorted out in a jiffy, so don't you go worrying yourself.... worse things happen at sea as they say."

Mr James was a kindly man; Nelly flashed him a weak smile. "Thank you," she said, "I'm so sorry to have troubled you...really I am... I'll be as quick as I can."

Alf James stayed sitting beside Clifford as Nelly scuttled off; he didn't like the look of things at all.

Clifford had been so hot. All night waves of sweat rolled over him; at times he'd felt as if he was walking lost in fog; a damp, clammy fog that clung to his skin and drifted into his mouth where it collected in the hollow of his tongue.

He dreamed of pulling an endless stream of cotton wool out of his mouth, frantically tugging the thick fluffy lumps that were choking him, drying up his spittle and weaving its way down his throat. He was suffocating.

The pain in his left foot was the worst. Clifford couldn't remember injuring it, but he felt a searing stab pass through the arch of his foot and rip through his sole. He felt as if it was being nailed to the bedclothes; vicious spikes of pain pinning him to the bed. He needed Nelly; he tried to shout but the cotton wool and fog was still in his mouth.

Someone lit a fire under his right foot torturing him; his toes tingled and burnt until they exploded into nothingness, fat pink sausages that split open their skins. The heat grew and grew, flames licking up his leg; he frantically patted at his leg to put out the fire; his fingers tingled and protested. So much pain. He knew he had to escape. He had to get out of bed.

In the half-light with aching hands he tried to pull back the covers; he so needed a cold drink. As he attempted to get up from his entangled prison Clifford knew something was terribly wrong.

His leaden legs would not obey him; for a moment he felt sure his feet had been nailed to the bed and the horror of it drove him forward. He scrabbled and clutched at the silky counterpane, wrenching it away from his lower body.

In his terror he launched himself forward towards the bedside cabinet desperate to grab something solid. It all seemed to happen in slow motion, as his hand grasped the wooden ledge his body seemed to slide and follow it with a slump and a crash onto the floor.

As a young boy, on a rare cycle ride to the countryside, Clifford had seen a calf being born. The grey, slimy slide and plop of the new-born animal fascinated him as it dropped out of its mother and lay helpless on the muddy ground, trapped in a thick, gooey membrane. He had watched enthralled as the cow had licked away the gelatinous covering and nuzzled it into life before the beast stood triumphant on wobbly legs.

As he lay helpless on the floor, he had felt the membrane creeping over him.

CHAPTER 24

Hospital

They had wrapped him in concrete, he was certain of that, the weight of it on his chest felt as if it was crushing the life out of him. As Clifford lay motionless, he felt sure they must have tied his arms to his sides preventing all movement, not even that of his smallest finger. He must be trapped somewhere. What other explanation could there be?

Clifford was scared to open his eyes. He knew from the warmth in front of his face that they were torturing him with bright lights. My God what had he done?

He tried to calm himself.... *think, think.* He remembered being lost in a fog; a dense invading fog that left him struggling to breath... so where was he now?

The clatter, the noise and mechanical groans and hisses worried him; what monster was this? Clifford dared not turn his head in the direction of the noise which seemed to be coming from the left...*courage man.... just do it...* to his horror he could not move his head.

"Oh hello... so you are back with us again this morning Mr Harris... that *is* good news." The owner of the angelic disembodied voice laid a cool hand on his brow; in the distance a bell rang.

Clifford made a superhuman effort to open his eyes wider; they seemed to be glued together with sand and grit.

"Oh, dear Mr Harris, that *does* look nasty and sticky, now don't get yourself agitated, I'll be back in two tics with some nice warm water and a flannel to wash your face for you.... we'll soon get you freshened up a bit. I've rung for Professor Atkins; he'll be along to talk to you soon." With that the soothing voice disappeared into the distance accompanied by the click of heels on a hard floor and the dull *thunk* of a swing door closing behind them.

"*Professor Atkins?*" Through his gummed-up lashes Clifford could glimpse a dazzle of overhead lights. A strong odour of carbolic disinfectant wafted over him. And then there was that noise; the constant rhythmic suck and hiss like waves sucking through beach shingle.

"*Where the hell was, he? Nelly... where was Nelly?*"

The hand came back. From behind his head he heard the splash and slop of something being immersed and wrung out. Images of a navy-blue swimming costume crashed into his mind.

"The water is nice and warm for you Mr Harris; we'll soon have those eyes feeling better."

But they closed the baths, he remembered now, they had closed the baths!

"Now then.... easy does it.... just try to keep your eye-lids closed for me until we're all finished. We don't want any soap getting into them and making your eyes sting, do we?"

He felt the hands making soothing gentle sweeps across his forehead with a moist cloth; moving carefully around his eyes, patting and dabbing. He winced as a stab of pain pierced his brow.

"I'm sorry Mr Harris, I'll try to stay away from that cut. That really was quite a deep gash you gave yourself; but it's healing nicely now. Professor Atkins might let you get those stitches taken out in a day or two; he usually likes to leave at least a week before removing suturing."

A week.... had he been like this for nearly a week?

The angel chattered on sweetly as soft hands fluttered away from his brow and eased gently down across his cheeks and mouth. "Once it's all healed together, I don't think you will notice a scar at all."

The angel had a slightly breathy lisp that reminded him of.... of.... of a little girl... of his little girl... of Jean!

His panic was intense. Newly released eyes darted to and fro, desperate to get his bearings Clifford tried once more to turn his head. A white cap atop a pretty upside-down face hoved into view as two soft hands cradled the sides of his head, keeping him straight.

"Now, now then Mr Harris, just calm yourself. My name is nurse Pollard and I've been looking after you whilst you've been very poorly. Professor Atkins is here now.... he will explain everything."

CHAPTER 25

Polio

"Polio!" Nelly visibly staggered under the crushing impact of the awful diagnosis. Polio.... she thought he'd had a bad cold that was all. Just a bit of muscle stiffness from over exertion at his swimming practice, but the horror of Polio had never crossed her mind.

Her legs turned to jelly; a wave of panic crashed over her. Only the steadying arm of Dr Thomas kept her from being a crumpled, snivelling, heap on the floor.

Dr Thomas was certain that Clifford was dangerously ill with Polio; he had seen several similar such cases in the last few days. The public baths were linked to the source of deadly virus and clusters of cases had sprung up as the contagion had spread. Cardiff was in the grip of a Polio outbreak.

All she could manage was a feeble little "Oh....Oh, please God, no." When the diagnosis was given; it was as if she had been slapped across the face by those few terrifying words.

"I'm sorry Mrs Harris....I'm afraid your husband is suffering from Poliomyelitis.... only time will tell now...we'll do the best we can for him."

A soothing hand patted hers, the world was a blur as she struggled to hold back the tears and concentrate on what Doctor Thomas was saying.

"Sit down for a few minutes and gather yourself together Mrs Harris. You've had a big shock...of course we must think of you now and little Jean....and" he added hesitantly, his eyes searching hers, his hand sweeping gently across her brow, soft white fingers palpating under her ears.

"and you Mrs Harris...are you feeling quite well in yourself? No odd aches and pains?"

She shook her head unable to speak. Polio!

By the time they took Clifford away to the City Hospital isolation unit he was unconscious and sinking fast. She had stood mute with shock as she watched the canvas stretcher carrying him being lowered down the staircase and out into the waiting ambulance.

The neighbours would certainly know by now, bad news always travels fast.

Nelly sat slumped in the armchair; whilst Mrs James made her a cup of tea. Alfred James had taken it upon himself to convey the news to her parents; there would be no visiting the Harris household today, or any day soon, for that matter, until the danger of infection was past. Nelly was to stay indoors. Dr Thomas had promised to pop by later with an update, but until then she was condemned to just sit and wait and hope.

Polio! The word ricocheted around her brain leaving her bereft of rational thought. Her mind raced in chaotic circles;

what would happen to Clifford now? What about Jean? What about herself?

Only the night before, she had kissed him and tried to persuade him to make love to her. She had rested her head on his shoulder, her face close to his until he had turned his back to get some sleep.... Polio!

And Jean... Jean had been hugging and cuddling her daddy; rolling her perfect skin against his cheek only the day before on that bright and perfect afternoon in the garden. *"Come give your Daddy a kiss."*

She tried to shut out the awful possibility that Clifford had brought this dreadful disease into their lives too; nobody told her what to expect next. How long before she would know if they had contracted it?

A rising tide of panic started to creep over her... she had so many questions; she needed to talk to Dr Thomas.

Jean was chattering happily to Mrs James in the kitchen; the clink and clatter of domestic life carrying on as it must. Nelly fought the urge to cry.

"There you are Mrs Harris, here's a nice strong cup of tea for you; I've put two sugars in it, for the shock my dear. Best thing for shock is strong, sweet tea... my mother used to swear by it." Ivy James stirred the tea and handed Nelly the strong orangey brew.

"I've made little Jean some toast for her breakfast with a nice warm cup of milk, so that should keep her going for a bit. She's out in the garden collecting some more rose petals in that tin bucket of hers... I thought it would give you just a few minutes peace and quiet to pull yourself like. She's such a little angel, bless her."

"Thank you er... Mrs James."

"Ivy... do call me Ivy, dear. What with all that kerfuffle this morning I think we should be on first name terms by now don't you? After all it's not many women I'd let see my Alf in his pyjamas is it now?"

Nelly raised a weak smile.

"That's right dear, that's what you need to do; put a brave face on things. No good crying over spilt milk as my mother used to say. Smile and the world smiles with you, that was her motto."

Ivy's mother sounded like a walking box of cliches, Nelly thought as she sipped the sickly tea; she let the gossipy voice of Ivy James wash over her.

"Now if you're *sure* you can manage, Mrs Harris, I'd best be going home. But remember, I'm only the other side of that wall, so if you give it a knock I'll pop around. Any time you need me, just a few taps that's all it takes, it's no bother at all and we'd be glad to help out."

Nelly mumbled her thanks.

"These walls are just like paper my Alf says. We always know when you are in; sound certainly travels in these houses; on occasions I almost feel I could be in the sitting room with you and Mr Harris."

"Clifford... Clifford and Eleanor, but everybody calls me Nelly," Nelly tried to raise a weak smile.

"And thank you... Mrs.... Ivy....thank you and Alf...thank you both for everything," Mrs James gave her a fierce hug as Jean clung to her mother's skirts.

"There, there, it's nothing my dear. Now you just take care of yourself and this little angel here," Ivy said ruffling Jean's golden curls.

"I'll see myself out Nelly... Don't forget now, just a tap the wall and I'll be straight around."

CHAPTER 26

The visit

On the tenth day she, and Jean, were pronounced out of any danger. In the days after Clifford collapsed Dr Thomas came to visit them every morning. He brought news from the hospital and monitored their health; finally, they had the all clear. It was the best news and Nelly's heart embraced it.

"I'm pleased to say Mrs Harris that you and Jean are definitely free from any signs of infection. You can go out and about now freely, see your family and of course you may wish to pay a visit to Mr Harris in the Royal infirmary. Visiting hours start at two thirty and finish at four." Nelly's eyes lit up. "Mr Harris is strong enough now to tolerate a short visit if you feel up to it. Children are not allowed on the tank respirator ward."

She would have to ask Mrs James to look after Jean that afternoon; Ivy had been such a good friend in the dark days following Clifford's illness. With no children of her own, when given half a chance, Ivy James showered Jean with outbursts of maternal affection.

"I'm sure it would do Mr Harris good to have a visitor, but I have to warn you Mrs Harris, you will find him much changed. Don't expect too much at first, he is on a very long, slow road to recovery. We can't predict how much progress he will make; only time will tell."

"But he *is* getting better isn't he Doctor? So, there's hope." Nelly asked anxiously.

"Yes, Mrs Harris there is hope. Every day he is improving, but the first two weeks are the worst with Polio. He was in great danger and he still needs help to breathe. It may be many months before we will know the full extent of his recovery."

Doctor Thomas chose his words carefully before adding, "It's a gradual process Mrs Harris and some people make a better recovery than others. Only time will tell." He saw the look of panic on Nelly's face.

"It's important that your husband stays calm and that *you* stay strong and positive for him. Do you understand me Mrs Harris?" Dr Thomas's voice was stern as he held her gaze.

"No weeping and wailing in the intensive care unit. He needs you to be strong Mrs Harris, the poor man has got a very difficult time ahead of him and he doesn't need to be worrying about you."

"Of course, Dr Thomas," she muttered like a chastised child.

Later that afternoon as she sat in the gloomy visitor's room of the Royal infirmary waiting to be summoned. Nelly steeled herself to be brave.

She had put on her best summer dress, a delicate rose-bud sprigged pattern with white string gloves and a small brimmed hat. Clifford always liked this outfit, she wanted to be pretty for him.

The nurse, a dour, matronly figure in battleship grey, had sailed off down the corridor some ten minutes ago *to get Mr Harris prepared for his visitor.*

Nelly's nerves were kicking in as she sat on the hard bench. She willed herself to be cheerful; to smile for him. She reapplied her lipstick and tucked a stray hair back under her hat.

Smile and the world smiles with you.... smile and the world ...She fought to swallow the tension collecting in her throat.

What would she say to him? Even worse would he be able to answer her? If he couldn't, then would she be able think of enough things to say to fill the time that she was allowed *"no more than fifteen minutes, we mustn't tire Mr Harris"* the battleship had said crisply when asked about visiting times.

Dr Thomas cautioned that Clifford was being aided by a respirator machine whilst the virus ran its course; an iron lung. She had never seen these new-fangled contraptions before; the very thought of it worried her.

"You can come with me now Mrs Harris." Nelly jumped a little as the battleship commanded her presence. "Nurse Evans is on ward duty this afternoon and can assist you if there is a problem... This way please."

A problem!

Nelly struggled to keep up as she followed the grey, starched back marching resolutely down the long, glossy corridor. The smell of carbolic was overwhelming.

Nelly hurried past numerous large wooden doors that punctuated the walls. Nurses wearing jaunty starched caps walked purposely in and out of wards with brisk efficiency; fresh faced young women carrying trays, bottles and bed pans discreetly covered in linen cloths went about the business of tending the sick.   The hospital reminded her of a hive.

Through porthole windows she caught glimpses of other patients resting for the afternoon. The sight of other men snoozing peacefully in their striped pyjamas settled her nerves. *Perhaps it wouldn't be as bad as she feared.*

At the very end of the corridor was a set of windowless swing doors; overhead a bold red sign screamed at her:
AUTHORIZED STAFF ONLY
ALL VISITORS MUST BE ACCOMPANIED AT ALL TIMES

As the door swung back Nelly saw three, glossy, pale blue, tubular coffins on wheeled trolleys. The huge metal caskets had bulbous riveted ends, portholes along the sides and a large, flared trumpet shape at the far end. Some sort of mechanical pressure gauge was attached to each trolley.

There were no beds with crisp sheets and hospital corners, no vases of flowers and resting patients in striped pyjamas, just machines. It was if they had just entered the bowels of a ship.

The room lacked any windows; three ranks of white lights punctuated the ceiling overhead, running in strips parallel to the metal tubes below. A rhythmic, mechanical suck and hiss reminded her of a steam engine leaving Cardiff station. But where was Clifford?

An attractive young nurse sat on a chair by the flared end of one of the trumpets. She stood up smartly when the sister entered and put down the book she had been reading aloud.

"Nurse Evans, this is Mr Harris' wife... I've told her that she can stay for a maximum of fifteen minutes and that you will guide her through things." The battleship checked her watch; promptly swivelled an about turn on her heels and left.

Nelly stood frozen to the spot, uncertain what to do next. She looked helplessly towards the pretty young nurse for instructions.

"Your wife is here Mr Harris to visit you. I'll mark the page so we don't forget where we got to and then we can pick up where we left off tomorrow. Now remember, take your time and don't over exert yourself." Nurse Evans spoke in a breezy tone in the direction of the machine.

From the end of the trumpet Nelly heard a low breathy *Yessssss... Nursssss* followed by a dull *Clunk* that caused her to start a little.

"Come and sit here Mrs Harris that way your husband can see you reflected in the mirror." Nurse Evans flashed Nelly a kindly smile and patted the chair for Nelly to take her place. Nelly felt her legs wobble as she approached the trumpet; she pinned a smile on her face.

"Now don't be nervous... this amazing machine is helping Mr Harris breathe until his lungs recover."

As Nelly made her way behind the trumpet, she saw Clifford's grey, wasted face poking out of the end of the tube. A large mirror was attached at an angle just in front of his face allowing him a wider view of his claustrophobic small world. Nelly positioned herself on the chair so that he could see her. Her upside-down reflection looked accusingly stiff, painted and garish.

"The way the machine works is by vacuum Mrs Harris; it helps draw the air through the lungs until the weakening effect of the virus subsides and the patient can breathe unaided. These dials monitor the pressure and an alarm sounds if the machine has a malfunction or is switched off." Nurse Evans chattered as she tweaked the angle of the mirror to suit Nelly's short stature.

Nelly tried to maintain a fixed smile.

"There that should do it. It's best if you don't ask Mr Harris to give long answers, he can only speak on the exhale motion of the machine. It makes conversation a bit disjointed, but Mr Harris has got the hang of it now, haven't you?" Nurse Evans flashed a warm smile over Nelly's shoulder.

"I'll be over by Mr Ellis in respirator number one if you need me at all. I'll leave you two to have a few minutes together." Nurse Evans said as she slipped out of view of the mirror.

"Hello Clifford." Nelly removed her gloves, there was no hand to hold. She didn't know if she could kiss him and she was too embarrassed to ask Nurse Evans. She tentatively stroked his hair away from his face.

"Nelly... wherrrrrs Jean... errs Jean?" His soft voice gasped out the few words until they trailed off in a hiss like a deflating balloon. A metallic *Clunk* punctuated the suck and draw of the iron lung.

"It's all right Clifford.... she's fine. She's staying next door with Mrs James this afternoon.... Children aren't allowed on this ward.... so, don't worry she's absolutely fine... we both are." she added brightly.

"It's *you* we have all been worried about." Nelly listened as the machine pushed air into his lungs.

"aa've been so fright...end Nelllll," Clifford's eyes darted to and fro scanning her face as the words drifted out of his dry lips.

Nelly watched Clifford's face contort as air flooded back into his lungs. She tried to imagine the horror of what he'd been through. He was trapped inside this machine as it sucked his breath in and out of him; giving him permission to speak every fifteen seconds. It truly didn't bear thinking about.

"Clifford, you've got to be strong and get better my love.... for all our sakes." She remembered Dr Thomas' instructions; *strong and positive.*

"Doctor Thomas says you're making good progress Clifford, so here's hoping you've turned the corner... If you keep it up maybe you will be able to come home in....in a few weeks or so.... when you've got better." Nelly spoke with an optimism that even she didn't believe.

Her sentence had been too long, the machine was now grasping his voice on the inhale. She waited. *Clunk.*

"You're not in any pain, are you?" Nelly said quickly. She waited.

"I can't feel any....thinnnng," Clifford hissed, his brow rumpling into deep creases as he gathered his thoughts. *Clunk.*

She bent closer to catch his words. It seemed an age before he rasped out his next effort.

"I'm par..a... lysed," he gasped as a small tear trickled slowly down the side of his face.

Nelly's resolve evaporated; unable to stem the flood of anguish that burst from within she turned her head away from the mirror and sobbed silently into her handkerchief.

CHAPTER 27

Cootes

"Ahem!" The small cough was polite, but purposeful.

Clifford sat propped up in bed with his eyes closed, he refused to be rushed.

One of the few useful things that Clifford had learnt from his nurses over the tedious, starched months he had spent being poked prodded and attended to, was that if someone thought that he just *might* do something, then they were prepared to wait for him to do it. The owner of the cough could wait.

This nugget of wisdom was one of the few tools of control that Clifford had left available to him, he was wielding it, with great effect, on the bespectacled, annoyance seated at his bedside.

"Ahem... Mr Harris.... if you please?" Alfred Cootes, the clerk from company accounts, looked at a loss. Mr Cootes consulted his watch.

"I'm afraid I'm going to have to press you for an answer *today* Mr Harris... after all it has been over two months since...." the small, weasel faced clerk let the rest of sentence hang in the air.

Visiting time was drawing to a close and Cootes was under instructions to get a resolution; he did not intend to leave empty handed.

Nelly glanced at Clifford; his torso was on a slight lean; she resisted the urge to straighten him and the pillows. A small tic of annoyance twitched at the corner of Clifford's otherwise impassive face.

The weasel decided to adopt another tactic. "It would save Mrs Harris such a lot of worry if we could get the documentation signed today, put the wheels in motion so to speak..." he cleared his throat with emphasis before ploughing on. "After all, I'm sure you must see that there's no point in delaying the inevitable.... is there Mr Harris?"

Clifford refused to dignify the comment with a response; he kept his eyes closed. The clock ticked.

"The doctors have confirmed that you'll be discharged soon for...er rehabilitation," Cootes chose his words carefully, his voice unctuous. A small bead of sweat graced his upper lip.

"And whilst we *all* hope you will make further progress it's just not possible, under the circumstances, for you to continue working for the company." His head inclined sympathetically towards Nelly.

Clifford's face hardened. He knew his limitations only too well. Only yesterday he caught the dead glance of Nurse Pollard as she helped turn his useless body in a blanket bath; pretty nurse Evans had gently washed his lifeless legs; soaping carefully around his half-dead penis that no longer seemed to belong to him.

The fact that he could now manage to produce a slow sloppy trickle of urine into a bottle was proclaimed a triumph; the fact that he would never make love to his wife again was slotted into the *"For better or worse category" that* he and Eleanor had signed up to only four years ago.

"The company has been very generous under the circumstances, very generous indeed Mr Harris; a nice little pension for life.... You can't say fairer than that, can you?" Cootes tossed the question vaguely in Nelly's direction. Nelly looked away.

The room was suffocatingly quiet. Clifford thought it ridiculous that the curtains had seagulls on them; he had studied them for days. Turquoise blue curtains, with scatterings of small white seagulls that arranged themselves in irritating patterns the more he stared at them. Who ever heard of seagulls in a hospital!

Perhaps Cootes would go away if he kept his eyes shut. Clifford's hands clasped and unclasped the waffle bed throw; his long nails scraping the threads rhythmically with an irritating *scritch, scratch, scritch, scratch*.

"Mr Harris!" Cootes barked.

Nelly looked horrified. "Really! There's no need to raise your voice in here Mr Cootes."

Clifford knew that Cootes would not be leaving without an answer; without obtaining the necessary squiggle at the bottom of a page. Cootes was bloody lucky his stiff hands could make the required squiggle at all.

Clifford didn't feel lucky, just angry. He decided to get it over with.

"It's all right Nelly.... I know Mr Cootes is only doing *his* job," he said bitterly. Clifford cast the luckless Mr Cootes a hard stare "I just don't appreciate being rushed in these matters."

Mr Cootes had the good grace to look a little sheepish.

"Well then, Mr Cootes I supposed you had better bring me the relevant document ... since, as you can see, I'm somewhat indisposed."

Mr Cootes couldn't stop his eyes from making an embarrassed glance at the tented hump in the bed that covered Clifford's lifeless legs.

"Of course. Yes of course, Mr Harris." Cootes scrabbled around in his breast pocket for his fountain pen. "Here we are Mr Harris.... Err, would you like me to read you the terms and conditions again? I mean I have gone through them several times with you and Mrs Harris already.... but if you need...?" His voice trailed off, Cootes couldn't bear to finish the sentence with any suggestion of conceding a bit more delay.

Cootes guided the pen between Clifford's stiff and uncooperative fingers. He willed him to bring the matter to a close by signing on the dotted line. Cootes raised a small sympathetic smile willing Clifford over the finish line.

"I know what I'm signing Mr Cootes.... I'm signing my life away.... that's what I'm doing. All neat and tidy... on the dotted line; an admission that it's not going to get much better than this.... pensioned off .... no longer fit for purpose.... surplus to company requirements.... I, Clifford Aubrey Harris formally accept that I am officially redundant!"

Mr Cootes maintained a fish like stare, the sympathetic smile still nailed to his face.

"That's what I'm signing and believe me I've had plenty of time to think about it. There's nothing to do but think in here." Clifford said. Cootes' face was rigid with anticipation.

"Oh, don't worry Cootes....I'll sign your dammed document." His heavy, uncooperative hand edged slowly across the page; Clifford made a valiant attempt to keep his signature on the line.

"Not a bad first attempt Nelly eh? A bit more practice needed, but not too bad at all," his voice had a bitter, triumphant tone.

Cootes shuffled the papers into the correct order; he stood to leave. "Thank you, Mr Harris..." The clerk bent forward; his small hand extended uncertainly towards Clifford.

"May I, on behalf of the Directors of the Empress Shipping Company, wish you and, of course Mrs Harris, all the very best for the future."

Clifford grasped Cootes' slender hand with as much force as he could muster; he longed to crush the man's dainty fingers. It pleased Clifford to see Cootes wince a little at the unexpected pressure. Clifford held the clerk's gaze; a glint of triumph in his eyes as he tightened his grip on his tormentor.

"As a *former* employee of the company you are, of course, entitled to certain annual travel benefits.... Should you ever find yourself in the position of being able to avail yourself of them, then please don't hesitate to let the company know." Cootes added spitefully as he removed his squashed fingers.

Alfred Cootes completed his petty victory by striding briskly out of the room.

CHAPTER 28

Clifford

Nelly decided to light the fire early that morning. Their back-sitting room was always chilly at the best of times, especially when the sun went down. Clifford would feel the cold after the warmth of the hospital.

The morning air was crisp and sparkling with an unexpected September frost.

The air was like wine and Nelly drank it down in deep gulps.

The weak morning sun was already melting the light crystal dusting on the leaves of the rose bush; later it would be a glorious, warm day. Her heart cheered a little, it was a beautiful day for Clifford to be coming home.

Nelly hauled the coal in from the shed in the yard. She leant to one side as she struggled to lift the laden galvanized bucket.

She cursed the bucket as it banged against her leg. Last Autumn the heavy work of keeping the coal bucket topped up had been Clifford's job. She needed to get stronger she thought ruefully as she headed for the kitchen.

Her two-handed lift caused the bucket to swing perilously close to her legs again and the metal handle dug reproachfully into her fingers; next time she would wear gloves. Bloody bucket!

The house looked unfamiliar, out of sorts. Ornaments were moved out of harm's way, spaces now appeared to offer strategic handholds. A new order reigned over the sitting room, an order dictated by arm's length and limitations.

Nelly had carefully re-arranged the back-sitting room to ensure Clifford's chair was close to the fireplace and opposite the room's one small window. The view out of the window was limited she had to admit, but at certain times of the year a few rays of sunlight did manage to edge through and brighten the room for an hour or two. A ribbon of blue sky was just visible over the side wall of the house next door.

Nelly had sat and re-sat on Clifford's armchair; fractionally altering and re-altering the angle of the chair in order to get just the best view for him. With careful negotiation she had managed to deliver a glimpse of sky whilst at the same time leaving just enough room next to his chair for a low side table to take cups of tea and the like.

Nelly glanced around as she laid the fire. The room looked lopsided and spare now with so many things ranged along one wall, but it was the best she could manage. It would have to do.

Yesterday, helped by Archie and Alfred James, the best front room had been transformed into a bedroom of sorts; Clifford's bedroom. She knew now that it was impossible for him to get upstairs to their bed; she must sleep alone... for now. *Surely not forever.*

As Nelly sorted out spare linen and pillows to take downstairs, she told herself all of this was only a temporary measure, until things got better. Things could change; she *had* to believe things could change.

A small single bed had been hauled down from upstairs by the two men and pushed tightly up against the sitting room wall, as instructed by the hospital. *To stop Mr Harris falling out in the night, we don't want any accidents.... always remember prevention is better than cure Mrs Harris.*

A sturdy side cabinet was placed at the pillow end to hold the nigh time urine bottle and other necessities. The room lost its formal reserved-for-best-occasions air and took on all the practicalities of an invalide's bedroom.

To make space for the bed the sofa had been banished to the upstairs bedroom; that too was only a temporary measure she had told herself. It could always come back downstairs if...no not if, but when things improved. Nelly couldn't bear to part with her lovely sofa; to lose that was to lose all hope.

In the corner of the front room were grey, metal, hospital issue callipers, a spare set of Clifford's new legs irons. The ugly contraptions stood upright, propped up against the wall; skeleton legs, with brown leather padding and straps to encircle the thighs. Like instruments of torture, they had locking mechanisms at the knees and tapered ankle braces riveted to a pair of sturdy brown boots.

The nurses in hospital had shown Nelly how to fix the heavy callipers over Clifford's wasted limbs. She remembered the look of grim determination on his face the first time Clifford was hauled upright on his metal legs.

Look Nelly I'm walking!

Aided by two strapping nurses, he'd made a jerky, crab-like, progress across his small hospital room. Clifford propelled his legs in wide arcs; hips swinging from side to side. A loud metal click sounded as his boots made contact with the polished floor.

After all the exertion Clifford's brow was covered in sweat. He covered a few yards before grasping hold of the corner of the wall for a rest. Walking!

Her fingers had fumbled; clumsy and nervous. She was shown how to wrap crepe bandages around his shrivelled legs on skin that could no longer feel rubbing or chafing as he swung his body forward in its metal cage.

He had not looked at her as she knelt before him and folded the wrapping across his thin thighs. As she touched his cool skin, she tried to banish memories of him thrusting into her, pushing forcefully against her sex; that man was gone.

Nelly hated the sight of those callipers; she decided to lay them down, out of sight, at the foot of his bed. There was no need for Clifford to stare at them day in and day out. She would get them when he needed them. The sight of a pair of boots peeping out from the end of the bed caused her to shiver.... they looked like dead man's legs.

Nelly looked at the clock, it was 9-30am already, the morning was slipping by. Clifford was due to be discharged at ten o'clock and even with all the fuss of leaving hospital it would not be long before he arrived. She needed to get a move on.

Nelly glanced at herself in the mirror that hung over the mantle-piece, a pale anxious face with a loose strand of hair trailing her forehead looked back at her. What a mess.... she'd better tackle her appearance before Clifford arrived with Archie. They couldn't see her looking like this.

Archie insisted on accompanying Clifford home from the hospital.

"Got to help you get him settled in Nelly, so let's have no arguing about it."

He wagged his finger as she tried to protest.

"It's a different world now for you both and believe me I *know* just how that feels." Archie said firmly. "You were very good to me when Molly was taken ill and I'll never forget that... I'm here for you Nelly for as long as you need me... for both of you." She kissed him on the cheek.

Archie. In the dismal weeks following Clifford's illness, Archie had been her rock, her comforter, her confidant. Archie was the only person who seemed to understand her mourning for the life that was gone... the life that used to be... the life she wanted back. The Clifford she wanted back.

Mother had told her over and over again that things between him and Molly were still distant and unchanged. Yes... Archie certainly had enough troubles of his own without taking on hers.

Soon she must take Jean next door to stay with Ivy for the rest of morning.

It had been Alf's suggestion. "Best keep that little lass out of the way for a few hours and give the man a bit of space love... you know...just to get the hang of things. These halls and doorways are pretty narrow in these old houses...

awkward like. It'll take a bit of manoeuvring before you get the hang of things; but you will. in time you will."

Alf's grasp of the physical practicalities of living jolted Nelly into a fearful reality. Up until that moment it hadn't occurred to her exactly *how* Clifford would get around the house on his callipers.

Alfred's observation set off a chain reaction in Nelly's head. How would Clifford be able to manage the little step down that separated the hall and the back parlour? Would the hall stand be firm enough to use as a hand hold? Could he even get to the outside toilet? What would she do if he fell or got stuck somehow?

How would they cope, just the two of them day in day out?

Clifford was such a big man, and now.... now he was nigh on helpless. The obstacles to overcome had suddenly piled up. She collapsed into a sobbing heap in Alf's arms.

"There now, "Alf soothed. "There's no point in running to meet trouble my lovely, just take it one day at a time." he stroked her hair as if comforting a small child.

"Chin up.... You'll manage it my girl, you mark my words...and there's plenty of people who will help you out if you just ask...there's always me 'n my Ivy, only next door... just you remember that... we're only a knock away." He mopped her tearful face with his handkerchief.

Clifford had regained the use of his once powerful arms and a limited amount of sensation had slowly returned to his wasted torso. But, despite her fervent hopes and prayers, the paralysis refused to retreat any further; below the waist he was as good as dead.

A cripple her father had said. The ugly word lodged spitefully in her head.... *Cripple*.

In the hospital teams of nurses had deftly pushed, pulled and manipulated him into position, straps and gadgets took the weight, units and beds were just the right size and height; armies of staff washed, cooked and laundered. Now there was only her.

And what about poor little Jean, how would she ever find time for Jean? She was at such a boisterous age now, she needed a mother's attention, she needed to play and have fun. Just going to the park would be impossible; how would they get out and about as a family?

The hospital had said that they would provide a wheel chair, but how would she get Clifford into it let alone push him along! Nelly's mind looped in frantic circles every time she thought about all the obstacles to overcome... *No don't think about it.... don't think!*

She refused to accept that Clifford would *never* regain the use of his lower limbs.

What did these Doctors know anyway? As Ivy James said they got things wrong loads of times.

Where there's life there's hope Nelly she'd said. Nelly clung to this simple belief. She churned the phrase over and over in her head. A mantra of hope. To think otherwise was the road to despair... and misery; it was to be like... like her sister Molly.

The thought of Molly trapped in a bitter, grey world of might-have-been jolted her back to reality. She was not Molly. She would not be Molly! Together they would make it work.

Today was the first day of her new life with Clifford, she must pull herself together for both their sakes. She took a deep breath, drew on a crimson mouth and fastened her hair with a grip. The bold, defiant colour gave her confidence.... There she looked a lot better!

"Mummy.... Mumeeee?" A patter of small feet scampered along the landing and down the stairs. "Mumeee!"

"In here Jean, Mummy's just getting herself ready and finding a nice vase." A small, tousled head popped around the sitting room door. Jean skipped and hopped into the room fizzing with excitement.

"Hello, my angel... shall we pick some flowers for Daddy to go in this vase?" Nelly chose a small crystal vase from the cabinet.

"We can cut some pretty roses to go in it and then we can put it beside Daddy's bedside so that he can see them.... Would you like to help Mummy choose the best ones from the garden?"

Jean jigged up and down clapping her hands.... her Daddy was coming home.

"Then, if you promise to be a very good girl, you can go next door and see Aunty Ivy." Jean's eyes widened with joy.

"Aunty Ivy said that you can help her make some cakes for Uncle Alf this morning. Would you like to help Aunty Ivy?"

"Yeth please Mummy. Oh yeth...yeth," Jean lisped as she skipped and bounced out into the garden on her quest for roses. Picking flowers, making cakes *and* Daddy coming home, for Jean the day just got better and better.

CHAPTER 29

A new life

Through the open doors of the ambulance Clifford saw old Mrs Jones peeping around the corner of her net curtain, watching the show. The lace twitched down; she made a big play of straightening the curtains. Nosey old cow!

The air was cold on his face after leaving the warmth of hospital. He took some deep breaths partly to rid himself of the stench of carbolic, partly for courage. After nearly four months stuck in hospital he was longing to be back in his own home. Back to his own things... back to Nelly and Jean.

Almost there.

Strapped in the canvas seat of his wheelchair, Clifford waited to be unloaded like a sack of spuds. He willed the men to get a move on.

"Best keep you covered up mate until we get you inside.... don't want you going down with a chill now do we?" The young orderly tucked a soft grey blanket around him bib style, draping it over his chest and tucking it in firmly behind his neck and shoulders.

He'd had months of being poked, prodded and examined. Clifford was sick of hands invading him.

He watched as Archie jumped out from the doors of the ambulance, an effortless spring down onto the street. The pavement now presented as a vertiginous drop away for Clifford, as treacherous as any cliff edge. The two orderlies manoeuvred him into position.

"Left a bit Charley... watch his arm like on that handle.... to my right a bit now.... that's the fella... carefully does it!"

Clifford's world see-sawed backwards, titling his face towards the sky.

"Easy there, not too fast.... that gulley is quite steep just there. Steady... Ok now let's turn him around.... That's the way."

The wheelchair bumped down onto the pavement. Clifford sat exposed to the street and longed to get inside. His eyes darted nervously towards the house.

"I'll get that front door open for you Clifford," Archie proceeded to rummage in his pocket for the Yale key.

"Two tics and we'll have you inside in the warm... Nelly says we're to take you straight through to the back parlour."

Since when did Archie have keys?

The two orderlies grunted and manoeuvred the wheelchair through the narrow doorway and carried him backwards over the threshold of Alma road. After the sterile reek of the hospital corridors the hallway smelt comfortingly familiar; dried tea mingled with soot and beeswax polish.

Clifford winced as the chair banged against the edge of the banister. A flake of brown varnish splintered onto his lap.

"Bring him through here please... that's it, keep going.... mind that step just in front of you... Oi, mate, just watch the paintwork!" Archie directed the two men into the parlour.

The room looked so different now, Clifford struggled to remember how things used to be before he left. He remembered playing Kim's game as a child with his mother on wet Sunday afternoons. *Good for his memory muscle* she'd said as a tray full of objects gradually disappeared a piece at a time. *Come on tell me what's missing there's a clever boy Cliff.*

Since he'd been gone so many things had been moved around; gone was the cosy clustering of chairs where he and Nelly had sat by the fireplace and chatted at the end of the day. Ornaments and objects, had disappeared he knew that for certain... But what were they? Where were they? It would irritate him for days as he tried to recall the way things used to be.

The new functional order with all the furniture ranged up against the walls reminded him of his hospital room. All he needed now was curtains with seagulls on them!

Nothing looked the same from the low vantage point of his chair.... In hospital with the high beds and chairs he had not really noticed how short he had become. Now with his neck stretched and head raised the world looked uncomfortably out of his eye-line. He inhabited a world of nostrils and people bending down indulgently to speak to him like a small child.

Nelly stood waiting for him in front of the fireplace. His heart melted a little as he saw how pretty she looked. She smiled a vivid red smile for him. Archie stood tall and strong next to her watching him being carried in. Centre stage all eyes were on Clifford now.

Act 1 Scene 2 Crippled man and stretcher bearers enter stage right. He thought bitterly as he jolted awkwardly into the room.

He always used to be at least an inch taller than his brother-in-law and now he felt dwarfed; half a man. Everyone, even Nelly who barely scraped over five foot, seemed to tower over him now.

How he wished they would all sit down.

"Where shall we put him for you Mrs?" The orderlies struggled to turn Clifford around in the small sitting room and set the chair down in the middle of the rug awaiting instructions. One of them started to unwrap him like a parcel, removing the grey blanket from his neck.

"Oh, umm...in this...." Nelly started to gesture towards the carefully aligned fireside chair.

"No, not there thank you Nelly...I'll stand... I haven't lost my tongue, or my marbles, if that's what you're worried about...." Clifford said as he flashed an angry glance at the young orderly with the greasy hair who had had the temerity to treat him like an idiot.

"Just help me lock these things into place and then I'll stand beside my own hearth... Thank you very much!" Clifford's tone was curt.

Nelly exchanged an embarrassed glance with the unfortunate men; it was not like Clifford to be so prickly. And why did he want to stand... why now? She thought frantically. His chair was all nice and ready for him, why didn't he just sit down until everyone had left?

She didn't know where to stand herself if he was going to use his "legs." In hospital she had always kept out of the way to one side when the nurses helped him practice... now what?

Please don't fall.... Please God don't fall!

Nelly moved quickly away from the fireplace to stand in the kitchen doorway, her face registered her confusion. Archie followed her lead and jumped effortlessly out of the way.

Easy for some, Clifford thought as he planned his route across to the fireplace. The calliper locks were clicked into place under Clifford's trousers and he was helped to his feet. He was now the tallest in the room, a good three inches taller than the weasel orderly with the greasy hair. He smirked with satisfaction.

The tension in the room was almost palpable. Clifford was sure he heard a sharp intake of breath from Nelly as he wobbled to get his balance on the young orderly's arm.

Keeping his head high, with three unsteady lunges Clifford made it over to the fireplace. "There we are," he said as he turned to face the onlookers, his hands dodging ornaments; fingers seeking out unfamiliar holds on the mantle-shelf. Clifford hung on to the narrow ledge for dear life, knuckles whitening with the effort.

"I just need a bit more practice over the next few days and then we'll be fine... Now when these two gentlemen go on their way, I'd like to have a *proper* cup of tea Nelly....It's been hours since I had breakfast." Clifford said.

Archie saw the men out and Nelly went off to make a pot of tea.

Standing marooned by the mirror, clutching onto the mantle shelf with both hands to retain his balance, Clifford realised he had a pressing urge to pee. How the hell could he unbutton his flies?... And a bottle.... he needed something to pee in! He heard the tap water rushing into the sink... Nelly was filling the kettle.

"I need a bottle Nelly." Clifford yelled.

Nelly stuck her head around the doorway, he looked at her anxiously.

"I daren't try getting out to the lavatory on these contraptions... not yet anyway... not for just a pee.... Come on Nelly hurry up! "

She ran to get him a glass urine bottle.

"Here you are Clifford." She held it out for him take. He felt frustration boiling up from deep within him. Couldn't she see he didn't have two sets of hands? How the hell did she think he was going to be able to hold the bottle, aim his flaccid penis into it without bending over to see what he was doing *and* hold onto the mantle-piece at the same time?

"And I'm going to need some help.... I haven't got time to sit down to do this. I've never done it standing up since...." his voice trailed off as he saw the penny drop.

"Oh, I see... I'm sorry Clifford. Sorry, I didn't think." Nelly said. She felt flustered.

She hadn't thought about actually helping him in such an intimate way... and in the sitting room too!

Clueless, she lifted his pullover and started to fumble with buttons on his trousers. She'd never undone a man's trousers before; she was all fingers and thumbs.

"No, no, not the very top one," he snapped "My trousers will be around my ankles at this rate....no, no, just the flies Nelly." His bladder throbbed.

Nelly, now on her hands and knees cast him an apologetic look; stiff buttons resisted her clumsy fingers.

"Look Nelly.... where's Archie... he could do this for me..." he cast his eyes around wildly, where was his brother-in-law?" He was starting to panic, still uncertain of his new dull body, he didn't know how long he could hold on. He couldn't wet himself... not here.

"What can Archie do?" a voice called cheerily from the hall. The sight of Nelly on her knees answered his question.

"Clifford needs to...." She was mortified to ask him.

"It's obvious what I need Nelly....I need to bloody well have a pee.... right now! And what's more, I've got no time to stand here debating the finer points of the matter Archie...would you do the honours?"

Dismissed, Nelly left the two men and retreated to the sanctuary of her kitchen. She mashed the tea leaves and clattered the teacups onto the tray. She was stupid... clueless and stupid, her face burned with embarrassment.

"There we are all sorted... Panic over!" Archie joked as he joined her in the kitchen. "Clifford's decided to sit in his chair by the fire for now.... So, I'll just empty this bottle for you Nelly, then I'll be back in a tic for a cup of that tea you promised me."

Archie slipped behind her with the brimming urine bottle and headed out to the lavatory. "And when I've rinsed this thing out, I'll top up the fire and then I'll refill that half-empty coal bucket for you," he called over his shoulder.

"Thanks Archie," Nelly smiled.

"Here we are then, all done... and I've even put the seat down," Archie joked as he returned to the kitchen with the empty bottle. He gave her a conspiratorial wink.

Her small face crumpled; brow furrowing, she took a deep breath, in an effort to control the rising tide of panic that was creeping through her. All day Nelly had tried to be brave, nonchalant even; take it in her stride. After all this was her new life... *their* new life together. For weeks she had so wanted him to come home, willed him to come back to her. Now the reality of it felt too hard to take.

"Oh Nelly....He's a proud man and in some ways it's as hard for him as it is for you. Life has changed for both of you." Archie's level, calm voice soothed her. Nelly bit her bottom lip in an effort not to cry.

He moved towards her. "Now come on... don't be too hard on yourself Nelly, it's early days yet." He kept his voice low; the door was open, sound travelled easily. Archie knew Clifford would be listening.

He put his arm around her slender shoulders and hugged her. She felt fragile and bird like as she leant against him, her body shuddering as she sought to regain control. Her small, prettily coiffed head that rested against his shoulder was so unlike Molly's spartan crop.

Molly.... distant, crisp and monosyllabic. She seemed to find no joy in anything; the two of them simply existed in the same sphere.

Recently Molly had taken to helping Father Thomas by tending to St Bartholomew's. Spending hours in the cold draughty church polishing the wood and brass, arranging flowers and kneelers, repairing books and vestments. And of course, visiting Billy.

It was always about Billy.

"Nelly....NELLY! What's taking you so long in there? Is that tea on its way yet?" Clifford's voice caused her to jump.

"Just coming... I'm just coming Clifford!" Nelly scurried into the sitting room with the tea tray.

Clifford's mood soon improved after they all sat down together and ate a sausage and mash dinner. The two men had tackled their meals with obvious enthusiasm and compliments about Nelly's cooking flowed thick and fast.

"Can't beat home cooking can you Clifford? That was perfect Nelly.... one of my absolute favourites." Archie mopped the last of his gravy with a thick hunk of crusty bread.

"Nelly's always been a wonderful cook. I've certainly missed her cooking these past few weeks." Clifford said loyally. "I must say I'm glad to be back home, thanks for all your help Archie."

"You're always welcome to join us Archie, you know that... Isn't he Clifford?" Nelly added flashing Archie a warm smile.

"Of course, he is," Clifford said.

Archie stayed until late into the afternoon. He knew he should go back to the flat... and Molly. Soon, but not yet... not until he could be sure Nelly and Clifford would be all right. Any way, he reasoned what was the rush to leave... there was nothing really to go home for? These days his wife barely noticed if he was there or not.

Nelly and Clifford needed him. For the first time in a long time he felt wanted about the place. Wanted and useful... no, he was in no rush to go home.

Earlier that afternoon he had assisted Clifford in a practice "run" to the lavatory. It opened Archie's eyes to the obstacles facing his brother-in-law's simple desire to relieve himself with some degree of dignity. Sharp edges, stiff latches and lack of handholds presented a daunting prospect. The short route outside suddenly turned into a major mission.

Archie found the screwdriver and tightened the lavatory door handle before fastening a piece of garden string to the latch so that Clifford could pull it shut when he sat down. He lowered the Izal box on the back of the door so that it was within easy reach and swept the moss and leaves off the garden path to stop them forming a slippery mush. After hacking back, the rose bush he exposed a stout handhold amongst the trellis and finally Archie hammered in raised nails on the coal bunker lid to provide a snag free surface to grab onto by the back door.

Archie stood back to admire his handy work...*Not a bad job Archie old boy.*

Now, with plenty of forward planning, Clifford would at least be able to get to the lavatory and take a shit under his own steam. It was a small step forward.

Archie tidied the tools away for her and tucked them back under a shelf in the shed until the next time... he knew there would be plenty of next times.

"Well, I'll be off home now Clifford." He shook his brother-in-law by the hand.

"Thank you once again for that delicious dinner Nelly... I haven't had a sausage and gravy dinner for... "he didn't know what figure of time to pick without sounding terribly disloyal to Molly who rarely cooked anything these days.

"Well not for quite some time any way... as I said you can't beat good home cooking can you Clifford?"

"Can't argue with you there... hospital food leaves an awful lot to be desired." Clifford said with a spark of good humour in his voice.

Nelly jumped up, "I'll just to see Archie to the door Clifford....and then I'll pop next door to collect Jean. I won't be long." She was anxious to speak to Archie before he left.

It was nearly five o'clock and the long evening stretched ahead of her, undressing Clifford, getting him into bed, washing and dressing again in the morning and the visits to the toilet. And Jean?

"Thank you *so* much Archie for being here today and for... well, you know... just for everything." Nelly's eyes looked tired, she felt bone weary.

"Do come and see us again soon Archie, won't you?... Only if you can spare the time, I mean... I know you have your own problems... I wouldn't want to put you to any trouble Archie...." she said, her voice hesitant, apologetic.

"Of course, I will.... you know you only have to ask Nell," he saw her face fall a little, he knew she didn't want to keep asking him for help.... probably *wouldn't* ask him for help.

He tossed her a lifeline. "Tell you what.... How about I pop by early tomorrow morning... you know, just to see if Clifford wants a bit of assistance with getting up and dressed. Man, to man like... just until the two of you have got a bit of a rhythm going?"

He could see a flood of relief cross her face.

"Oh, thank you Archie.... Yes, I'd like that just until I.... I mean until we.... as you say, get the hang of things.... If you're *sure* you don't mind."

She kissed him on the cheek. "Bye Archie."

As he walked down the street, Archie glanced over his shoulder just in time to see Nelly leaving Ivy Harris' house with Jean in tow. He waved to them both before ambling his way home to Molly.

On second thoughts, Archie decided he would pop into the Maltsters Arms on his way home for a pint of beer and maybe a smoke with Jack the landlord.

The sight of poor Clifford hauling himself about the place all afternoon in his callipers, had made him feel the need for a drink or two.

After all he had nothing to rush home for.

Sarah

Cardiff September 2012

And so there it was in amongst my mother's things; a small announcement that shocked me to the core: Leonard William Smith deceased 1/07/1929 - 2/11/1932. Much loved son of Mr and Mrs Archibald Smith.

Much loved; I turned the phrase over and over in my head; much loved... poor Aunty Molly, it must have broken her heart to lose her baby. I hunted amongst the other yellowing scraps of paper hoping to find another announcement of a happier kind for Molly and Uncle Archie but there wasn't one.

No more births, no more announcements at all relating to Uncle Archie and Aunty Molly.

No wonder my mother had spoken so kindly about poor Aunty Molly. A wave of guilt swept over me as I recalled my teenage sneers about plain, old Aunty Molly.

I straightened out the clippings, placed them inside the "Red Run" flyer and tucked them back inside the manilla envelope. As I pushed the flyer inside, my fingernail snagged on a small piece of card still trapped at the bottom of the envelope; it was a small, faded photograph.

Written on the reverse of the tatty black and white picture in an elaborate, flamboyant hand was... Archie x.

It was an image I had never seen before. In the background of the picture were old fashioned shop fronts and a bustling Cardiff street scene; everyone wearing hats, all heedless of the photographer. A picture of a long-forgotten world just going about its everyday business.

In the foreground of the faded image, my grandfather smiled broadly for the photographer from his wheelchair; young and handsome with a full head of thick wavy hair, dressed in his best suit. My tiny Grandmother, looking even more slender than I ever could have imagined her, was pushing Grampy's big wheelchair. A small girl with a mop of Shirley Temple curls, evidently my mother aged about three years old, was trotting beside him.

Without her mother's hand to hold Mum was grasping on to the wheelchair handle; her pale face showing her determination to keep up, her small hand, for some reason, shielding her eyes.

It was most peculiar- Gran and Mum were not even looking towards the photographer at all, no poses or happy smiles. Camera shy faces avoiding the person behind the lens in their desire to rush past. Who took this picture-and why? Could it be Uncle Archie?

It hit me like a train; my own Mother must have had a very constrained childhood. With all the pressures of an invalid in the household; a home short on comforts and modern facilities, it was easy for a little girl to be lonely and lost.

The age-old regret of the living washed over me; I wish I'd asked my Mum about it before she passed away. Now it was too late. Only the whisperings of these bits and pieces packed up in my mother's boxes could speak to me now.

A glance at my watch showed that it was already one o'clock; the morning had flown by. At this rate I wouldn't have a hope of finishing the task today if I didn't get a move on. I decided to grab a quick snack for lunch before tackling the last few packets and folders.

CHAPTER 30

Outside

From the cool gloom of the sitting room Clifford over-heard chattering and giggling in the garden. Half heard snippets of conversation reached his ears; a murmured buzz that stayed tantalizingly out of reach.

Jean's sing song demands *"play with me, play with me.... please Uncle Archie....pleeeese play with me,"* bounced like pebbles across his chest.

Cardiff was in the grip of an Indian summer; early morning chills gave way to cloudless blue skies and waves of shimmering heat. The weather forecasters said it was unprecedented and couldn't possibly last. Today was yet another beautiful, soft, warm afternoon and Clifford longed to feel the sun on his face before the weather broke. He longed to be able to pop into the garden to see what the fuss was about and the lack made him irritable.

Clifford had been home for over three weeks now and he was beginning to get cabin fever. It was hard to find hope in the few small achievements he had gained over the past weeks: lumbering visits to the outside toilet that took twenty minutes and left him exhausted. Devising a makeshift grabber from Nelly's wooden back scratcher in order to reach a fallen newspaper without calling for her, falling asleep without tormenting himself about the thought of his wife lying alone in the bedroom above him. Small victories.

The prospect of a wet dreary Autumn and then a long dark winter being just around the corner filled him with dread. Peals of laughter and shrieks of outrage trickled through the half open door into his world. The gloomy news commentary on the wireless about mounting unrest in Germany struggled to compete with the hullabaloo coming from outside.

"Oh no Jean.... Arrgh you little scamp!"

"No.... No Jean don't splash Uncle Archie like that please... Oh you little madam... look what you've done... you've made Uncle Archie's trousers all wet now.... That was *so* naughty.... I'll have to go and get Uncle Archie a towel to mop up this mess .... You say sorry young lady." Nelly stubbed out her cigarette and headed into the kitchen.

Nelly, Jean and Archie were having larks in the glossy sunshine. A large, galvanized tin bath served as a makeshift paddling pool and now poor Archie sat on his stool dripping wet, the victim of a well-aimed bucket of water. He feigned a stern look at the guilty offender and tried not to laugh.

"Sor...reee uncle Archie." Jean said sheepishly. Her china blue eyes appealed at him from under the brim of her white, cotton sun hat; he thought of Billy.

Clifford caught a brief glimpse of Nelly as she dashed into the kitchen in search of a towel. "Nelly.... Er Nelly?" he called after her retreating back.

She popped her head around the door. "Just a moment Clifford, I've just got to give Archie this towel.... He's absolutely soaking wet, poor man. Jean's being a proper little Madam this afternoon throwing water about.... Look..." She pointed to a damp splodge on the front of her blue, cotton dress," she almost got me as well, the little monkey. Lucky for me Archie caught the worst of it!"

Nelly laughed.

Nelly's hair was tousled, her cheeks tinged pink with the strong sunlight and as she swished her dress a faint whiff of tobacco drifted towards him; they had been smoking together. "I'll be back in just two tics." She called.

He waited for her to return. A fat bluebottle looped annoying figures of eight around the light bulb, occasionally it taunted him by zipping past his chair just out of reach of his rolled-up newspaper; he would have to ask Nelly, or Archie, to swat it down for him.

"Now you go tell and Daddy what you've been up to you scamp.... trying to drown your poor old Uncle Archie," Archie strode into the room patting at his sodden trousers with a towel. He gave Clifford a broad wink. Jean, standing in her damp vest and pants, looked every inch the sinner.

"Mummy won't let me put that pool out in the garden again... not after we've made all this mess for her...will she?" Archie said. Jean shook her head.

"Your poor Mummy's got water everywhere now; everywhere except on the flower bed that is!" Archie joked. The sinner hid bashfully behind his legs.

"I think I'd better get a broom and sweep that path for Mummy, don't you?" Archie tried to maintain a stern face, he caught Nelly rolling her eyes at him as if to say *don't overdo it.* Jean jutted out her bottom lip and did her best to look contrite.

"Still no harm done poppet.... Uncle Archie needed to cool off any way, its fair roasting out in that garden," he said chucking her under the chin. She rewarded him with a mischievous grin.

Clifford, in his grey cardigan, noticed that Archie's already tanned arms looked red down one side, an angry line showed at the margins of his rolled-up sleeves, his brother-in-law would need some calamine lotion later on.

"That shed certainly shelters the garden from the wind... it's a real sun trap out there today, absolutely boiling for the time of year.... I reckon I'm going to pay for this later on." Archie inspected his pink arms as his eyes adjusted to the gloom of the sitting room.

"Yep, definitely no more sun for me...I think I ought to come inside for a while and keep out of it." He glanced at Clifford's pale, moon-like face staring up at him from his chair, his lips set in a joyless line; legs propped on a stool covered with a plaid rug.

"Sorry Clifford.... that was thoughtless of me." Archie mumbled as he moved to sit down on a small armchair.

"It's a real shame you being stuck indoors on a glorious day like this... Oh I'm being such an idiot! Why didn't I think of this before? I could try to take out this other armchair into the garden for you, if you like?" Archie pounced on the smaller of the two armchairs that served as Nelly's chair. "That way you could get to go out in the garden for an hour or two... you know, get a bit of fresh air for a change.... it would do you a power of good." Archie screwed up his eyes and assessed the width of the chair.

"Yep it should just about do it...I reckon I could get it out through that scullery doorway if I shift it onto its side... It would be a bit of a squeeze, but what do you say Clifford?" Archie beamed.

Clifford looked dubiously at the narrow doorway. "I don't know if it's going to fit through that gap; that doorway is quite tight..." Clifford craned his neck to get a glimpse of the azure strip of sky that tantalized him, ".... but I suppose it's worth a try since the weather is *so* nice. I'm going stir crazy looking at these four walls day in, day out", he admitted.

"That's the spirit Clifford, nothing ventured... and all that." Archie up-ended the chair in one swift easy movement and manoeuvred it towards the doorway.

"Hey, hey... careful with the woodwork. What on earth is going on?" Nelly said as she saw Archie struggling to manipulate her precious armchair through the narrow doorway into the kitchen and out into the garden.

"It's going to be a bit of a mission but if Clifford wants to sit out in the garden in the sunshine... then sit he bloody well shall." Archie puffed as he heaved the chair through the gap with only inches to spare.

"Bingo!" he said triumphantly.

Nelly looked on with admiration as Archie effortlessly lifted the chair over the path, cleared away the water mess and then helped manoeuvre her husband into the newly positioned armchair nestling in the lee of the shed wall.

In the afternoon sunshine clusters of fat bees hummed and dithered over the full blown spicy Sweet Williams. Tiny hover flies skittered over the untidy jumble of golden rod that scattered a haze of pollen over the path. In the garden next door, a luminous white sheet flapped idly to and fro against the backdrop of a cloudless blue sky.

Jean busied herself collecting drifts of fallen rose petals in her bucket and chasing orange and red patterned butterflies that drifted over the garden wall drunk on the nectar of Mrs James' Buddleia.

It was deliciously hot and bright. Clifford sat propped against cushions in the small armchair, with a floppy, white, cotton hat to shield his head from the sun. He drank in the sights and sounds of the tiny scrap of garden. The effort of getting into the garden left him feeling in need of refreshment.

"A nice pot of tea is just what we all need," Nelly said brightly," if Archie would fetch the card table, I think we could squeeze it in next to Clifford."

The bath tub removed, Archie busied himself bringing out two dining chairs and a folding card table that sat shakily on the uneven, narrow path. In the kitchen Clifford heard the kettle whistled on the hob; Nelly would be out soon with a tray of afternoon tea.

"Oh, that tray looks heavy.... here, I'll carry that for you Nelly.... go on take the weight off your feet... you go and sit with Clifford, and I'll be mother."

Clifford looked on as his brother-in-law, with casual ease, wrested the laden tray from his tiny wife.

"Thank you, Archie....I don't know how we would manage without you. It's marvellous for us all to all be able to sit out in the garden on such a beautiful afternoon. It was a brilliant idea." Nelly flashed him a dazzling smile. "Sorry to say, you've got to put it all back again though..."

"Think nothing of it. Now onward and upward as they say. What we need is to think big... no need to stop at the garden!" Archie winked at Clifford.

After the success of cracking the garden expedition, exciting plans were now being hatched for Clifford to get a wheelchair out on loan from the hospital services unit. The glorious Indian summer wouldn't last much longer; they needed to make the best of it before the blustery winds of Autumn arrived.

"I've got two strong arms Clifford, I'm absolutely certain we can get you out and about again... Nelly couldn't push you in one of those contraptions, but I certainly can!" Archie announced.

Clifford looked uncertain; the memory of being unloaded like a sack of spuds, trussed up in a blanket and being gawped at on his first day home, flashed through his head.

"Oh, please Clifford, please let's give it a try.... Jean would love it and so would I.... being out together again as a family." Nelly's eyes pleaded for him to agree. "But only if you're *sure* it's not too much trouble for you Archie." she said anxiously.

"Of course, I'm sure.... any way it's bound to be a bloody sight easier than lumping these armchairs all over the place. Once we get you a wheelchair old man, if we plan our route properly there's no telling what we could get up to... We could visit the park... or even go to the pub. The world's your oyster!" Archie enthused.

For the first time in a very long time Clifford felt something approaching contentment.... no not contentment.... acceptance.

"Oh well, as the old saying goes- Nothing ventured nothing gained. Let's give it a go then Archie." Clifford said.

Nelly clapped her hands with delight; the prison door had opened a chink and the outside world beckoned.

As Archie ambled his way home to the unappealing prospect of reheating yet another bowl of Molly's greasy mutton stew, he pondered the unfairness of life.

The day spent with Nelly and Jean in the garden had been a delight; he'd been laughing all afternoon and it was a good feeling, really good. He felt alive, strong, and best of all *needed*.

In his own joyless household laughter was a distant memory, he thought ruefully. He certainly didn't feel needed or wanted. He and Molly seemed to just slip pass each other each day like two twigs caught in a current. He felt lonely.

He wished that he and Molly could find their way back to each other, back to what they once had together... back before Billy. The very thought of a world before Billy made him feel guilty.

But Archie was angry.... why couldn't Molly be a bit more like her sister; making the best of things... trying to cope, instead of shutting him out and wallowing in misery? Even Clifford, despite being crippled seemed buoyed up and willing to try to move forward. Why not Molly?

It had been so many months now since Molly had so much as touched him, let alone allowed him to make love to her. There was only lovemaking *before* Billy, now she shuddered if he even so much as tried to hug her. Stiff and unyielding Molly would flinch and move away from him, a perfunctory peck on the cheek before retreating to Billy's old bedroom to sleep alone.

Archie yearned to be touched, to feel like a man again; surely his wife couldn't expect him to go on like this; he watched her shrink with revulsion every time he went near her; the vague excuses of needing *time.*

How much time could anyone need? He thought bitterly. He'd been patient after Billy had gone.... too bloody patient his mates said.

There never seemed to be any end in sight, he thought angrily. The whole world seemed to be going to hell in a hand cart if the newspapers were to be believed and his wife spent her days on her knees polishing the brass work in St Bartholomew's like a penitent recluse.

"Fucking, self-indulgent lunacy, that's what is," Archie muttered under his breath.

As Archie ambled homewards, he reflected that it was a bitter irony that he and Clifford shared one cross at least.... *neither* of them could make love to their wives.

He turned on his heels and headed back to the pub. If there was nothing to go home for then he wouldn't go home!

CHAPTER 31

The Excursion

October 1937

"Look at me.... Oh, come on Nelly, do be a sport... just watch the birdie please!" Nelly looked away bashfully trying hard not to return a smile. Her eyes not daring to meet her tormentor's gaze she struggled to keep the wheels in a straight line and weave a path amongst the shoppers.

Jean gripped onto the slippery bamboo, chair handle and shielded her eyes from the late afternoon sun. Her legs felt chilly as she trotted beside the invalid carriage. The sun was getting low and she was tired from the visit to Roath Park lake with Mummy, Daddy and Uncle Archie.

"Smile at the nice camera man Clifford! That's the way.... all say cheese now.... That's it Clifford.... good man.... at least some one looks pleased to see me!" Archie teased as he clicked away.

"Just one more picture and I'll take back the chair.... promise!" Archie wheedled. Nelly laughed despite herself.

"Atta girl! You can swap places with me now. I think that's the end of the roll." Archie tucked his camera back into the brown leather box that hung around his neck.

Nelly felt foolish trying to push Clifford over the uneven paving slabs, but Archie had insisted on recording the *grand expedition* as he insisted on calling the trip to Roath Park. After much coaxing Nelly had agreed to at least go through the motions of trying to propel Clifford in a straight line whilst Archie recorded the event for posterity on camera.

Now it was the end of the day; Jean was getting grumpy and tired. It had been a very long, exciting afternoon; her first proper outing in a long while. The little girl had fed the ducks on stale crusts; chased the squirrels collecting acorns on the huge green park lawns and had played hide and seek with Uncle Archie in the formal rose garden; skipping and jumping behind the bushes until Archie collapsed into a heap on the lush grass.

The journey home felt long and tiring for little legs, "I'm tired Mummy...." Jean rubbed her eyes and pouted her bottom lip.

"I know, darling.... You've been such a good girl and you've walked *such* a long way. Not long now and we will be home for tea.... you can have a nice, boiled egg and some soldiers for your tea if you like." Nelly coaxed and cajoled the tired child into a reluctant trot.

"Your Uncle Archie has brought Mummy some lovely brown, speckled eggs this morning.... a pretty brown egg for your tea...won't that be nice?"

Jean gave a wan smile; her eyes fluttering with exhaustion.

"*Chick, chick, chick, chicken lay a little egg for me....* *Chick, chick, chick, chicken I want one for my tea!*" Archie trilled.

"Come on Jean sing along with your Uncle Archie...." he coaxed flashing the small child a big grin.

"*Oh, I haven't had an egg since Easter and now it's half past three! So, chick, chick, chick, chicken lay a little egg for me!*"

"You do look silly Uncle Archie!" Nelly laughed as she watched him capering around Jean flapping his arms and feigning to lay an egg.

He'd have been such a wonderful father to Billy, she thought sadly. Her sister was being a fool neglecting a man like Archie, an utter fool. Her mother was right it *was* time Molly came to her senses.

"Come on Clifford I think we'd better get a move on and get you back... there's one tired young lady here who looks fit to drop," Archie said. He took over the chair and headed back to Alma road.

CHAPTER 32

Rain

The Autumn of 1937 rolled in with a flurry of bad-tempered storms; winds tore the leaves from the trees and put an end to the outings. Evenings drew in and the mornings were relentlessly grey and gloomy.

For Clifford the cramped sitting room took on the air of a prison.

Within just a few days it was as if that long, hot, Indian summer had never been. Mother nature was making up for her late bounty by punishing the earth with torrents of rain driven on by freezing winds that whistled nagging draughts through the house.

When it wasn't coming down in stair rods the weather settled into a heavy, grey, greasy drizzle that slicked the walls and windows, sucking the light and casting deep shadows

Day after day Clifford sat in his armchair, lamp on, gloomily watching rivulets of rain trickling down the windowpane.

Day after day he gave up any hope of leaving the house. Clifford dreaded the coming months.

The tick of the mantle clock nearly drove him mad as he marked the hours and hours of rain and heavy drizzle. The weather forecast gave no hope of respite and the year was dragging to a miserable close.

In the dark days as Nelly struggled with all the chores, the wireless became Clifford's constant companion, his window on the world. He listened avidly for hours, but there was precious little to lift his mood. The world news was fractious and ominous. Whispers of oppression and hatred of Jews, pro-German uprisings in the Sudetenland. Tensions and pacts between countries, all interwoven with strikes at home and waves of job losses.

The world seemed to be turning in on itself.

After the joy of going out, feeling the fresh air on his face and seeing a world outside his own four walls, Clifford started to despair of being trapped indoors for months on end.

As the days grew shorter and more miserable, so did Clifford's temper.

"Nelly!... Nelly, there's someone at the door!" he barked impatiently. "Nelly can't you hear that knocking!"

"I'm coming.... I'm coming Clifford. Just a moment will you.... I need to dry my hands for goodness sake."

Nelly abandoned the brimming sink that was almost overflowing with soaking bed sheets and striped pyjama bottoms and hurried through to the hallway to answer the door.

She hastily unbuttoned her damp, sprigged house coat as she went; patting her hair in to shape for good measure. Who on earth could it be? They weren't expecting visitors and her mother wasn't meant to be coming until tomorrow.

Her heart contracted a little as she could see the familiar outline of Archie peering through the glass panes. A mixture of pleasure and panic surged through her. Archie always cheered her up, but Clifford was in such a fractious mood today, who knew what he'd say to an unexpected guest.

She caught sight of her reflection in the hall mirror; she looked a fright; her hair was dishevelled through her exertions over the steaming laundry and her jumper had sprouted a small stain near the neckline.

Nelly groaned. There was nothing for it she would have to let him in mess or no mess.

"Hello there, Nelly.... I was just passing by and I thought I'd pop in... hope I'm not intruding." The rain dripping off his hat gave lie to his excuse of a casual afternoon's stroll.

"No, no of course not... do come in Archie. My goodness you're soaking. Here, let me take your coat.... you're always welcome, you know you are." She added.

Clifford gave her an affectionate squeeze and pressed two packets of Craven A cigarettes into her hand. "Don't tell the boss," he whispered pressing his finger to her lips.

Even in the gloom of the hallway he noticed the dark, blue-grey circles under her eyes. She looked tired and careworn; a small strand of stray hair looped over her eyebrow; her shoulders drooped slightly under a scruffy jumper. Her collar bone looked prominent; she was losing weight.

"How's tricks Nell?" He tucked the stray strand gently behind her ear, his voice oozing concern.

For one brief moment she absorbed the sensation of someone caring how *she* felt, she shrugged her shoulders "Oh I'm...."

Her words hung in the air as Clifford's tetchy voice shattered the moment.

"Nelly! Nelly who on earth is it? There's a hell of a draught coming through the hall! Is that front door still open.?......Nellie!"

She took a deep breath and steadied herself, Clifford was trying her patience today. His constant shouting was making her feel nervy and unsettled. She mouthed *sorry* towards Archie.

"It's only Archie, Clifford," she called back, as she hung Archie's dripping mackintosh on the coat stand.

"Come on through," she said. Her hands seemed to flutter as she ushered him towards the back-sitting room.

He could sense her agitation.

"You'll have to excuse him today Archie; the weather is really getting him down and...." she lowered her voice, "and he's having a few problems at the moment... you know." Nelly gestured down below.

"The nurse said it's a bladder infection, probably caused by sitting about so much.... so, he can't help it, really, he can't... we've had a few night-time "*accidents* "and I'm up to my eyeballs in washing whilst he's barking out orders like a sergeant major." Nelly managed a weak smile.

"Come on through I'll make us all some tea."

Clifford felt the draught and the interruption to his wireless programme keenly; there was still another fifteen minutes to go; he hated missing the end of the world news broadcast, it had taken him positively ages to locate the European news channel. He glared impatiently at Nelly and Archie as they clattered into the small sitting room.

"It's all right Clifford...." she could see a dark cloud of irritation gathering on his face. "Archie can come into the kitchen whilst I finish the chores *then* we can come back in and all have a nice cup of tea together."

She ushered Archie through into the steamy kitchen leaving Clifford to his broadcast.

Even to Archie's eyes the kitchen looked like a disaster area with dripping washing oozing over the draining board and two galvanized pails of soaking linen demanding attention. "Where's tuppence then?" he asked.

"Oh, Jean's next door with Ivy," she said, "that woman's a God-send, an absolute God-send, especially today."

She lowered her voice a little, "I'm sure she must have heard all the kerfuffle going on in here, what with one thing and another," she rolled her eyes in the direction of the sitting room. Clifford's radio chattered loudly.

"... any way Ivy popped over first thing this morning to take Jean off my hands for the day."

"Good old Ivy," he said. He lit a cigarette and lit another for Nelly; he popped it in between her lips.

"I think you deserve one of these my girl ...." he said as he opened the back door. He knew the regime.

"You take a breather Nell and I'll tackle the last of this bloody washing.... go on make yourself useful and hand me that tea towel to shove around my waist, there's a good girl."

"But I can't let you...."

"Rubbish of course you can. The army certainly taught me lots of things when I graced them with my presence and washing my own kit was one of the more useful things they managed to drill into my thick head." Archie said with a wink.

"Any way what with Molly being the way she is I'm used to fending for myself. So, stop arguing, chuck us that tea towel and I'll have this lot rinsed out in no time at all."

Archie thrust his strong arms into the grey, soapy water and set about wringing and plunging the washing with vigour.

"You can't be expected to do everything around here, you'll wear yourself out at this rate," Archie looked at her with concern.

He slapped and agitated the laundry several times before tipping out the slop.

"You need to keep your strength up, for Jean's sake." he added.

Nelly stood in the door frame dragging heavily on her cigarette as if her life depended on it.

She gave him a weak smile, "I know.... thanks Archie....Oh Good Lord.... just look at the time! I better get that kettle on... he'll be wanting that tea soon, and it's nowhere near ready," she said glancing anxiously at the kitchen clock.

"Don't panic Nell, he can wait a minute or two, can't he?" He saw her shake her head at the very suggestion of Clifford being made to wait for his tea.

"Oh, come on Nelly all this charging about and getting yourself in a tizz is going to do you in .... I mean," he added hastily. "Who's going to look after you my girl if you don't look after yourself. You're no good to any one if you go to bits."

"You listen to Uncle Archie," he wagged his soapy finger theatrically.

She nodded and gave him a small smile that trsformed her careworn face. Archie thought how young and pretty she looked for a fleeting moment.

" Nelly....Nelly!" Clifford's voice travelled through to the kitchen.

"Nelly.... can you hear me?" he demanded, "I'll have that tea now.... Nelleeee!"

"Coming Clifford, just two tics," she called. She shooed the grey smoke out of the kitchen; tossed her cigarette butt into the flower bed and made a mental note to retrieve it later before it was noticed by Clifford on his way to the lavatory.

Archie shook his head as Nelly sprang in to action.

She popped her head around the doorway. Clifford looked mutinous.

"I hope that tea won't be too long Nelly, I'm gasping," he said testily.

"The kettle is just coming to the boil Clifford," she fibbed. "I'll send Archie in to keep you company, while I make that tea."

Nelly glanced at her reflection in the mirror "Oh my goodness just looks at the state of me." She started to unbutton her house coat; Clifford couldn't abide house coats.

As she stood in the doorway Clifford sniffed the air theatrically.

"Can I smell smoke coming from the kitchen Nelly?"

"Smoke Clifford?"

"Yes smoke … cigarette smoke Nell." he added for good measure. "Have you been smoking again?" he demanded, his voice carrying through to Archie in the kitchen.

"Oh …. umm." Before she could answer, the door to the kitchen flapped open behind her.

"Hands up…. I'm guilty as charged Clifford......all my fault entirely," Archie said chirpily as he strode into the sitting room with a tea towel still tied around his waist and a cigarette dangling from his lips.

"Sorry old man. Just not thinking." He tossed his cigarette into the fire.

Archie glanced at Nelly who stood nervously in the middle of the room.

Nelly reminded him of a chastened child standing before the headmaster. *Clifford was being a bully.*

"I was just helping Nelly wring out a few of those bed-sheets and I was simply dying for a ciggie; I couldn't exactly go out into the garden in this awful weather could I now? I mean, just look at it…. It's positively raining cats and dogs out there." Archie gestured towards the torrents of rain bouncing off the windo- pane.

Clifford glowered at the weather.

"Not to worry Archie…." Nelly jumped in before the lie was explored. "Now how about I make us all that nice pot of tea? You take a seat and chat to Clifford, I'll only be couple of minutes," Nelly headed for the kitchen.

"Biscuits?" Clifford barked as she turned her back, "I'd like a biscuit with my tea, have you bought any more biscuits yet?"

Clifford's voice had a petulant tone that grated on Archie, he resisted the urge to roll his eyes.

"Honestly Clifford I haven't had any time to get out to the shops, what with the rain and ... and everything," She gestured in the direction of the washing that lay festooned all over the kitchen.

"So, I'm sorry, there aren't any biscuits Clifford. But I've got some nice fresh bread if you'd like some.... with maybe a little of Ivy's black-currant preserve?" Molly coaxed.

Her husband clicked his teeth with undisguised annoyance. He wanted biscuits and nothing else would suffice. He gave a brief shake of his head. he would not be mollified with bread, butter and jam.

"I'm sorry," she repeated. "It's been one of those days today Clifford and I'm all sixes and sevens.... this awful weather will be the death of me." she said as she shut the door behind herself.

Clifford will certainly be the death of you at this rate, Archie thought angrily as he took a seat opposite his stony-faced brother-in-law.

He watched as Clifford folded his half-read newspaper into exact quarters, smoothing and organizing the pages with precision. Archie heard clattering in the kitchen and imagined Nelly rushing about to get the tea things together. He resisted the urge to help her.

Selfish old sod, can't he see he's dragging her down with all his demands and moods? Nelly do this, Nelly do that... barking orders at her all the time like some jumped up bit of military brass. Couldn't even bring himself say a bloody please or thank you.

He won't be happy until he's turned her into a servant and a drudge; worn out before her time.... Well, he's not going to.... not if I've got anything to do with it. Archie fumed inwardly.

After witnessing Clifford's display of bad temper Archie felt he simply couldn't bring himself to try to make conversation with the man. *Let him stew.*

Only the ticking of the mantle clock punctuated the stultifying silence that draped over the room.

Archie longed to leave and he longed to stay. He vowed to himself that he would pop in more often, that way he'd really see how Nelly was faring. And if Clifford didn't like it then Clifford would just have to lump it.

"Here we are a nice pot of tea," Nelly smiled broadly as she carried the heavy tray into the room. Archie could see she had tidied her hair.

"And, surprise, surprise Clifford, I found there was one biscuit left in the bottom of the barrel after all." She handed him the offering of one slightly tatty rich tea on a fine china plate.

Clifford harrumphed a small thank you and accepted the peace offering.

"Can't manage to dig up another one for you though Archie," she added by way of apology.

"Oh, don't worry about me Nell," he said airily, "I'm very easily pleased; a nice cup of tea from a pretty lady does it for me every time." He was pleased to see her blush at the small compliment.

Clifford slurped his tea noisily. "Did you warm the pot Nelly? This tea seems a bit tepid to me." He fixed her with a beady stare over the rim of his cup.

"Ungrateful bastard," Archie muttered under his breath.

Clifford sobbed as she helped him out of his callipers and into bed that night. His eyes were fearful dark pools; he clutched her arm as if his very life depended on it.

He hated himself, his white shrivelled legs disgusted him. What sort of man was he now?

Without his callipers he was trapped in his bed, in his room... trapped in his bloody useless body. An overwhelming tide of panic started to build from deep within him.

"Please don't leave me Nelly... Promise me you'll never leave me.... I couldn't bear it if you left me." He scanned her poor, beautiful, tired face.

"Of course, I'll never leave you Clifford," she soothed, "no matter what.... I'll never leave."

CHAPTER 33

Curtains

Nelly didn't know how it happened.... it certainly wasn't meant to. Events of that morning had cracked the tectonic plates of her small world causing her to question everything and now she didn't know where it would lead.

That night as she replayed the events of the morning over and over in her head, she tossed and turned under the chilly sheets unable to sleep and unable to pray. The ground had shifted from beneath her leaving her giddy and tormented with doubt. No, she hadn't meant it to happen!

Weeks and weeks had dragged by with uneventful, monotonous regularity. The cold rainy weather had kept her cooped up indoors trying to amuse Jean and placate Clifford. Nerves were getting frayed and the house began to feel like a prison. If it wasn't for Archie's visits and the kindliness of Alf and Ivy James, Nelly felt sure she would have gone mad.

Clifford had developed an irrational fear of being left for any length of time. He needed to know where she was, how long she would be gone and who she'd seen. His endless questions scratched on her nerves, making her feel like a wriggling insect under a microscope; pinned down and examined.

Nelly felt shackled to the house and overwhelmed with day-to-day chores. Each day drifted into the next, lacking colour and purpose. As Clifford clung to her for support, she felt dragged under by the sheer weight of his needs.

If his mood was dark, then even short visits to the shops proved impossible for days at a time; she relied all too often on the good- hearted Ivy James to get her groceries and take Jean out for an airing.

Cooped up in doors for days on end she felt restless and dispirited. Occasionally her mother popped by to collect or deliver Jean and sometimes Kathleen stopped for a cup of tea and a chat with her daughter, but so often the talk turned to her mother's concern for "poor, dear Molly" who still drifted colourlessly through life.

It was always about Molly, Nelly raged inwardly. Sympathy for her and Clifford seemed to be in short supply.

Perversely on these visits from her mother Clifford often seemed energized and animated, "he's making the best of it" Kathleen passed on to the neighbours who enquired after his health. It was only when his mother-in-law left that his spirits slumped; drained by the effort of putting on a brave face. Nelly would be left to pick up the pieces; to nurse the grudges and fend off the criticisms.

It seemed that the only thing she had to look forward to the were the regular visits from Archie; he buoyed her up when she felt she was drowning under the sheer, monotonous drudgery of it all. Without Archie's titbits of news and scraps of information from the world outside, she felt sure she would have suffocated under the tedium of her dull existence.

She knew Clifford couldn't help his moods, and sometimes, just sometimes, flashes of the confident, witty man she had fallen in love with shone through. She lived for those moments when he actually noticed her. But too often a bitterness crept into his voice; and he pushed her further and further away from him.

She was beginning to feel more like a nurse than his wife.

Even Jean's lively childish chatter seemed to give him little pleasure; her clatter and whirling about the place grated on his fragile nerves and caused him to snap.

"Why don't you be a good girl for mummy and perhaps I could take you next door to visit Aunty Ivy? I think Daddy needs a bit of peace and quiet today," became Nelly's regular refrain as she struggled to keep the lid on their lively daughter.

Her husband had sought to gain control of his life and emotions by ruling his little domain. Alma road ran to Clifford's timetable and to his alone. As his world shrank, his power grew and soon he was master of all he surveyed, even if all he surveyed was to be found on the ground floor of their small, terraced house.

So that Tuesday morning, to escape his forensic, beady eyes, Nelly decided to take refuge in the upstairs middle bedroom. She intended catching up with some chores; she needed some space.

There was plenty that Clifford liked to listen to on the wireless on Tuesday mornings so there was a good chance she could be excused for a couple of hours. Nelly planned to spend the morning enjoying the peace and quiet.

The stairs might prove a barrier for Clifford, but for Nelly they offered a small route to freedom. A bridge into a world where she wasn't being summoned and watched every moment of the day.

"I'm only going upstairs Clifford to sort out that middle room and then I really must put these curtains back up, its freezing up there with no curtains up at the windows.... It shouldn't take me too long, but it's got to be done." She said brooking no argument. Nelly tossed a heavy pile of sprigged floral cotton curtains over her shoulder.

Now that Mrs Pugh had decided not to return Nelly had been trying to sort out the middle room. Putting up some curtains was next on her list.

The old curtains had been donated by her mother, being surplus to requirements in the Fowler household. Nelly had made good use of the gift. The heavy cotton sateen had been turned to remove the faded edges and shortened to fit the window in the middle room, now they looked almost as good as new. She had spent hours delicately unpicking the seams and then hand stitching the cloth. Nelly was very pleased with the results of her efforts; no matter that only she would ever get to see them, it was a job well done.

"I've made up the fire; so, you should be fine for an hour or two," she added hastily as she saw a thinly disguised look of irritation cross his face. Clifford preferred her to sit opposite him in her chair and keep him company.

260

"Oh, and by the way, Archie said that he might pop by to see us sometime this morning,"

"Oh Nelly... I really would rather..."

"Don't worry Clifford he can let himself in when he arrives... I can leave the door on the latch for him." She cut him off before he could object.

"Well what time did Archie say he would call?" Clifford asked peevishly consulting his watch. It seemed to him that Archie had visited nearly every day for weeks now. Clifford felt that he didn't really feel the need for *another* visit quite so soon; he'd been visited more than enough already!

"He didn't Clifford.... he only said that *he might and* left it at that. So, I really don't know, is the answer," Nelly said firmly.

Clifford harrumphed at the prospect of an uncertain visit. After all, there were morning programmes he liked to listen to on the wireless; he needed peace when tackling cryptic cross word clues and visitors only got in the way of these things if they turned up when it suited them. He liked his visitors to arrive to schedule, *his schedule.* Spontaneous drop ins by all and sundry were a great inconvenience in his opinion.

"You know I don't like you putting that door on the latch Nelly, a strong draught at this time of year might blow it open. The house is cold enough as it is, without letting all the heat out," Clifford said as if denying his brother-in-law access on a chilly day was the most reasonable thing in the world.

"All right, all right, I'll put the key under the mat then... Archie knows not to knock," she said trying to keep a note of exasperation out of her voice. She would not be diverted from her task in hand.

"I've put your newspaper next to your chair and a pen in case you want to do the cross word." she said hitching back up the heavy curtains that were starting to slip off her thin shoulder.

"Ivy will bring Jean back after lunch so unless there is anything else you need me for Clifford, I'm *going* to tackle that middle room, before the morning runs away from me."

Before he could raise any further objections, Nelly disappeared out of the room and shut the door firmly behind her.

Nelly trudged up the stairs with her load. With the aid of a wooden chair to reach the curtain rails she felt able to tackle the prospect of hanging the heavy curtains single handed.

The middle room sash windows were particularly ill-fitting and draughty. The new curtains would help enormously. *Yes, there was certainly plenty to keep her busy,* she thought to herself.

Nelly couldn't avoid the disagreeable fact that the windows were actually very grimy and in need of a good clean. *Bother she needed to tackle them first before nice the clean curtains were hung up.*

She set about the dirty panes with a rag, some Windowlene and plenty of elbow grease. Nelly smeared and rubbed the pink, creamy liquid, straining from her perch to reach into all the tricky corners. With a soft rag in either hand she worked away vigorously at removing the smeary film; buffing and polishing each window-pane to fine shine.

Later on, at night as she lay alone in her bed trying to make sense of events that followed, she realized that she must have been so engrossed in the job in hand that she hadn't heard a tread on the stairs, or even the small click of the bedroom door. But the strong masculine voice behind her had so surprised her she had fairly jumped out of her skin with shock.

"So, this is what you're up to them!" A voice chuckled behind her.

"Oh...Oh" for just a moment visions of Clifford standing behind her raced through her mind. As she began to turn towards him, she felt herself losing her balance; the chair began to rock and wobble precariously. With cleaning cloths in her hands, she was powerless to stop herself from falling.

"Steady on there Nell," Archie rushed behind her and caught her before she toppled over. His hands grabbed her firmly around her waist and he pulled her towards him.

She felt so light as he swept her up in his arms.

Her heart was thundering in her breast. *Idiot, you fool...of course it couldn't have been Clifford, what a ridiculous idea!*

"You frightened me Archie.... You really did. I thought it was.... well didn't know what to think... you gave me such a start, you idiot... I could have broken my neck!" she said accusingly.

Her face looked pale and her blue eyes glittered as he lowered her gently to the floor. "Honestly Archie you are the limit.... creeping up on me like that.... I could murder you!"

And then it happened. As Nelly started to entangle herself from his protective embrace, he kissed her.

His mouth found hers and he kissed her with a desire and urgency that took her breath away. He devoured her. In his need to drink in her kisses, he was like a man dying of thirst; consuming her as if his very life depended on it. And she, in her need, responded with equal passion.

Nelly broke away, her cheeks flushed, her heart aflutter like some giddy school-girl.

"Oh my God Archie...why?" she panted unsure of herself. Terrified what she may do next.

"I'm sorry Nell, I just couldn't help myself...actually I'm not sorry," Archie said vehemently. "I'm not sorry at all...I'm glad I kissed you. I want you Nell and I think you want me too."

"Archie we can't... we mustn't" her eyes darted around the room, like a frightened faun trapped in a clearing, uncertain of where to run. She took a step towards the door.

"I ought to go Archie before we do something, we will both regret.... really, I should," she said willing herself to be strong.

"Neither of us is happy Nell; not with how things are. Life is such a bloody mess. It's a mess for the both of us.... We can't go on like this." He saw her flinch a little.

"You know what I'm saying Nelly," he said, his eyes blazed with passion. "You must know how I feel about you.... well... you do, don't you?"

It had been so long since any man had looked at her with such desire. Over these long months she had felt invisible, a faint, colourless echo of herself. It hurt her to admit it but she was so very, very lonely.

At times, late at night she often had raged at the unfairness of it all; crying herself to sleep. She so wanted to be loved but Clifford no longer even wanted to kiss her, certainly not kiss her properly like he used to. When challenged his response had cut her to the quick. *What's the bloody point in its Nell, it's not as if it will be leading to anything...? we both know that,* he had said.

Now they parted each night with a perfunctory peck on the lips and a formal *goodnight.*

She had grown very fond of Archie and she could not deny that her heart gave a small flutter every time he came to call. He lightened her life; he was her rock.

But she never expected this. *They mustn't do this.*

"Can't we just try to make each other happy? Please Nelly," Archie pleaded.

She stood before him trembling. She knew that he was giving her a choice and the prospect of it terrified her.

"We don't have to hurt anyone, truly we don't." He took her by the shoulders and pulled her gently towards him. "You deserve someone who cares about you.... someone who really *wants* you.... like I want you Nell." His hand cradled her head, fondling her soft, delicate neck; tilting her face towards his. Her lips parted exposing her small white teeth.

"Tell me you don't want this and I'll leave," he said throatily as his lips fluttered across her neck. "You are so beautiful," he murmured.

His fingers fumbled with the small, round pearl buttons on her blouse. As he slid his hand inside the silky fabric his hand caressed her breast causing her to moan.

"I can't... Archie we shouldn't," she said half-heartedly, making no attempt to resist him as he covered her mouth with urgent kisses. In her heart she wanted him; her head told her it was all wrong; her body yearned for his touch.

He led her towards the small, hard single bed that ranged against the wall. He undid his flies as Nelly removed her skirt and lay down on the dingy chenille bed spread. His desire to make love to her almost overwhelming him. He would not be able to wait long.

He ran his hand across her thigh and hips caressing her soft skin that lay just above her stocking top. As he kissed her, his fingers were searching the silky fabric of her underwear for the fasteners to release her. She lifted her hips slightly.

Sounds of laughter from Clifford's wireless drifted up through the floor as if mocking her.

"Don't worry, I promise I'll be careful Nell," he said as he removed her drawers.

She lay with her generous firm breasts exposed and her eyes half closed as she waited for him. She felt flickers of desire wash over her...*It had been so long... much too long.*

"My God you are magnificent," he drank in the soft curve of her belly and the firm, milky-white of her thighs. His fingers probed between her soft golden pubic hair as he prepared to enter her.

"It'll be all right, don't worry," he murmured, "trust me Nell everything will be all right."

She felt the comforting weight of him as he thrust inside her. The pent-up desire to feel a man within her after such a long time caused her to writhe and moan. She knew she was lost.

"You've taken your time with those curtains Nell. I was beginning to wonder where on earth you were.... and where's Archie by the way?" Clifford demanded the moment she re-entered the sitting room.

"He's had to go." she said as she drifted towards the kitchen. She craved a cigarette to calm herself.

Clifford's face fell a little; he had been quite looking forward to a cup of tea with Archie.

"I *only* said that I wanted to catch the last half an hour of "Old Mother Riley" and then the news headlines." he harrumphed.

"I didn't expect him to just up sticks and leave.... *Go upstairs and have a chat with Nelly for half an hour,* that's all I said to the man," Clifford said pettishly....."I mean to say if Archie's just going to turn up on the door step whenever it suits him, then he can't exactly expect people to just drop everything in an instant can he now?"

Nelly caught sight of herself in the mirror, her hair looked messy and a pink flush still bloomed on her neck.

"I thought he would at least stay for a cup of tea. Oh well, I expect he'll be back again soon enough; he's usually around here every five minutes these days."

Clifford picked up his newspaper with his soft white hands. "I think I would like that cup of tea now please Nelly," he said without lifting his eyes from the newsprint.

To Clifford she was invisible.

CHAPTER 34

Guilt

It was nearly two weeks before Archie visited Alma road again. In the dark days that followed their brief lovemaking she paced about the house restless and racked with guilt.

Why didn't he come? She couldn't remember a time when he had stayed away for so long. As the days passed, she was beginning to think he despised her. She had been a fool and she knew it.

It was almost the end of November now. Cold, dark days meant frequent back-breaking trips to the coal bunker with the hungry coal bucket; festoons of damp laundry garlanded the small kitchen refusing to dry and, on the doorstep the milk bottles popped their silver caps in the sharp morning air.

Nelly dreaded the long winter months stretching ahead.

Occasionally Alf James would stop and stay for a fleeting visit after returning little Jean from a morning spent with

Aunty Ivy. Clifford did little to encourage the man to stay. He found Alf superficial and gossipy with his incessant chatter about the highs and lows of his favourite football team, Cardiff City.

The vicious fire that had recently engulfed the Ninian park stadium had exercised Alfred deeply; the fate of Austria and violence of the Gestapo that exercised Clifford were dismissed as a ripple in someone else's pond. They had nothing in common except Jean and soon Alf came and went with only some ritual social pleasantries to mark his visits.

"How are you doing today Clifford?" or "I think it looks like rain again," became the extent of Alfred's repertoire before he invariably left with a cheery "give Uncle Alf a hug my little angel, you're always such a good girl for your Aunty Ivy.... see you soon poppet."

And Nelly knew they would.

With little to shape his long day, Clifford listened to the wireless as if his life depended on it. If the stories on the programmes were to be believed, then the world was beginning to be an increasingly fractious place; he fretted about the future.

For Nelly, cut off from the looming chaos and woes of the world outside, their lives inside the four walls of Alma road rumbled on with a turgid monotony. She felt cooped up and restless like a caged bird.

Every time the wind rattled the letter box, she waited for a rap on the door that didn't come. Her nerves began to fray.

Where the hell was Archie.

After so many days without a proper visitor, Archie's absence had been noticed.

"You don't think he took umbrage do you," Clifford asked. "I mean I wasn't rude the last time.... I only asked him to wait while I finished listening to "Old Mother Riley", I don't think that was too much to ask.... Do You?"

Clifford was somewhat puzzled by this unexpected turn of events. He liked Archie and was missing manly conversation; even more he missed the chance to chew over the latest developments in Europe.

Over the last week or two Clifford had become increasingly alarmed as news of Herr Hitler's ascendancy dominated the airways; reports of the rounding up of "habitual" criminals and Jews hinted at difficult times to come. He really wanted to discuss it with Archie. *Where was the man?*

"I mean to say, if people just turn up unannounced then...."

Exasperated she cut him off, "I really don't think Archie is like that Clifford, there's probably some other perfectly simple explanation."

"Like what?" He seemed genuinely puzzled that other people had lives to lead.

"Oh, I don't know.... how could I?" She said giving her full attention to the jumble of darning on her lap. "I mean it could be anything.... couldn't it?"

Clifford returned his attention to the wireless. A wave of whine and static grated on her nerves as he twiddled with the dial.

In the first few the days after Archie's visit Nelly had tortured herself with guilt. She tried to absolve her sins by cleaning the house within an inch of its life; scrubbing and polishing the crime away. One day as she was down on her knees scrubbing the front step, an image of Molly on her knees polishing the brass work at St Bartholomew's sprang unbidden into her mind. *"Damn and blast the man!"*

She felt frightened; it was as if day by day she were slipping noiselessly into a gaping void that she could not escape. *Where the hell was Archie?*

At least Clifford did not seem to notice the flurry of cleaning activity and he certainly didn't notice her; he only ever noticed her absence. *Nelly...Nelly, where are you? Nelly! What are you up to now?*

She hated herself for resenting her lot, she knew Clifford couldn't help being the way he was, and she struggled to keep alive a small glimmer of hope that a miracle *could* still happen.

Father Edwards and the congregation regularly included them in their prayers for the sick, but in her heart of hearts Nelly did not think God was listening.

At the start of each day, she struggled to gain control of her emotions, to will herself to be strong, not mourn the life they had had before polio. But the reality of their new life was sinking in and she found the prospect terrifying.

She was only twenty-six; she felt seventy-six.

Together she and Clifford merely existed in a world of repetitive routine, their days simply dawdled by.

Her fierce optimism in those early, warm summer days when Clifford had just returned home from hospital had tempered into a dull acceptance of their lot.

Nelly no longer dared to think about how things would be *when* Clifford got better. She forced herself to face up to the fact, that as far as Clifford's health was concerned, this was almost certainly as good as it was going to get.

Trapped in the house for dark days on end, a suffocating tension crept between them. Jean was fractious and bored with being cooped up. To spare Clifford's nerves Nelly made sure the little girl spent more and more time away from her joyless home.

"Shh Jean, don't clatter about so, Daddy's got another one of his headaches. How about going next door to see Aunty Ivy, you'd like that wouldn't you." became a regular refrain.

On other occasions Jean would spend her days with Nanna and Grandad Fowler who showered their only grandchild with oodles of affection; even they had accepted there was little likely hood of either of their daughters having any more babies.

Somewhere along the way Jean was getting lost and Nelly knew it. But what could be done, she had to look after Clifford.

The loud, triple knock on the front door caused Nelly to start. She had been engrossed in her work mending Clifford's socks; the sharp rapping jolted her into life.

"Who on earth can that be at this time of day?" Clifford said glancing at the mantle clock; it was almost two o'clock and an interesting programme was about to start.

"Tell them to go away, Nelly," Clifford grumbled. The radio crackled and fizzed with static and he strained to hear the commentary.

Nelly put down her darning and jumped to her feet, "I'll just go and see who it is Clifford."

"If you must.... but close that door behind you, I don't want all the heat getting out."

She pulled the door behind her and hurried up the gloomy hallway, wrapping her grey shapeless cardigan around her thin frame. Through the frosted glass she could see the familiar outline of Archie standing in the porch.

Her heart contracted a little. He'd come at last. She took a deep breath to calm herself.

"Hello there Archie," she said levelly, as she opened the door a little.

"Aren't you going to let me in then?" the half-opened door sought to bar his way.

"Come on Nell....You can't keep a man standing out on the door step in this weather; it freezing my what's-its off!" He joked, his warm breath huffed clouds of vapour.

She stood to one side and let him through.

"I thought for a moment there you weren't going to let me in and then I'd have to break the door down." Archie stamped his feet against the cold.

She frowned a little and looked as if she was about to cry.

"Hey there, is everything all-right Nell?" He took her by the shoulders, his dark brown eyes searched her face. "Come on them. Out with it... is something up?"

"Why haven't you called Archie.... I mean it's been ages since... since, well you know." She was hesitant, uncertain of what to say next. "I've.... Well, I just haven't known what to think. That's what's the matter!"

He could see the misery in her eyes.

"Oh, I'm sorry Nelly love, I've been longing to see you, believe me I have. But I *couldn't* come. My father has been so very poorly these last few days and I've been stuck in the house looking after him." He tilted her chin and caressed her face; her cheeks were so pale.

"Needless to say, Molly hasn't been able to help out with the old man," he said with a bitter edge to his voice. "All her time and energies are still taken up with that blessed church, and my poor old Dad was bed ridden with tonsillitis. He could barely swallow his own spit poor man.... I simply couldn't leave him to his own devices Nelly; he needed me to play nurse, get him things, fetch and carry.... you of all people should know what that means." Archie pleaded.

She nodded, yes, she knew only too well what that meant.

"Any way, I couldn't risk bringing an infection around here to little Jean and Clifford could I now?"

"No, I suppose not." Nelly felt guilty for doubting him.

"I came as soon as I possibly could Nelly, truly I did." He gave her a gentle lingering kiss.

"There.... am I forgiven?"

"Nelly....Nellie!... Who on earth are you talking to?" Clifford's voice travelled along the corridor and made her spring away from Archie's embrace as if an electric shock had passed through her.

"Coming Clifford, I'm just coming," she called. "It's only Archie."

Sorry she mouthed as she quickly hung up his damp coat and hat on the hall coat pegs.

"You'd better go through to the sitting room ... you know what he's like," she kept her voice low.

"Only after you've given me another kiss first," he said softly. He stooped to kiss her before she could object and then marched purposely down the hall to the sitting room.

"Hello there Clifford, long time no see." Archie said with a cheery lilt in his voice. "I was only saying to Nelly that I'm sorry I've not been around for a few days, but my father's been rather ill with tonsillitis."

"Oh......" Clifford's face registered alarm, he hated the idea of illness coming into the household.

"Don't worry Clifford, Dad's had the all clear," Archie added hastily. "I came around as soon as I could." he shook Clifford warmly by the hand. "I've *really* missed my visits." He added giving a winning smile.

"Well, I am pleased you've come." Clifford said as he extended his hand to shake Archie's. "It certainly has been a bit quiet around here lately, hasn't its Nell?"

"Yes.... yes, it has." She mumbled. Her heart was jumping around like a frog in a box, pounding so violently she felt sure they must hear it.

"And this awful weather is enough to drive a man mad, nothing but heavy drizzle for days on end.... I'm sure it interferes with the wireless; bloody static renders the damn thing useless for hours some days." Clifford said as he snapped off the hissing annoyance that squatted at his elbow.

"Well come and sit down and make yourself comfortable man.... take the weight off your feet before I get a crick in my neck." Clifford gestured towards the other armchair opposite the fire where Nelly usually sat of an evening. "Tell me what you've been up to these last weeks."

Archie settled his large frame into the armchair opposite Clifford's raised legs resting on a footstool.

Nelly hovered in the background, gathering up her sewing things and balling the socks into pairs. Cat like she watched the two men to see any signs that Clifford could sense a change had come over their relationship. She felt absurdly jittery and on edge. She willed herself to be calm.

There was an almost a palpable new energy in the house that had been lacking for days; she waited to see where it would lead.

Nelly fretted and fiddled as she tidied her things away. She didn't know if she would get to talk to Archie that afternoon, she had barely caught his eye. All his attention was focussed on Clifford.

Clifford on the other hand, was obviously enjoying having a new set of ears; someone who could pick up on the finer points of his analysis. He held forth with his views of world affairs and Archie listened with intense interest. The two men chewed over the implications of Herr Hitler's growing power and speculations of conflict. The conversation ebbed and flowed between the two men and she seemed to be forgotten.

Surplus to the room, Nelly decided to take refuge in the damp and gloomy kitchen and to calm her fractious nerves with a sneaky cigarette.

She made scones; her mind soothed a little as her fingers gently lifted and rubbed the powdery mixture into a fine crumb. Every so often she paused to listen to the gentle buzz of voices coming from under the door as the two men went over the finer points of their arguments. To her relief her heart had finally stopped pounding.

Over tea and warm scones, the conversation between the two men continued in a companionable rhythm. It was as if nothing in the household had changed.

Archie was an animated speaker. She watched his long fingers being tented and stretched as he gestured the finer points of his argument. It was hard to believe that only two weeks ago those same hands had caressed and cupped her breast; seeking out her nipple. Those same fingers had probed her sex and guided his manhood into her. She felt a flicker of desire between her legs as the memory came flooding back to her.

The mantle clock chimed five, it was almost time for Archie to leave; they had barely exchanged a dozen words; she didn't dare look at him. He made a move to go, rising from the low armchair stretching out his long limbs.

"Time I was getting along Clifford," Archie said.

She rose and drew the curtains against the night, in the darkness of the window-pane she saw his reflection looking back at her.

"It's been good seeing you Archie," Clifford said.

"And it's been good to see you both Clifford," his voice was warm, effusive almost. She could see Clifford smiling.

Nelly began to clear away the tea dishes, nervous fingers placing plate on plate. The click, click and chink of her best china being stacked signalled the end of their afternoon. She gathered up the crumbs from the cloth with a knife and placed the napkins on the tray. She would re-fold and use them again.

She must not look at him.

The fire was starting to get low. Standing now with his back to her by the mantle-piece, she could see the look of concentration on Archie's handsome face in the over mantle mirror.

Archie bent over the fire and riddled the clinker vigorously. A cloud of ash fell through to the hearth in a glowing heap. "Well, I'd best be off now Clifford.... I think I'll just pop out to the lavatory before I leave." he said.

Archie turned to face her, his eye caught hers and held her gaze for just a moment.

"Tell you what Clifford, whilst I'm about my business.... Shall get a couple of buckets of coal in before I go? It would save Nelly going out to that old bunker in the dark later on."

"Thank you, Archie.... that's a kind thought,"

He held the door open to let her pass with the tea tray. She murmured a small "thank you" as she brushed past him.

"And when I've finished getting that coal in, I'll fetch the cinder pan and get rid of some of that ash out from under the fire... that should see you both right for the evening." He started to follow Nelly into the kitchen. He paused.

"I'd better shut this door for you Clifford whilst I'm in and out to the yard. Wouldn't do to have all your heat go flying out the door, would it now?"

"Yes, yes Archie... thanks again." Clifford agreed with alacrity; he felt draughts acutely.

"I just want to try catch the evening weather forecast.... if I can locate the blessed thing again on the wireless. Don't know what's the matter with the thing is these days!" He harrumphed and turned his attention to the dial.

Archie closed the door behind him with a purposeful click; it would not blow open.

It was neatly done; he would have a little time with her before he left.

The whine of the wireless trickled under the door.

Nelly stood at the Belfast sink scraping and rinsing plates. As soon as the door was closed Archie stood behind her, he slid his arms around her waist. He kissed the small, soft piece of skin just under her ear. His lips barely grazed the wisps of downy fine hair at the base of her neck as he fluttered kisses towards her throat. He felt her tense slightly.

"Come here you, and put those dishes down," he said tenderly as he turned her around to face him.

He cupped her face in his hands and held her gaze. The gloomy acid-yellow glow of the pendant light picked up the mauve shadows under her eyes. Her shoulders were drooped a little and the life seemed to have ebbed out of her. The bouncy vibrant Nelly was nowhere to be seen.

She was so tiny and fragile looking, like a small bird gazing up at him. His heart melted, he knew she was struggling, but he wanted her.

He wanted her and he was not prepared for her to send him away. Not now.

"Look Nell....I'm really sorry you were worried; I'd never want to hurt you.... or Clifford for that matter. You know that don't you Nell?" He soothed as he stroked her face.

She nodded, her eyes darting towards the sitting room door. "Please Archie, I...."

He put a finger to her lips.

"Shh Nell....I just need to talk to you.... I promise I won't rush you. But things just can't go on as they are.... you must see that.... Don't you?"

She nodded dumbly.

"I care about you Nelly. You deserve life and happiness too; you can't just keep yourself tied to this house day in day out; everything revolving around Clifford and his needs."

"Oh, Archie that's not fair...It doesn't!" She protested, her eyes flashing.

"Oh, but it does... and you know it!" he retorted.

"Happiness isn't the sole preserve of just one person in this household... what about you and what about Jean? And where is Jean by the way. I haven't seen Jean in weeks now?" He challenged.

"She's just staying with my mother for a few days," Nelly said her face flushed with indignation. She hadn't expected this.

"Your mother, Aunty Ivy.... whoever. Nelly you know the truth is that anything that gets in the way of Clifford's needs and rules gets smothered or dismissed... and that includes poor little Jean! You drop everything for Clifford." He hissed struggling to keep his voice low.

"How dare you come here and criticise me?" She gasped.

"I dare Nelly, because I know just how it feels to be on the receiving end," he said bitterly.

"Because of what's happened to Clifford you're denying yourself a life and what's more you're shutting out Jean and everybody else for that matter...... just like Molly does because of our Billy!... Even after all this time she still only thinks about Billy.... Every day it's Billy, Billy, Billy and there's no room for anyone else in her life!"

Nelly could see the anger and hurt in his eyes. It was the first time in a very long time that she had heard him mention

Billy. She suddenly realized the date; it had been just over a year since Billy died.

"You know I'm right don't you?" There was a catch in his voice.

"I know, I know" she muttered.

"That's exactly what Molly says!" he retorted. "Clifford's not your gaoler Nelly; don't turn him into one."

She looked defeated. "I just can't help it......"

He hugged her, "but I know you can Nelly... and I can help you; we can do this together." He kissed her gently.

"Tell you what... how about I go home tonight via your parent's house, I haven't seen them in ages...."

"Why... what on earth will that achieve?" She said puzzled.

"I can offer to bring Jean home for you tomorrow, that'll save them a trip and at the same time I can check out the lie of the land with regard to giving you a bit of a break now and then." He explained.

"I can't.... Clifford... really I can't," she spluttered.

"Oh yes you can.   After all, If I don't ask for you, then it's never going to happen is it? ... *You* need a life outside these four walls and you need help." He pulled her a little closer.

"The trouble is Nelly everyone thinks you are coping.... And you are... but at what cost? At the end of the day, you aren't a machine.... no-one is."

"I can manage, really I can," her voice trembled a little.

She felt the warm comforting manliness of him as he held her close, his fingers gently stroking her hair. She hadn't been held like that in such a long time and she missed it so much.

"Let me care for you Nelly," Archie soothed.

She did so want to be taken care of, to feel valued. Clifford needed her and once he had truly loved her, but now he pushed her away. He could not stand and wrap his arms around her, she knew that.... but what was worse, he refused to kiss her.

Archie's soft words dripped seductively into her soul. Tearing at her resolve.

Oh yes, he was right, she did want to be cared for but most of all she needed to be wanted; to be kissed, to be made love to before she turned into a drab old frump.

She lifted her face and put her arms around his neck; she kissed him. He had his answer.

"You really should go now, Archie." She said softly.

"Not before I've done one more thing." he said untangling himself. "I'd better get that coal in or else there will be hell to pay," Archie said with a grin.

CHAPTER 35

The Plan

"Honestly Archie, I had absolutely no idea things have been that bad," Kathleen looked to her husband for support, Ernest remained firmly behind his newspaper. Only a small clearing of Ernest's throat indicated he was listening.

"She never said a word to me. I know she's had a bad time of it but.... I mean if she'd only said something...." Kathleen searched her memory for evidence of Nelly's cries for help. There were none. Yes, she'd noticed Nelly's sad looks and loss of bounce but then, that was only to be expected, all things considered. Her Nelly was a coper; she wasn't given to self-pity, her Nelly just got on with things.

Kath shook her head sadly; Archie's revelations about a weepy Nelly run ragged at the beck and call of an irascible, demanding, husband shocked her to the core.

"I mean when I saw them only last Monday.... Clifford seemed positively chipper.... I *actually* said as much to you didn't I Ern?" She looked to her husband for support.

Ernest gave a small non-committal grunt from behind the newspaper.

"We're talking about Nelly," Archie reminded her.

"Well of course Archie. I admit I have seen a few.... er.... *tensions.*" Kathleen groped for a catch all word to describe her daughter's predicament, "but only now and again.... and *certainly* nothing as bad as you're describing. I mean if only she'd said something...."

"Well I'm saying it for her," said Archie firmly. "Nelly is at the end of her tether and needs time out of that house, to have a bit of fun... a bit of life. And even more importantly.... she needs time to be with Jean."

Jean was squatting on the floor sorting buttons into coloured piles, at the mention of her name she lifted her golden head and flashed Uncle Archie a winning smile. She rummaged amongst her pile of treasures and picked out a choice specimen.

"Well now Jean.... is that pretty one really for me?" Archie reached to take the small gift of a gilt button embossed with flowers from the toddler's chubby fingers. "You're very kind. Thank you my little darling." Happy with the praise, Jean returned to her task.

"But the point is Kathleen .... she *won't* ask. Nelly's struggling along, stuck in that house day after day and Jean is being palmed off here there and everywhere so that Clifford can have her complete and undivided attention. Something has got to give," Archie said firmly.

"Jean's not *palmed off as* you put it Archie. We love having her here don't we Ernest? We thought we were helping the matter not hindering!" Kathleen bridled.

"No-one is suggesting you're hindering Kathleen... far from it. I'm simply saying there is more than one way of helping," he said, trying to smooth her ruffled feathers.

"We've all had a dreadful year one way and another. We've lost our Billy, and what with Molly the way she...." Archie hesitated uncertain of how to frame his next few words. "Well, you know what's happened to Molly... and all I'm saying is that we can't let Nelly go the same way."

"What do you mean...*go the same way!*" Kathleen looked terrified, memories of Molly descending into a kind of madness; long weeks with her locked away in Whitchurch and the whispers of gossiping neighbours were still all too raw in her mind. She despaired of her pretty, eldest daughter ever finding happiness.

Molly seemed to float about in a world of her own; terse and uncommunicative. But surely *not* her Nelly, that really would be too much to bear.

"What I mean is... can't we try to find a way to make next year better... better for everyone?" Archie pleaded. "A way to let Jean and Nelly have a bit more life and fun?... Take some of the burden off her.... we could *all* help.... isn't that what families are for?"

Kathleen looked bewildered. Archie had laid down the gauntlet and she had no idea what to do with it.

"Ernest?" She lobbed his name over the top of the newspaper willing him to put the damn thing down.

"Archie's right Kathleen. Just because Clifford is a cripple doesn't mean our Eleanor's life must be over too." Ernest opined from behind his newspaper.

Kathleen winced at the word *cripple*. To spare Nelly's feelings she invariably referred to Clifford as an invalid... but then her Ernest always did call a spade a bloody shovel.

Up until that point Ernest Fowler had stayed out of the matter; Kathleen was a strong woman with fixed opinions, and he knew better than to chip in when she was in full flow. Matters of emotion were best left to the women folk in his opinion.

Ernest had a reputation for being a man of few words, only speaking on matters of importance. But once his views were unleashed, they were invariably brutal and to the point. He had no truck with euphemisms; plain speaking and no nonsense, that was Ernest's mantra.

"Well, it's obvious Kathleen that the man isn't going to walk again so let's stop kidding ourselves! He's lost the use of those legs and no amount of praying on your knees in St Bartholomew's is going to bring them back. Praying and twiddling with rosary beads hasn't helped Clifford.... or our Molly for that matter!" He folded his paper and tossed it down beside his chair.

"Ernest!"

"Now don't you Ernest me!" he glared. "As Archie said we need to come up with a plan and that plan must include our Molly; she's spent far too long moping about polishing the pews at the church, or whatever it is she does all day. Her sister needs her, and Molly needs to pull herself together. She needs telling Kath, and the sooner the better!"

"Molly! Oh, for heaven's sake Ernest! What on earth are you thinking of! Are you really saying that we should somehow expect our Molly to...to..." Words failed her? Kathleen threw her hands in the air and looked flabbergasted at the very suggestion of asking Molly to help out. Lost for words Kathleen left the rest of her sentence flapping in the air; testament to the ridiculousness of the proposal. *Molly, for heaven's sake what on earth would Ernest think of next!*

Archie was equally stunned by this unexpected turn of events. His Molly helping out... well, well, well.... that certainly would be a turn up for the books! He didn't hold out much hope that old man Fowler would work a miracle on that front.

If the truth be told he felt that Molly was now absolutely lost to him, beyond reach. These days she barely so much as spoke to him and each day they simply drifted past each other. Archie was furious at her self-imposed, drab misery, beating herself up with blame, relishing her affliction as if doing penance for her loss.

In his opinion with Molly, it was all about Molly's pain, no-one else was going to get a look in. He felt it was more than about time that she pulled herself together.

Archie didn't give Ernest's new idea a hope in hell of succeeding, but he certainly wasn't going to say so.

"You can roll your eyes at me if you like Kath, but Archie is right. The *whole* family needs to pull together on this." The line of Ernest's mouth was set, he would brook no argument.

His wife folded her arms and stared back at him in defiance. How dare he speak to her like that in company, she was inwardly seething, but held her tongue. She would be having words with him later.

"I've sat by for far too long watching this family tearing it's self apart and it's time something was done about it." Ern said firmly. He stood up and planted himself four square in front of the mantle-piece; commanding the room. He was a short and stocky man with a grey toothbrush moustache and grey blue eyes that flashed with irritation when he was riled.

Archie could not deny that old man Fowler certainly had a presence about him

"Well *I'd* like to know how earth you plan to get Molly out her shell?... Go on Ern, if it's all so simple tell me how you're going to set about it." Kathleen's voice dripped with sarcasm.

"Well....I shall start by tackling that young Father Edwards, for one thing" he said tersely.

Kathleen flinched as if Ernest had slapped her. She had a soft spot for Father Edwards. The fresh-faced young priest had proved a great comfort to her and Molly over the dark months; she would not hear words said against him.

"What's Father Edwards got to do with it!" She squawked.

"Father Edwards needs to understand that *this* family needs Molly to pull herself together and do her bit. It might suit him to have her turning up as regular as clockwork, with Brasso and lint in hand spending hours polishing for Jesus..."

"Ernest Fowler....now don't you dare blaspheme!" Kathleen crossed herself.

"Oh tosh.... I'm sorry Kathleen but all this pussy footing around is not helping our Molly move on and it's certainly not helping the family. We've all let it go on for far too long." He fixed his wife with a steely glare that dared her to defy him.

"Archie needs his wife back and Nelly needs her sister and it's starting today.... As a priest it's Father Edwards' job to get Molly to see where her duty lies. She needs to see that there are others in this world with bigger problems than her own.... and if you won't tackle your precious Father Edwards about it...... then I shall!" Ernest said with emphasis.

Puzzled by grandfather's fractious tone Jean broke off from sorting through the button box. Her china blue eyes were like saucers peering out from under a mop of golden ringlets.

"Don't worry my chic.... Grandad's got a plan." Ernest said sweeping the little girl up in his arms to give her a big hug.

"We Fowlers aren't quitters!" he said. "Now, how about your Uncle Archie takes you back home to Mummy today, to save Nanna a journey? And then tomorrow Nanna and Grandad will come and visit Mummy *and* Daddy for a change. Won't that be fun poppet?"

Jean's eyes lit up and she nodded furiously in agreement.

Kathleen knew there was no point arguing, Ernest's mind was made up and there would be no shifting him on the matter.

"Come on my little luvvie, according to your Grandad it looks as if we'd better get you dressed to go back home with your Uncle Archie." Kathleen flashed her husband a withering look.

Jean scrabbled about trying to pick up the scattered buttons. "Never mind those my darling. Run along now, there's a good girl, and fetch your coat for Nanna, it seems Grandad. has got plans." Kathleen scooped up the buttons and Jean dashed out into the hallway to grab her hat and coat.

Ernest turned to Archie, "And if *I've* got anything to do with it, I'll get that Father Edwards to persuade Molly to pay

Nelly and Clifford a visit before the week is out" he said firmly.

"After all," Ernest reasoned, "if Molly can get out the house to spend hours visiting a plaster statue of the good Lord in a damp old church on a cold November day...... then she can *certainly* get out the house to visit her sister and brother-in-law in t*heir* hour of need...."

Kathleen folded her arms across her bosom, her head tilted to one side looking like a woman about to do battle.

"What is it the good Father Edwards preaches about charity beginning at home Kath?" Ernest left the question hanging in the air defying her to answer.

He knew Kathleen would not argue with him in front of Archie. His wife could have a very sharp tongue when riled but she knew not to cross him in public, this storm would brew and crash in on his particular shore later on.

Kathleen resisted the urge to snap back and merely rolled her eyes theatrically as if to say that the proverbial snowball had a better chance in hell than Ernest Fowler had of persuading Molly to visit Nelly, with or without any help from Father Edwards. She would have something to say about the matter when Archie had gone home. Ern could be such a fool sometimes- laying down the law to her indeed!

The thrust of her bosom and jut of her head as she marched out of the room conveyed her opinion of Ernest's hare-brained plan.

CHAPTER 36

Penance

The seductive sweet smell of incense, bees wax and old leather calmed Molly as she worked. She did not notice the dank cold. The long-pointed feet of the crucified Jesus oozing with thick gobbets of red blood against deathly white flesh seemed to speak to her. Those Holy feet invited her devotion and reminded her how His own dear mother must also have suffered at the loss of her only son.

Molly lovingly rubbed and buffed the alter rail; her finger-nails dark with wax, her heart lifting a little as the late morning winter sun glinted through the stained-glass window behind the stricken Lord. A brief kaleidoscope of green, blue, red and gold scattered across the floor transforming the dark nave, touching her pale hair with a lambent beauty.

Father Edwards watched from the vestry door as Molly bobbed and bowed on her knees before the alter, her slender arms reaching for nooks and crannies to be cleaned. Her devotion to St Bartholomew's was a credit to her. Never had the small Victorian church looked so beautiful, so tended, so loved. His heart swelled with gratitude that the good Lord had moved his servant Molly to devote herself to the service of the church.

When he first arrived at St Bartholomew's as a fresh young priest, a mere two years ago, he could not fail to notice the air of damp neglect that hung over the building, the lingering smell of mildew, the cobwebs and the tarnished lack lustre brassware. Now everything was calm and orderly, gleaming to the glory of God.

Father Edwards gave a small prayer of thanks for the gift that was Mrs Molly Smith and asked the Lord to help him with the difficult task that lay ahead.

He stood watching Molly as she went about her chores, captivated by the glowing scatter of light shards that danced across her back as she worked. The fleeting rainbow transformed her, illuminating her fragile form.

Molly lifted her dainty head; swept her slender hand across her brow to wipe away a strand of hair and a vivid image of a supplicant Mary Magdalene kneeling at the foot of the crucified Lord gripped him. The image was so powerful it caused him to gasp. "Jesus, Lord God, have mercy," he murmured fervently.

The young priest dipped his fingers into the small water stoup on the wall and crossed himself in holy blessing.

It had been the most difficult of mornings. Whilst preparing his thoughts for an Advent homily, tucked away in the small office attached to the vestry, he had been interrupted in the most disturbing way by an agitated Ernest Fowler.

Father Edwards had been quietly contemplating his Advent theme of *walking humbly with God* when Ernest Fowler fairly barged in his office, at just before ten o'clock and shattered his thoughts.

"Ah there you are Father Edwards, I thought I might find you here.... sorry to be disturbing you like, but I *must* speak to you on a family matter.... it's very important." Ernest blurted out. "I can see you're a bit busy like, but this really can't wait Father."

It had been three days since Archie's visit to the Fowler household. Ern had said he would speak to Father Edwards, and today was to be that day.

On the way to the church Ernest had rehearsed his speech over and over in his head. Words were not Ernest's strong point, but his mind was made up; things needed to be said and despite all of Kathleen's protests and pleas for tact he was going to give Father Edwards both barrels.

"Of course, of course, Mr Fowler do come in and tell me what's troubling you, the door of St Thomas' is always open." Father Edwards put away his papers and gestured for Mr Fowler to take a seat.

The priest saw the agitated look on Ernest's face. Mr Fowler was not a regular attendant at Mass to put it mildly, but his wife Kathleen was as devoted a Catholic as the young priest could have hoped for. Mr Fowler would need some work.

Father Edwards was quietly pleased that Ernest Fowler had turned to him in his hour of spiritual need. He flashed him a beatific smile

"Just ask away Mr Fowler and of course I will do *all* I can to help.... please sit down, calm yourself now and tell me what's troubling you," he soothed; his lean white face composed into a look of professional concern.

"Molly!"

"Molly.... er, er... do you mean Mrs Smith?" Father Edwards was thrown off kilter by the unexpected reply.

"Yes, of course I mean Mrs Smith...*our* Molly.... look I'm not going to beat about the bush Father Edwards.... you and I both know she'll be in here again this morning- just like she is *every* day, day in day out, regular as clockwork."

Ernest glanced around the tiny study cum office that only boasted a few sticks of utilitarian furniture and a small gas burner. It looked sparse and orderly.

"God only knows what she finds to do all the hours she's moping about here.... But it's *our* family that needs Molly far more than the good Lord does.... and so, I'm asking....no I'm *telling* you that it's your job to get Molly to see some sense."

Ernest registered the shocked look that crossed the young priest's face and the crimson flush that ran up his cheeks making the man look more like a young choir boy than a priest old enough to be in charge of a flock. In Ernest's opinion he still looked very wet behind the ears and the priest certainly didn't look old enough to be counselling parishioners about the troubles of the world.

"See sense? I *really* don't know to what you are referring Mr Fowler," Father Edwards said. "Perhaps you could enlighten me, and then maybe I can be of service." His voice was calm and courteous.

Father Edwards pursed his small pink lips into a pious rosebud and folded his hands across his cassock.

Ernest could feel his impatience rising; he felt sure the priest was patronizing him and it riled him.

"Well then to make myself perfectly clear, Father, I'll start, again shall I?" Ernest said enunciating each word as if talking to man a who was somewhat slow witted or hard of hearing.

"I'm here to have words about our Molly .... our Molly moping about in this church of yours, day in and day out for hours at a time when her own family needs her at home.... our Molly spending too much time helping *you* when she should be helping us! That's what I'm talking about Father Edwards...... And don't go giving me any excuses about Molly serving God...."

"Mr Fowler! Molly *is* serving God in her own way.... we are all called to serve God and some of us heed that call." He said pointedly.

"I'm sorry Father, but Molly needs to listen to some calls for help rather closer to home. If someone doesn't make her see sense, sooner rather than later, she'll end up losing her husband and her sister- *they* both need her as much as, probably *more* than, God does at this moment in time.... Our family is struggling, nay drowning under problems and I want to know what *you* are going to do about it.!" Ernest jabbed his finger back and forth.

The priest seemed to shrink visibly into his chair. "I see," he spluttered.

"Well.... what do you mean by *I see*" Ernest sneered? "It seems to me that you *don't* see what's under your very nose and that's the problem. ..... So, will you help Molly see sense about where her duty lies, or not?" he said firmly.

"Mrs Smith is a grown woman Mr Fowler.... far be it from me to tear her away from her service to our Lord."

"Rubbish! So that's how the land lies is it?" He fixed the young priest with a fearsome glare. "Pah... Call yourself a priest...... It looks to me as if you are quite content to see my daughter abandoning her marriage vows of loving, honouring and obeying her husband *and*....." Ernest searched his memory for scraps of Sunday school scripture, "and honouring her father and her mother," he boomed.

"Mr Fowler, please control yourself, and lower your voice!" Father Edwards pleaded. "Remember you are in God's house."

"I'm sorry Father. I'm a plain-speaking man and I can tell you now, I'm at the end of my tether with all this.... this malarkey. It makes me want to tear my hair out!" Ern threw his hands up in frustration, jumped to his feet and paced around the small room.

Father Edwards shrank even deeper into his chair. The small office suddenly seemed a rather dark and hostile place.

"Please calm yourself Mr Fowler. I'm sure we can find a way forward. Now that you mention it, I can see you *may* have a point," he said slowly. "Perhaps I could offer Molly, er Mrs Smith a little more spiritual guidance to help her move forward."

Ernest stopped pacing and fixed the priest with a beady stare.

"I do feel that Mrs Smith's devoted service to our Lord has helped her to....er heal over these last few months...... and I certainly don't think we should take that away from her...." Father Edwards added quickly.

Ernest opened his mouth to argue.

"But....but I agree that maybe we... er, er *I, ought* to try to make her see that God would want her to embrace all that life has to offer.... a good Christian always puts others before themselves."

"Exactly... my point exactly Father! Well, I'm pleased that's settled then.... I'll leave it with you to do, err" Ernest groped for the right expression, "err the necessary.... and I'll tell Kathleen that you have agreed to help." He fixed the priest with a steely stare.

"And..." Ernest said with emphasis, as the priest wriggled somewhat under his gaze. "And ... I can tell Kathleen that Molly can be expected to visit her sister in the *very* near future?"

Father Edwards nodded realizing it was futile to resist the wrath of Ernest Fowler; he was pinned to the spot like a prize specimen moth and there was no escape. "Yes, of course.... I will try my very best to...er"

Ernest cut him off mid-sentence. "Excellent! Well, now that's settled I shan't disturb you any longer, I'll leave you to your work and bid you good morning Father."

With that a victorious Ernest Fowler donned his hat, turned on his heels and marched out before the young priest could say another thing.

And so, it was that Father Edwards had found himself promising Mr Fowler that he would do his "best" to tackle the dilemma that was Molly Fowler. The only problem was he had absolutely no idea where to start.

"Oh goodness Father you startled me!" Molly gasped as she stood up and caught sight of the priest standing in the deep shadows of the vestry doorway.

"I mean.... I don't usually see any one in here at this time of the morning.... I shall be finished here in just a minute Father," she scrabbled to scoop up her cleaning cloths into a large wicker basket. Molly looked startled and flustered. "I just need to put this cleaning stuff away and then set out the prayer books for Mass and ...."

"I'm sorry if I made you jump Molly," Father Edwards said as he moved towards her in the rainbow light of the nave. "But I think those things can wait."

She looked puzzled. Father Edwards picked up her basket and led her gently by the arm "How about we go into my office and have a nice cup of tea instead?"

"But...." she protested.

"No buts...I have something I *must* discuss with you and it can't wait" he said firmly guiding her towards his office.

Her heart fluttered like a small bird in her chest and a wave of panic crashed over her. What had she done wrong?

Molly took a chair and sat perched on the edge, her hands rubbing frantically on her bony knees through her housecoat. She looked like a runner ready to spring out of the traps.

Molly watched as Father Edwards put a kettle on to boil on the small two ring burner. He placed some cups on a small tray and gave a delicate sniff at the rim of the open milk bottle sat on the window ledge.

"That's the marvellous thing about these draughty old buildings; milk keeps for ever at this time of year, put it on a windowsill and it's almost frozen some mornings...." He glanced around the office, "Now I'm not sure if we have any sugar to go with it.... ah yes, you're in luck, there is a smidge at the bottom of the bag if you'd like some?" Molly shook her head.

The young priest knew he was gabbling, uncertain of where to start. As he busied himself with tea making, he could see Molly was a bag of nerves, her eyes were a deep cornflower blue and looked like saucers in her small delicate face.

Until that morning Father Edwards had not noticed before how truly beautiful Molly Smith was. Her short cap of hair framed her face and threw her delicate features and sensitive mouth into relief. She had a young soulful air that reminded him of an image of St Therese of Lisieux that sat beside his bedside. For a moment the likeness was uncanny, he felt as if he was looking at her image made flesh; the same trusting eyes and heart shaped face gazing up at him.

Every night he prayed to St Therese to grant him resolve and faithfulness before God. Like her he too had known from a very young age that he must devote his life to the Lord, but unlike the blessed Therese he had struggled with his vows. That morning, as she sat in his office Molly, with her beautiful face looking to him for answers, pulled at his heart in a way that disturbed him.

"Lord, give me strength," Father Edwards muttered to himself.

He handed her the teacup and sat opposite her in a scruffy old armchair. In the tiny office their knees were almost touching. *Where to begin?*

"Molly, er..." he cleared his throat. "I'd like to say how truly grateful I am for all you do for us, really I am.... the church has never looked more lovely."

"Thank you, Father," her faced relaxed a little.

"So, I'm not quite sure how to say this but...." He stared into her eyes as they searched his face.

"Say what?" she said slowly.

"Well....I'm asking you to.... to spend less time here in the church and more time at home with your family."

Her cup clattered into the saucer. Molly looked devastated.

"But I haven't got any family.... not now. I only had Billy.... you know that Father. And Billy is here, here lying in the church yard. I visit him every day.... I must visit him! I must.... You can't ask me not to come and see him." Tears started to spring from her eyes.

"Please don't stop me coming Father... I'm begging you, please don't send me away!" She fell down on her knees before him and clutched his hands between hers.

"Come, come Molly don't upset yourself." Father Edwards tried to raise her from the floor. She flapped him away. On her knees she swung to and fro wringing her hands.

The priest felt helpless. He did not know how to handle a weeping woman beside herself with searing emotion. Long hours in the seminary had prepared him for theological studies but not for the complexities of the human heart.

"Why are you telling me this.... what have I done? You must tell me Father... have I done something wrong?" Molly pleaded.

"No... No of course not.... it's just that this morning your father said that your family......"

"My father! What on earth has he, or any of them for that matter, got to do with this? "She challenged, cutting him off before he could say any more. "The last time my father and my family interfered in my life they had me locked up in Whitchurch with the mentally feeble!" She spat.

She saw the shocked look on his face. "Oh, you didn't know that they had me sectioned in Whitchurch, did you? It was for my own good apparently." She sneered. "Have you ever been to that awful place Father?" She challenged him. "I mean- do you have any idea what it's like to be shut away in a place like that?"

The priest shook his head sadly. She was right- he had no idea. His heart went out to the broken young woman kneeling at his feet.

"Oh, I expect, at the time, to satisfy the gossips Mother put about some face-saving nonsense that I was taking the sea air or some such convenient lie... It doesn't do to admit there is a lunatic in the family, does it? ... I mean what would the neighbours think... no, no let's keep it all under wraps, bury the evidence, lock it away.... out of sight out of mind.... It was like being in prison." Molly said bitterly.

He could see the pain and anger in her eyes. She sat on her heels, her thoughts reeling.

"Perhaps I was mad.... mad with grief." she muttered. "'I'd lost the most precious thing in the world to me.... I'd lost *my* Billy Father Edwards.... I lost both my babies then.... Is it any wonder I was the way I was?" She held his gaze.

"Both?"

"Yes both.... God saw fit to take away another baby when He took my Billy," She gestured towards her taught flat belly.

"I used to think God punished me because.... because it *was* my fault Billy...." Her words became lost in the huge gulping sobs that overwhelmed her. Until now she had not dared to speak her fear of a vengeful God. With her head in her hands, she wept; hot tears coursing down her face.

"Hush now Molly.... you must believe that God loves you. When he carves out a path for us, we cannot always see where it will lead, but He does love you." Father Edwards knelt down beside her.

"Let us pray to Him for His help and guidance Molly," he said.

"I can't Father," she gulped. "I don't know how to pray any more.... I don't think God has been listening to me." She sat with her head bowed, the storm subsiding a little.

"God *always* listens. In the darkest of times God is always with you; just because you can't see or hear Him doesn't mean He isn't there with you sharing your pain. We cannot know God's purpose for us Molly, but He does have a purpose for all of us... Trust in Him Molly, His plan *will* unfold." Father Edwards urged.

He placed his hand gently on her head "Oh Lord, bless thy servant Molly. Help and strengthen her in her hour of need. Show her the light of your countenance and grant her the wisdom to accept the heavy cross you have given her to bear. Guide her back to the bosom of her family who need her and grant her peace of your love.... Amen"

Molly muttered a small "Amen."

He raised her off the floor. "I'm not sending you away Molly I would never do that. My door is always open .... and St Bartholomew's needs you, but...."

"But what about my Billy?" She pleaded.

"Billy is with God *and* he is in your heart. His earthly remains are in the churchyard, his soul is with God.... Billy will always be a part of you, no-one can ever take that away." He held her gaze, willing her to place trust him "and I promise you that from this day onwards I will remember Billy's soul every day in my prayers,"

"Thank you." Molly muttered.

"But your family *and* your husband need you too."

Molly hung her head "I can't." She whispered.

"What do you mean by can't Molly?"

She sat silent in front of him, eyes down cast, her faced contorted as if struggling to reach something deep within herself. Her fingers agitated and twirled the small buttons at the bottom of her cardigan, turning the small bead over and over.

"I just can't." She said miserably not meeting his gaze.

"Molly it always helps to unburden yourself; let God share your load, let Him help you." he said fervently. He could feel an ecstasy of love and compassion washing over him. This was to be his ministry; this was God's purpose for him. With God's help he could lead Molly Smith to salvation. She needed Father Edwards to lead her back to the Lord. He was fighting for her very soul.

"Father it's been.... er... years since my last confession.... could I, could I make ...." she stumbled, as if the words were reluctant to leave her mouth.

"Yes, yes Molly. Confess your sins to God and obtain His blessed salvation" He urged.

"I .... It's just that I'm just not sure where to begin," Molly said her eyes brimming with tears.

"Just take your time Molly and God will guide you. Say the sins that you remember and try to start with the sins that lie heaviest on your heart." He sat and waited for her to begin. The small clock on the office wall seemed to tick away at a snail's pace. He must not rush her.

She took a deep breath, closed her eyes and crossed herself. Her hands fluttered across her bony chest before she clasped them together in her lap, her knuckles blenched white with tension.

He nodded for her to go on.

"Bless me Father for I have sinned. It's been.... it's been such a very long time since my last confession.... Father I've been guilty of so many terrible sins in my heart; I have desired that which was not mine to have...... I covet another woman's child." She glanced at him nervously. "Father, wretch that I am, I cannot bear to see my sister's little Jean without wishing I could hug her to me and run away with her. Even now, with all that's happened to her husband, I'm envious of what Nelly has.... she has her child!"

"I know it's a wicked thing to say, but.... but I wouldn't care if *my* husband were afflicted if I could just have my Billy back....... And....I know I have neglected my family... but just the sight of Jean.... oh, the sight of all of them, just reminds me of my Billy and..... and of that place they sent me to." Her bottom lip trembled as she breathed short shallow breaths.

He heard the pain in her voice and his heart went out to her.

"For a while after Billy died, I hated my husband Archie.... he scrubbed him out Father.... every little bit of him tidied away out of sight, I couldn't forgive him for that." Her voice was bitter as she recalled the empty cot room devoid of Billy's things. The accusing stack of papers piled up against the empty nursery wall.

For a moment he thought she had finished. Silence stretched between them and the clock ticked.

"Also..." Molly faltered..." I confess that I have... have forsaken my marriage vows; pushed my husband away.... We don't.... I mean... I can't bear him to....to touch" she gulped before gathering herself together. She took a deep breath "and so I have denied him my body and I can't bear...." the words seemed reluctant to leave her mouth. She looked wretched, unable to say any more about her loveless marriage and she broke down, overwhelmed with racking sobs. "So please Father.... please don't ask me to.... because I just .... just can't!" She pleaded.

"Hush, Molly, don't upset yourself.... I'm sure with God's love you will find a way to rekindle your marriage vows. Sometimes these things just take time; be patient with each other."

She looked at him askance and shook her head.

"Trust me Molly. God knows *and* understands the trials and tribulations you have been through. You can do this. But He does expect the truly penitent sinner to try change their ways.... *and* their heart." His eyes glittered with intensity.

He played her like a fish on a line gently pulling her back towards God

"But that's the problem Father.... when my Billy died a part of me died with him.... Without him I feel dead inside" She banged her fist on her chest. "Every day I simply exist.... that's why I come here.... to be near my Billy and to ask God and the Holy Virgin to look after him.... I'm sorry Father.... but I just don't know how to live without him." She gulped trying to contain herself.

"He is being loved by God Molly... as a good Catholic you *know* that.... God gave his only Son to save us all.... to save Billy. In time you will feel God's blessed healing" He held her thin cool hand in his. "God has heard your confession Molly and I believe you are truly contrite...." he held her gaze as she nodded dumbly. A small tear trickled down her face.

"So, I am asking you to say a prayer of Contrition and six Hail Mary's," he still held her hand. "I'm also asking that you find it within yourself to visit your sister and her husband.... just for a few hours each week."

"But I can't." Molly gasped and pulled her hand away.

"If you are truly repentant Molly, then you *must*," Father Edwards cleared his throat. "If you are to join Billy and the angels in heaven then you *must* abandon the sin that you have confessed to and reconcile yourself to your family.... including your husband."

She looked as if she had been dealt a terrible blow. Her fragile, beautiful face looked to him for help, for reassurance. The rows of dutiful, elderly ladies in their black mantillas reciting their prayers by rote every Sunday did not need his ministry as much as the tragic Mrs Smith did. She would be his mission. She would be his quest.

This is why he trained as a priest. This was God's divine purpose unfolding. Molly was a fallen lamb who needed leading back to Christ. He knew then that it was his blessed duty to fight for the heart and soul of Molly Smith.

"Molly I know this will be hard for you," he soothed. "But as your priest it *is* my duty to tell you how to find your way back to God.... It will take time; the road to salvation is never easy, but you must try to walk it a step at a time.... You will never be alone, I promise... I will walk with you.... Trust me." His eyes glittered fervently, two bright splashes of pink tinged his cheeks.

"Oh, Molly it will be such a huge weight off your soul if you take the first steps towards reconciliation." Father Edwards said.

Molly felt backed into a corner. The thought of not being reunited with Billy because of her refusal to recognize her sin was almost too awful to contemplate.

"I'll try Father," she muttered.

"Bless you Molly. So, you will promise to visit your sister in the morning?... Just for an hour," he added quickly before she could protest.

"All right.... I promise Father.... and will you...?"

"I'll pray for Billy and I'll pray for you to find the strength." He held her hands firmly between his. "Go visit your sister ....and then we can talk again in the afternoon; I'm free after midday mass. I'll be here all afternoon.... I will be here whenever you need me." The priest held her gaze willing his strength to flow into her.

"Thank you," she smiled a small smile that didn't quite reach her eyes, but even so it gladdened his heart. He released her hands and watched as she slowly walked out of the office. She would return tomorrow afternoon and he would be waiting.

CHAPTER 37

The Visit

The sharp rapping on the door knocker roused Clifford to a fury. *Who on earth could that be at this hour of the morning? People seemed to be coming and going at all hours lately.* He felt a stab of irritation grip his chest. He took a deep breath and bellowed.

"Nelly the door... Nellieee!"

Nelly hastened to dry her hands. The bundles of washing sat steeping, greasy and grey in the sink. Jean was next door with Aunty Ivy. She had hoped to have a productive morning tackling the mountain of laundry scattered around her ankles. Now she was needed in the sitting room. *Bother she was just enjoying a quiet ciggie too!*

"Door Nelly!" he barked. "Door!"

"All right.... Just coming Clifford," she trilled injecting a false brightness into her voice.

The shirts and smalls would have to wait. Her once pretty hands looked chapped and sore. "Bloody dish-pan hands," she muttered under her breath. She ditched the dog-end of a cigarette into the slop of a te cup on drainer and flapped her house coat to disperse the odour of tobacco.

Despite the fact that it was only early in the morning, Clifford was already in a foul mood. He had just resumed his seat in front of the fire and was busy unlocking the hinges on his callipers. The unavoidable journey to the outside lavatory to perform his business had been a particularly hazardous one that morning. More than once his boots had skittered wildly on the icy path; only the handhold on the rose trellis stopped him from losing his balance, he'd wrenched the trellis loose and gained a thorn in his thumb for his pains. Today would be a day for bottles; he would not venture out again.

To compound Clifford's bad mood the fire sat smoking miserably in the grate. The coal was tarry and reluctant to catch on the overnight embers. His cup of tea had gone cold. It was a poor start to the morning and now, to cap it all, someone was knocking on the door.

"Nelly!..... There's someone at that blessed front door again.... tell them to go away will you. It's only just after nine o'clock for heaven's sake."

Nelly slipped into the small room rubbing her damp hands on the front of her rather stained house coat. "For goodness sake Clifford, give me a moment, for the love of God... You know I'm doing the laundry. I can't answer the door with wet hands can I now?"

He frowned. He was not used to being crossed.

She left the question hanging in the air and scurried towards the door, looping a stray piece of hair behind her ear as she went. "Goodness me, I must look an absolute fright," she muttered.

"Find out who it is.... and then tell them to go away," Clifford called after her retreating back. "People are trooping in and out of here like Cardiff terminus. I don't know what everyone's playing at.... tell them I don't want visitors today.... No visitors!"

She shut the door to the passageway to keep out the draughts and, just as importantly, to drown out her husband's petulant cries.

Her heels clicked on the grubby hall tiles. Her mind was racing. Who on earth could it be? Clifford was right, it was awfully early in the morning for visitors.

Archie came to visit them every other day now without fail and today was not his day. It couldn't be him again could it? She dared not hope.

She stole a glance at her appearance in the hall stand mirror. A dowdy, pale, scarecrow stared back at her.

"Just coming." she called out to the shadowy figure on the doorstep.

Her mother and father had already visited them twice this week and it was only Wednesday. Ivy James wasn't due to bring Jean back until after eleven when the washing was supposed to be finished. Who on earth could it be?

Perhaps it was a tradesman looking for business, or maybe one of those Salvationists who wanted to save her soul. Nelly reached for the door lock.

Through the patterned glass of the frontdoor she strained to see the outline of a figure wearing a greyish mackintosh waiting on the doorstep.

Well, it certainly wasn't the post man.

She opened the door cautiously and peeped through the small gap.

"Molly!" She gasped. The surprise of seeing her sister after all these months left her speechless. Her mother hadn't mentioned a visit and Archie certainly hadn't said anything of the sort.

In an instant her mind raced guiltily back to yesterday's hurried love making. So why had her sister come, and why now? Surely Molly couldn't be suspicious about her and Archie, could she?

Yesterday morning on the pretext of fixing the faulty catch on the bathroom door Archie had followed her upstairs. Their coupling had been briefing and urgent. A need satisfied for a while.

She knew it was wrong but their need for each other didn't seem too great a sin when Molly lurked in the shadows, never visiting, refusing to be a wife to Archie. But now here she was large as life, on Nelly's doorstep.

Nelly was lost for words. She felt a flush of embarrassment rise on her neck, certain that her guilt must be etched all over her face. Unable to move; blocking the doorway, she tried to gauge her sister's demeanour; waited for the outburst that didn't come.

"Hello Nell." Molly removed her neat, brown gloves and extended a bony hand of greeting towards Nelly, "er...can I come in?" Molly's voice faltered, unsure of her welcome; it had been such a long time. She tried to manage a small smile.

Relief flooded through Nelly, whatever the purpose of her sister's visit, it was not a visit in anger.

She roused herself. "Of course, Molly. Oh, my goodness sis... *what* a surprise. Come in, come in before all the heat leaves us." Nelly ushered her sister into the gloomy hallway. "Here Molly- let me take your coat."

With Nelly's assistance, Molly slipped her arms out of her mackintosh. Nelly briefly glanced at the rumpled grey cardigan that looked two sizes too big, it was oddly buttoned up over a worn-out blouse and a tweed skirt that had seen better days. Her sister looked shabby too. *What a pair we make.* Nelly thought grimly.

"Nellieee... what on earth are you doing out there?" Clifford bellowed from the small sitting room.

Molly shot her sister a worried glance. "Oh...If I've come at a bad time...."

"Not at all," Nelly lied. "Clifford is just having one of his mornings. I'm pleased you've come really, I am... Come on through." She took Molly by the arm; her fingers registered the scrawny lines of her sister's bony wrist.

"Just coming Clifford." she called. "We've got a visitor," Nelly announced praying he didn't say something rude about the unexpected guest. She ushered her sister into the gloomy sitting room that reeked of tarry, damp coal and soap suds.

"Oh, for goodness sake Nelly....I said *no* visit...." he began, his voice tetchy and bubbling with frustration. Nelly glared.

Clifford halted mid rant when he caught sight of Molly.

"Oh, it's you," he said ungraciously.

"Good morning Clifford," Molly said stiffly.

"Well... it's certainly has been a *quite* a while since we saw you last."

Molly flinched slightly as he drawled out the word *quite*, rolling it around in his mouth as if challenging her for an apology. His mouth set into a thin line and he fixed her with a hard stare.

Molly stood twisting her hands like a prisoner under cross examination in the dock. She thought of her promise to Father Edwards and took a deep breath in an effort to calm herself. The urge to make her excuses and leave was overwhelming, only the thought of confessing her failure to the young priest stopped her fleeing. Clifford did not look pleased to see her. She held the man's gaze as he glared up at her from his armchair.

"I hope I'm not disturbing you Clifford?... I could always..." she offered.

He cut her off mid-sentence. "No, no. Since your here, I suppose you'd better sit down and take a cup of tea with us." he said. "Nelly you'd better put that kettle on and make us all a cup of tea."

Dismissed from the room Nelly headed for the kitchen.

"Well don't just stand their Molly, take a seat, take a seat," Clifford said as if it irritated him to see her cluttering up the sitting room with her long, lean, able body. He flapped his hands in the general direction of the spare arm chair.

Molly took a seat as instructed; folded her neat white hands and came down to his level. She waited for him to speak.

Clifford had to admit his curiosity was piqued. He was somewhat intrigued by this unexpected turn of events.

"Well... this certainly is a turn up for the books. So, Molly, to what do we owe this unexpected pleasure?" Clifford gave her a small, considered smile and waited.

Nelly stood behind the kitchen door and strained to hear what was being said. Voices were low, murmured words that stayed annoyingly out of ear shot, but at least there were no raised voices. Her heart pounded and the dull throb of a headache inched its way across her brow.

Why had her sister decided to come?

CHAPTER 38

Sin

Archie arrived at Alma road as usual just after 10am. He had volunteered to tackle the rickety trellis, that was now hanging onto the wall by a thread and the spiteful overgrown rose bush that caused Clifford such grief the previous morning. Repairs were in order.

Archie disappeared off into the garden to get the tools; there was plenty to keep him busy. After settling Clifford with the newspaper and wireless Nelly headed for the garden. It might be her only chance to talk to him alone.

"Honestly Archie I nearly died, when Molly showed up, I didn't know what to think." She hissed before taking a deep drag on her cigarette...

"My nerves are absolutely shredded." Nelly leaned against the toilet door and exhaled another plume of smoke into the chill morning air.

"She stayed for absolutely ages chatting to Clifford *and* she said she'd be back again at the same time next week. Why on earth is she doing this...And why now? Nelly hissed...

"I mean has something happened?" She scanned his face for clues. She didn't dare ask if her sister suspected anything about the reasons for Archie's frequent visits.

They huddled by the tangles of the frost burnt rose bush. Nelly felt the rush of nicotine calm her frazzled nerves a little. Ever since her sister's visit her mind had been in turmoil. Nelly had barely slept a wink.

All night she had struggled with her conscience and her guilt. Tossing and turning until, in the early hours, until she had finally given up the battle and got up to make herself a cup of tea and rake the last few embers of the fire together. At least it would be warm when Clifford got up that morning, although he was sure to grumble about the scandalous waste of coal.

It had been such a long time since Nelly's last Holy Communion and her soul felt dirty...polluted with sin. *What had they done?*

In the early hours her mind had been made up. This madness must end. She would tell Archie that morning.

On the greasy path lay a tatty dead Robin, stiff legs jutting in the air, a small pool of rust and cream feathers scattered in the flower bed. She hated next door's cat.

"Did you know she was coming?" Nelly demanded.

"Umm No... not really." he mumbled. He dragged heavily on a cigarette, giving himself time. His face impassive.

"What do you mean by *"not really?"* Nelly hissed keeping her voice low for fear of being overheard by Ivy James.

"For heaven's sake Archie what on earth's going on? I don't see my sister for months at a time and then without so much as a by your leave she pitches up on the doorstep.... Why?"

"All right, all right, calm down Nelly. Your father did mention something about getting Molly to help you out last time we spoke.... but that was weeks ago and....and I didn't take him seriously, honestly I didn't."

Archie stubbed out the cigarette and tucked it up into the small gutter that ran along the outhouse roof safe from Clifford's sharp gaze.

"Come on Nell... you know what she's been like these last few months, it's been like living with a silent order nun; all church, prayers and penance .... I didn't think she'd actually come here, not in a month of Sundays." He tried to take Nelly's hand, but she pushed him away.

"Well, she has come... and she's told Clifford she's going to keep coming, every week! Apparently, she told Clifford that according to Father Edwards, it's her Christian duty to visit the sick and support her family."

"Bloody Father Edwards." Archie grumbled.

"Archie!" Nelly remonstrated. "Any way it's Father Edwards we have to thank for this sudden change of heart.... she even tried to make a fuss of Jean when Ivy brought her back, but Jean was having none of it."

Nelly shook her head at the memory of Jean hiding shy and uncertain behind her skirts when Aunty Molly tried to give the child a kiss.

"Oh, Archie this is such a mess.... Did she say anything about her visit to you when she got back?"

"No."

"What.... she just breezed back in without saying anything?"

"Not a word! Molly didn't come home until after three o'clock. I'd no idea where she'd been all day."

"Well why didn't you ask her?" Nelly snapped.

"Don't be ridiculous Nell...I've given up asking her what she does all day. We're just two ships that pass in the night... All I know is she left the flat just before nine o'clock without a word and that was the last, I saw of her until she strolled in some six hours later." He said peevishly.

"So, if she didn't go home, then where did she go after she left us?" Nelly was puzzled.

"I expect she went to St Bartholomew's in the afternoon as usual... But I've really got no idea what she's up to Nell, really, I haven't. I'm flummoxed and that's the truth." He reached over for her hand. "Come on Nell."

She pushed his hand away. "Don't," she said miserably. "Can't you see Archie... that this changes everything.... It has to."

"Why?"

"Oh, you are a fool... we both are." she added hastily. "How did it ever come to this Archie? All this skulking about like criminals, hiding in corners, carrying on under Clifford's nose. Well, it's got to stop.... We... I mean I..." her voice started to crack.

"What do you mean Nell? I don't want it to stop.... I don't want us to stop," Archie hissed as he pulled her towards him.

"There is no us Archie. It's madness to think otherwise." She snapped.

"I've been up half the night worrying about it.... You're my sister's husband and if she is trying to make a go of things then..." she looked up at him with eyes brimming with tears.

Molly felt tired and confused. What had seemed so clear cut the night before seemed less certain in the cold light of day.

"Then what?" He said softly. He put his arms round her, drawing her nearer.

She was caught up in the enveloping warmth of him. She leant against his chest and drank in for one last time the comforting smell of him; a spicy tang of soap mixed with tobacco. Her resolved weakened a little as his thumbs drew small circles under her ear lobes, fingers caressing her face.

"Please, don't be like this.... I need you Nell." he murmured stroking her hair.

"Clifford needs me..." She tried to pull away from him, "...and Molly needs you. So, we've got to stop this Archie before someone gets hurt...."

He cradled her face and kissed her forehead-a soft sweet butterfly kiss that made her heart melt.

Archie. Please don't make things any worse than they are." She added miserably, her voice trailed off as she dis-entangled herself from his embrace.

He stood strong and handsome in his blue check work shirt; his hands balled into angry fists. "Don't go in Nelly.... please," he pleaded, feeling her slip away from him.

"I must go, before Clifford misses me. He'll be wanting his morning tea soon.... and well know how he gets if he's kept waiting," she added lamely.

Archie tutted loudly "For goodness sake Nelly you're not his skivvy!"

"And Jean's playing upstairs," she added hastily, "if she comes down fussing and wanting attention, well...." She left the rest unsaid, gave his hand a small squeeze and turned to go.

"I'm very fond of you Archie.... you know that don't you?" she said over her shoulder. She did not trust herself to look at him again.

She headed into the kitchen, her shoulders drooping as if the whole world was resting on them.

He watched her through the grimy scullery window as she busied herself in the kitchen, clattering china and pots, making Clifford's tea. Every so often her hand fluttered up towards her face.

He felt sure she was crying.

He lit another cigarette and took out his fury on the battered trellis, hammering in the nails and hacking back the spiteful rose bush to within an inch of its life. Archie wasn't going to give up that easily.

It was the tapping and whistling that had caught Jean's attention as she played upstairs with her dolls in her bedroom. Her bed ran under the window ledge giving the little girl a good view of the tiny garden and over the wall into Aunty Ivy's garden next door.

From her bed Jean spent many an hour watching Aunty Ivy's cat hunting birds and Uncle Alf's shirts fluttering on the washing line like angry men waving their arms.

Looking out of her bedroom window she could just glimpse the little shed and the outside toilet. This morning Uncle Archie seemed to be very busy and he whistled as and knocked nails into the wooden trellis.

Jean loved her Uncle Archie. He was such fun. Mummy must love Uncle Archie a lot too because she came out to give him such a big hug and a kiss.

Sarah

Part of me toyed with the idea of just scooping up all the various bits and cuttings into a large envelope and then dealing with anything non-urgent another day. It had been too easy to get sucked into looking at photographs and pondering over nick knacks and the morning had drifted away from me with very little to show for my pains. Mum's table was still covered in piles of stuff and the box of rejects was accusingly empty.

But any thoughts of me packing up and calling it a day vanished when I discovered the puzzling envelope lurking right at the bottom of the box.

The A4 sealed buff envelope had a rather mysterious message on the front in my mother's spidery hand that demanded attention. It was addressed to me.

The curious words banished all thoughts of packing away.

"Dear Sarah

Perhaps the contents of this envelope should have been consigned to the dustbin of History a long time ago. I know as the eldest will be dealing with things so I'm sorry, but I've left this decision to you.

Feel free to decide to let by-gones be by-gones and throw it away unopened or you may wish to read it as part of our family history -the choice is yours. I am only sorry I wasn't brave enough to deal with it in my lifetime, but perhaps the "right" time never came and, as you are reading this, that time has now gone. I'll leave it up to you. Your loving Mother Xx"

Over a steaming mug of coffee, I pondered the dilemma. If it was a family secret, kept hidden for years, did I really want to know it now? Let sleeping dogs lie and all that...

As Gran always said, "curiosity killed the cat,"
And as I always said, "satisfaction brought it back."
I opened the envelope.

CHAPTER 39

Consequences

It was almost Christmas; the days were long and dark. Nelly made every effort not to be alone with Archie, not even for a few minutes. She could see from his eyes he was angry; a fierce brooding presence that dared her to change her mind. She didn't, but he still came.

Sometimes he took Jean out to the park, sometimes he helped with the heavy work loading the coal up or beating the dust out of rugs. Other times he simply sat with Clifford discussing politics and the prospect of Britain being dragged into conflict as tensions mounted abroad. But he never came with Molly.

Molly's visits had settled into a twice weekly routine; every Monday and Wednesday afternoon without fail. Nelly had to admit that her visits certainly did give Clifford something to look forward to. Her quiet calm demeanour seemed to sooth him.

Often the two of them simply sat by the fire for hours at a time listening to the radio with only the occasional observation on the weather or world politics breaking the stillness that draped over the room.

Frivolous chit chat and gossip from the world outside never burst through; Molly had entered Clifford's world on his terms.

Clifford was also teaching Molly to play bridge. From the kitchen, whilst Nelly prepared fish paste sandwiches and a pot of tea, she could hear Clifford patiently explaining the "art" of reading your partner; she recognised the irony that he couldn't read his own wife.

Molly's visits allowed Nelly to slip unnoticed into the background.

As the kettle came to a noisy boil Nelly retched and heaved over the sink; it was not the first time that day. In her heart of hearts Nelly knew she was pregnant. She couldn't hide the truth from herself any longer; she was going to have a baby and it was a product of her sin.

The smell of the bloater paste was revolting her stomach and she struggled to control the gagging that forced its way up her throat. She felt hot, and clammy.

The only other time she had felt like this she had been carrying Jean and they had both been so happy. Her and Clifford giggling at the prospect of being parents, so deliciously happy to be having their child together. The whole family had rejoiced.

But there would be no happiness with this child, this cuckoo. No congratulations and wishes of joy, no happy planning for the new arrival; no welcome for another little grandchild to gladden her parent's hearts. That happy, dutiful Eleanor was long gone.

Who was that person she thought ruefully as she swirled water into the sink; watching stringy mucus collect in the plug hole? Nelly opened the back door and took huge gulps of icy air in an effort to calm herself.

This was such a bloody mess! How could she have been so foolish? What would she do now?

Shame washed over her. A fallen woman.

Every day she had prayed for her period to appear. Every night she appealed to God to forgive her and make things right. Every morning as she heaved over the small basin in the bathroom, she knew her sin had grown a little more.

She would have to tell Archie-how could she not? And Clifford-Oh God what would this do to Clifford?

And Molly, how would she face Molly?

Please God I can't have this baby.... there's still time. Please God.

CHAPTER 40

More lies

It was Christmas Eve. The violent retching was subsiding a little. Nelly had escaped discovery; well almost.

"Just a little tummy bug, my sweetheart" had been the swift lie when Jean had caught sight of her mother heaving over the bathroom sink one morning, "no need to worry it will soon pass Jeanie." Nelly had become an accomplished liar.

"But don't tell Daddy, we don't want him to worry about Mummy do we poppet?"

As the nausea retreated a corner had been turned and there was no turning back. As the sickness subsided Nelly knew her pregnancy was firmly established. God had no intention of taking her sin away.

A rosy bloom started to appear in her cheeks. It had not gone unnoticed.

"You're looking rather well this morning Nelly." Clifford said.

Nelly was startled that Clifford even remarked on her appearance. He never remarked on her appearance.

"Oh err...am I?" Nelly distracted herself with plumping up cushions; perhaps the vigour with which she did so would give a reason for the accusing blush that graced her cheeks.

"Yes....I thought that you've looked a little peaky of late, even Molly remarked on it when she came last week. I said you'd probably been over doing it a bit, what with Christmas coming and everything." Clifford looked at her with his cool brown eyes, she felt he could peer into her soul.

Unable to hold his gaze Nelly crossed over to the fireplace and made a noisy effort to knit the fire together.

"Yes.... well, I had felt a little under the weather for day or two," Nelly admitted.... "but I'm better now," she added hastily keeping her back to him.

"There, that's the fire sorted, it should be fine for an hour or two, "she rubbed her hands down her baggy house coat.

"Are you going out then Nell?"

"Yes, Clifford.... I'd better pop around to the greengrocer before the morning runs away with me. Mr Hallit promised to put my Christmas order up, but you know how things are these days, I'd better not leave it too late in the day or that dopey lad of his might sell it to another customer."

Satisfied with the explanation Clifford returned to his newspaper." Well don't be too long," he ordered over the top of the broad sheet.

Nelly strolled around to the of shops clutching her coat against the raw wind, her mind whirled hither and thither-. *what should she do, what on earth should she do?*

As she walked immersed in her thoughts her eye was caught by the large number of perambulators that were parked outside the various outlets on the busy parade. Chatty mothers queued to purchase their Christmas provisions and as the queue of mothers snaked into the dark recess of the butchers, their babies took an airing.

In her misery Nelly looked at the ranks of babies laying snug in their knitted hats and mittens, swaddled up against the December chill, noses pink and rosy in the sharp air.

"Ah good morning to you Mrs Harris."

Molly jumped as a chirpy voice close to her elbow wished her good morning. It was Edith Teasdale, a gossipy woman in her early fifties who lived just two doors away from her mother.

"Morning Mrs Teasdale." Nelly watched as Edith tucked a stray corner of blanket back into the pram." The baby stirred in his sleep; little pink starfish hands flexed.

"There you are darling that's it...we can't have you getting cold, can we?" Edith flashed Nelly a smile. "He's such a bonny baby... of course mine are all grown up now." Edith gazed at the sleeping infant. "Just makes you want to bundle up one of these little darlings and run away with it doesn't it? Gorgeous that's what they are at this age.... scrumptious.... all God's little angels." She cooed in a sing song voice.

Nelly hmmed in vague agreement.

Edith poked her head into the first carriage in the queue, "This is Sally Perkins' little lad Frank, he's an absolute charmer; just like his father aren't you my precious." Mrs Phillips gave a throaty laugh. "Well, my baby days are long gone, but as I said to my Jack, when they are little like this, I wish I'd had dozens instead of just the two boys. But my Jack

330

wouldn't hear of it. *Two lads are more than plenty Edith, he used to say... double trouble."*

Edith chucked the dozing child under the chin. "Ooh but I'd have loved a little girl. They always say girls cleave to their mothers." Edith sighed at the absence of a daughter.

"Mind you I never left *my* boys outside like this though. Goodness me no... I always worried some poor childless soul would spirit them away. Never took my eyes off them for a minute I didn't. People can be desperate you know."

Edith Teasdale chattered on, barely taking a breath as she opined on the craft of parenthood.

"I mean you've got to pity the poor souls who can't have one of their own haven't you? It doesn't bear thinking about... not being able to have babies of your own... Tragic it is.... Oh, just look at his little face!" Edith oozed.

The tiny bundle started to squirm and thrash in the pram, with mouth agape like a fledgling chick, Frank twisted his little head from side to side until he was nearly swallowed up by his knitted bonnet.

"Come on let Aunty Edith sort that out for you my little man... we can't have you tying yourself in knots, now can we?... There, there, Mummy will be back in a minute." She cooed as she gently straightened the baby's bonnet and tucked the blanket up around his chin.

Mrs Phillips caught sight of the pained expression on Molly's face. "Oh, I'm sorry to be prattling on so Mrs Harris... now tell me, how is that poor husband of yours dear?"

As Nelly trundled home with her basket of vegetables, groceries and Christmas nuts a thought started to blossom in her mind. The idle chatter of Edith Teasdale had set a hare running that was beginning to offer a small glimmer of hope.

Nelly was beginning to see the outline of a plan, but first she must get rid of Archie.

CHAPTER 41

Nelly

"What do you mean I *can't* come in Nelly?" Archie was flummoxed.

Why on earth was he being denied entry to the Harris household on boxing day morning? He had said the day before Christmas Eve that he would pop in with Jean's present and now Nelly wouldn't let him in. He could barely conceal his agitation as he hovered on the doorstep. She had been very distant of late, but this was very odd indeed.

Being barred from entry spoke of contagion. The dreaded measles was rampaging through Cardiff...*had someone in the household gone down with measles or worse?*

"What's wrong Nell.... is someone ill.... is it Jean?"

"No....No-one is ill...Jean's fine thanks, Archie." Nelly had only opened the door a few inches, but it was quite obvious from her stance that she had no intention of letting him in.

Archie visibly relaxed a little at hearing no-one was ill, but Nelly still blocked his way. He could not read her expression. He edged a little nearer.

"What I mean is that you can't visit us anymore, not this morning, not now," Nelly held his gaze as he recoiled as if she had slapped him. "Not ever," she added.

He stood with his mouth gaping in disbelief, lost for words.

"What do you mean.... why what's happened?" He said suspiciously.

"Nothing....It's just for the best Archie." Nelly started to shut the door.

"What do you mean *it's for the best* "he parroted her prim pronouncement.

"Who says it's for the best" Archie fumed as he slipped his foot in the door, "Who Nelly?"

"Father Edwards," Nelly lowered her eyes as she spun the lie.

"I've made a *full* confession to Father Edwards and he has offered me absolution if I repent of my sin and return to my marriage vows. He said I must give you up ... completely.... so, I am." She didn't dare look him in the eyes.

"Bunkum...that's religious mumbo jumbo and you know it Nelly! What does that snivelling, sexless, ninny know about... about anything?" Archie hissed.

Nelly looked shocked, "he's a man of God Archie and please keep your voice down or the neighbours might hear."

"Pwah.... bloody nosey neighbours, who cares what they think?" He spat.

"I care! Please Archie don't make a scene." She could see he was totally wrong footed by this unexpected turn of events. She willed him to walk out of her life, out of their lives. For her plan to work Archie must never suspect she was carrying his baby.

All night she had lain awake hatching her plan she could not afford to weaken now. If she allowed Archie to come in then she was lost. "I'm begging you Archie....don't make this any more difficult than it is.... Please go.... I want to you to go for all our sakes." Nelly added lamely.

"If I go now Nelly.... I won't come running back," Archie sneered. "I love you Nelly but I'm not being taken for a fool.... dancing around on a string *just* because you need a man to do odd jobs about the place occasionally." He knew he was being cruel, but the sting of her rejection goaded him to a fury. How could she just toss him aside like this?

"Don't say that Archie... that's not true and you know it" Molly said miserably, "I'm sorry.... really, I am. But it's because I care for you, that I mustn't see you again.... Try to make it up with Molly, for all our sakes," she pleaded.

"Don't tell me what to do," he snapped, "You lead your life Nelly and I'll lead mine. I've obviously made a very big mistake and from now on I'll start looking after number one... I've obviously misjudged you Nelly."

"What will you do?" she said anxiously.

"I'll get a very long way away from here, that's what! From now on what goes on my life is absolutely none of your business." He blustered determined to lash out.
Archie removed his foot from the door and turned to go.

"Oh, I nearly forgot...You'd better take this; it's for Jean," he handed her a small, wrapped parcel tied up with a silvery cord. "Tell her it's from Uncle Archie and if she ever asks where Uncle Archie is, then you'd better have a good excuse ready and waiting because blaming it on Father Edwards isn't going to wash." Archie said bitterly.

She fought to hold back the tears; shamed by his anger. She watched his retreating back as he stomped off down the road, hands thrust deep in his coat pocket.

You don't know how sorry I am about everything Archie. You can never know.

Nelly trailed down the passageway back to the sitting room. Before she entered the room, she pasted a bright smile on her face.

Jean was sat cross legged by the fire chattering to her daddy about her wonderful new pop-up book from Nana and Grandad; the little girl was blissfully unaware of the drama that had unfolded on the doorstep.

Nelly's heart lurched as Jean jumped up and rushed to look behind her into the hall "Mummy, Mummy where's Uncle Archie.... is he hiding?"

"No Poppet, Uncle Archie couldn't stop this morning.... but look he left this present for you...Isn't that nice." Nelly swiftly distracted the little girl and the crisis passed in a frenzy of torn paper and string. An exquisite, small cloth doll emerged with long brown plaits and a pink gauzy dress.

"A new dolly!... I think I'm going to call her Margaret. Isn't she pretty Mummy?"

"Yes, very pretty, now why don't you take her upstairs to meet all your other dollies, I'm sure she would like to make friends."

Jean scampered off with her prize.

Clifford raised an eyebrow. "So why didn't he come in Nell.... it's not like Archie to miss a visit."

Nelly took a deep breath and started on the next stage of her plan. "It's my fault Clifford.... Archie has taken offence at something I said and I told him he wasn't welcome in our house."

"I see.... and what did you say that could have caused this reaction... you haven't said anything to me about it," Clifford said crisply.

She took a deep breath, her eyes darted about nervously. "Well the other day Archie made it clear he was going to seek "comfort" outside his marriage because he was fed up with Molly and the way things were between them."

"I see... so why would he say that to you?" Clifford's dark brown eyes pierced her.

This was the dreaded question that Nelly knew would come.

"Because he wanted to know if I felt the same." She stared straight back at him, holding her nerve. "I'm not *exactly* sure what he meant by it... you know about me feeling the same way.... but I told him straight that his duty lay with my sister. After all it's not Molly's fault she's been ill is it?"

"True." Clifford kept his thoughts to himself letting her spin her yarn.

"I'm not absolutely sure he meant anything by it Clifford really I'm not.... I mean he didn't make a pass or anything.... and perhaps I got the wrong end of the stick.... But when I got cross at the thought of him wronging my sister like that, he got very angry and said that I had been just using him to do odd jobs about the place. He accused me of moralizing and then this morning he told me I was a busy-body and refused to come in."

She made a mental apology to Archie for maligning him.

Clifford bristled at the man's accusation of "being used" as an odd job man. He was only too aware of his helplessness and the jibe hit home. He had obviously misjudged the man. He resented Archie's high-handed manner. How dare the man embroil his wife in his sordid plans to seek gratification elsewhere. They would manage without him.

"Well under the circumstances, if he's going to be like that, it's just as well he didn't come in. I do wish you'd told me about this before, Nell then *I'd* have had something to say to him.... man, to man" Clifford chided. He was irritated that his wife had gone over his head.

"Sorry Clifford I didn't want to make a fuss; I know how much you dislike unpleasantness. Perhaps I overreacted.... but I was thinking of Molly, and then when he started accusing *us* of using him, I thought it was all too much. I said if he thought like that then he was ...." she ran her fingers through her hair distractedly. "Well, I said it was a bloody cheek and that I'd rather he didn't come at all if he felt like that!"

"I'm sorry I've messed things up, especially for Jean.... and for you," she added lamely.

"You did the right thing Nelly. If the man's got an ounce of sense he'll work at his marriage and if things work out between Molly and him then.... then we'll see. *Handy man* indeed! In future if we need any help, then we'll pay for it.... We're not a charity case.... The nerve of the man!"

"And please don't say anything to Molly, will you?" Nelly pleaded. "You know how fragile she is... I couldn't bear it if something were to set her off again. Things are bad enough between her and Archie as it is....and I don't think my poor mother could cope with any more upset if Molly were to be taken poorly again." Nelly screwed in place the final nail in her coffin and was gratified to see Clifford give a small nod of agreement. With Clifford's help, Molly would be none the wiser.

"We'll say no more about it Nell.... I think I'd like that cup of tea now please."

"Yes of course Clifford, "she said meekly.

That evening as Nelly lay in bed between the ice-cold sheets, she pondered her next move.

Now she just needed to get fat. For things to go smoothly she would have to hide herself under her baggy house coat, add a few socks for padding and appear to eat her way into her new shape. With the use of corsetry and baggy clothes she felt sure she could keep up the deception. After all, when she was carrying Jean, she barely showed for the first six months, her generous bosom always gave her a matronly appearance at the best of times- now it could come to her aid.

When her time came Nelly had decided that she would deliver her baby into the safe hands of the church; a small precious bundle that would be discovered within hours by the sisters of St Bartholomew's. With Clifford unable to go upstairs or leave the house she felt sure she could do this... it was her only hope.

As Mrs Teasdale pointed out on Christmas Eve some childless soul would be desperate for a little baby to call her own. Nelly could give someone else the joy of bringing up her baby.

"Don't worry" she crooned as she stroked the small swelling in her abdomen. "It's going to be all right.... everything is going to be all right."

She felt a small flutter deep within her; for the first time she felt her baby move.

"Please God forgive me," Nelly murmured.

CHAPTER 42

Decisions

It was the beginning of February and Archie had kept away from Alma road for weeks on end.

The long, dark days were trying Clifford's patience and, even though he wouldn't admit it, he was beginning to regret the decision to deny Archie the right to visit. Perhaps they'd both been a bit hasty.

As Nelly had said herself, perhaps she had got the wrong end of the stick and made a mountain out of the proverbial mole hill. After all what went on in Molly and Archie's marriage was really none of their business. Clifford reasoned.

The kitchen tap had developed a persistent leak that created an annoying drip, drip, drip, into the sink. No matter how many times Clifford urged Nelly to turn the tap off fully the tap continued to drip. It grated on his nerves whenever Nelly left the kitchen door open. It was like Chinese water torture. *Drip! Drip.*

Clifford tried to concentrate on the news on the wireless but the sharp, penetrating noise of water hitting porcelain drove him to distraction. *Drip, drip, drip.... drip.* Sometimes he would think it had stopped and for a few blissful moments his irritation subsided, he held his breath waiting to see if his torment was over. Then like some malevolent being it would start to torture his nerves again. *Drip....*

Bloody washer needed fixing, that's what it was.

Clifford had told Nelly to make sure she closed the door properly that very morning before she went out; he'd insisted on it. He'd even heard the click of the latch as it landed home. But now the door was well and truly open again. *Drip..............drip.* It was the damn draughts that whistled through the old house that caused the door to pop open.

The dripping seemed to worm its way into his brain. *Drip....drip.* Clifford would either have to wait for Nelly to come back from the shops or he would have to fix his callipers into position make his way over to the door to shut it again.

Neither option would resolve the matter of the faulty tap and anyway in all likely hood the blessed door would spring open again as soon as he resumed his seat. *Drip, drip,............drip!*

Archie would have sorted it out in a trice.

Apart from Molly's twice weekly visits few people troubled Clifford's world. Since old man Fowler had had a bad fall over Christmas Nelly's parents tended to stay at home fearful of slipping on the icy pavements. Father Edwards came once a week to dispense the Holy sacrament to him, but otherwise it was just him and Nelly... Oh and of course Jean.

From his chair in the back-sitting room Clifford could just glimpse a leaden skyline and the watery, winter sun that rarely broke through the clouds and never managed to pierce the gloom of his sitting room.

Even the view through the net curtains from the vantage point of his bed in the front room only showed a few hardy souls braving the element. Those who could stay indoors did. He hated the winter.

Drip...

Thank goodness it was Wednesday at least he would play Bridge with Molly that afternoon. Clifford always won of course but she was improving and soon she would be a worthy opponent. Maybe he might just drop a small hint to Molly about Archie dropping in, the man should have learned his lesson by now. After all Archie was family.

Drip....

Molly's day was also not going to plan. She sat in their chilly flat surrounded by her thoughts and the wreckage of her marriage. A Hessian bag of Archie's cast-off things sat in the middle of the floor, his winter felt hat sat perched rakishly on the top of the lumpy bundle, as if it were a makeshift guy waiting for coins.

Molly had spent the morning at St Bartholomew's rubbing bees wax into the church pews until the old oak fairly glowed a glossy treacle colour. Afterwards she visited Billy with a few sprigs of fragrant Winter sweet to lay on his grave. She liked to keep his memorial looking nice; spring bulbs would soon be breaking through.

When she came home the flat had seemed oddly quiet, as if the life had finally gone out of it somehow. She hadn't really expected Archie to be there; he so often wasn't. But flat seemed to know something was up and the silence was unusually heavy.

The letter left propped on the mantle was short and to the point.

"*Dear Molly,*

There's no point us tormenting each other any longer. I have waited for you long enough, but it seems that you have decided to embrace the past whereas I need to reach out to the future. I'm a family man Molly and without Billy or even the hope of another son I cannot see the point of us.

I'm sorry it had to come to this, but I have decided to leave Cardiff. I have accepted a job with the Malaysian Rubber Company managing their exports. Business is booming over there now, it seems that a man with no attachments can go far. There seemed no point in discussing the matter with you as we no longer have anything to say to each other. I have made arrangements for you to stay in the flat for as long as you want. I will send you a monthly allowance so that you will not want for anything.

Tell anyone who asks that it's all my fault, but I won't be coming back. Cardiff holds nothing for me now......By the time you read this letter the Lady Eloise will have set sail.

Goodbye...Archie"

The lumpy bag contained his heavy winter clothes and a note to drop them into the church collection point for the down and out; he would have no need of them in the tropical heat. Archie was gone.

She should have cried for the death of her marriage, but all her tears had been shed for Billy. A small part of her felt that it was no more than she deserved but on reflection at least she was no longer bound by her promise to Father

Edwards. No more promises to keep. She felt oddly at peace.

   -Archie was gone.

CHAPTER 43

Gone

It was already nearly a quarter to twelve. Nelly had stopped chatting for far too long as she went about her errands and now the morning was slipping away from her. She scurried back from the shops with her few groceries including some pig's liver for a dinner of liver and onions. She knew Clifford would grumble about the lack of his favourite lamb's liver, but the butcher assured her there was none to be had. Pig's liver it had to be.

"Soak it in milk Mrs Harris for a few hours before cooking.... a nice dish of milk will remove any trace of bitterness, that's the secret.... Fairly transforms it, it does......Nothing wrong with a nice bit of pig's liver.... Succulent it is and, in my opinion far tastier than the lambs.... I bet you a pound to a penny you'll never notice the difference."

She knew Clifford certainly *would* spot the difference but there was nothing to be done about it. The shops were worryingly empty of late and beggars couldn't be choosers. Pig's liver would just have to do.

Nelly tried to clutch her brown; woollen coat closer to her chest to fend off the bitter North wind that wanted to cut right through her. The struggle to get the coat to meet in the middle was beginning to defeat her. She'd already moved the top and middle buttons over an inch or so to accommodate her swelling abdomen. At this rate she would have to try moving them again and soon she would run out of spare cloth.

She hoped Spring would arrive early this year; there could be no new Winter coat.

Every day she inspected herself in the wardrobe mirror; it was getting harder and harder to hide the growing bump. She lived in baggy cardigans, *to ward off the cold Clifford.*

Nelly practised her angles in the long mirror in order to present herself to best advantage. From the front she had to acknowledge her figure looked unchanged, but in profile however it was a rather different matter; her breasts were fuller and she looked decidedly rounded.

When she been carrying Jean, she hadn't even started to show by twenty-two weeks. She'd had the smallest, neatest bump with most of her pregnancy weight evenly distributed around her hips and thighs. Everyone had commented on how neat she was. This baby however was determined to make its presence known and seemed to resolutely thrust itself forward. Perhaps it was a boy?

She didn't dare let herself think about the baby-it was not hers. She told herself over and over it was to be her gift to some poor couple that would love it; she would never know it's future, never experience the suckle on her breast and drink in that warm oatmeal smell of a new-born after she had rocked it to sleep. That would be her penance.

Father Edwards would find the baby a good home she was certain of that. It was not her baby. It could never be hers.

She picked up the pace as she cut through Inkerman street. She would soon be in Alma road.

Molly would join them this afternoon for her usual game of cards with Clifford- Nelly would be sure to sit with a basket of darning on her lap; there was always plenty of mending to do. Under a jumble of socks her lap would be hidden from view. Once the two of them were engrossed in their game, she could slip out into kitchen to prepare the sandwiches. Her sister had gimlet eyes.

Luckily Molly's chair at the card table meant her back would be to Nelly for most of the afternoon, with some deft serving of the afternoon tea Nelly would be safe from her sister's prying eyes.

Nelly stepped up her pace, her small heels clicking rapidly on the greasy paving slabs. She needed to get a wriggle on or Clifford's dinner would certainly be late. There would be no time for soaking the offending liver. Pig's liver would cause enough of a grump; late pig's liver would be beyond the pale!

The dinner had gone as badly as Nelly had feared it would. Clifford had pushed the fried pig's liver around his plate grumbling and tutting at the lack of tender lamb's liver. He made a huge play of finding stringy bits of veins that seemed to have piled themselves onto Clifford's portion; they were arranged accusingly around the rim of his plate like grey, dead worms that had somehow drowned themselves in gravy. With every forkful the tally grew.

To add insult to injury, in her haste, Nelly had salted the potatoes twice making the mash and onion gravy as salty as Lot's wife. Even the savoy cabbage seemed tough and lack lustre. Clifford, who abhorred waste picked his way through the wreckage of his meal with a face like thunder.

She had hoped that Molly's afternoon visit would be a welcoming distraction from the dismal dinner; Clifford was in dire need of cheering up. Beating Molly at Bridge that afternoon might do the trick and take his mind off the vexed subject of pig's liver.

She had not expected Molly to drop the bombshell that threw Clifford into a complete tailspin! It certainly knocked all discussion of stringy liver out of the question.

"No, I'm afraid Archie can't pop around to help fix that tap Clifford," Molly said coolly. She didn't even raise her eyes as she contemplated her hand of cards.

Clifford looked dumbfounded. He had just spent a good fifteen minutes indulging in casual chit chat before slipping in a request for Archie's services to silence the drip. He had not expected to be rebuffed. "Oh...I see," he said, when he plainly didn't see at all.

"He can't come, because he's left." Molly added as she arranged her cards into suits. Her face was impassive as if this announcement was of no great consequence what so ever.

"Left!" Nelly gasped.... "What do you mean by left?"

"I mean exactly that Nelly.... he's packed his bags and he's left. He's left me and he's left Cardiff.... some nonsense about finding a new life on a rubber plantation out East."

Molly pursed her lips as if considering her next move. Bridge required concentration.

"A rubber plantation!" Nelly's heart started to pound. Archie gone and apparently gone for good.

"Yes, I know it sounds bizarre.... but apparently, he's gone to Malaysia to some rubber company that needed a manager.... well, that's what his note said anyway."

"Note!" Nelly was starting to feel a little dizzy. "You mean he only told you all this by a note?" A sense of dread was creeping up through her stomach. What had Archie done? She felt the baby squirm within her.

"So, what did it say.... this note.... I mean did he give any reason for.... for" Nelly didn't dare contemplate the awful possibility that Archie had left some sort of confession.

"As I said it seems he just wanted to make a break from everything. From here.... from me." Molly paused before adding as an afterthought. "He's left me well provided for so I'm sure I'll manage." Molly's tone was final there was no more to tell. She continued to shuffle her cards to best advantage.

Nelly allowed herself a small sigh of relief. Archie had not betrayed her in a fit of anger and rejection. She was sorry though for her sister's plight, being abandoned was very hard.

"I'm very sorry to hear that Molly, very sorry indeed," Clifford said. He really *was* sorry in more ways than one.

"I think we'd better give cards a miss this afternoon, in the circumstances.... don't you? You've obviously.... err got a lot on your mind."

"Not at all Clifford not at all.... I insist we play. There's nothing to be done about it now. Let's carry on with the game" She flicked one more card into place and fanned her cards out for inspection. "Especially since it appears, I've got rather a good hand this afternoon."

CHAPTER 44

The Secret

March was roaring in like a lion. The heavy rains of February had eased up only to be replaced by a biting wind that blasted the City with a bitter intensity. Huge gusts ripped through the streets toppling trees in Roath Park and bringing down an advertising hoarding, killing a poor paper boy out on his rounds. The killer gales were vicious and relentless.

The old house was riven with draughts; icy blasts cut through the sitting room every time Nelly ventured out into the kitchen or hall. Clifford felt the wind was determined to torture him.

A plumber, at not inconsiderable expense that Mrs James refused to countenance paying for, had finally sorted out the dripping tap and had added some extra lagging around their hot water tank in an effort to conserve the meagre amount of hot water supplied by the back boiler. Despite this small improvement the house was miserably cold, and for Clifford, the tyranny of the drip had now been replaced by the treacherous, biting draught.

In the sharp snap the bedrooms were so chilly that even with a piping hot water bottle Jean often had trouble getting off to sleep at night. Her little nose peeping over the heavy coverlet took on an icy glow.

"I'm soooooo cold Mummy," Jean chattered, her teeth clicking together like castanets as she snuggled under the covers. "And I'm frightened of the Wooo! Wooo...."

On gusty nights Jean focussed on the high-pitched buzz that reverberated through the old sash window edges and it terrified her.

The high-pitched humming, when the wind caught it just right, sent Jean into a wide-eyed Tizz "I don't like it Mummy, please stop the Whooooo noise." She pleaded as if some angry monster was threatening to creep through her bedroom window.

And when the wind blew from the East the pane in the little back bedroom window rattled so violently that Nelly felt sure it would break one day. Today the wind seemed to come from each and every direction with a fair cacophony of rattles and a high pitch buzzing torturing the house.

"Mummy will try and fix it for you today when you are around visiting Aunty Ivy," Nelly soothed as she got Jean dressed that morning.

"I'll make some nice fat strips out of one of Daddy's old work shirts to block up the gaps and that way the nasty draughts won't be able to sneak in. We'll fix that naughty old Mr Wind, won't we?"

Jean, suitably mollified, nodded her head vigorously.

Later that morning, armed with twisted strips of cotton rags Nelly set about pushing the fabric into the gaps with an old kitchen knife. She started at the bottom of the window ramming the padding deep into the cracks. It was vigorous work.

Of course, the sash could no longer open, but she could always remove them when the warmer weather arrived in the spring.

The top pane was proving tricky and a difficult stretch; everything seemed to be just at the limit of Nelly's arm's length.

Don't give up, you're nearly there, she told herself as the muscles in her arms screamed from working directly above her head. She felt almost dizzy with the exertion, bending and adjusting to reach into the tricky corners, teetering on tip toes to reach into crevices, her expanding bump pushing her even further away from her target. Fighting back a nausea that bubbled in her throat she rammed home the final shred. *Almost done....... Done!*

She collapsed onto Jean's small bed sweating with the exertion. She had to admit for all the effort she had done a good job but now she was exhausted. Her eyelids fluttered shut and just for a few moments she allowed herself to drift off as a crashing sensation of tiredness overwhelmed her. She jerked herself back to reality. The morning was slipping away. *No rest for the wicked Nelly!* There was still all the shopping to be done before Jean came home.

Laden with two shopping baskets crammed with potatoes, carrots, cooking apples, a pound of sausages, sugar and flour Nelly felt as if her arms were fit to drop off. Her back ached and her neck had developed a crick from all her efforts that morning.

Only the promise of a crafty cigarette when she got home gave her heart. *You've earned it my girl.*

As Nelly tackled the washing up after lunch her back seemed to throb as she hunched over the sink. The baby wriggled and squirmed, her abdomen hardened in protest beneath her house coat. Her body yearned for a rest, and her feet and fingers looked pudgy and swollen. She knew she ought to sit with her feet up; but, how could she?

"Nelly!" Clifford called. "Nelly.... that fire is getting very low."

"I'm coming... I'm coming Clifford." she lumbered into the sitting room to check. Yes, the fire certainly needed coal and the bucket was almost empty; it would not last the rest of the afternoon and evening. She banked up the fire with the remaining fuel; there was nothing to be done for it, she had to refill the coal bucket.

She trudged out to the coal shed and began shovelling nuggets from deep within the bunker. Her aching back grumbled in complaint as she reached into the dark recesses, the tension stretched across her shoulders and radiated all the way to the base of her spine.

Laden with anthracite the heavy bucket swung against her legs as she struggled to find her balance. All day she struggled to keep going when her body cried out for rest.

The day dragged on in a never-ending chore of bending and lifting; swinging Jean into the bath, carrying the drowsy child upstairs to bed, banking up the evening fire, helping Clifford with his unwieldy callipers on her hands and knees and steadying her husband as he leant heavily on her for support.

By the time Nelly collapsed into her own bed that night, she was almost crying with an overwhelming sense of exhaustion. She sat on the edge of the mattress peeling off her layers of clothing. Tearful and tired she caught sight of herself in the mirror, her belly looked undeniably swollen now; not plump but accusingly six months pregnant. She cradled the bump and rocked herself to and fro.

Dear God I'm not sure if I can keep doing this.... I'm so sorry....so very sorry little one."

Despite her crashing exhaustion Nelly could not rest. No position gave her any relief. Her back throbbed and the baby seemed to thrash about inside her pushing its little fists high up under her ribs; her body spasmed in protest.

As the night wore on the baby gave up tormenting her but her back continued to radiate sharp pains that caused her to gasp; a cramping sensation that refused to be stilled.

Nelly got out of bed and tried to ease the cramps by walking around the bedroom. As she paced, careful to avoid the creaky boards for fear of waking Clifford, her worst fears were confirmed. This was no ordinary backache she was in labour.

Panicking now her instinct was to protect; Clifford and Jean couldn't be alerted. She must do what she had to do and do it silently.

Nelly stifled a gasp as another pain ricocheted around her body. Like animal mothers fearful of alerting prey, her only hope of survival now was in her silence.

The baby was coming far too soon of that she was certain. *It's much too soon....* Nelly gasped as the pains grew faster and stronger.

She struggled into the middle bedroom and found an old newspaper blocking the draught, some clean towels, sheets and pillowcases stored in the tall boy. The plaster statue of the virgin Mary looked at her accusingly.

Holy Mother help me. She prayed silently as she set about her lonely task.

Back in her bedroom Nelly rolled up the mat and covered the floor with the newspaper and topped it with an old sheet folded into a thick pad. She removed her nightgown and slipped her bed jacket over her shoulders.

Naked from the waist Nelly knelt on the floor her with her head resting on her folded arms on the bed. She placed another towel between her legs. All she could do now was wait and pray she was not found out.

As the hours trickled past, she willed the baby to be born. When the pains became overwhelmingly intense, she bit down on the edge of the mattress and suppressed her moans. When the first streaks of silvery dawn broke through the clouds with one final push the tiny baby slipped silently into the world.

Sweating with the exertion Nelly panted with relief; the ordeal was over.

The small body lay motionless on the floor. It was a boy. A thick, grey, greasy rope wrapped tightly around his neck. The tiny baby looked, for all the world, like skinned rabbits she saw hanging on the butcher's hooks in the market.

Nelly bent down and put her ear close to his mouth; a faint bubbling sound seemed to come from his chest, but he did not move, and she could not bring herself to try and chafe and fret him into existence.

In the cold blue light of the bedroom the baby lay motionless on the striped towel beneath her; with one small almost imperceptible twitch it was over. She watched him slip away. Soon the little body started to take on a chilly waxy hue and she knew she must act quickly before the household sprang into life. She must hide his body.

Gathering up the tiny grey corpse she bundled it up in the striped towel along with the fleshy afterbirth and cord. She placed her son inside a pillowcase only pausing to place a brief kiss on the linen that covered his small head. *I'm sorry.... so sorry...forgive me my little one.*

On top of her wardrobe was an old brown suitcase still sporting a travel label from their honeymoon-*they would never need it again.* Nelly dragged the case down and gently placed the swaddled body inside.

She let herself cry bitter tears for a few moments before cleaning herself up as best as she could. She ripped off a wide strip from the blood-stained bed sheet, formed it into a thick pad and packed it between her legs to staunch the bloody flow that trickled between her thighs. She then placed the rest of the sheet and stained newspaper in the case. All the evidence of her son's brief life was erased.

Was she so very wicked to be grateful his little life had slipped away?

The twin locks were clicked into place and the case shoved under the bed. Tomorrow Nelly would find a hiding place deep inside the loft. No-one must ever know.

Sarah

Sarah needed to know what terrible secret her mother had kept for so long.

Inside the brown envelope was a large yellowing front page from the Cardiff Evening Post and another smaller clipping folded into quarters. The front-page headline screamed at Sarah.

"Mystery mummified body of baby found in Cardiff attic."

Police have confirmed that the mummified remains of a baby have been found hidden in a suitcase in Alma Road, Roath Cardiff.

It appears that the terraced Victorian property had been rented for nearly forty years by the late Mr Clifford and Mrs Eleanor Harris. Neighbours confirmed that the house had been empty at the time of the ceiling collapse.

Surviving tenant Mrs Eleanor Harris, 73 years, is currently a resident of the Forest Fach nursing home and she is believed to be suffering from terminal cancer.

Mrs Alice Chisholm, Matron of Forest Fach, confirmed to our reporter that the Police had visited the nursing home, but that Mrs Harris was considered by doctors to be too frail and unwell to be interviewed.

The property has been inspected and deemed unfit for human habitation. The owner, Mr Mathew Pugh, has been served a slum order by Cardiff City Council. Mr Matthew Pugh, was unavailable for comment.

Mrs Harris' only daughter, Jean Matthews, asked for the media to respect family's privacy at this difficult time.

The City coroner has been informed.

The second newspaper clipping tucked in the envelope was brief and final.

"Mummy baby death remains a mystery. Case now closed say police."

The City Coroner has returned an open verdict on the tiny mummified corpse discovered in a Cardiff slum attic two months ago. Mr Jones, coroner, confirmed that the body was that of a male pre-term foetus that had probably been still born. A newspaper found in the suitcase alongside the remains indicated that the birth had probably occurred around March 1934.

The previous long-term occupant of the property, Mrs Eleanor Harris, has recently passed away from cancer at the Forest Fach nursing home. The Police say that they are not looking to interview anyone else in connection with the discovery and consider the case closed. The baby's body remains unclaimed and when released will receive a pauper's burial at the City cemetery.

Sarah's mind was in a complete whirl. She had no idea any of this had taken place. Tucked away in Bristol, immersed in the heady world of student life, nothing had ever been said. The family shame had been buried.

Poor Mum, poor Mum...poor Gran! A small tear trickled down Sarah's cheek.

The terrible revelation raised so many questions, questions she would never know the answer to.

Is the dead baby the reason why Gran would never leave Alma road?

How did the poor little thing die?

Sara felt sure the baby must her grandmother's, after all who else could be the mother- surely not Aunty Molly?

And who was the father of the baby? Was Grampy aware of the secret. Surely not!

But Sarah wasn't sure about anything anymore. Her world had tipped on its axis.

All those years she had visited as a child she had no idea about the grim secret hidden in the attic. The attic her father was never allowed access to.

Sarah wished her mother had talked about it before she passed. Now the secret was hers.

That was the thing about secrets, once you know them do you share them or keep them?

Sarah looked at the detritus scattered over the table; the family pictures, snippets of leaflets, locks of hair, rose petals. Cherished memories, and that ghastly bloody envelope.

When Sarah started on her quest to sort out her mother's papers, she had such fond memories of her darling Gran. Alma road had been her joy, her haven. Gran had been perfect.

Did this one scruffy envelope change any of those memories? Did this sad, miserable secret that so tormented her mother she kept it hidden in her wardrobe for decades, deserve to crash once again into a new world and cause ripples in the family.

Sarah made her choice. She took the envelope and the two faded press clippings and tore them into hundreds of pieces. She scooped them into the bin.

As far as Sarah was concerned the secret died with her mother. As her mother had said "consigned to the dustbin of history."

Sarah vowed never to mention it to Beatrice or anyone else. The tiny corpse that received a pauper's burial all those years ago should be allowed to rest in peace. She would not rake over old wounds.

I loved you Gran and this doesn't change anything.

Just like you asked me all those years ago in Forest Fach. I'm not judging you harshly…. I'm not judging you at all.

About the author

Anne was born in Cardiff in 1957. The product of an ordinary working-class family she was educated in the Bishop of Llandaff Primary and secondary schools. She went to Swansea University in 1975 to study English and graduated in 1978 when she married Stephen Tonks who she had met at university. Anne qualified as a teacher and went on to have three children with her husband Stephen. Anne and Stephen were living in Bristol when he died aged 35 yrs. of cancer.

Anne went on to rebuild her life and marry Andrew Main in 1995. They have Anne's fourth child together and now live in a tranquil village in Buckinghamshire.

Anne entered parliament in 2005 and served as the Member for St Albans until 2019.

Follow Anne on Facebook @annemainauthor
www.facebook.com/annemainauthor

Printed in Great Britain
by Amazon